D1528825

SCIMITAR

ALSO BY ROBIN RAYBOULD

NON-FICTION

An Introduction to the Symbolic Literature of the Renaissance
Emblemata: Symbolic Literature of the Renaissance

SCIMITAR

Robin Raybould

TB

Tetrabiblion Books
New York

`

Scimitar is a work of historical fiction. Apart from the well-known actual people, events and locales that figure in the narrative, all names,
characters, places and incidents are the product of the author's imagination or are used fictitiously. Any resemblance to current events or
locales or living persons, is entirely coincidental.

Published in the United States by Tetrabiblion Books

Raybould, Robin
Scimitar/a novel/Robin Raybould
p. cm.

ISBN
978-0-61-543316-5
Library of Congress Control Number
2011920597

Set in 10pt Garamond
Printed in the United States of America on Acid Free Paper
Cover design by www.allmond.eu

www.scimitarthebook.com

Contents

TRANSLATOR'S PREFACE

I discovered the manuscript which tells the story of the life of Eduardo Ferrucci in the Laurentian Library in Florence during the summer of 2003. At the time I was researching a book on the Peplos of Aristotle, a long lost collection of mythical stories of which only a series of funerary epigrams remain, and the Codex Bombycina which had been acquired by the library in 1492 was one of a series of links in the long chain of references leading back from the 19ᵗʰ century to the origin of the Peplos in classical times. I had arrived from Milan the afternoon before with a tight schedule of literary field work following up on the leads I had accumulated while working in the libraries of New York. The temperature and humidity of the reading room of the Laurentian are monitored and controlled for the better preservation of the manuscripts so that quite apart from the pleasure of sitting in the peace of Michelangelo's vast reading room, it was a delicious relief to get out of the heat of the Florentine summer and settle down for a day's work.

I had washed my hands in the basin provided for the purpose just outside the locked reading room doors and when the Codex was delivered to my seat I was given a pair of thin rubber gloves, a heavy cord to stretch over the stiff pages to hold them open and a pencil to write my notes. No question of ink spills here! The Codex, which from the outside looked like a small printed book bound in a hard blind-stamped pigskin cover, was placed for me in a pair of foam book rests at a forty-five degree angle so that I would have to bend from side to side to read each page. I was amused to hear that, according to the Library records, I was the first person in the last 104 years to ask to see the Codex!

It was much thicker than I had expected. I knew that the epigrams I was looking for would only take up only a dozen pages and the commentary which I was hoping to find would add only a few more. On the other hand, it was common for early manuscripts, if they were bound at all, to be bound together indiscriminately even if they were of a completely different subject matter and origin so I would not have been surprised to find other texts included in the Codex.

I found my epigrams quite quickly and made my notes. Then I gingerly turned the following pages which were written in a sober Greek majuscule script so precise and regular that it could have been printed. After a few moments, I came across something which was obviously different, a new and long text – it went on to the end of the Codex, some hundreds of pages - in a very small spidery hand, much more like what we today would call handwriting. Indeed, it gave the appearance of a modern manuscript; the color of the ink was strong, there were frequent deletions, insertions, marginal notes and even ink-blots. It was in Italian and the first page was headed "Il Studiolo" but neither there nor elsewhere in the manuscript was there any indication of the name of the author. I started to read; the Italian was early modern but not difficult to understand, obviously from the 15th or 16th centuries. It appeared to be a memoir but quite sophisticated in its structure, the product of a cultured hand. As I read, the dating became clear from the detail and the events recounted in the first chapter which took place in the mid 15th century. The author was apparently a participant in the events he described.

I postponed my next appointments which were in Paris and Oxford and the next day returned to the Laurentian and continued to read. The story of Eduardo Ferrucci was compelling and, even if it were not to prove of historical importance, I realized that if the manuscript were unknown, its publication might be an academic triumph for me. A memoir from that era is most unusual. Prose works of any kind, apart from the novella or short stories in which readers of the period delighted, are quite rare.

Surprisingly perhaps, it is not uncommon for new manuscript material to be discovered in the libraries of Europe which hold tens of thousands of volumes which have never been examined in modern times. The Laurentian alone holds 100,000 volumes, the library of the Monastery of St. Gall in Switzerland has 170,000, many of which are not catalogued and many other of these ancient libraries are hard put to catalog even their current input let alone that from centuries past. After two days of reading in the Laurentian, I began to believe that I had found something of real interest so I arranged for the library to copy the whole text of "the Studiolo" and send it to me at home. They charged two Euros a page for the each of the 250 pages which in the circumstances seemed to me to be excellent value.

I have since transcribed and translated the whole text and present it here adding a few notes where it seems appropriate. I believe that the text is of true historical importance not only for the accounts of the events described but also as a witness of Ferrucci's literary discoveries which helped to catalyze the Italian Renaissance. It is seldom that one is fortunate enough to read let alone discover a chronicle which reveals contemporary life on both an intimate and a historical level. Ferrucci describes in turn his experiences as a scribe both in Florence and Constantinople, as an Italian spy operating in the turmoil of the last years of Christian Constantinople, as a participant in the great siege of that city by the Turks and after the siege had ended, in a reversal of fortune, as the ambassador of the Turkish Sultan to Florence where he clashes with the ruler of that city, Duke Cosimo de Medici.

The text is also an interesting comment on an important and continuous thread of Renaissance thought with its insistent references to the helplessness of the characters in the book in the face of fate. It was one of the features of the development of the concept of the individual by the humanists of the age that it came to be believed that man with his new-found self-confidence could finally triumph over the vagaries of fate and fortune. This evolution of individual confidence is reflected in the events of the book, in the development of the character and fortune of Ferrucci himself and in the serious writing of the time. It was a recurring obsession of the great Renaissance philosopher Marsiglio Ficino who was apparently a protégé of Ferrucci. Ficino summarizes his thoughts on the matter in his commentary on Plato's dialog, the Kalliope, and I have included this as an appendix to the present book since it was by coincidence the first work that Ferrucci commissioned Ficino to translate.

During the summer of 2004, I returned to Florence, this time prepared for a longer stay and finally found in the city archives, in document T349.stran1454, a reference to Eduardo Ferrucci's visit to Florence as the ambassador of the Sultan Memet II to Cosimo de Medici. This gave me further confidence in the authenticity of Ferrucci's story.

I emphasize that nowhere in the manuscript does the name of the author appear but I believe that there is no doubt that we can assume 1) that in view of the frequent comments on contemporary history and events embodied in the text it was written by someone who had living knowledge of them and in many cases was an actual eye-witness and 2) that Ferrucci was the only person who was present at or could have had knowledge of all these events. It is unclear why he would not have acknowledged his authorship. This may have been an instance of the reluctance of important persons to make public the fact that they were writers at a time when the profession of a writer was not regarded as compatible with high social status. Or it may have been that the manuscript was intended to be passed directly to the printers who would, of course, have known who the author was and would subsequently have added his name to the published version. We do not know how long Ferrucci lived but since he was apparently about 20 in 1439 he could have lived until 1500 or in any event well past the advent of the printing press. It is possible that his book may have been printed and subsequently lost. Or maybe in years to come someone will find it in the Laurentian.

PROLOGUE

The Studiolo

Count Eduardo Ferrucci sat at his desk in the peace and beauty of his study, the Studiolo. For a few moments he looked up from the letter he was reading and gave thought to the progress of his mission during the three months since he had arrived back in Florence. His first task on his return had been to purchase the Palazzo Gasparini, one of the largest and grandest mansions in the city. He had offered the owners a price well above its value with the condition that even if the formalities of the purchase could not be concluded within a short time, and they were not, he would be permitted to take possession immediately. They did not refuse him and, during those first weeks, he had redecorated the whole building and to the existing furnishings he had added the most beautiful and exotic objects, paintings, fittings and furniture that could be found in the city. The result was a display of opulence that vied with the greatest of all the noble palaces of the city.

One of the few rooms he had not touched was the Studiolo where he was sitting. Small, with a low ceiling and lit almost entirely by candelabra, the entire room was paneled in rare woods which, in turn, were inlaid with detailed and finely wrought images of the instruments and expressions of the arts and sciences, each image accompanied by an inscription in Greek. This room, the history of which was known throughout the city, was the principal source of the reputation of the Palazzo Gasparini.

Ferrucci himself had learned of the remarkable origin of the Studiolo many years earlier directly from the bookseller Patrizzi who had been instrumental in the bargain which led to its acquisition. The Count Gasparini, after whom the palazzo was named, had exchanged the Studiolo with Montefeltro, Duke of Urbino, for a manuscript Gasparini had purchased from Patrizzi. Montefeltro was well-known as a zealous, not to say eccentric, collector of books and manuscripts and that, to satisfy his passion and provide employment for his numerous scribes, he was known to go to extraordinary lengths to obtain rare or unusual works.

Gasparini himself, on the other hand, was neither knowledgeable about nor had any interest in bookish matters for their own sake. Indeed, from his youth, he had preferred the sword to the pen, since swordsmanship, he had always believed, was a more suitable accomplishment for a man as well favored as he himself. But he prided himself on his shrewd grasp of character and he sometimes undertook the practice of acquiring beautiful or expensive objects when he saw an opportunity for an arrangement with one of his peers. Thus it had been with the manuscript. Patrizzi had assured him that it was extraordinarily rare, possibly a unique copy of a work by one of the Greek philosophers, A_____, a name Gasparini had not recognized and had quickly forgotten, and, Patrizzi added, a work which, to his knowledge, was not even possessed by Montefeltro. Hearing this, the eyes of Gasparini gleamed with even more than their usual brilliance, and the bargain with Patrizzi was quickly concluded. And so Gasparini had acquired the Studiolo, since Montefeltro's obsession had even overcome his distaste at seeing a signal part of his patrimony, of his home, literally torn down to satisfy his passion for books.[1]

Gasparini, in one of the few successful exercises of his imagination, had hit upon the pretentious title of Studiolo, which was intended to resonate with the name of the Florentine Studio, the small, nascent, university in Florence. At least he had had the sensitivity occasionally to experience a nagging sensation that he was not the man best suited to take advantage of the inspiration afforded by the ancient images on the walls but this slight discomfort was always overcome by his satisfaction at the continual surprise and admiration of his visitors and by the reputation he had acquired throughout the city as the guardian of the room and its mysteries. He had successfully nurtured this reputation by refusing to allow those who wished to investigate the meaning or significance of the images to copy them or even examine them closely.

As Eduardo Ferrucci silently savored these memories and his own contribution to the events of the last fifteen years, there was a light tap on the door and, without any response from Ferrucci, the door was opened and Vittoria Orsini entered, accompanied by two maids carrying food and wine.

"You may go," said Vittoria to the maids after they had set a table in the center of the room opposite Eduardo's desk and then she went over to him smiling a wide and intimate smile. He waited until the door was closed, pulled her onto his lap and gave her a passionate kiss, which without hesitation she responded to.

Eduardo was tall, good-looking, with brown eyes and long light brown hair curling down over the nape of his neck. He must have been in his late thirties but the lines of his face betrayed an experience beyond his years and hardships beyond the knowledge of his peers. He smiled easily but when he did not smile, his gaze was intense and direct. Vittoria was some ten years younger, with golden brown hair bound in a single braid which went almost down to the waist of her scarlet gown. She was beautiful with brown eyes of a similar color to Eduardo's and a light complexion complemented by the freckles on her cheeks.

"No," whispered Vittoria in Eduardo's ear, "Let us eat. That is enough for now."

"Very well," said Ferrucci with a sigh and then a smile and they went over to the table and sat down.

"I had a letter from my mother," said Vittoria. "She says that Venice is scandalized by what they hear about me."

Eduardo laughed. "Whatever Venice knows about you, I have no doubt she described herself. So she only has herself to blame."

"It's true. I can just imagine it. It is the only excitement she and her friends have had in years."

"And how is your brother? You haven't mentioned him since that extraordinary lunch we had with the family."

"Are you surprised?" replied Vittoria. "He is a bore. His wife is a bore. I don't even like the children. They are spoilt and stupid. But forget about them – tell me, have you heard anything from the Duke this morning?"

"No. And I am beginning to wonder if he will ever respond."

"What will you do if he does not?"

"There is nothing I can do except wait. To approach the Duke again is diplomatically impossible. It would be seen as demeaning for the Sultan. I have two more months here and then we will have to swallow our pride and leave as we have long arranged. I have been talking to Bryseis. He agrees that the only thing we can do is be patient and in the meantime we should spend our time as best we can."

And he allowed himself a brief smile and continued.

"But I have however found out much more about Lucchese."

"I cannot imagine how you did that. Whenever I bring up his name, people refuse to talk about him. Everyone seems to be very much afraid of him."

"That does not surprise me in the least. He knows too much. He appears to know something about everyone in the city. For nearly twenty years he has been compiling personal information and now he knows every peccadillo, great and small, of every family in the city. He has agents in the city and outside. All the banks report to him. I have absolutely no doubt that he makes money by taking payment to suppress information which might be scandalous if made public. He is by far the most powerful and one of the wealthiest individuals in the city apart from the Duke himself. And he hates me so we must continue to be very careful. I tell you again, that if you leave the Palazzo alone, you must always take four of the janissaries with you."

"I know. I always do. I am careful," and then she started to raise her voice. "But that's not the point. What can you do? Time is running out. What can you possibly do to dislodge him, to get your revenge? I know you will never relax until you do and I know that he will always see you as a threat and you will never be safe until this antagonism is resolved. And I want to see you safe and happy."

He smiled briefly again. "Darling, you are right. I must and will do something and soon. I have discovered that his daughter, Roberta, is affianced to one of the sons of the Crescenti family from Rome and they are to be married shortly. The Crescenti are impoverished but Lucchese regards it as a good match – both an alliance with an ancient family and a tie to Rome which could help his political ambitions. I shall offer the Crescenti a bribe much larger than the Lucchese dowry to break off the engagement. That would be a blow to Lucchese's pride and his prestige."

"Well you can do that but does he not deserve a much worse fate? People will forget about the broken marriage within a few weeks. And he will guess what has happened and how it happened. He will continue to be powerful and will be just as intent on destroying you as ever or even more so."

"I am also considering the possibility of enticing him into the wool business and trying to bankrupt him in the same way that the Gasparinis were bankrupted years ago. I told you that story, did I not?"

"Yes you did and you can also try that but I don't believe from what you tell me he will ever fall for it. He is much too astute and in any event it would take months to bring about such a scheme and you don't have the time. I think you should consider the plan that I have suggested."

"I have already told you that I don't like it,' said Ferrucci. "It is much too dangerous for you."

"Nevertheless," replied Vittoria, "I have heard that he is estranged from his wife."

"Yes that happened years ago. Rebecca Lucchese has and always has had a very unfortunate reputation."

"Well that would make him vulnerable to the attractions of a woman and I don't believe what I propose would be dangerous. I am used to dealing with strong men and it would be exciting. I would enjoy it. Don't you still have that letter, the letter that shows that he betrayed you, you the hero of Florence? I believe I can provoke him into taking some rash action to recover it and that would be our opportunity. Trust me. In this way you could dispose of Antonio Lucchese once and for all."

Eduardo looked at her admiringly.

"You are a wonderful woman, both brave and beautiful and I love you for it", he smiled. "I have no doubt you could do it but I am very concerned whether it is worth the risk? But tell me again what you propose and I will give it further thought."

Part 1 Florence 1439

CHAPTER 1

The Banquet

Count Federigo Gasparini, the Countess Maria and their two daughters, Juliette and Cecilia Gasparini, welcomed their guests at the top of the great staircase on the second floor of the Palazzo Gasparini. The hallway reached up to the third floor of the palazzo so that in the dim and flickering light of the candelabra it was almost impossible to make out the beamed and painted ceiling high above the waiting guests. Behind the Gasparini family, at the back of the hall, was an elaborate fireplace with an open fire and, on each side of the fireplace, tall windows which looked out on to the street beneath. Opening from the opposite sides of the hall were the doors of the dining hall and of the grand salon, the principal rooms of the palazzo. There was surprisingly little furniture: a dark oak credenza with gothic tracery and linenfold columns beneath each window and round the walls a few sgabelli, small dark octagonal wooden chairs with accompanying tables. The severity of the funishings was offset to some degree by small tapestries on the walls which gave color to the otherwise forbidding grandeur of the Palazzo.

The guests left their carriages within the courtyard and before mounting the staircase were greeted by footmen in the Gasparini livery. The name of each of the guests was announced by Alberto Grimaldi, the General Secretary of the Council, standing next to the Count. The gentlemen nodded to their host and hostess and occasionally exchanged a few words of greeting while the few ladies that had been invited held out their gloved hands to be kissed. Many if not most of the guests were dignitaries of the church and the brilliance and color of their vestments was only matched by its extraordinary variety reflecting the fact that almost every denomination in Christendom was represented that evening at the great banquet in the Palazzo Gasparini.

Isidore of Kiev, Metropolitan of all the Russias, was there as was Cardinal Bessarion, Archbishop of Nicaea, the Imperial Chamberlain, Dermokaites, and Gemisto Plethon, whose assistant Philip Shamash was betrothed to Cecilia Gasparini, with others from the Greek delegation. Representing the Latin Church was Cardinal Nicholas Albergati, President of the Council together with Andrew Chrysoberges, Archbishop of Rhodes, Cardinal Cesarini, Alberto Grimaldi and others. The leaders and representatives from the remaining Eastern churches who had participated in the Council were at the banquet also but no doubt it would be tedious to name them all.

The banquet had originally been planned on a small scale merely as one of the working dinners, hosted by different families in the city, that were held at intervals to allow members of the delegations to discuss the doctrinal issues that remained between them. But fortunately for Gasparini, the successful end of the Council had come so quickly and so unexpectedly, and the Greek delegation was so insistent on their desire to depart immediately, that there had not been time to prepare another venue for the celebrations other than that already planned at the Palazzo Gasparini. Gasparini's only regret was that the small size of his hall which would seat only one hundred and eighty guests would limit the prestige of the occasion.

The long line of guests continued to pass up the staircase and through to the dining salon and, after a time, it became more and more difficult for the host to hear any of the brief exchanges with his guests above the echoes of conversation from the dining hall, the crackling of the fire behind him and the soft tones of the lutenists playing in the gallery. Gasparini found that his concentration was wandering and as the line of guests passed into the dining hall, he began to dream how Fortune had dealt kindly with him. He loved his family. His wife Maria still, as she had always, fulfilled his expectations in private and public. His daughter Cecilia's engagement to Philip Shamash, the assistant of Plethon, the doyen of the Greek delegation, was, he assumed, the envy of the whole city. Juliette, Cecilia's twin sister, was, it was true, obstinate and headstrong and had an alarming obsession with reading and writing but this, he conceived, was no more than a youthful fancy which she would quickly grow out of. The negotiations for her own engagement to Antonio Lucchese would shortly be concluded and the liaison with such a prominent family would add further luster to his own. Above all, the hosting of the great banquet was a unique, not to say historic privilege, which would confirm his position in the highest rank of Florentine society, a position already enhanced by his recent acquisition of the Studiolo.

This last thought gave him a sudden moment of disquiet. On the one hand, he could acknowledge that the bookseller, Patrizzi, was indirectly responsible for what had become his greatest pleasure; and yet, on the other, he despised him as beneath the consideration of an aristocrat of his stature and as being a tradesman and peddler of books, the purpose of which he, Gasparini, man of action, could not understand and did not approve. And Patrizzi was getting old and his judgment, it seemed, was becoming less reliable. He was leaving more of his affairs to his assistants, in particular to one Eduardo Ferrucci of Ferrara, a young man of good education who had settled in Florence within the last few months. Ferrucci, who was evidently connected to the ancient family of that name, had had the misfortune to see his close relatives stricken in the outbreak of plague in Ferrara during the previous year as a result of which he had apparently been left penniless. Ferrucci had been taken on by Patrizzi as a scribe but he was clearly intelligent and ambitious, he would not be satisfied for long with his current employment or position and he was already assuming a more responsible role in the Libreria of Patrizzi.

Ferrucci was a frequent visitor to the Palazzo Gasparini, perhaps too frequent. Gasparini experienced a twinge of that sensitive awareness possessed by all parents and focused particularly on the well-being of their daughters. It was all very well for Patrizzi to bring books for Gasparini to consider, but, in the past, these visits had occurred only once every few months. Now, the house of Patrizzi, in the person of Eduardo Ferrucci, seemed to have something of interest for him, or more likely for

Juliette, almost every day. And no doubt there were visits that he did not even know about. When the banquet was over, he would have to question Garzon, his steward, on the matter.

Apart from his own family, Gasparini had invited to the banquet only a few close friends and associates. These necessarily included the Count and Countess Lucchese and their son Antonio and in addition the Lord Octavian Fregoso and his brother Friderick, Messer Peter Bembo, Lord Cesar Gonzaga, Count Lewis of Canossa, Lord Caspar Pallavicino, Lord Lodovico Pius and Nicholas Phrisio. Gasparini had accepted the instruction of Grimaldi that, in view of the restrictions of space, this small selection of his friends would have to suffice.

The Duke, Cosimo de Medici and his Duchess, Eleonora of Toledo, were the last to arrive and, after they were seated at the top table on the dais at the far end of the hall, upon a discreet sign from Gasparini, the banquet began. Gasparini himself had arranged to sit between the Duchess and Leonardo Bruni, the Chancellor of the Signoria of Florence, with whom he was anxious to ingratiate himself. Bruni, as titular head of the government, although not in practice the most powerful man in the city, would be most able to help him in his continuing social ambitions. Amidst the clatter of the service of the first of the many dishes of the banquet, Gasparini opened the conversation with his neighbor, Bruni.

"Finally," he said "the efforts of the government have borne fruit. I imagine that you and your colleagues are most pleased with yourselves, as you well deserve."

This suggestion of Gasparini only demonstrated his ignorance of the true state of affairs since, although it was only a few days since the historic and unprecedented decree of union of the Eastern and Western churches, *Laetentur Coeli,* had been formally announced to the world in the great new cathedral of Santa Maria del Fiore, the Florentine government had actually had little or nothing to do with the deliberations of the Council.

Bruni regarded his neighbor with some disdain. Of course, the Gasparinis were known to him but he had never had intimate relations with them. He only knew of the reputation of the Count as a mean-spirited, small-minded man whose family was from outside the city and who, unlike many of his peers, did not engage in or was incapable of engaging in banking or trade. Surprisingly perhaps such occupations were viewed as not merely acceptable, even amongst the aristocracy of the city, but as admirable, since it was recognized by all that such enterprises contributed to the prosperity of the city as a whole. Furthermore, like many of his peers, Bruni could not understand, when he gave it thought, how Gasparini was able to maintain his costly life-style when he appeared to rely solely on the income from his country estates.

Bruni could hardly bring himself to reply to Gasparini but since the latter was the host and since he would be in his company over a long evening, he knew he had to make some effort at civility.

"You are kind, sir, but mistaken," said Bruni. "I fear our government has had little to do with this success. All we have done is bear the cost of the expensive needs of a thousand delegates to the Council, so I am as much pleased as anyone that it now appears to be drawing to a close."

"Yes," said Gasparini, "it does seem that these Greeks have been here for a long time but, in reality, it must be less than two years. That is not long, when you think of the momentous success they have now achieved. Who would believe that after a thousand years that we will once again be united with our Greek brothers?"

"I believe, before raising our hopes, we should wait to see whether the decrees of union are ratified by the Greeks. I personally have strong doubts that they will be. And even if they are, I also doubt very much whether the Emperor's true aim will be achieved."

"His true aim?" asked Gasparini.

"Yes, his true aim. This is no secret. It is obvious. His true aim is to obtain military assistance against the infidel, against the Turk."

"Why would we not give that?" asked Gasparini, by now completely out of his depth. He regretted that he had started this topic of conversation and in an effort to put an end to it he looked around him as though suddenly distracted with some domestic responsibility. But he could not immediately detect any problem which might require his attention. The guests beside him and on the long tables below the dais appeared either to be happily engaged in animated conversation or just as noisily focused on the multitude of dishes which were being served to them in a never-ending succession. In spite of the open windows and the strong draught of the fire, the great room was beginning to fill with smoke from the tapers and the hot coals heating the serving dishes on the side tables. It would soon become unbearably warm.

"Signore, give it some thought," said Bruni who refused to give Gasparini the break that he was looking for. "Would you send money and men to defend a city, half a world away, that is completely surrounded, that has little or no means of supporting its population, whose citizens have always been unwilling to defend themselves and that represents the rump of an empire now with no meaning nor purpose?"

Gasparini remained silent.

Bruni continued, starting to enjoy the sound of his own voice, "As you know, the Turk has designs to conquer Constantinople as one more step towards the invasion of our own country. Naturally, an alliance of the Churches has, shall we say, many temporal advantages which will of course enhance those that are spiritual."

"But in that case, why then would the Greeks not ratify?" asked Gasparini, by now completely out of his depth.

"It is, of course, always important to pay attention…" said Bruni, with a supercilious curl to his lip, "to what is lost and to what is gained."

"Nonetheless the Turks have to be stopped. They are now but one day's sail away from Italy. And do we not have to help our Christian brothers?"

Gasparini was raising his voice in his alarm and conversation around them slowed.

"Well, Signore Gasparini," said the Chancellor in an acid tone, "you can be sure that when the time comes for the city to ask for contributions to the campaign, you will be the first I shall approach."

All eyes were on Gasparini and he reddened and said nothing. He tried to change the subject and asked hurriedly, "I do not see the Patriarch here. He should take some credit for this success. Has he left the city?"

Bruni could not help himself. He laughed aloud and was echoed by his neighbors at the table.

"Indeed he has," said Bruni. "He died a month ago."

Overcome by embarrassment, Gasparini turned away again and this time to his other neighbor, the Duchess, who regarded him with a kindly but blank smile. It well known that her Italian was poor and her accent worse but Gasparini felt that there might be some salvation in a simple conversation on the matter of his daughters and their marriage prospects. But he was not sure if the Duchess understood what he was saying or, if she did, whether she had any interest.

Finally, after an arduous meal, from every point of view, the moment came for the speeches that would celebrate and consummate one of the great moments in Christian history. Bessarion spoke first, on behalf of the Greek delegation, through Nicholas Sagundino, the interpreter:

> Great is the beauty of harmony. May Christ Our Lord, who died to restore harmony between man and God, grant it to the two Churches and join them together in mind and will, and not let them remain divided. May the Holy Spirit, Giver of all good gifts, the Spirit of truth, inspire us with the truth and, as in the Blessed Trinity there are three Persons but only one substance and nature, yet the plurality does not destroy the identity, grant that we, though many and of diverse nations and, alas, from the machinations of the arch-enemy of beliefs and faiths, may rid ourselves of the diversity and prove ourselves one in belief and faith in regard of You.[2]

And Albergati replied:

Let the heavens be glad and let the earth rejoice. For, the wall that divided the western and the eastern church has been removed, peace and harmony have returned, since the corner-stone, Christ, who made both one, has joined both sides with a very strong bond of love and peace, uniting and holding them together in a covenant of everlasting unity. After a long haze of grief and a dark and unlovely gloom of long-enduring strife, the radiance of hoped-for union has illuminated all.[3]

Of the many other speeches at the banquet in the Palazzo Gasparini, I now record the opening remarks of Gemisto Plethon since his speech was destined to have a profound influence on the future cultural history of Florence and Western Europe. It was also, as fate allowed, the only lasting legacy of the grand ambitions of the Council of Florence.

Our ancestors, both Hellenes and Romans, esteemed Plato much more highly than Aristotle. Plato's view is that God, the Supreme Sovereign, is the creator of every kind of intelligible and separate substance; and hence of our universe. But most important of all is Plato's theory of Forms. God in his absolute perfection is not the immediate creator of our universe but rather of another prior nature and substance, more akin to himself, eternal and incapable of change in perpetuity, that he created the universe not directly but through that substance. That substance is composed of an intelligible order called Ideal or Formal. And they make an assemblage of all those Forms of all kinds and minds and place a single perfect mind over the whole of the intelligible order, assigning to it the second place in the sovereignty of the universe after God in his absolute perfection ....[4]

By now the Duchess, Eleanora, had fallen asleep and was snoring gently. Who can blame her, after a dinner with nine courses, eleven speeches and a lecture on an unknown Greek philosopher, who had died two thousand years earlier? This put the rest of the company in something of a quandary and Gasparini, again, in acute embarrassment. What was the protocol in such a moment? Should he, out of courtesy, also fall asleep or should he follow the lead of the Duke, Cosimo, who seemed, as always, not to hear his wife and who had been, by contrast, taking a keen interest in Plethon's speech, leaning forward, listening intently and occasionally interrupting and asking questions.

This speech awakened Cosimo's interest in the work of Plato, a philosopher hitherto unknown to him as he was to most scholars in the West. Plato's work inspired Cosimo to found the Platonic Academy in Florence as one element of his extensive patronage of the arts and culture of humanism. He entrusted the leadership of this Academy to the young Marsiglio Ficino who was also given the task of translating all the known works of Plato from the Greek, a task which, as we shall later see, he largely fulfilled.

After the dinner ended, some of the guests remained and strolled with their hosts in the loggia of the palazzo, taking advantage of the cool night air to refresh themselves. Eventually, even these last descended to their carriages waiting in the courtyard and departed. Gasparini sat with his family for some minutes in the grand salon, discussing the highlights of the evening and experiencing a mixed sense of anticlimax, exhaustion and satisfaction.

"Well," said Gasparini with a smile on his pinched features, disguising his silent shame at embarrassing himself in front of his peers, "I think we can say without reservation that the evening was a great success."

"Yes, Papa," said Cecilia, "Congratulations. I really enjoyed myself. Philip was so attentive tonight. He said that now his diplomatic duties are over, he will be able to spend more time with us. My heart was filled with pride hearing him converse so knowledgeably about the union of the Churches. He knew all the different political ramifications for both countries. He is going to be a great, kind man, I feel…."

Gasparini looked at his daughter hopefully. "I look forward to benefiting from my son-in-law's political understanding. And what did you think, Maria?

"I found the Duchess difficult to talk to. She has an impossible accent and I could not understand most of what she said. And I think she was rather bored with all those speeches."

"She was not the only one," said Juliette. "I almost went to sleep too. Those Greeks go on and on – they seem to think very highly of their own ideas."

She blushed slightly when she realized that this remark might refer also to her sister's future husband but she did not really care. She did not like Philip Shamash and could not understand what her sister saw in him nor why her father was promoting the match.

Sure enough Cecilia, sensitive about these matters, was furious.

"How dare you say that about Philip? What do you know of men and speeches – you are only interested in books. You are so, so ….", she struggled for words, "you are so self-absorbed. You think you will find a man who wishes to be with a woman who thinks about nothing but the Scriptures?"

"Yes, Cecilia, I don't seem to be spending my time cultivating the attractive female qualities of gullibility and passivity. Perhaps you are right, I do not know how to attract a man," said Juliette quietly, knowing full well that it galled Cecilia that, of the two of them, she was the one who had always attracted men the more.

"Girls, this is ridiculous. Cecilia has made a wonderful match and you, Juliette, you will be doing so shortly also," said their mother, sharply but wistfully, for, as she spoke, she realized with a pang of real sadness that only for a very little longer would she have occasion to lecture the two girls after their frequent disputes. The fact was that the girls did not get on well and never had. They had been rivals most of their lives and Cecilia, like her father, had become increasingly resentful of Juliette's intelligence and her independent nature.

"Really, Juliette," said Gasparini, "you must have more respect for our guests and more interest in them. Do you not understand that the people who have been in our house tonight are some of the most important and influential people in the world? For my part, I had a very good conversation with the Chancellor himself and I have no doubt he will be helpful to us."

"And", said Maria, "I thought the Duke looked very handsome tonight and...charming." She waited a bit, and continued with an almost embarrassing expression of desire, "As a Duke should be. A man of authority. Quite admirable."

Juliette said nothing. She did not care in the least for anyone who had attended the banquet and she wanted, as much as Cecilia did, to get away from her parents with whom, she believed, she had nothing in common. She had no interest in politics or the events leading up to the Council and her thoughts the whole evening, had only been on that man whom she saw, in her imagination, as the one Fate had already chosen for her.

"You may both retire," said Maria. "Thank your father for an evening which I believe to be the most important occasion in our family's history and, as your father says, one you should never forget. Now, go to your beds. We will be doing the same shortly. Sleep well my little ones."

CHAPTER 2

The Libreria

Eduardo Ferrucci was seated at his writing table in the front room of the Libreria, where he could work and at the same time keep watch on and serve the customers. There were only two other young men in the room, almost certainly students from the university, who were copying texts on the table across from him. Presumably they not been able to afford to buy an original text, or possibly Patrizzi was not prepared to release the only copy he had, so they had to copy it out themselves, a process which was much less expensive than buying the original but obviously more time-consuming. Nevertheless, this was a common task, one from which Patrizzi derived a useful income and one of the first which new students had to get accustomed to. Books that were to be copied were not bound but kept in *peccia* or pieces so two people could copy from the same book at the same time. Alternatively, a book could be rented for a short period so that it could be copied at the student's leisure.

Behind this front room of the Libreria, there were several others in each of which a different stage of book production was undertaken. In the first, parchment was prepared. Animal skins, sheep, goats or calves, were delivered at intervals and were first soaked in a mixture of lime and alum, to remove dirt and any remaining animal flesh. They were then stretched on frames to dry and scraped with a *lunellum,* an instrument with a blade shaped like a half moon, to bring the parchment to the necessary and uniform thickness. The finished product was cut into the required size, normally about twelve inches by sixteen, and then folded. Each half of the folded sheet was a folio, the front of which was the recto and the back the verso.

Patrizzi's illuminator, a man by the name of Arturo, worked in another room. Illuminated books were much more expensive and therefore rarer than the others and since the demand for new illuminated books was not very great, Patrizzi did not need to employ more than one illuminator. If the book was to be illuminated, Eduardo or one of his fellow scribes would finish the text and then pass it over to Arturo. In yet another room, the books were bound. Sheets of folded parchment were gathered together in groups of four so as to make a signature of sixteen pages and placed on a frame, where they were sewn together into a binding of soft vellum or of board covered with vellum or pigskin. The last room on the ground floor was a large, locked and windowless chamber where the finished books and manuscripts were kept. Patrizzi, his wife and family and his unmarried employees, including Eduardo, lived in the rooms of the large house above the Libreria.

Eduardo at his table was surrounded by the materials and the instruments of his new trade: sheets of clean parchment, a pumice stone for scraping the parchment in case it still showed any impurities, an awl or spike, with which he made holes in each side of the sheet at regular intervals down the page and a plummet, another sharp instrument of lead or silver, which he used to draw faint lines on the parchment between the holes as a guide to his writing. His quill pen was accompanied by a knife, since the pen needed frequent sharpening, and it could also be used to scrape away from the parchment any errors he might make. Finally, he had his inks, both black and red, the latter being used for initial letters or paragraphs that were to be emphasized.

Eduardo was diligent, by nature, but his thoughts were not on his work which progressed mechanically and not without frequent pauses and even sighs, sufficiently audible to cause his two companions at the table to glance over at him. He could not help it; the doctrinal subtleties of Gratian's *Decretals*, which he was copying, were a long, long way from being sufficient to absorb the image of Juliette's dark eyes, surrounded by long black lashes which had smiled at him so gently. And the flawless white skin framed by curling brown hair which she tossed just slightly when … when may be she knew he was looking. Just the thought of her made his breathing quicken, and he dropped his pen leaving a large blot on the side of the parchment. He stood up and starting walking slowly around the shop. When would he see her again, he wondered? Was her father beginning to suspect the true nature of his frequent visits? Did she care about his reduced social status? How could he ever aspire to the social rank of the Gasparinis? And the most insistent question of all. Did she return his feelings?

Eduardo had a somewhat diffident air about him. He was a dreamer but this belied a determination to fulfill his dreams. He did not like his job but he did like the atmosphere of the book shop and the books and manuscripts that surrounded him. He was a romantic; the thought of the vast tracts of knowledge contained in all those books excited him immensely. He hoped that one day he might be able to contribute in some little way to this great corpus of human knowledge. And yet, although he was grateful to Patrizzi for offering employment to him, a stranger and one destitute at that, he knew that he could not remain long in the Libreria.

Patrizzi was a wealthy man but he would always remain what he was, a tradesman, someone for whom acceptance in the salons of Florentine society was inconceivable. What's more, Eduardo knew that whatever his literary dreams, a life as a writer or in the university could never bring him the financial rewards that would be necessary for him to be accepted by the likes of the Gasparinis. The Ferruccis were a large and respected Ferrara family but his father was the youngest of several brothers and had not been wealthy. Now that his parents and his own two brothers were dead, he did not know what, if anything, was due to him as an inheritance. With the plague at its height, he had left Ferrara much too quickly to be concerned about anything of that nature and, in any event, he had been too shocked at the death of his family to give any thought to it. Eventually, he could return and make inquiries but at present he did not even have money for the journey.

He had gone over these thoughts many times as he had pursued the lonely and long hours of his new profession. Already he sympathized with the words that he had found at the end of a manuscript he had copied not long before: "just as the sick desire health, so the scribe yearns for the end of the book." But now, all such and similar thoughts were banished by his absorbing visions of Juliette. All memories of the past, all ambitions and calculations for the future, were obliterated by the images of the woman he loved. Not only was she beautiful in every respect but she shared his interest in books, in reading and apparently in writing. He had never seen anything she had written but from hints she had dropped, it was clear that this was her passion, even more perhaps than his own. His interest was in the manuscripts themselves, their origins and their history and apparently hers was writing.

Eduardo knew that this interest of hers, if she wished to pursue it seriously, would inevitably create for her enormous if not impossible difficulties. For any aristocrat, a writing career would be scandalous and, for a woman, out of the question. Writers were socially lower than merchants or tradesman, on a par with actors, strolling players and mountebanks. Anyone with literary pretensions who also belonged to the aristocracy invariably used a pseudonym or the name of a real person who was paid to act as a front for his noble patron. He did not know of a single example, past or present, of a woman who had done this.

His visits to the Palazzo Gasparini, which was only two hundred yards away on the other side of Santa Croce, had become more and more frequent. He knew that they would eventually arouse suspicion despite how remarkably distant the Count and Countess seemed from their daughters. He had started to run out of ideas for even remotely interesting books for Gasparini, and even Patrizzi was starting to get curious. Although sales were brisk since Juliette would buy anything and everything he brought with him, Patrizzi could not afford to offend Gasparini. Even before the latter's recent rise in status with the Duke as a result of his famous banquet, just one complaint from Gasparini to the authorities might have severe consequences for Patrizzi.

Eduardo was contemplating these matters with something approaching desperation, when the two students got up to leave. As they opened the door, they stepped back to allow entry to another visitor. Eduardo's heart sounded with a beat he thought could be heard all over the room.

Juliette was wearing a cloak with a dark hood, which allowed her to remain hidden and almost unrecognizable. She came forward keeping her eyes on Eduardo. They stood very close for a few seconds in the center of the room and then he clasped her to him. He could feel her heart beating rapidly. Eventually, she pulled away. He pushed down her hood and she shook her long curls free. They looked at each other again and she asked:

"Where is Patrizzi?"

"He is out. I don't expect him to return for at least two hours. The others are working in their rooms at the back."

He pulled her to him again and they kissed, at first soft and gentle and then greater urgency. He covered her cheeks and ears with kisses, she put her neck back, abandoned herself to his caresses. Finally she pulled away breathing heavily.

"I cannot stay," she said, "but I have something to show you."

She pulled from a pocket of her cloak some papers, which she laid on the table. They contained writing with drawings on each page.

"This is something I have written," she said. "You must advise me what I should do next. There are many more. I know that they must be kept secret but maybe you can copy them and tell Patrizzi that they were written by someone else."

"Tell me what they are," asked Eduardo.

"They are a series of allegories," she replied. "I have tried to make them mysterious and a little difficult to understand by concealing the meaning as in an enigma. In this case, the meaning is hidden in the combination of the title, the image and the poem, all three, which makes it more interesting to decipher. I believe that this is a new kind of writing. My tutor, Signor Manzoni, told me that St. Bonaventure has said that we can contemplate God with the sensible things, not only since they are signs but by themselves as his essence, presence and power. That is what I am trying to do with my writing: to find God through the symbols I create. I feel that God has called me to do this and I should devote my life to it."

"And the titles – they are in Greek. Do you read and write Greek?" Eduardo's tone expressed surprise and admiration.

"No," she said reddening slightly "I copied those from my father's studio. They are some of the inscriptions inlaid into the wall. I shall try and learn Greek. Then I shall discover what they mean."

At that moment there was a frantic knocking on the front door. Eduardo opened the door and her maid, whom Juliette had asked to remain outside for exactly this reason, cried that someone was coming. Juliette went white, put on her hood over her hair and held her hand over her face but it was too late. In strode Philip Shamash.

Whatever else he was, Shamash was a gentleman and a diplomat. When he saw the hooded and slightly disheveled figure just inside, he stopped, gave a slight bow, held the door open and watched as Juliette left the room and walked slowly down the street followed by the maid. He turned and looked at Eduardo with an almost imperceptible smile playing across his lips. If he had recognized Juliette, he gave not the slightest indication of having done so but we have to assume that since he was engaged to be married to Cecilia, Juliette's identical twin sister, it would have been extraordinary if he had not done so.

Shamash was of average height with a sallow complexion, long dark hair and a classic profile. He had not achieved his position as assistant to one of the most famous men in Europe without good reason and his time with the Greek delegation in Florence, and the experience this had given him in the diplomatic arts, had increased his reputation. He was about thirty but appeared older. He radiated the confidence of a man who had the ear, the friendship and if necessary the aid of some of the most powerful men in the world. He had a piercing, intelligent but unsettling gaze and when he smiled, his eyes did not. He was, in short, not a man to be unnecessarily antagonized.

Shamash, surprisingly, was a frequent visitor to the Libreria. The Greeks, both those in the delegation and other visitors in the years before the Council, had long been bringing books from Constantinople to the West. The motivation was no doubt partly to conserve unique literary treasures, which otherwise might have been lost, but mostly it was in the hope of financial windfalls. There was possibly an element of both, but the fact was that, as the revival of classical learning had taken hold in the West, there was an obsessive demand for the works of the classical authors of ancient Greece and Rome. Book collectors in the West would pay extraordinary prices and go to extraordinary lengths to obtain rare manuscripts. Montefeltro was just one amongst many and the Duke Cosimo himself was a dedicated collector.

It is one of the oddities of history that the long age of the Eastern Greek Empire, had produced little or nothing in one thousand years in the way of original literary or visual art. The great contribution of the Byzantines to Latin history was their zeal in securing and, for whatever reason, bringing to the West much of that classical literature which had hitherto been assumed to be lost. The new found enthusiasm is indicated as much as anything by the example of the Emperor John Palaeologus himself who took advantage of his journey to Italy for the Council of Florence to bring some books from the Imperial Library, which he sold to defray his expenses.

The booksellers of Italy profited from this enthusiasm and Patrizzi was amongst them. He was no longer surprised by the extraordinary treasures that the Greeks would suddenly produce without warning and he knew that when the time came, for whatever reason, if he was patient, another rarity would be brought into the Libreria.

Shamash, in this respect, was no different from the other Greeks. And, on this occasion also, he had brought something to show Patrizzi. It was a thick folio volume bound in stamped pigskin and secured by clasps. He took it from the loose bag that he was carrying and laid it on the table. Eduardo, who did not have the authority or indeed the experience to conduct a negotiation to buy such a book, explained that Patrizzi was not there but would be returning shortly. Shamash said that was no concern, he would leave it and return at another time to discuss the matter with Patrizzi. Eduardo had now met Shamash on several of these visits and while recognizing and respecting the latter's age, experience and status, felt able to be open with him and speak without reserve. Hoping to forestall any questions about the identity of his recent visitor, he immediately started studying the book.

"Can you tell me anything about it?" he asked, undoing the clasps and opening the book at its title page.

He saw immediately that it was in Greek, which he was unable to read. All educated Europeans read Latin, which was the language of the Bible and the church and which had been the lingua franca of Europe for more than a thousand years. But very few read Greek. The influx of Greek texts and Greek speakers into Italy during the early part of the century offered an opportunity and a solution. Scholars wanted to be able to read texts in the original and now there were translators and teachers who could help with this. As we shall see shortly, Plethon himself acted as such a teacher. Patrizzi could read Greek. When or where he had learnt, Eduardo did not know, but it was obviously an essential attribute for a book-dealer in such a time.

"Yes," said Shamash, "I would be happy to. The book is a collection of sayings by the ancient Greek philosophers which was made by one Stobaeus in the 5th century of our Lord for his son Septimius. It is called the Eclogues of Stobaeus. Do you know what Eclogues are?"

"I am afraid not," said Eduardo uncertain as to whether this was an admission that he was almost illiterate or whether an eclogue was actually a rare thing which he could not be expected to know.

"Eclogue means material or collection." continued Shamash. "But what is also interesting is that there is another meaning for eclogue, coming from a different root, and that is as a pastoral poem. So that is the origin of the Eclogues of Theocritus and Virgil. You know of Theocritus and Virgil, I assume."

"Yes, of course," said Eduardo slightly coloring, although if he had been asked to name one of Theocritus' works he would have had some difficulty.

Shamash continued. "There are more than two hundred and fifty different authors in the index of this book and to my knowledge many of these dictes are not quoted elsewhere in Greek literature. It is an extremely rare and valuable book and may be the only copy in existence. It is however rumored that there is another volume containing further sayings. In the Bibliotheca of Photius in Constantinople from the ninth century, two volumes of Stobaeus are recited. I do not know whether this means that there were two copies of the same book or whether this refers to the fact that the present volume is divided into two books or whether there was indeed another volume which has now been lost."

The two men were quiet while Eduardo turned the thick parchment pages slowly, contemplating the antiquity of the knowledge within them and frustrated but curiously excited by the fact that he was wholly unable to decipher the Greek script.

"How old is the manuscript?" he asked, not so much because this was the first question that any potential purchaser of manuscripts should ask but because he was excited by the touch of the ancient pages.

"Not so old," said Shamash "I would think about three hundred years but Patrizzi will be able to tell more exactly."

"How long would it take me to learn Greek?" asked Eduardo almost without realizing that he was saying this aloud.

"That depends on how hard you work at it. I could find you a tutor if you were serious but of course tutors are expensive."

"I would like that," replied Eduardo, knowing immediately that he could not afford it and knowing that Shamash knew it too and was laughing at him. He admired Shamash for his worldliness, but he also knew that he could never be friends with him and did not wish to be.

"And now," said Shamash pulling out of the bag some papers. "I have some more lecture notes for you."

"Ah yes" replied Eduardo and he took out from a drawer in the table some sheets of parchment covered with his fine script. "These are the ones I have just finished. I hope they are satisfactory."

"I hope so too," said Shamash with an edge to his tone, not a threat but just a hint that, if they were not satisfactory, there would be consequences. At the same moment, he noticed the sheets that Juliette had left lying on one side of the table. He picked one up and started to read it. "Is this yours?" he asked.

Eduardo said yes, not knowing whether he was telling the truth or not.

"I like it." said Shamash. "May I keep it and this one?" And, without waiting for a response, he pocketed two of the sheets, gave his leave and indicated to Eduardo that he would return in a few days when Patrizzi had had time to consider the Stobaeus.

Eduardo's heart went cold. He knew that something terrible had happened. He had not had time to think; he should have stood up to Shamash but he had not. He had betrayed Juliette even at their first private encounter. He was sure now she had been recognized and was compromised. He sank into his chair and put his face into his hands.

As for the lecture notes, I have said before that Shamash was assistant to George Gemisto Plethon who, during his years in Florence for the meetings of the Council, had found sufficient time to give public lectures on Plato, on the Zoroastrian oracles and on his own brand of universal religion of which Christianity, in his view, was just one manifestation. Shamash had asked Eduardo to correct and copy out a Latin version of these lectures so that they could be distributed to those who only understood Latin. Eduardo had enough work to do and enough on his mind but he had wanted to help Shamash in view of the latter's connection to the Gasparini family so he had agreed. He had informed Patrizzi about this additional work and he did it in the hours after the Libreria was closed. Shamash seemed keen to offer the work to Eduardo and, although the latter had not been sure how Shamash could help him in his suit with Juliette, he had, at the time, taken the perhaps naïve view that any ally was better than none.

A little later, Patrizzi returned and found Eduardo still seated at the table with the Stobaeus in front of him. He, at least, had had the presence of mind to put the remainder of Juliette's parchment sheets into the drawer and he had not even been able to look at them.

Patrizzi never made any attempt to hide the fact that he was a man of very great learning. Why should he? His white beard and long craggy face, piercing black eyes, black gown and the flat tasseled hat he always wore, betrayed his calling; that of a man of science and letters. He was greatly respected for it. Along with such humanist luminaries such as Poggio Bracciolini and Niccolo Niccoli, he had been one of the first people to learn Greek in Florence and this from the legendary Byzantine academic, Manuel Chrysoloras, on the latter's stay in Florence at the beginning of the century. Since books were very scarce outside the church establishments, monasteries and the cathedral libraries, and since the booksellers were the only secular source of books and also the main source of new books, bookshops had become centers of learning. The booksellers, those with the aptitude and the time, became teachers and leaders of the new humanism.

When Patrizzi came in, he did not seem to notice Eduardo's disconsolate look, and his gaze immediately lighted on the volume in front of him. He took off his hat and cloak and sat down opposite Eduardo, turning the book around and opening the title page, merely asking, "Who is this from?"

Eduardo told him and repeated, as best he could, the information that he had learned. Patrizzi studied the book in silence, reading the title page, going slowly through the several indices and leafing through some of the pages.

Finally, Patrizzi said without visible excitement, "This is a very important book, possibly one of the most important I have ever seen. I have never heard of this writer but he is what is called a doxographer, from the Greek *doxon*, meaning opinion; he wrote the opinions of other people. The first and most famous doxographer was Theophrastus, a student of Aristotle himself and afterwards head of the Academy in Athens. It may be that this book contains unique information about ancient Greece not available anywhere else. I do not know the value of it but we shall have to pay whatever he asks. I want you to go through it leaf by leaf and record any imperfections which we can use to bargain with him."

Eduardo asked, "What about the second volume he talked about?"

Patrizzi said, "I know nothing about this volume so I cannot speak about a second but, if there is a second, it would obviously be all the more important."

Eduardo then asked, "Would you teach me Greek?"

Patrizzi looked at him and smiled. "You are an intelligent and ambitious young man and you could have a great future in this business but I doubt whether you will have the patience for it. I know that you already have your thoughts elsewhere. But yes, I will teach you Greek. It will take time. But I believe you will enjoy and profit from it. We will start tomorrow. Now, you must examine this Stobaeus carefully."

So saying, he turned the book round so it once again faced Eduardo and walked up the stairs at the back of the Libreria. Eduardo sighed, took a spare piece of parchment to make notes and started turning the pages of the Stobaeus. He came across few imperfections, nothing worth noting. There were no worm-holes, no water stains, the parchment was fine and in good condition. As he progressed, in his excitement, or at least enthusiasm, to start on his lessons in Greek, he started to copy some of the letters, particularly the large illuminated letters which began each section of the book.

It took him an hour to go through all four hundred pages of the manuscript by which time he had also a line of Greek letters on his parchment. Of course, he did not know the language but when he studied the line of script, it did seem to him that the letters were not randomly placed; there seemed to be, for instance, an excess of the letters which he assumed to be vowels and these were positioned at seemingly significant intervals.

kaituposantituposkaipemeptiketaiegeezoefooroskatekeiaia

He was so curious that he decided to settle the matter there and then. He picked up the parchment and took it up to Patrizzi, who was seated comfortably in his small salon on the floor above, reading a recently completely manuscript, no doubt checking it for errors. Eduardo explained what he had done and Patrizzi took a quick look at the line of letters, picked up a pen and rewrote the letters as follows

Kai tupos antitupos kai pemep... ti ketai e ge e zoefooros katakei aia.

"You do indeed seem to have discovered something, my boy", smiled Patrizzi. "Such a game was quite common amongst ancient writers and indeed still is but it is always interesting to find a new one and to work out its purpose."

"But what does it mean?"

"Well, I can't be exactly sure," said Patrizzi, "since there appears to be some word or words missing in the middle. It seems to be something like this. 'And there is beating and beating back and woe .....the life-giving earth holds the thing that you are seeking.' The word 'kai' at the beginning means 'and' so it looks as if there is another part of the phrase before this. It may be that the other volume which Philip Shamash talked about would yield the first part of the saying."

"Have you ever come across such a phrase before?" asked Eduardo.

"No I have not and I cannot throw any further light on it at all. But," said Patrizzi, with a further smile, "this will give you added incentive to find the other volume although how you will set about this without alerting Shamash or going to Constantinople yourself, I would not know."

Eduardo thanked Patrizzi and returned to the floor below where he put the parchment with his Greek script safely away in the table. He now had to work on the next series of lecture notes for Shamash.

CHAPTER 3

Antonio Lucchese

The Palazzo del Podesta was an impressive and forbidding building, more of a fortress than what we today would call a palace. Constructed about two hundred years before the present, it was at first the seat of the one-time governor of Florence, the Podesta, who as an independent and neutral outsider had been appointed to rule the city in the hope that he might be able to restore order between competing political factions. This hope had proved illusory and the Podesta's period of rule had been temporary. But the city, fuelled by its growing prosperity, had over the years experimented with various kinds of governance including elections for public officials and the sharing of power between the aristocratic families, the guilds and the merchants.

The history of Florentine politics had been complex and sometimes bloody but throughout this period the city and its citizens had grown in wealth and prestige. The wealth of the bankers had grown at the same time until the Medici family, the most powerful of them all, bankers to the Popes themselves, had, not long before the time of which I write, taken over the government of the city and ushered in a period of political stability and cultural splendor.

It was thus not unusual in the least that a young aristocrat such as Antonio Lucchese should seek employment and be welcomed in the city government. The Bargello, the Florentine chief of police, had his headquarters in the Palazzo del Podesta and this is where Antonio too had his office and spent his working day. In view of his connections, his education and his foreign experience, Antonio had been appointed head of security for the city, and his duties included providing escorts and guards for the foreign dignitaries who had been attending the Council. More important from the city's viewpoint, he employed and supervised a large network of agents to oversee the clandestine and unwelcome activities of these visitors. He also controlled all foreign agents who spied for the city throughout Italy and the Orient. It was a vital position which reflected the high regard in which he was held by the city officials including the Duke.

Antonio was tall, with dark eyes and black hair, an aquiline nose and a natural air of authority, even arrogance, enhanced by his experiences in the army in its recent campaign against the forces of Milan, in which he had distinguished himself both by personal courage and by his qualities of leadership. He was an excellent choice for a job that was becoming one of the most responsible in the whole city administration.

It was not just that Florence, the wealthiest state in Italy, had to be continually on its guard against the depredations, incursions and alliances and even invasions by its neighbors including the Papal States, but that all the Italian cities were becoming increasingly aware, not to say alarmed, by the more distant although recognizably greater threat posed by the spread of Islam towards the West and the success of the Turkish conquests in Greece and in the Balkans. For this reason, although the reality was masked by the polite and learned disputes on doctrinal differences between the Christian factions, the Pope and the secular authorities of the West, as much as the Eastern Emperor, were receptive to the idea of the Council and the possibility of the reunification of the two Churches.

Antonio sat at his table surrounded by piles of parchment. The room was dark and uninviting and the stone walls were covered only by small tapestries. There was only one window about three feet square, appropriate for a building which had been intended as a fortress. Additional light was provided by candelabras on the walls and by candles on his table.

Sitting on the other side of his table was Giulio Scamuzzo, the agent he had assigned to watch Philip Shamash.

"Signor Shamash has made several visits to the Libreria Patrizzi over the last few weeks. I assume he is selling books to the Libreria rather than buying them."

"Yes," said Antonio, "I am acquainted personally with Philip Shamash. It would not be unusual for such a man, a member of the Greek delegation, to visit a bookseller. What was the purpose of telling me this?"

"There was an incident I noted when he visited the Libreria yesterday. I thought I should report it to you. A young woman was waiting outside the shop as he approached and, as he did so, she knocked on the door violently as though to warn someone within. Immediately after he entered, a lady came out. The first woman was obviously her maid. The two of them then walked hastily along the street out of sight."

"Did you recognize either of the two?"

"No, I could not see the second woman, she was wearing a cloak and hood. I might recognize the maid again. I did not see where they were going since I remained to watch the Libreria. Signor Shamash stayed about half an hour and then left without further incident."

"Why would someone not want to meet Philip Shamash?" said Antonio more to himself than to Scamuzzo. "Or what would this lady be doing in a bookshop which she did not want to be surprised at? What was she doing in a bookshop at all? Something is going on here. You did well to report this, Scamuzzo. Did you get the impression that the lady did not want to be recognized?"

"Yes, Signor, I did. It was a clear day but she had the hood right over her head so it was impossible to see who she was."

"Was she carrying anything? Anything that would identify her?"

"No, Signor. Nothing."

"I will give it further thought. You should continue to track Signor Shamash and if you need help, I will make it available. You will circulate descriptions of the two women and coordinate any responses that you receive and report to me. If you see her at the Libreria again or you recognize her or the maid anywhere, you should follow her. Do you have any questions?"

"No, Signor."

"Good. You may go."

Antonio knew, of course, that the Greeks were bringing books to the West and selling them; Shamash's business with the Libreria was therefore not out of the ordinary and his last visit might be completely unconnected to the unknown woman but nevertheless Antonio determined to give a higher priority to the supervision of the man. He knew him socially, of course; they had met several times in the salon of the Gasparinis, and he himself was of similar age to Shamash but he did not like him and did not trust him. He had been surprised that the Gasparinis had acceded to the suit by Shamash for Cecilia and there was now even the real possibility that the two of them might become brothers-in-law.

His thoughts turned to Juliette. He had known her distantly most of her life. It was a good match; the Gasparinis were an old family and, although not of the first rank, in recent years the family's fortunes had improved. Why this had been he was not sure. Federigo Gasparini did not have a reputation as one shrewd at business, he was an irascible small-minded man who relied on the income from the family estates and unlike many of his contemporaries had never engaged in trade or banking.

Antonio came to the sudden realization that, since there was a possibility that he was to be allied with the Gasparinis, he should investigate (who better placed than he to do this) the financial affairs of his prospective in-laws. It would do him no good if there was subsequently any trouble on that score. Nonetheless, he believed that Juliette would make a good wife and, with her intelligence and independence, a real partner in his ambitious plans for his future life in the city. He knew that she was headstrong but this made her more attractive to him. He believed that this was one amongst several characteristics they had in common. She was tall, beautiful and a little distant and although it had always been assumed without question by himself and his family that his wife would be chosen primarily for social or financial reasons, he was beginning to be drawn to her.

He remembered the last time he had seen her at the Palazzo Gasparini during one of the family's weekly salons. Since his recent appointment, he had little time for visiting or the other social activities which were the continual pursuit of many of his peers but in view of the discussions which were going between the Gasparinis and his own family on the terms of their betrothal, he felt that the least he should do was to visit his future bride's family and make himself agreeable to them if not to her.

She had been standing alone in the salon, looking out through one of the tall windows, bound up in her thoughts and apparently unwilling to join in conversation with any of the dozen other guests. She wore a long green silk dress trimmed with white lace which contrasted with her dark hair falling in curls on to her bosom. When he approached, she looked round at him with her dark brown eyes which, despite their clarity and beauty, did not smile. It was she, he was sure, but since, all the time he had known her, he had never been absolutely certain, at first glance, whether it was she or her sister, he addressed her with the phrase which had come to be traditional amongst all her acquaintances.

"Signorina Juliette, I presume."

She inclined her head in acknowledgement.

"You seem distracted," he said.

"Yes and no," she replied. "I am distracted by this noise of conversation but not by my own thoughts."

"In that case, your thoughts must be very weighty. Perhaps you would like to share them with me."

"No," she said sharply, "I would not." There was a pause and then, "I apologize, Signor Antonio, I have forgot myself. Welcome. Will you take some refreshment."

"I would prefer not to."

"Very well," she said, "And how are you? We do not see much of you these days. I hear you have been appointed to an important position in the city government."

"I am pleased to say that I have placed in command of the security services of the city."

"That does indeed sound important," she said, "and what exactly does that entail?"

What he did was, of course, confidential, but he was young and anxious to impress a beautiful woman, particularly one who might become his wife.

"I supervise and direct the many agents we have at home and in foreign territories."

"Ah," she said, finally with a glimmer of interest but still without smiling. "Spies. That indeed sounds interesting and important. What have you discovered recently?"

"I wish I could tell you, Signorina Juliette, but you will understand that I have had to learn quickly the most important lesson of my appointment which is to keep a secret."

"Oh, come now, is there nothing you can tell me? Do I look like I work for the Turks? You are amongst friends here, family. Tell me an exciting story about spies in the city. And besides, we citizens have the right to know what the government is doing on our behalf!"

So saying, she moved closer to him and looked directly into his eyes. He could smell her scent and almost feel the movement of her body. But at the same time he was becoming irritated, not just by her persistence, but by the knowledge that she was deliberately baiting him, that she did not have any real interest in his work, that she was trying to break him down, to make him submit to her will. It was a game. If he told her more, she would lose respect for him in the knowledge that he had not been able to sustain that first duty of his position.

"Signorina, you know I cannot say more even to you," he said, forcing a smile, "except that with the conclusion of the Council and the departure of the delegates, I will have more time to pay my respects to your family and to you. I shall look forward to that. It will give me great pleasure to see you more often."

This first attempt at intimacy did not receive the slightest reciprocation from Juliette. In any event their conversation was interrupted by Maria Gasparini who was much more welcoming to him than her daughter had been. She took Antonio by the arm and led him off to meet other of their guests introducing him with excessive enthusiasm about his importance in the city government. But Antonio soon excused himself. He had been left without the slightest indication of what Juliette felt for him and this irritated him considerably. He was not accustomed to being left in doubt about his own intentions or those of others but he had meant what he said. He did want to see her again.

His reverie was interrupted by a knock on the door of his office which without any response from him opened to admit Francisco Bardini, the Bargello, Antonio's superior, the Chief of Police. Bardini was a man of medium height, in his fifties, with a swarthy complexion, a goatee beard, dark piercing eyes and a sharp voice which could penetrate any conversation. Antonio rose from behind his desk and offered Bardini a chair.

"The conclusion of the Council will ease your work within the city," said Bardini after he was seated and without waiting for any preliminaries. "The Greeks are returning home. Other delegations from the Eastern churches remain, but we know that their combined numbers are far fewer than those of the Greeks. We must consider how you should now best deploy your resources."

"Your honor," responded Antonio. "I have already been giving this some thought. I believe we should start to retrain some of the agents that have been monitoring the visitors in the city to prepare for work beyond the borders of the Republic. It is there that the greatest dangers to our security now lie."

"Yes," said Bardini, "That shares my own belief. And I believe we have to focus our efforts. I reflect the opinions of the highest circles of our government when I say that the greatest priority should be given to reporting the activities of the infidel and discovering their future plans. I need hardly remind you that it is clear that the ambitions of the Turks have no bounds. It is now more than a century that they first crossed the Bosphorus into Europe and since then they have slowly been taking control of much of the Balkan States and of Greece. I would say that there is no doubt that they intend to continue in this expansion. Don't you agree?"

"Yes, your honor, it does indeed seem that they are permanently and irretrievably entrenched on the frontiers of Italy and indeed the rest of Europe and poised for further advance. It concerns me and it concerns us all."

"Personally, I believe that the Greeks are irrelevant to our security, that the whole Council has been a waste of time and of our resources," continued Bardini, with scarcely any interruption in his train of thought. "We all know that Constantinople is just a small Christian island in a Moslem sea. Despite the renowned city walls and despite any help that we may give them, the Greeks cannot and will not withstand any determined onslaught on the city."

Antonio shared the ambivalent attitude of all his countrymen towards the Greeks. On the one hand they were regarded as decadent and effete, culturally and doctrinally inferior, despised because of the feeble resistance they had put up to the advance of the infidels and with an Emperor and a Patriarch who ruled over a few square miles of territory with all the anachronistic and functionless trappings of a vast but long-lost empire. On the other hand, it was recognized that the Greeks were fellow Christians, that Constantinople was a final bulwark against the advances of the enemy and that the fall and destruction of the city would be an immense psychological blow to the West.

"I have recited these dangers," continued Bardini, "because I want to reiterate the importance of focusing your future work on the activities of the Turks. You should do this even if you reduce the supervision of our political and trading rivals in Italy itself. Please provide me as soon as possible a detailed plan of what you propose."

With that Bardini rose and left the room and Antonio remained to contemplate the difficulty of his task. He knew that there were Turkish spies in the city as there were in all the Italian cities and from the start of his appointment he had been instructed to concentrate his efforts on detecting them and neutralizing them. It had been a particularly difficult task in view of the number of foreigners in the city and the impossibility of supervising them all. Now, in addition, he would have to expand his efforts beyond the borders of Florence and even into Turkish territory itself.

CHAPTER 4

Philip Shamash

Deep in contemplation, Philip Shamash walked slowly around his room, which was dimly lit by a few candles and by the fading light of dusk from the tall windows in one wall. He had spent the day with Plethon with whom he shared a large apartment in a palazzo in the Via dei Pecori. Plethon had given one of his final lectures on the dialogues of Plato and Shamash, in attendance, had circulated to the audience the Latin notes that Eduardo Ferrucci had edited and copied. Now that Plethon was leaving Florence, Shamash would have to find other accommodations at least until his marriage with Cecilia, after which he was expecting to be able to acquire a comfortable house with the dowry that she would bring. To move was an inconvenience but it was only for a matter of weeks since the date for the marriage was already set. Like most of the other participants and in spite of the urgency of a decision in the matter, he had not expected the Council to be concluded, at least as far as the Greeks were concerned, as soon and as suddenly as it had.

He had managed the matter rather well, he thought, although the timing of it had been quite fortuitous. If it had not been for the marriage, he would not have had any good excuse for staying on in Florence, and the marriage would give him the funds which enabled him to do so. Cecilia's parents would be quite content and indeed would presumably encourage his plan to remain in Florence, so that their daughter, after the marriage, would be near at hand. Up to now Shamash had been living on a stipend provided by Plethon as his assistant, which was by no means generous, and, indeed, some of his colleagues in the Greek delegation secretly wondered how Shamash could present such a striking figure supported by what was presumed to be a modest income and how, in spite of his connections and his learning, he had persuaded the Gasparinis that he was sufficiently well matched to be allied with one of their daughters.

The fact was that the Gasparinis, being unlettered and incorrigibly provincial, had been taken in by Shamash's familiarity with great men, his prominence in the Greek delegation, his diplomacy and ease of speech and by his understated elegance, which gave every appearance of deriving from substantial wealth. To some extent this was true; Shamash had, like many of his compatriots, brought with him from Constantinople a large number of books and he was selling these at enormous prices. And he made no attempt to deny appearances. But even the Greeks, although they had no reason to say so, did not know of his origins. He was an orphan who had been educated in the schools of Constantinople, where he was rapidly singled out as being of exceptional intelligence and promise and, in due time, came to the attention of Plethon himself who had adopted him as student and then assistant in his work and his travels. He had been become Plethon's secretary and amanuensis but during the time of the Council, with the constant interaction between the different factions and with diplomacy stretched to its utmost in both secular and spiritual matters, he had gained a reputation, on his own account, as a man who had a political and diplomatic future. He was admitted to many of the meetings of the delegates, his advice was sought, given and valued and, in some instances, his opinions were adopted by his superiors. He had begun to achieve a career and persona independent of Plethon.

He thought again of Cecilia. She was tall and beautiful but, in character, a complete contrast from her sister. When the two girls were together, it was difficult to tell them apart unless they were engaged in conversation, when it became obvious that Juliette was intellectual and curious but Cecilia, it must be said, was not. Nevertheless, she was lively and intelligent, with a hard edge of practicality, and this suited Shamash. He needed a wife for two simple reasons; to gain respectability in Florentine society and to find an excuse to remain in Florence for as long as possible. He had not the slightest wish for a woman who might challenge him personally or intellectually. He did not seek a loving relationship with Cecilia but one of convenience, although, for the time being, at least up to the day of the wedding, he would not be and could not be faulted in his attentions and his devotion.

He thought also of his visit to the Libreria Patrizzi the day before. He had returned there again to negotiate with Patrizzi for the sale of his book and had come away with a fair price and a very large sum of money, sufficient in fact to fund his expenses for the wedding. This was an absolute necessity if he was to continue the front that he had been projecting for the benefit of Gasparinis. He also gave thought to the young lady he had encountered in the Libreria on his earlier visit. Not only had she concealed her identity but the maid whom she had left outside the bookshop had betrayed the clandestine nature of her mistress' business by her frantic knocking on the door when he had approached. That her mistress was from a wealthy family was indicated by the very fact that she had a maid. He felt that he recognized her, he was not sure how or why and, although he had not seen her face, he had a strong feeling that they had met very recently. He was also sure that the pages he had taken, and which he knew that Eduardo did not want to give him, were connected with the visitor. He had an idea that would solve his doubts on the matter and might, somehow, he was not yet sure how, act to his advantage.

He again took out the two pages from his locked cabinet and studied the first. It was in a striking and easily recognizable hand and consisted of a motto in Greek. The picture was erotic, not to say obscene, and showed a woman dressed in the skins of a cow coupling with a bull. The poem was in French and read:

> "Knowing that this Pasiphae was a fool
> In no wise learn thou not of her school
> Though that some women do so amiss
> Yet right many good there be I wiss."[5]

Shamash recognized the reference, which was to the myth of Pasiphae, the daughter of Helion, on whom a spell had been cast so that she lusted after a bull. After intercourse she gave birth to the Minotaur, half man and half bull, to whom the young men and maidens of Athens were sacrificed and who was eventually slain by Theseus in the Labyrinth. The "Allegorie" on the sheet that Shamash held was a rather facile rationalization of the myth in Christian terms suggesting that the myth of Pasiphae was the classical prefiguration of the biblical parable of the prodigal son; as the Allegorie stated "there is no greater joy than a soul returned to God." The whole ensemble seemed to Shamash to be no more that a puerile and prurient doodle but it was one which, if he was right about the identity of the author, would be devastating if made public. The only element that struck him as being out of place was the Greek motto, *Kalliope*, which did not seem to have any direct relevance to the subject matter and which had obviously been taken by the author from some other source. It was just more evidence of the amateurishness of the whole composition. He picked up the other sheet he had taken; this was headed *Phaedrus,* a title which also seemed to have no relevance to the rest of the composition.

Smiling to himself, Shamash placed the sheets back in his cabinet, gave it a further moment's thought and then went to the door of his room and locked it before settling down again at his desk. He first studied with care the pages of lecture notes in Eduardo's hand. After a few moments, he sharpened his pen and wrote what appeared to be two paragraphs on a separate clean sheet of parchment. Then, examining alternately one of the pages of Eduardo's notes and his own composition, he wrote a series of figures on a third piece of parchment. This process took him nearly an hour but he was still not finished. Under the first series of figures he then wrote a second series of figures which appeared to be adjustments to the first series, since he referred continually to the first before adding to the second. Finally, he took out from his cabinet a flask of fluid in which he dipped another, this time rather blunt, pen and very gently inscribed the second series of figures between the lines of one of Eduardo's pages of notes. He then cut up the two extra sheets of parchment that he had been using into very small pieces until the contents were completely illegible. He wrapped Eduardo's pages in a further piece of parchment and writing an address on the outside, tied the whole package up neatly covering the knot with sealing wax, which he melted with one of his candles. He did not however seal the ball of molten wax even though he was wearing a signet ring which he could have used for the purpose. He determined that he would give the package the next morning to one of the couriers who made the regular passage to Constantinople with other correspondence for that city.

The whole process had taken Shamash two hours. He could hear through his windows that the streets of Florence were still awake but he was tired and he immediately prepared himself for sleep.

CHAPTER 5

Twins

Some weeks after the banquet, Cecilia and Juliette were spending the morning in the sitting room of their own small apartment in the Palazzo Gasparini. It was here they had grown up and been educated and where they had spent most of their time in each other's company. They were very close and in spite of the differences in their character they had always shared with each other almost all their thoughts, feelings and aspirations. Cecilia had long recognized that her sister was much devoted to books, to learning and writing than she, but only occasionally now did she allow frustration on the matter come to the surface. She knew that her sister's special interests would not make life any happier for her, quite the contrary since there would be no opportunity for her to pursue these interests when she was married which would, as both of them assumed, be very shortly. Juliette had little social life and few friends unlike Cecilia who mixed with the children of many of the great families of the city.

Juliette was sitting in the window seat with a book in her hand. But she was not reading. She was thinking about Eduardo. Cecilia, for her part, was once again going over the lists for the wedding: the guests, the preparations for the ceremonies and the details of her trousseau. She was, at that moment, studying her hands and considering the appropriate color for her wedding gloves but she finally interrupted this difficult task to ask her sister: "What are you thinking?"

Juliette reddened slightly and replied hesitantly, "I was thinking about Ferrucci."

Cecilia giggled. "That's nothing new. You are always thinking about him."

"It's true. I can't get him out of my mind. Tell me, Ceci, what is about Philip that attracted you to him? Why did you fall in love him, in particular?"

But she didn't wait for an answer. She was longing to share her all-absorbing thoughts.

"I love Eduardo's eyes. And his smile through his half closed lids. I love the way little wrinkles appear around his eyes. And his brown curly hair, a little lighter than his eyes. I love the way he looks at me. He can't take his eyes off me when he comes round with books. I love to tease him and look severe. And then I smile at him and he blushes."

"My God," said Cecilia, "you really are in love with him. But are you sure that this is just not your clever way with words. Do you really love him, like that, as much as that? If you do, it is going to lead to disaster. Mama and Papa will never agree to a match, you know that. He doesn't have any money, we know nothing about his family and he doesn't have any prospects at all, working in a bookshop – it's just hopeless."

Juliette bridled, her short temper immediately ignited.

"Well, it's the same for you. We know nothing about Philip, his family, his background and his prospects. I respect your wishes and your love for him but, whatever you think and whatever Mama and Papa thinks, I think that your marriage will also be a disaster. As for Eduardo, I want to care for him because he is penniless. I shall make a living from my writing. We will run away and travel the world together."

Cecilia who had long known her sister's views of her fiancé, and was quite accustomed to her sister's outbursts, laughed. She was well aware that Juliette did not share her own practical sense, was careless of the details of her future and lived much of her time in a private world of romance, idealism and contemplation.

"I love Philip," she said, "he is important, good-looking, well-regarded by his peers, and very clever. We are going to stay in Florence and be close to Mama and Papa. It will be a wonderful life."

"Well," said Juliette, "Just because Eduardo lost his family doesn't mean he does not have a good name. I feel so sorry for him. The plague is a terrible, terrible thing. Just thinking about it frightens me. I hope God protects us and it never comes to Florence. Every night I pray for forgiveness for my wild thoughts. I hope God doesn't think I am presumptuous, being only a small thing in this world, but I do ask that he does not punish us as he punished Eduardo and his family."

"Stop worrying about Ferrucci! You have to think of the reality of your future. You should marry Antonio Lucchese. You know that's what Mama and Papa want and they are talking to his parents about it. Then we can all continue to live here in the city and have a wonderful life together."

Juliette got up from the window seat, threw her book down and stamped her foot, once again a rage.

"I hate Lucchese. He is much too old for me. He has no interest whatsoever in reading and writing."

"Don't be so silly. They say he is brave and has a wonderful career ahead of him. You would have a splendid home, a large family and position in the city. And he is attractive. You know that."

"He is arrogant and overbearing. We would not be partners. He would have no interest in me for myself and would just see me as a helpmate for him and his career. I am not interested in 'family', although I am interested in his job which sounds quite exciting. I was talking to him about that the other day. He is in charge of all the spies in the city. But he would never let me help or contribute anything. It would never work."

"Well, it's going to be your life so it's your decision but do think carefully – you may never have another such wonderful opportunity. And you really have to be more careful about Ferrucci. I can't imagine that he can have more books to sell you. Hasn't he sold you every book in the shop? Garzon told me that he was round again the other day."

"Garzon, Garzon, what business is it of his?" said Juliette, again in a fury.

"Actually, I think he was dropping a gentle hint. I think he was, for once, being nice. I think he wanted me to pass on to you, that things are going too far. You have got to stop him coming round."

Juliette raised her voice. "It's none of Garzon's business, I tell you. I don't care what Garzon thinks. I shall do what I want." Then there was a pause. "Actually, I have to tell you a secret. You must not tell anyone."

Cecilia laughed. "Haven't you been telling me to keep secrets ever since we could talk. Have I ever let you down?"

"I went and saw him at the bookshop. I went with Francesca. I left Francesca outside to keep watch. We kissed. It was wonderful. But then there was a disaster."

Cecilia had put down her work and was now staring at Juliette with an open mouth.

"Guess who came in," there was a pause, "....your betrothed, Philip."

Cecilia now stood up and lost control. "Are you absolutely out of your mind," she shouted. "Don't you realize what this means. Don't you realize? This is the end for both of us." She put her head in her hands and started to sob. "Philip will give me up and you will be ruined." She fell back into a chair and lost all color. "We are both ruined."

Juliette put her arm round her distraught sister. "Don't worry. I am almost certain he did not recognize me. I had my cloak and hood on. He couldn't see me and I left at once. It will be fine, I promise. If he was going to say anything he would have done so by now."

That was true and after a short time Cecilia calmed down a little.

"You have got to stop seeing Ferrucci," she said. "You have got to stop. This could happen again."

Juliette said nothing, picked up her book and sat down to read again, trying to ignore the implications of what her sister had said though she recognized that what Cecilia said was true. If she was ever discovered and exposed in such a compromising position, both she and her sister would be ruined. But the fact was she was careless, not to say reckless, of her own future and reputation and found it hard to contemplate curbing her own behavior for the sake of her sister.

"What are you reading?" asked Cecilia still shaking.

"This is the latest book Eduardo brought me. It's called De Ludo Globi, On the Game of the Ball. It's the latest by that Cardinal Cusanus whom Signor Manzoni is always talking about. I can't make out what he is trying to say. It is either that life is a game which God plays with us – we are just His puppets, He keeps us on a string and we live according to the whims of His will or it could be saying that trying to understand the nature of God is as difficult as playing with a misshapen ball. I don't know. I shall have to ask Manz about it."

Cecilia was not listening and had returned to her lists.

"One of the best things about getting married," she said, "is that I shall never have to have another lesson from Manzoni again. I can't tell you what a relief that is. He tried so hard with me but it was hopeless. You are his favorite and I don't mind."

"I think he is sweet," said Juliette. "He is so serious. I love to tease him. I shall tell him that I have found love. How I have found the path to oneness, to my God. How I am going to be one with God. And he will be very excited and suggest that I go into a convent to contemplate God. Then I will tell him that my God is Eduardo and how I love him and how I am going to become one with him."

"Juliette," exclaimed her sister, "this is too much. You have got to control yourself."

"Yes." said Juliette, pursuing her thought. "I shall tell him that and he would probably faint with shock and we would have to sprinkle water over him to bring him round or may be that would finish him off altogether. I mean he is so old. He must be at least forty."

"That's not old. Mama and Papa are much older. But I agree he is kindhearted and he never shouts at us; I shall miss him in spite of everything."

"I am going to continue with my lessons as long as possible." said Juliette. "I am going to be a writer. I am going to write about how we can find God. Eduardo gave me some copies of the lectures of this Greek, this Plethon. You should know him, Philip is his secretary."

"Of course. I have heard him speak of Plethon. What of him?"

"Well, he says, that all the confusion of this world, the fears, worries, aggravations, distractions, irritations, the many, many individual things of this world become one in God. So every part of the world, every tiny piece, every one of our problems, our actions and our good and our bad thoughts are part of God so whatever happens in life it really must be good since it is part of God."

Cecilia who had listened to these meandering outbursts for many years and had never had the interest to contribute to or respond to her sister's profound observations, said nothing. She turned her mind back to her own plans for the future, to the wedding and her life with Philip Shamash.

Juliette returned to her seat in the window and began wondering what Eduardo thought of the pages she had given him. Then she decided she would go again to the Libreria. She didn't care what happened or who was watching them. She must see him.

CHAPTER 6

The Salon

Each week the Gasparinis were at home to visitors. This was the custom of Florentine society and the Gasparinis, being what they were, were no different from their peers. Usually, such affairs were held in one of the smaller rooms in the palazzo but this week, for good reason, the family received in the salon, the great hall of the Palazzo.

The grand salon was a long room with a high beamed ceiling lit by tall windows which overlooked the courtyard in the center of the palazzo. Without the heat and focus given by a winter fire, the salon had a severe, even forbidding aspect, the only decoration being the painted beams in the ceiling, tapestries on each side of the fireplace and, beneath them, Cecilia's two cassoni or marriage chests. The decoration on these was not yet complete, a work in progress which would be finished by the wedding, which was now only two weeks away. The cassoni by tradition would contain the practical elements of Cecilia's dowry, clothes, linens and other items which would enable her to set up a household as a married woman.

Recently it had become the Florentine custom, amongst the best families, to emphasize the splendor and size of the dowry by having the cassoni of their daughters decorated by the greatest artists of the age. Gasparini of course was no different in this respect and he had employed for the task one Paolo Ucello, an artisan much in demand at the time. It could already be seen that the end result would be magnificent; painted on the panels between the Gothic tracery of the cassoni was a series of scenes depicting incidents from the lives of the Roman emperors. When his visitors on that day looked upon and admired the beauty of the work, the Count could, modestly and genuinely, be pleased with himself.

One person who stood in the background in his customary deferential pose and attire and who did not admire and was not pleased was Garzon, the steward of the Gasparinis. In the absence of the slightest interest in these matters from the Count and Countess, it was Garzon, who selflessly shouldered the burden of administration of all the Gasparini domestic and business affairs. He ran the household, kept the books, paid the staff and collected the rents from the Gasparini estates.

Garzon appeared to be the ideal manager, his air of deference and confidence never faltered, there was never a ripple in the calm progress of life in the Palazzo, the books were balanced every year, there were no complaints from tradesmen, no creditors to appease, not a single whisper of impropriety. The reality was however different. Garzon was indeed shrewd, but he had never believed it necessary to waste this valuable commodity on the affairs of someone other than himself. He had been systematically looting the Gasparini estates for years. Under his stewardship, there were as many thieves in the Gasparini household as there were servants and it is not clear whether or not they were the same people.

The situation was by no means desperate for the Count and Countess. Garzon had seen to that. But he was becoming anxious, very anxious. The Count had instructed him at quite short notice to employ Ucello and although this latter was only an artisan, he was very expensive. Garzon could not argue with Gasparini but what with the additional cost of the unexpectedly large Council banquet and with the wedding approaching rapidly, he was for the first time experiencing some trouble with the household finances. Not only was the Count himself completely uninterested in these matters but, buoyed by the success of the banquet, he was flinging caution to the winds and demanding ever greater extravagance for the wedding, which he believed should accord with his rising social status.

Even more worrying for Garzon was that he had been informed by a friend, Mario Cartari, a courier for the Bicci bank where Gasparini kept his accounts, that an agent of the Bargello had visited the bank the day before and according to a colleague of Cartari, a scribe, who worked within the bank, this agent had inquired about the state of the Gasparini's accounts.

Garzon had for some time been considering that it would be prudent for him to conclude his activities with the Gasparinis. He had a plan in place for this eventuality but he was now concerned that he might have left it too late. As one would expect from a man of such shrewdness, he had backup plans, including information he had been collecting over the years on the peccadilloes of each of the members of the family. But this information would only be used as a last resort if all else failed and as a means towards his own defense, if he was somehow discovered.

While Garzon was silently contemplating these matters, Gasparini walked about the room waiting for his guests. He was expecting the Luccheses among others and this was the reason he had used the salon even though he was not anticipating a large gathering. He was hoping to advance the discussions regarding the betrothal of Juliette and Antonio and what better venue to impress the visitors than the grandeur of the salon, with the beauty and expense of Cecilia's cassoni on view.

The Luccheses were one of the most respected families in Florence and a liaison with them would continue the improvement of the Gasparini fortunes. Antonio was a splendid young man who had all the advantages of wealth, family and reputation, with a stable and possibly brilliant career ahead of him. The Luccheses had both landed estates and interests in the wool trade, the trade which over recent generations had been responsible for the rise in reputation and power of the city of Florence and which accounted for the wealth of many of its leading citizens. Gasparini knew that he had no head for business and that, at the least, he had to align himself and his family with those who did. He was relying on Juliette's beauty and intelligence, which Antonio appeared increasingly to appreciate, to achieve this.

Maria, the Countess Gasparini, a handsome woman, known for her devotion to her husband, was seated gazing steadily out of a window while she waited for the guests. She appeared oblivious of her surroundings, in a moment of religious contemplation, an occurrence which, for her, was so frequent that she had acquired, amongst her friends, something of the reputation of a mystic. There was a light smile playing over her lips as her thoughts wandered elsewhere.

"Giorgio. Where are you darling? Why are you not beside me naked as you usually are in the heat of the afternoon? I know you are not telling the truth when you say you love me. I know what you love is that I pay for your apartment. But I don't care. All I want is that you make love to me at every moment that I can get to you "

This pleasurable yet deeply spiritual meditation which, for Maria, was of frequent occurrence, was cut short. Someone was addressing her.

"Your ladyship. What a pleasure it is to see you".

She shook her head and looked round. It was Caspar Pallavicino who was paying his respects. She languidly lifted her hand for him to kiss. He noticed that she appeared to be flushed and he put this down to the depth of the mystical connection which he and all her friends understood that she constantly experienced.

Garzon knew better. He knew who lived above the milliner's shop in the Borgo Santa Croce and why it was that Maria had such a passionate interest in hats and headwear and why she had such a large collection that it was becoming increasingly difficult to find discreet storage for them even in the endless chambers and closets of the palazzo.

Pallavicino was a mincing little man, an old friend of her husband who always came to the weekly salons, who knew all the gossip which he never failed to share, but whom even Maria found boring.

"Milord", said Maria, "It is my pleasure, as always, to welcome you to my home."

Before the words were out of her mouth, Pallavicino had embarked on a long and breathless story of how there was rumor that a young unmarried noble lady had been detected unchaperoned in the company of a young man. The Countess listened politely but was thankfully saved by the arrival of the Luccheses, whom she rose to greet. She was aware as much as her husband of the advantages of a match between Antonio and Juliette and she wanted to play her part in bringing it about.

Gasparini took Emilio Lucchese aside and, after a pointed stroll past Cecilia's cassini, the two of them went up to the far end of the room, sat down where they could not be overheard and engaged in earnest conversation. Maria wanted to have a similar conversation with the Countess Lucchese but she could not get rid of Pallavicino especially since no other visitors had yet arrived. And so the two women exchanged pleasantries while my lord Pallavicino bowed, scraped and nodded.

The only other occupants of the large salon were Juliette and Cecilia, the latter with two of her friends, Elisabetta Bembo and Marina Fregoso. These last three, with frequent giggles and conspiratorial whispers, were discussing the upcoming wedding in which the two girls were to have important function as chief attendants to Cecilia. Juliette who, against her will, had been forced to attend the salon by her father, sat alone reading. This in itself irritated her father.

Other guests arrived. Gasparini's conversation with Lucchese had been concluded apparently to their satisfaction and Gasparini was now by the door welcoming the latest arrivals, Peter Bembo and his wife, Julia. Their daughter, Elisabetta, was already sitting with Cecilia in the salon. Lord Cesar Gonzaga and the Count of Canossa both of whom had also been at the banquet were announced. Cesar Gonzaga had recently lost his wife but this had not prevented him from continuing to appear in society and he was now very popular with the ladies. Maria Gasparini gave him special attention.

Lord Paulo Catania had also made an appearance with his wife, Lady Joia. Gasparini was particularly pleased to see Catania and welcomed him effusively. His lordship was a member of the Florentine Committee of Security, a body of eight senior advisers to the Duke, which met on an ad hoc basis, usually in times of crisis. It was this committee which had appointed Antonio as head of security although in practice, since the Committee did not meet often under the stable regime of Duke Cosimo, Antonio reported to the Bargello. It was Catania's first visit to the Palazzo Gasparini. It had in fact been noticeable that since the banquet the number of visitors attending the Gasparinis' salons had increased. Over the years, jealous gossips had intimated that

Gasparini was one of those who did not like his acquaintances to know his friends but the elite of Florentine society appeared now to have accepted him as one of their own.

A small crowd gathered round Catania who began to talk about the successful conclusion of the Council.

"I believe", he said, "that this is a moment that will change the course of the history of our country and indeed of Europe as a whole. The prestige of the city has been enhanced and", with a nod towards the Count, "every citizen can be proud of the part he has played"

This well-honed speech was apparently intended to continue for some time but was interrupted by Cesar Gonsaga who said quite diffidently:

"Is it not true that the Decree of Union has still to be ratified by the full Greek and Russian churches and that the delegates from the other Christian communities in the East are still in the city with hard negotiations to conclude?"

Catania literally waved this objection aside but was interrupted again.

"It seems to me," said the Count Canossa, who saw the practical aspects of the matter quite clearly, "that even if Paleologus was sincere in his desire to unite the Churches, his real aim, and we all know it, was to obtain material assistance for his struggle against the infidel, from us, from Milan, from Venice and from any and every other state in Latin Christendom. The only real question is whether we or anyone else are going to provide such assistance and indeed if all this discussion on dogma has or will make any difference or whether it has all just been a waste of time. After all whether or not the churches are united, we are all brothers in Christ. It is," he said with a slight bow towards Catania and with the expectation of a significant response from the powerful politician, "a political decision and not a spiritual one."

"It is much too early for that decision to be made," said Catania diplomatically, "but when it is we shall take into account all the relevant and necessary factors. Our first priority is always the security of the state and decisions as to how best to achieve this are always complex."

"It is a practical decision," said Bembo, also wanting to be heard. "Is it likely that any help that we send the Greeks can actually prevent the inevitable? It is a miracle sent by our Lord himself that has enabled the city to hold as long as it has – without proper arms and supplies. All it has is three great walls. I fear the worst; I see fate taking its inevitable course."

The party fell into silence. They all knew what that course would be and no one wished to dwell on it.

Juliette pointedly ignored the company and their chatter and remained with her book seated next to the great fire-place.

"What is it you are reading?" asked a voice which Juliette recognized before she even looked up.

It was Antonio. He had what she thought was quite a kind smile on him and a gentle look in his eyes. She handed him the book, *The Romance of the Rose*, an epic poem written about one hundred years earlier, which was as notorious as it was unreadable, the poem being interspersed with long sections of commentary both on the poem and on completely unrelated subjects.

"Have you read it?" she asked mischievously.

"Of course not," snapped Antonio and she immediately realized that he did not have a sense of humor or, if he did, it was not one she could relate to. She had apparently already challenged his masculinity, something she realized that if, God forbid, they were ever to be married, he would never be able to accept. She looked right into his eyes and he looked away. She took the book back, put it down beside her and then rose.

"Let us take some refreshment," she suggested. A liveried footman, wearing the badge of the Gasparinis, a rabbit rampant, and carrying a tray with cakes and drinks came up to them.

"How are the plans for your sister's wedding proceeding?" Antonio asked.

"I know nothing about them." Juliette replied. "I have not wished to interfere with my sister's preparations or detract in any way from her enjoyment of such an important day. I am not even taking any prominent part in the ceremonies."

"That is very thoughtful of you indeed. And I have no doubt that it will be a magnificent occasion. Your family is getting something of a reputation for splendid hospitality."

Juliette nodded in acknowledgement.

"And what is there new to report with the spies?" she asked, a little too loudly for Antonio's liking. "I would hope you are now concentrating on the Turks. They are getting a little too close for comfort, are they not?"

Antonio looked at her in amazement and she continued.

"You know there is something I have never understood and that is why the Turks have never been able to get themselves a good navy. If they had that they would be able to blockade Constantinople without difficulty."

Antonio was speechless. It was not only a question to which he had no answer, one which he, being a soldier, had never even asked himself but it was one which obviously needed an answer. In fact, he would raise the question himself when he had his next meeting with the Bargello. He looked at Juliette sharply and frowned, not, as she immediately felt, that he disapproved of her stating her opinion but because he did not want to reveal to her that he had never even considered the matter.

For her part, she felt again that she had said too much and came to the sudden realization that, in his company, she would never be able to state her mind. This is ridiculous, she said to herself, this is never going to work. I have now gone as far as I will for the sake of politeness and in the interests of the family.

She excused herself abruptly and went over to join her sister and her two friends.

Antonio, who had appeared to be put out by Juliette's remarks, was actually fascinated by the brief exchanges between them. This was the first woman who had ever stood up to him, who did not appear in the least intimidated, who was obviously of the highest intelligence, who seemed as well informed as he, and was possibly better educated. She was undeniably beautiful. Again he thought that if she could only be tamed she would be a wonderful partner for him, possibly for life.

It was the first time he had ever thought of a woman as a partner, as someone for whom he might be prepared to spend time, energy and emotion to make her happy. He realized at the same moment that this was a dangerous thought, one that would inevitably interfere with his own grand ambitions, one that might result, at the least, in antagonism and jealousy, antagonism between the two of them and jealousy over other relationships that she might have. Was such a liaison worth it, he wondered?

He looked round to follow Juliette and was momentarily taken aback by seeing Philip Shamash in the midst of the group of girls, apparently the center of attention and talking animatedly. He saw Shamash sit down and, with a pen that he was holding, invite each of the girls to write something on a piece of parchment, which he then folded and put in his pocket. Antonio's immediate reaction was proprietary and aggressive; he went forward to join the group and get close to Juliette, to claim his girl, even though she had never given him the slightest hint that she was or would be his.

Philip Shamash turned towards him, met his gaze calmly without the slightest indication that their encounter was anything but the most normal social intercourse. The two of them were the only men of their age present and it was right that they should exchange greetings if not confidences.

"The wedding is very soon, is it not?" said Antonio.

"Yes, indeed," replied Shamash, "and we are all very busy in the preparations," making it clear with the slight emphasis on "we" that he was already part of the family.

"And have you decided where you are to live?" asked Antonio, innocently.

"I am discussing this with the Count," said Shamash, "but we are looking at a house on the Via dello Sprone which will accommodate us well. I hope you will come and visit us when we are settled in."

"I would be delighted to," said Antonio and then turned again to Juliette to find that once again she had moved away and in fact had left the room. As he looked around to see if he could locate her, he noticed some new arrivals, more friends of the Gasparinis, Messer Nicholas Phrisio, his wife, Angelica, and their daughter, Rebecca. Phrisio was a wealthy man, who had made money in the wool trade and now had shares in the Bardi bank.

Antonio had known the family for years, as indeed he knew most of the Florentine families, and he also knew that Rebecca for a long time had been and still was very fond of him. For lack of anyone else he knew well to talk to, he joined them as they were being welcomed by Maria Gasparini. Rebecca was undoubtedly attractive, but in a very different way from Juliette. She was about 20 years old, of average height, with long black hair and dark eyes, which contrasted with her intensely clear skin, an aquiline nose and a full figure, which she had no inhibitions in displaying to its advantage. She had always been passionate and uninhibited and, unlike Juliette, had no intellectual pretensions whatsoever. She was clearly delighted to find Antonio, greeted him with a kiss on his cheek, which she could only reach if he bent down a little, and then drew him off to one side.

"There are rumors going around amongst our friends that you are to be engaged to be married to Juliette Gasparini. Are they true?" she asked in a half mocking tone.

"Nothing is settled yet," he replied truthfully but evasively.

"I should hope not," she said managing to pout even at the same time as she spoke. "You know that I for one would not allow it. She is not right for you. She would only cause you continual trouble. Look, she is not even here now to be with you in her own house. She is not made for the discipline of marriage. You know that I have loved you for years and will always love you. I am the one for you."

Her voice was rising, her bosom heaving, genuine tears came to her eyes and the other guests turned to look at her. Antonio, whose exploits and bravery on the battle-field were already talked about in the salons of Florence, was not so well equipped to fight on the field of love. Unusually for him, he was not sure what was the right thing to do, so he did what anyone else would have done, he did the natural thing. He put his arms round her to comfort her and to the shock of both his parents and of the Count and Countess Gasparini who had just ended their discussions on Antonio's betrothal to their own daughter, Rebecca pulled him down to her and, without warning, gave him a passionate kiss on the mouth, which he appeared to have difficulty extricating himself from. The deep silence which invaded the great salon was finally broken only by Rebecca's sobs as she ran out of the room.

CHAPTER 7

Jealousy

Antonio was furious with himself. He still suffered from the embarrassment of the incident at the Gasparinis, which no doubt was now known by everyone in Florence who mattered, including and especially, Juliette. How was it that he of all people, recently appointed to one of the most important posts in the city government should have been subjected to such indignity and just when he was gaining a reputation for sagacity, respectability and reliability? His mother and father were also embarrassed and furious and had had to apologize on his behalf to the Gasparinis. No one seemed certain whether the engagement to Juliette was still to take place. Why were women so unreasonable and troublesome? Why could they not see and observe the proprieties? And what had Juliette thought when she heard of it, as she undoubtedly had? He was confused. On the one hand he was thinking about Juliette constantly, he could not get her face out of his mind and on the other, he had to admit that he had, for a moment, enjoyed, not so say become lost in, the kiss with Rebecca. He admired her for her passion and directness and he suspected that life with her would be much simpler than with Juliette.

He was seated at his desk toying with his papers and turning these things over in his mind, when he was interrupted by the delivery of further reports from his agents within the city. The first, Giulio Giovio, had just been to the Bicci Bank.

"Everything seems to be in order with the financial dealings of the Gasparinis," said Giovio. "They have taken out a number of loans over the last few years but these were all repaid at the proper time."

"What was the nature of their transactions?" asked Antonio.

"Gasparani invested his loans in wool shipments. These shipments are sold in another city, and the bank's local office is repaid with interest. Gasparini retained seventy five percent of the profit. I have learned that the financial affairs of the Gasparinis are conducted in the main by their steward."

Antonio saw all this as good news and it further confirmed his decision to pursue Juliette. He would not have credited Gasparini with the good sense to engage in such affairs but they were standard practice and he did not give them a second thought other than sending a request to the Bicci Bank that he should be informed each time Gasparini undertook any further such ventures.

The next report concerned Shamash. The agent who was watching Shamash had seen him on several occasions hand over packages of papers or letters to the courier for Constantinople. While this in itself was not the least unusual, the agent thought that since Shamash was under suspicion, it might be worthwhile, if and when he were to send another package, to seize it and examine it. Antonio agreed and dictated and signed the authority for this to be done.

Finally, he met with Scamuzzo who had been watching the Libreria Patrizzi. Shamash had been to the bookshop twice in three days and Antonio had felt this sufficiently unusual that he had decided to station Scamuzzo to watch the Libreria during the day.

"I was outside the Libreria all day and towards evening last night the woman in the cloak and hood, again went into the bookshop. I am sure it was the same woman although the maid was different. The maid again remained outside. Although my instructions were to remain only until nightfall, I decided to stay on watch."

"You did well," said Antonio.

"After two hours, the lady came out of the shop and, in accordance with your instructions, I followed her and the maid back to the Palazzo Gasparini in the Via dei Neri which I assume was her home. I was able to see her face as she entered the palazzo. She was young and had long brown hair."

Antonio pushed back his chair and stood up. His face had lost its color.

"Are you ill, Signore?" said the agent in alarm.

Antonio slumped back into his chair and waved his hand.

"No, no, I am well," he said heavily. "Go on. Go on."

"This morning, I went back to the Libreria and inquired further. I have here a list of the names of the owner and his employees. The owner is Patrizzi who lives in the house. I was able to ascertain that the only person present in the bookshop the previous evening, at the time of the young lady's visit, was one Eduardo Ferrucci. He is an immigrant from Ferrara who has been in the employ of the Libreria Patrizzi for about four months. If you wish I can make further inquiries about the origins of Ferrucci."

"Yes, yes, do that. You have done well. You may go", said Antonio tonelessly.

Antonio realized at once that it must have been Juliette. Cecilia would never have dared go out on such an expedition on the eve of her wedding, quite apart from the fact that she had no interest in books. Antonio's features hardened and his heart froze with jealousy, although this is not nearly an adequate description of the mix of emotions which assailed him. What was Juliette doing alone with a young man for two hours? He just could not bring himself even to contemplate it. How could she risk her reputation in such a way? Did she not know that if it came out there was absolutely no possibility for her to make a suitable marriage? Had anyone else seen her? What was he to do with this information? Could he or should he now proceed with his suit with the Gasparinis? Who was this young man who was prepared to compromise a noble lady in such a manner?

He could concentrate on his work no longer. He got up and strode out of his office, slamming the door in his turmoil. For an unaccountable reason, such reckless behavior made Juliette even more attractive to him and, motivated by the twin engines of jealousy and power, he began to consider how he could proceed so that Juliette's reputation would be safeguarded and his rival eliminated.

CHAPTER 8

The Wedding

The day's celebrations began with the traditional procession through the streets of Florence. At about 10 o'clock in the morning, Cecilia mounted a splendid carriage on top of which lay a white marble bull decorated with flowers and ritual ornaments. She sat on a marble chair behind the bull wearing a dress of green silk and gold, matching gloves and a long train which descended down the back of the carriage, a dress which was rumored to have consumed more than ten yards of silk. She wore a long veil secured on the top of her hair by a crown of gold. The chariot was pulled by six white horses, on the necks of which had been constructed models of human torsos to give them the appearance of centaurs. The horses were mounted by six of Cecilia's closest friends including her chief attendants, Elisabetta and Marina, and of these, three were seated to the left and three to the right, each of them playing a musical instrument. In the many subsequent accounts of the legendary Gasparini wedding, it was said that these young nymphs played in heavenly harmony but this, in the circumstances, seems doubtful.

Accompanying the carriage were attendants on foot. Two of these carried golden vases in the antique style made of topaz from each of which a cloud of smoke escaped diffusing a priceless perfume. Behind them were two more attendants, blowing golden trumpets to which were attached pennons of fine silk woven with gold. Two others had ancient horns, which they played together. Behind Cecilia's carriage on horse-back rode some of the male guests and beyond them in carriages the remaining members of her family and other friends. They in turn were surrounded by revelers who carried cymbals and flutes, wore wreaths of vine leaves or garlands of laurel or were dressed as animals.[6]

The people of Florence, who had, of course, been alerted to the imminent wedding festivities, lined the route of the procession with the same excitement and enjoyment as they did during one of the saints' day festivals. The onlookers applauded, cheered and danced, waved ribbons, threw confetti over the bride and, after the last carriage had passed, followed the procession through the narrow streets in an ever-growing, chanting mass. After two hours, the carriages returned to the Palazzo, discharged the bride and the wedding guests, and as many of the populace as could be safely accommodated were allowed into the palace courtyard.

The formal ceremony itself was performed by a notary in the salon. Shamash, who had not been in the procession, now stood next to the bride, splendidly attired in tight scarlet leggings, a gold embroidered surcoat over a black velvet jacket and a scarlet velvet cloak trimmed with ermine. Around his neck he wore a heavy gold chain. The ensemble was completed with a velvet hat and long pointed slippers. After the vows were taken and the couple kissed and were embraced by family and friends, the whole party moved into the dining hall where the wedding breakfast awaited them.

The Gasparini hospitality was already legendary but Garzon had outdone himself. The table that he had prepared was one to delight the eye and the palate of the most jaded Florentine. There was grey partridge, calves' heads gilded and silvered, capons and pigeons, a sheep roasted whole, a great variety of roast birds, a suckling pig, and a dressed peacock, different tarts, and an abundance of candied spice (as well as much else).[7]

But the centerpiece of the meal was the wedding oration. This traditional laudatory epithalamium had recently, and especially in Florentine society, developed into a monumental rhetorical exercise, another expression of the wealth and status of the bridal family. As these things do when it is a matter of status, a momentum had developed so that, with every wedding ceremony, the oration became longer and longer as each family strove to out-do the next to the point that many of the guests began to view a wedding as something to be dreaded rather than enjoyed.

Of course, Count Gasparini was not one to be perceived as someone less than his peers and he had employed one of the most celebrated orators of the time, who went by the professional name, in the best classical tradition, of Claudius Ciceronianus. He could be relied upon to entertain the guests for at least two hours without pause although entertain was not the word that some of them subsequently used.

He began as fulsomely and sonorously as he was to continue since he needed to be heard above the general conversation, the noise of the service of the meal and the crowd outside the open windows.

"How great is the worth of marriage which had its beginning in paradise, which removes the evil of concupiscence, which embraces within itself a heavenly sacrament, which preserves the faith of the marriage bed, which maintains between the husband and the wife an undivided life together, which preserves children from dishonor, which frees carnal intercourse from guilt."[8]

Antonio was seated at the top table in a place of honor next to Juliette but uncomfortably close to Ciceronianus. He idly wondered how often this latter had used these words before; he was sure he had heard the same introduction at one of the many other weddings he had been to in the years he had been in town. This was the first time he had had the opportunity of being with Juliette since the embarrassing incident at the salon two weeks earlier. Fortunately, even though the Phrisio's and Rebecca had been invited to the wedding, since the invitations had been sent out many weeks earlier and they had then accepted, tactfully they had not come.

Antonio was fascinated by Juliette; the fact that she pointedly preferred to talk to Octavian Fregoso, her neighbor seated to her other side, and ignored Antonio to the point of rudeness, did not deter him in the least. Fregoso was an older man than Antonio but he was a bachelor and Juliette's attentions to him were giving Antonio twinges of jealousy, an effect that was no doubt intended by Juliette. Her closeness to him, her stifling perfume, her creamy neck mostly turned away from him on which lay a few loose curls which had fallen from her hair pinned on top of her head and which he had the greatest difficulty in preventing himself from touching, her provocative eyes which seemed always to challenge him, all of these made her more and more attractive to him.

He had already determined that when the celebrations were over he would remain behind and ask Count Gasparini for his daughter's hand. This was a formality since the affair had already been settled between his father and Gasparini but convention required that Antonio should still make the request. He believed that time was against him. He had to act quickly to prevent any further meetings between Juliette and Ferrucci, since the longer that liaison continued the greater the risk of its discovery. It was not for nothing that Antonio had obtained the reputation of a man of action; the existence of a potential rival, even though Antonio knew that a match between Ferrucci and Juliette would never receive her father's consent, was something which increased his determination to win her for his wife.

Ciceronianus had now reached the stage in his speech dealing with the beauty of the bride about whom he, in the custom of the time, was frankly sensual.

"What is more pleasing, more delightful and more lovable than a gorgeous face? Nor are women graced only with beautiful faces but with hair, breasts and thighs and an entire body, whether they be tall, white complexioned and luscious or well-proportioned."[9]

The Countess Maria, mother of the bride, not unnaturally, was also seated at the top table and next to Shamash. Conversation which, in any event, was almost impossible beneath the rolling cadences of Ciceronianus, had become increasingly desultory and now was completely stifled by the great weight of the ninth course, the roast suckling pig. Maria's eyelids were drooping and only when she heard these last words of Ciceronianus did her imagination awaken. She thought of Giorgio, whom she had not had the opportunity of visiting for at least a week and this, quite apart from the demands of the wedding, was making her quite irritable. Maria, of course, had had nothing to do with the catering arrangements but she had had to attend to the increasing excitement and nervousness of Cecilia who, not unnaturally, had been demanding of Maria's time.

"Giorgio, Giorgio," thought Maria. "Where are you?   Here I am losing Cecilia. Soon I shall lose Juliette. You are the only person I can turn to for comfort, for consolation. Once, perhaps, Gasparini would have given me that comfort. I do not even remember the time, if there was such a time, when he would have been willing or able to do that but now I just have you. I don't care that others may discover the truth about us. I need you."

Her mood changed from elation to despair and silent tears started to roll down her cheeks, which she dabbed with her napkin. Her neighbors at the table, other than Shamash who could hardly conceal his disgust at his mother-in-law's emotion, guessed rightly that this was the natural manifestation of maternal grief over the loss of her daughter and displayed, to no avail, token signs of comfort and condolence.

Ciceronianus, having provoked this demonstration of deep sentiment, was unstoppable. He had now passed on to the attractions of the groom.

"Who after diligently observing him and contemplating the dignity of his beauty, would not think that so decorous a face, such joyful eyes and so happy a look do not signify and promise a noble and unheard of generosity of spirit? Philip burns with an unbelievable fire of love and longs that Cecilia might burn with an equal flame so that they might be joined in joyous and perpetual love."[10]

Unlike his wife, Gasparini was enjoying himself hugely. He enjoyed the meal, he enjoyed the festivities, he enjoyed particularly the thought that, once again, he, his family and his home were the center of the attention of Florentine society.

Mindless of the fact that this honor was only open to citizens who were members of the merchant guilds, he began to harbor the thought that he would now be asked to become a member of the Signoria, the governing body of the city. He saw his recent social successes as an inevitable and unstoppable progress in his family's prestige. Determined to do justice to his own feast, and to show that he was a gourmet with the best of his peers, he made his way noisily through the final course of quinces cooked with sugar, cinnamon, pine nuts, and artichokes served with various preserves, made with sugar and honey. With exquisite timing and a final encomium, Ciceronianus also drew to a close.

"In choosing a wife four things are to be considered: beauty, nobility, good habits and wealth. In all these Cecilia excels and Philip in his choice demonstrates a wonderful discretion and sagacity."[11]

He closed with a deep bow and Gasparini started to applaud loudly which at least had the effect of arousing the other guests from their somnolence; they too joined in prolonged applause but more from relief than appreciation.

The meal ended, the guests rose from their places and crowded round the married couple who, after many exchanges with their friends, with both salutations and farewells, moved towards the grand staircase from which they would go up to the bridal chamber. The assembled guests, in the ancient tradition, broke into a great shout of bawdy remarks and suggestions and the crowd outside who knew what to expect, joined them in an uproar of cheering and chanting, expressing the universal desire for healthy progeny and many of them.

This was the climax of the celebrations but not the end. The party continued all evening; there was music and dancing and later another meal although on a lesser scale. Seizing an opportune moment, Antonio approached Gasparini and made his formal request for the hand of Juliette. Gasparini who would have agreed to anything, he was so happy, readily consented and was prepared to make the announcement at that very moment. What better time than when all his friends present. It appeared however that Juliette had again disappeared and was not to be found even in her rooms. Gasparini was so distracted that he did not or could not at that moment pursue the matter. Antonio, however, who had hardly exchanged a word with the woman to whom he was now engaged even though he had been her companion most of the day, certainly had an idea where she might be found and this overwhelmed him again with rage and jealousy.

CHAPTER 9

The Prisoner

Antonio walked slowly around his office. He was nervous. The interview he was about to conduct would require more than the usual degree of tact and diplomacy and he was concerned that Philip Shamash might be more experienced than himself in such things.

His agent had indeed detained the courier to Constantinople and had brought all the letters and documents that he was carrying to the Palazzo del Podesta. It was impossible for either the agent or the courier to know which of the packages had been given him by Shamash and so, of necessity, they were prepared to open all of them. Although it was recognized that he had had no part in the affair, the courier was detained pending completion of the investigation, at the end of which the letters and packages would be returned to him.

Cesar, one of Antonio's assistants, had the task of checking the documents. He started with those which were not sealed since it was assumed that the sealed documents were the most likely to be innocent. The sender would be apparent from the seal and Cesar recognized the seals of many if not most of the families in the city. He would open any package or letter with an unfamiliar seal and, later, if Antonio deemed it necessary, he could then open those which had recognizable seals. This latter was not something that Antonio relished and he had to have good reason to do this since the powerful families of Florence believed that they had the right to keep their correspondence private.

Cesar was an expert in the deciphering of codes and hidden writing. The first step in examining any of the documents brought to his attention was to pass each sheet over a candle. From experience he knew the height and the speed at which he should do this without singeing the parchment. Heating the document would reveal in most cases the presence of secret writing and, in this case, almost immediately after opening the first unsealed package, he found between the lines on one page of notes of Plethon's lectures, rows of numbers and letters that could only be a message.

Antonio sat at his desk and Cesar sat opposite him making a first attempt to decipher the hidden text.

"I have tried a simple substitution of the numbers and letters in the message and find nothing," said Cesar. "This means that, at the very least, multiple substitutions have been made using a key. This makes it almost impossible to break the message without knowing the key."

"Explain," said Antonio.

"The next level of complexity in such a code would be to use a long number as the key. We could take the number 75423 as an example. With this number as the key, the first letter of the message would be shifted seven letters to the right in the alphabet, the next letter, five letters to the right and so on until you get to the end of the key and then you start again."

"I understand," said Antonio. "Go on."

"Since we don't know the numbers of the key and we don't even know how long it is, as I say, it is impossible to decipher the message. Obviously the sender and the receiver know the key so it is easy for them."

"So," mused Antonio, "we have to persuade either to reveal the key."

"Indeed," said Cesar with a broad grin as he savored the thought of "persuasion". "Of course, Signore, to make my job easier," he suggested, "you could just "persuade" them to reveal the message itself!"

Antonio had therefore a delicate task. Quite apart from the fact that Shamash had just married into one of the most prominent families in the city and that he himself was preparing to do the same, Shamash had quasi-diplomatic status from his position with the Greek delegation. He had spent the last year in Florence cultivating the attention of both the secular and religious leaders of the city; furthermore, his mentor, Plethon, was one of the most famous men in Europe. On the other hand, Antonio knew that Plethon was leaving the city within the week, as were most of the delegates who had not already left, and Shamash would soon be left without his colleagues to protect him.

Antonio could not even be certain that the package they had opened was the one Shamash had sent but, since it contained the Plethon notes, that was extremely likely. He knew that Shamash would deny any knowledge of the secret message and would never reveal the code number or the contents of the message without the physical persuasion which Cesar, for one, had relished.

Philip Shamash was ushered in and Antonio rose to greet him.

"It is good of you to have come," he said. "Please sit down."

Shamash took the chair he was offered and sat down calmly, saying with the utmost grace but with an unmistakable edge to his tone,

"I assume I am not making a social call. I know one cannot refuse an invitation to the Palazzo del Podesta but I must tell you I find the timing very unusual, even discourteous. Only two days after my marriage. I assume you have a very good reason for wishing to see me in your official capacity."

Antonio had expected more sarcasm, more bluster, and so was not in the least surprised by this opening protestation.

"Yes," he said, "I am, of course, aware of your circumstances; nevertheless I trust you will see the importance of the matter, at least from my position which is the point of view of the city itself. You may take it from me that, knowing as I do your present circumstances, I would not have asked you here unless the matter was of the gravest concern."

Shamash nodded without speaking and waited. Antonio took out from his table one of the sheets containing the notes of Plethon which they had recovered from the courier.

"These papers have recently come into our possession and if they are what I believe they are, namely the lecture notes of Gemisto Plethon, there is no one better than yourself to tell us about them. I assure you that the matter is one of the highest national security so I hope you will excuse us for having asked you here at such short notice. I believe we will be able to clear the matter up very quickly."

So saying, he handed over the sheaf of papers for Shamash to look at and said, "Do you in fact recognize these?"

"Yes," said Shamash, "I do recognize them, of course. They are, as you say, the lecture notes provided by my teacher Plethon for his students on the subject of that great seer, the philosopher, Plato. Where did you get them?"

"I cannot answer that," said Antonio "but we would like to know as much about them as possible. For instance, how many copies were made? To whom were the copies given? How many different scribes were there?"

"I should say that for each lecture there would usually have been about twenty copies and the scribe for all these copies was a young man called Eduardo Ferrucci who works at the Libreria Patrizzi in the Via San Cristofano. I can give you the names of some of those who attended the lectures and some of those who received the notes. I do not know the names of all of them. Different people attended different lectures. Not everyone who attended wanted a copy of the notes."

"Do you keep a copy of these notes yourself?" asked Antonio.

"In general, I do not," said Shamash, "unless there are copies remaining which, in some cases, I might put aside somewhere. I am familiar with the subject matter. I do not need them. Now perhaps you can tell me what this is about."

"Later, maybe," said Antonio. "What can you tell me about this Eduardo Ferrucci? How is he involved in this matter?"

"He seems a nice young man, intelligent and curious. I understand he is a newcomer to the city. I have no knowledge of his background. He is apparently without means except for what he is paid at the Libreria but I can tell he is ambitious and when I suggested he might earn a little more by correcting and copying the lecture notes, he seemed enthusiastic."

"How did you come to meet him?" asked Antonio.

"I have made several visits to the Libreria with a view to obtaining offers for manuscripts which I have in my possession. I met him there. And now," he said, his voice displaying more than a little impatience, "I have done my part, I have answered your questions in good faith. As I am sure you are aware, I am not accustomed to being treated in this way. Either you tell me why this matter is important to you or I shall take my leave."

"You have been very helpful," said Antonio but without changing the grave and steady tone of his voice. "I need not detain you further. I know you are in the midst of setting up your new home and have many important things to attend to but I should tell you that the city authorities view this matter with great seriousness and I may very well ask you to come in again and assist us further. I should like to have the names of anyone you remember giving the notes to. My assistant will collect the list from you tomorrow. In the meantime, I hope you will give my respects to your wife."

"Since you have not told me the nature of this matter which you describe with such seriousness," said Shamash in a voice heavy with sarcasm, "I doubt whether I shall be able to help further than I have already."

He rose and turned to leave. Neither of them said anything further.

Antonio could not believe his good fortune. Ferrucci, his rival, whom he believed to be Juliette's lover had been delivered into his hands. He immediately summoned one of his assistants and instructed him to go to the Libreria Patrizzi with two guards, to arrest Eduardo Ferrucci, bring him to the Palazzo del Podesta and detain him pending interrogation. The assistant should also search Ferrucci's effects and seize any suspicious or unusual material.

Within half an hour came news that a search of Shamash's rooms had been fruitless. They were empty. He had already removed all his effects to his new home on the Via dello Sprone. Antonio had asked Shamash to come to his office for good reason although they both knew that this was an insult for a man of the latter's diplomatic standing. In view of their existing acquaintance, it would have been more appropriate for Antonio to have requested an interview in Shamash's home. No doubt Shamash put it down to their personal rivalry and the animosity between them but Antonio had wanted to ensure that Shamash could not interrupt the search that he had authorized. Apparently, this precaution had been unnecessary and Antonio would have to rely on his interrogation of Eduardo Ferrucci to make further progress. He decided to leave Eduardo in custody overnight in the dungeons of the Podesta on the excellent grounds that this would make the prisoner more malleable for his interrogation. Doubtless, Antonio had a vicious streak in him, which had served him well as a soldier and leader in the field and would continue to do so in his present position.

The next morning Antonio reviewed the materials belonging to Eduardo that had been found in the Libreria Patrizzi. Naturally, there had been uproar in the Libreria at the arrest and at the search but there was nothing that Patrizzi could do about it. Many unusual, not to say suspicious, items had been found. There were more copies of lecture notes, obviously those of Plethon, similar to the ones which Antonio already had in his possession, pages of work in Latin and Greek, some pages with long lines of script in Greek, and other pages with Greek titles, images and Latin poems and essays. According to the report of the search party, there were other manuscripts in Latin in Ferrucci's hand which appeared to result from his normal work in the Libreria and which had been bound and, according to Patrizzi, were available for sale in the normal course of business. These had been left at the Libreria but could be brought over for Antonio to review if necessary.

Antonio could not read Greek but he had a Greek translator on his staff, one Hieronymus Este, to whom he gave the Greek papers for translation. The lecture notes as we know were in Latin and these he gave to Cesar to search again for hidden writing. Cesar reported that on this occasion he could find nothing and the translations of Este indicated what appeared to be, in the main, merely the notes of someone who was learning Greek. The lines of Greek script, however, Este deemed suspicious; they seemed to be part of a riddle or adage that could easily conceal some secret message. Neither Cesar nor Este could immediately decipher the meaning of these lines nor of the sheets with the Greek titles, images and Latin commentary, which were in formats they had never seen before, where the Greek titles did not relate to the rest of the page and where the enigmatic nature of the whole could easily consist of some secret code.

After considering all this, Antonio summoned Eduardo, who was brought into the room with shackles on his hands and feet. He had not eaten for twenty-four hours. He had spent a sleepless night both from fear and discomfort, lying on a stone floor with a little straw for a pillow, without the slightest intimation of what it was he had done to deserve this treatment.

Eduardo stood there shivering from the cold of his imprisonment.

"Would you like some water?" Antonio asked.

Eduardo nodded and, after he had gulped down the draught, Antonio motioned to the guard to stand immediately behind Eduardo.

"Your name is Eduardo Ferrucci?" asked Antonio severely.

Eduardo nodded.

"You come from Ferrara?"

He nodded again. There was a pause while Antonio gazed at Eduardo with a frown that suggested that this already represented something treasonable. In reality, he was studying Eduardo's features, the soft brown eyes now bloodshot, the white face and curly long brown hair. This was the man for whom Juliette was willing to lose her reputation. He was almost ten years younger than Antonio and looked even more.

"What are you doing in Florence?"

"I am a scribe in the Libreria Patrizzi," whispered Eduardo.

"Yes, I know that," snapped Antonio. "But what is the reason you came to Florence?"

"I came because of the plague in Ferrara, because my family died and I had nowhere else to go to."

"What was your address in Ferrara?"

Eduardo gave it to him and Antonio wrote it down.

"Do you have money apart from what you earn?"

"No", said Eduardo. "I lost everything."

"Whom have you met in Florence?"

"Practically no one, apart from Patrizzi and his family and the other scribes and workers and the customers of the Libreria. What have I done?"

"We will come to that," said Antonio. "Now, which customers in particular have you met?"

Falteringly, Eduardo mentioned some names but he did not mention Shamash or the Gasparinis which, of course, Antonio noted with suspicion.

"Do you know Philip Shamash?" he asked.

"Yes."

"Was he a customer?"

"Yes."

"Then why did you not mention him?"

"Well, there are a lot of customers. I did not think of him."

"But do you not have a special relationship with him, to the extent that he gives you extra work to do? Is he not for you the most important customer?"

"I suppose in one sense he is," said Eduardo whispering hoarsely.

"And conveniently you do not mention him. Why is that?" repeated Antonio.

"I forgot," said Eduardo, who, in his exhaustion, was certainly not thinking clearly.

"You forgot. That is not very likely, is it? In fact, it is very unlikely that you just forgot to tell me about your best customer. The truth is that you were afraid to tell me because you are engaged in an affair with him that you do not want to tell me about. Is that not the case?"

"Well, yes," said Eduardo almost inaudibly and certainly miserably. He was hanging his head, looking the picture of guilt but Antonio knew he would look much worse within a very short time after he realized what he was being accused of.

"Now tell me what it is that he asks you to do", said Antonio who was, of course, immensely enjoying the discomfiture of his rival.

"He asks me to correct and copy out some notes of the Plethon lectures, which are then distributed to the audience."

"Yes, yes, yes," said Antonio irritably. "I know that already and what else does he ask you to do?"

"That's all,' said Eduardo. "He collects them every week and gives me more to do. There is nothing else."

"Of course there is," said Antonio and he showed Eduardo the copies that had been taken from the courier. "Are these the copies?"

"Yes."

"And this is your script?"

"Yes."

Then Antonio showed him the copy with the secret message, parts of which were still visible. "And you wrote this?" pointing at the secret script.

Eduardo peered at it and shook his head. "No, I did not write that. I have no idea what it is or how it could be there."

"I do not believe you," said Antonio. "You admit that you wrote the rest of this document and you try to deny that you wrote this message. That's ridiculous."

"But I have never seen this before," said Eduardo, his voice rising as he began to appreciate what he was facing and what this was all about.

"Oh yes, you have," said Antonio. "And now what about the key to the message? Let me have that please."

"What key? I don't know what you are talking about."

Antonio looked at Eduardo for a long time until the latter could no longer hold his gaze and dropped his eyes. Antonio could hardly resist a smile. Guilty or innocent, Eduardo had admitted enough that he was completely in Antonio's power and completely at his mercy. He smiled because Fortune had favored him in delivering Eduardo into his hands, because it was amusing that Eduardo was saying what all accused criminals and traitors had said throughout the ages and because with persuasion nearly all of them eventually admitted their guilt.

"What you have done," he went on, "is a crime against the state of Florence. It is no less than treason and treason is punishable by death. Your fate will be decided by the court based on my recommendations. The recommendations that I make will be based on whether you are or are not cooperative. If you are not cooperative, you will die – it is very, very simple. Do you understand?"

Eduardo who could now hardly breathe, slowly nodded his head.

"Then I ask you again and for the last time. What is the key to this message?"

Eduardo looked at Antonio. Both men waited. Finally, Eduardo, in bewilderment, slowly shook his head. Antonio motioned to the guard who pulled Eduardo to his feet and then shuffled him out of the room.

Antonio leaned back in his chair extremely satisfied with himself. Nothing but good could come of this. He would enhance his standing in the government from the discovery of what appeared to be a major conspiracy against the state. He would save Juliette's reputation since the principal witness to her visits to the Libreria would be eliminated and he would immediately be free to consummate his own relationship with her. He summoned a secretary and asked him to arrange a meeting with the Bargello himself as soon as was convenient.

Later that day, Antonio was sitting in the comfortable office of the Bargello, a large room with a beamed and decorated ceiling, tapestries hanging on three walls and tall windows that opened on to the interior courtyard of the Palazzo del Podesta and from which a light breeze gave some relief from the August heat. Antonio had been surprised and a little embarrassed to find that Lord Catania, who had been a witness to the unfortunate incident at the Gasparini's salon, was also present. He had apparently been reviewing other matters with Bardini and had remained to be part of the discussion with Antonio, no doubt to gauge for himself the character and merits of the new chief of security.

Antonio explained the findings of his agents and the details of the interrogation of Shamash and Ferrucci.

"We are unable to decipher the message unless we have the key to the message," he continued. "And the only persons who have the key is he who wrote it and he to whom it is addressed. I am convinced that both Philip Shamash and Ferrucci are in league in this conspiracy and that one or both of them knows the key to the message. I think it is likely that they are spying for the Greeks but that is not certain; it could be that they are agents for another country. I cannot know for certain until we have deciphered the message."

He pointed to the Greek scripts Ferrucci had secreted at his work place, which appeared to be codes and were, at the least, puzzling and enigmatic. He called attention to the fact that Ferrucci, unusually for a mere scribe, was attempting to learn Greek and that he had withheld information about the nature of his relationship with Shamash. Finally there was the fact that he was a foreigner who only very recently had been admitted to the city.

"I believe it is very likely that it was Philip Shamash who deposited the notes with the secret script with the courier but I cannot be certain and, even if he did do this, it is not certain that Shamash knew of the message. I believe that the evidence shows that Ferrucci is the more likely of the two to have written the message and that further persuasion should be applied to obtain the key."

"I congratulate you again", said Bardini after Antonio had completed his recital of the facts, "and now I take it that you are recommending that we submit Ferrucci to the rack?"

Antonio nodded.

"And what is your recommendation for Signor Shamash?"

"I shall leave that to your excellencies. I certainly believe that he has knowledge of the plot and may be the ring-leader but whether or not it is diplomatically wise to put him to torture, I do not know."

"And you yourself are in a difficult position in this decision, are you not?" asked Bardini pointedly.

"Yes, your excellency. As you know, Philip Shamash married the Lady Cecilia Gasparini only a few days ago and I myself am betrothed to her sister, the Lady Juliette. I shall have to consider carefully my relationship to the Gasparinis."

Catania spoke for the first time.

"There can be no question of submitting Signore Shamash to torture. Our relationships with the Greeks are too sensitive at this time. He has powerful friends and whatever he knows, if anything, it is not worth the least risk of jeopardizing the aims of the Council and giving ammunition to those who might wish to refuse to ratify the Decree of Union."

"Very well," said Bardini, "but since it seems highly likely that this man has been involved to some degree in a conspiracy against the state, we cannot risk him staying in the city. He will have to be asked to leave."

"It has just struck me," said Antonio, "that this marriage might very well have been an excuse and an opportunity for Shamash to remain in the city to continue his activities. My inquiries show that he is not a wealthy man and that he has supported himself largely by selling books. It seems an extraordinary coincidence that the marriage has taken place at the same moment as the conclusion of the Council by his delegation."

"Yes," said Catania, "I must say I have had difficulty understanding why the Gasparinis acceded to his suit. He must have been very persuasive. I met him briefly at the Gasparini's Salon recently – I believe you were there, Lucchese, were you not? He struck me as a very clever fellow and not at all someone to be satisfied with a union with such a provincial family. I tend to agree with your analysis, Lucchese. There is something odd about that marriage."

Antonio went cold from the insult from Catania. But, at the same time, he realized it was as much a warning as an insult. He recovered his composure sufficiently to ask Bardini, "in view of my relationship with Philip Shamash and in view of his diplomatic standing, I think it would be appropriate if you would give him the order to leave the city."

"Very well. You must inform him that he should come to my office tomorrow. And now, about Ferrucci. As I understand it, is your opinion that he should be put to torture to reveal the details of the conspiracy and the message. Is that it?"

Antonio nodded and watched as Bardini eyed him with a slight smile, stroking his beard as he always did when contemplating a solemn decision.

"No," he said, "we will do better than that. You can threaten Ferrucci with torture, you can threaten him with execution, you can threaten him with anything you can think of and then you will persuade him that in return for commuting such pleasant exercises, he is to become a spy for us, a double spy. If he refuses, you can do what you like with him. If he accepts, he is to go to Constantinople and report to our existing agent there. With his background, he may be able to get information from the

Greeks at a level of society which our other agents cannot reach. He is of noble birth, he is intelligent and well educated. We will tell him that we expect him to shadow Shamash and discover his true identity and allegiance. If Ferrucci is already a spy for the Greeks, he may or may not tell us anything of interest. If he is not, he may be very useful. He must give monthly reports to our agent. You will tell him that if he betrays us in any way, he will be immediately assassinated. You will tell him that we have informed Philip Shamash that he, Ferrucci, under torture, betrayed the true identity of Shamash so that if he attempts to contact Shamash no doubt this latter will take an immediate revenge. You will further tell him that if he carries out his duties to Florence faithfully, after ten years he will be released from his obligations to us and will be free. I myself, when I give Philip Shamash the order to leave Florence, will inform him that Ferrucci has betrayed him. You will keep Ferrucci in custody until Shamash has left."

These curt instructions concluded the meeting. Antonio rose from the table and left the room. On the one hand, he was full of admiration for Bardini's plan, a sentiment he could tell was shared by Catania, who remained seated, giving Antonio no more than a nod as he departed and, on the other, a little irritated that he was not to have his way with Eduardo whom he would have dearly loved to see on the rack. What's more, he realized that he was now going to have to monitor the activities of the man for years to come. The only consolation, which was a major one, was that Ferrucci would immediately be leaving Florence and it was very unlikely that he would ever see Juliette again.

CHAPTER 10

Love

A week later, Philip Shamash and Cecilia left the city. Shamash had been called in to the Podesta by the Bargello himself and informed that he was suspected of spying, that he no longer had permission to remain in the city and that he must leave with the remaining members of the Greek delegation. Shamash, with the utmost urbanity, denied the accusations, asked for details and for proof but was given none. He was informed merely that Eduardo Ferrucci had fully revealed the details of the affair, including the role of Shamash. The latter was also told that Ferrucci would likely be executed for his own part in the plot. This last was an added twist conceived by Bardini to make it more likely that Eduardo would not contact Shamash when he reached Constantinople. If Shamash ever discovered Eduardo, he would be certain to realize that the only reason that Eduardo's sentence had been commuted was the real reason: he must have turned counter-spy.

After Shamash had left, Eduardo was, once again, brought to Antonio's office from the cells.

"Good morning, Ferrucci," said Antonio, amiably.

Eduardo, who, in spite of better treatment at the hands of his gaolers during the past week, was looking no better than on the occasion of his first interrogation, returned the greeting.

"We have given you a little time to reflect on your options," continued Antonio, "and I will remind you of them again, indeed for the last time. You must tell me the key to the message which you wrote. If you refuse again to reveal this now, you will be put to the rack to help persuade you. Eventually you will tell us any way. You can save us all some trouble and speak now."

Antonio spoke in an even, friendly, tone, with a slight smile, just as he might as if he had been inviting Eduardo to sell him a book. As he spoke, he watched the prisoner carefully. Eduardo began to breathe heavily and turned white. He did not speak but just shook his head.

"Come on, my boy", continued Antonio in his most cajoling and condescending tone. "We know you came to the city as a spy, we know you were learning Greek, we have the parchments on which you were preparing secret messages. Your co-conspirator, Shamash, has been banished from Florence and has already left. He has implicated you in the affair. There is no one left to protect you and there is absolutely no reason for you not to tell us. Think about it. Think about it. This is your last chance."

Eduardo dropped his head and was apparently too over-come to speak.

Antonio pushed back his chair, got up and walked round the room. Then he went over to Eduardo and slapped him hard on each side of his face and then again.

"Tell me, you fool" Antonio shouted. And he hit him again with his closed fist, cutting his face.

Blood poured down Eduardo's face and on to his clothing. Antonio kicked over his chair and Eduardo fell heavily on to the floor. After a short while, since there was no sound from the prisoner, Antonio shouted at the guard.

"Pick him up and clean him up."

Antonio finally began to believe that his prisoner did not, in fact, know the key to the message. Eduardo had not even asked what would be his punishment if he did reveal the key. If his fate was to be death, whether or not he confessed, any sane person would have made some effort to avoid the rack.

Eduardo was cleaned up, given a new shirt and reseated in his chair and Antonio addressed him again.

"Very well", he said "I will give you one more opportunity to avoid the rack and avoid execution. Quite simply, I offer you the alternative of becoming one of my agents. You will become an agent for the City of Florence. You will go to Constantinople and obtain information about the Greeks. If you need it, I will give you twenty-four hours to make your decision or you can decide now. Either execution or Constantinople. What do you want to do?"

Not surprisingly, it was not a difficult choice and Eduardo spoke for almost the first time.

"I will go."

"Very well," said Antonio again, masking the disappointment that he felt.

"You will have one week to clear up your affairs and prepare yourself. You must conduct yourself in the utmost secrecy. You will be accompanied everywhere and the Libreria will be guarded until you leave. You will be escorted to Venice and put on a boat to Constantinople."

Antonio continued to give Eduardo instructions. He would be given one hundred florins for his journey and instructions how to meet a contact who would arrange lodgings for him. He would be paid for information when he provided it; otherwise he was free to take employment as he wished. He would be followed to Constantinople by other agents so escape was useless. If then or subsequently he attempted to escape, sooner or later he would be found and killed. He was warned that he should under no circumstances contact Shamash who would undoubtedly have him executed if he knew Eduardo was in the city. Nevertheless, the initial focus of his work was the real identity of Shamash. Eduardo was to discover who Shamash was working for and what if anything he had learnt. Over the longer period, it was Eduardo's role to obtain information by reaching into the highest levels of Greek society. He was further informed that, with good behavior and results of his mission, his exile would last for only ten years. His cover-story was to be simply that he had been driven out of Ferrara by the plague, that his family had all perished and that he had come to seek his fortune in Constantinople, attracted by fantasies of the glamour and wealth of the city.

He would be given a new identity as a further precaution and new papers. From henceforth he would be known as Nicholas Camerino and the public record would show that Eduardo Ferrucci had been executed for treason.

Eduardo was exhausted by his stay in the Podesta, although his living conditions had improved since the day of his interrogation. He was bewildered by the rapidly changing events and terrified by the prospects of his future life and his role as a spy, for which he saw himself as completely unsuited by character. He still had virtually no knowledge of Greek, no knowledge whatsoever of the tradecraft of a spy, he had never been off Italian soil and was much more interested in books than in the more vigorous pursuits that would now be required of him. His confusion was compounded by the fact that, at the beginning of his imprisonment, he could not conceive of how or why he had gotten into this mess although, as time went on, he began to realize that he had been framed or made a scapegoat by someone who could only be Philip Shamash.

Eduardo returned to the Libreria accompanied by an agent who assured him that he or a replacement would be watching the building at all times. Patrizzi was not pleased to see him. Any sympathy that he might have had for the young foreigner had been quickly dispelled by the knowledge that, if he himself was not careful, he would be implicated in this affair and his reputation and his business, built up over a lifetime, would be ruined at a stroke.

As it was, Patrizzi had immediately set about visiting his best clients, including the Gasparinis, to assure them of his loyalty to them and to the city and to emphasize this he gave each of them a gift of one of his most precious books in which he incorporated a specially written and fulsome dedication to the patron. Indeed, unsure of the gravity of the crime committed by Eduardo, since nothing but rumors had swept the Libreria and then the city, including the Gasparini household, he decided to present to Duke Cosimo himself, the *Hieroglyphica* of Horapollo, one of his most precious manuscripts.

Since this manuscript was in Greek, which he knew the Duke could not read, Patrizzi secretly harbored the thought that the Duke might ask him to translate it. If he did, he, Patrizzi, would have turned a disaster into a personal triumph and he would certainly have been able to recoup his financial losses. Unfortunately for Patrizzi, and indeed for Western culture, Cosimo did not accept the bait although he did accept the manuscript, which was not to be translated for another seventy years.

The upshot of all this was that Patrizzi wanted Eduardo out of the Libreria and out of his house at once. Eduardo assured him that he was leaving Florence for good and would be gone in three or four days. Patrizzi did not speak to him again. He refused to pay Eduardo's meager outstanding salary on the grounds that he had cost Patrizzi many times that amount and in any event he was a criminal if not a traitor.

The perils and uncertainties of his future were completely swamped in Eduardo's mind by his overwhelming need and determination to see Juliette again. She could not come to the Libreria and he would not be allowed access into the Palazzo. Finally, he decided to take Arturo, the illuminator, into his confidence. It was a risk but the two of them had been friends and Eduardo sweetened his request with one of his precious silver florins and this Arturo could not resist.

Just as he had in the old days, Eduardo chose a book that Juliette might consider purchasing into which he inserted a letter and asked Arturo to deliver the package to the Palazzo. Twenty-four hours later he received a reply delivered by one of the Gasparini servants to the effect that Juliette would buy the book. Hidden within the first letter was a second, instructing him to come to one of the rear doors of the Palazzo at seven that evening.

This was Eduardo's last day in Florence. Antonio had seen no reason to prolong his stay. Eduardo had nothing to do in the Libreria, Patrizzi wanted him out and even if Eduardo had had the means to transport them, he had virtually no possessions to gather up and take with him. There was no purpose in increasing the agony of waiting. Eduardo did, with Patrizzi's permission, take his Greek textbook and he also had the presence of mind to recopy the Greek characters and text that he had found in the Stobaeus. He had recovered something of his strength since his stay in the Podesta and with this he had recovered his determination and some little optimism. If he was to spend ten years in Constantinople, he would surely have time to search some of the libraries of the city and search for the great books that he knew must still exist there. But another side of him was deadened by a great emptiness; as he walked the short distance to the palazzo, he knew that this was the last time he would see Juliette again, perhaps for many years, perhaps forever.

Eduardo knocked on the appointed door which was opened by Juliette's maid. He was carrying another book as some little excuse for his visit. He knew that he was being followed by one of Antonio's agents but this latter would not be able to gain entry to the palazzo and, by the time he could make his report, it would be too late. He was met by Juliette's maid and they made their way up a back stair to her apartment.

Juliette was standing in the middle of the room and she dismissed the maid. There was no point in her remaining, even to keep watch. No one would visit Juliette at this hour and, if they did, there was almost nowhere for Eduardo to hide. Cecilia had, of course, already left and her room was empty apart from some childhood baubles she had abandoned. In any event, neither of them cared. There was no worse punishment that could be inflicted on them than what they were already facing.

They hugged each other for a long time and then sat down on a sofa in front of the fireplace, with their arms around each other,. It was already dark and the light from the tapers on the wall flickered around them. She asked him to tell her what had happened and he related the story of his arrest, incarceration and interrogation. When he came to the interview with Antonio, her face grew taut and she put her hand to her mouth.

"Oh, my God!" she exclaimed, immediately grasping what had happened. "It's he."

"What is it?" said Eduardo.

"It's my fault, it's all my fault," she said. "It's because of me."

"Why? How?"

"Because he must have found out about our visits together. And .. and," she hesitated and blushed, "My parents want me to marry him and I believe he is in love with me."

Eduardo looked at her and the weight that was on his heart became even heavier. She again flung her arms around him and covered his face and hair with kisses.

"But I shall never marry him. I promise you. I promise you. It is you I love. It is you I love." And she started to cry.

Now they sat beside each other, slightly apart, while she stifled her sobs and they both absorbed this last revelation.

"You may be right," began Eduardo, the tone of his voice rising and with uncharacteristic bitterness and even malevolence, he continued. "It is nothing to do with Shamash, it is nothing to do with spying. I could not understand what this was all about but now I do. He wants to get rid of me. He trumped up this spying charge to get rid of me. *Quel figlio de puttana. Quel cazzo.* But I shall get my revenge. If I do anything more in this life, I shall get my revenge."

He stood up and started pacing round the room in fury. Juliette watched him. It was the first time she had seen him express such emotion, such anger, such bitterness and she loved him for it.

"So what is going happen to you? Why did he let you out?" she asked in almost palpable fear at what he was going to answer. He stopped his pacing; they looked at each other and he answered only after a long pause.

"I have to go to Constantinople. I have to become a spy for him. If I don't go, they will kill me." He paused for a long time. He could hardly bring himself to say it. "I have to go for ten years. I am leaving tomorrow."

She put her hands to her face and again they were silent, both of them lost in sadness. He drew her to him. They both knew that fate had unaccountably taken control of their lives, that there was nothing more to be said, there was nothing that either of them could do, only that there was a great void ahead of them which nothing could fill.

In defiance of fate, she took both his hands and placed them on her breasts and he covered her face, hair and neck with kisses. They stretched out on the small sofa and pressed to each other. She began to cry again.

"I love you," she said.

"I love you too," he replied.

And without any hesitation, she stood up, and not letting go of his hands, she led him into her bedroom.

94

CHAPTER 11

The Betrothal

After the wedding, the palazzo had become quiet and lifeless. Maybe this was how it had always been. Unaccustomed to the strenuous activity of the previous few weeks, the servants were justifiably lethargic and even Garzon seemed unusually distracted. The Count himself experienced an intense feeling of anticlimax, which was probably natural in the circumstances. But this momentary depression was nothing to what he felt when, a few days later, Shamash informed him that he was leaving Florence immediately. He could not or would not elaborate except to say that permission for him to live in Florence had been withdrawn, that he would of course be taking Cecilia with him and he would return to Constantinople where the two of them would again start to set up a home.

Maria was frantic and urged Gasparini to do something, so he first asked Antonio who suggested that he approach the Bargello, who, in turn, told him that for reasons of state he could say nothing. He wrote a letter to the Duke himself but this also got him nowhere. One of the Duke's secretaries eventually replied referring him again to the Bargello.

Since no one seemed to know anything substantive, Gasparini took every opportunity to relate to his friends that the reason for the change of heart was quite simple: Plethon had put pressure on Shamash to return with him to Constantinople. Apparently Plethon felt that Shamash had become indispensable to him and, what's more, it appeared that the Emperor was likely to offer Shamash a diplomatic post which inevitably would make the latter's career even more glittering. After discussion with himself and his family (Gasparini went on) it had been agreed between all of them that this was by far the best option for the newly-weds. And thus with Gasparini's spin, the departure of

Shamash and Cecilia did not excite any particular attention and Gasparini felt that he had successfully blocked undesirable gossip and, with his usual acuity, turned the whole affair to good account.

His next problem was the announcement of Juliette's engagement. On the one hand, this would entail a further celebration which he would enjoy and which would once again bring the Gasparini name to what was now its rightful prominence within the city. On the other, he was beginning to experience some anxiety on the matter of the expense of the family's recent festivities. Garzon continually assured him that all was in order and that he, Garzon, was taking care of everything. His confidence and imperturbability could not be questioned and certainly, if Gasparini had wanted to go into the matter himself, he would not have known where to begin. The account books which Garzon showed him every month always balanced and the bottom line, which was all that Gasparini ever looked at, was always positive.

But more than anything, Gasparini was dreading the discussion he had to have with Juliette to inform her of the arrangements with the Luccheses and her engagement to Antonio. If she refused to go forward with it and he had the terrible feeling that she might, however unprecedented it was for a daughter to oppose her family's wishes in this respect, he would find himself with an awful decision to take. He loved his daughter, both daughters, but he knew Juliette's temperament and this was the moment he had been anxious about for years, the climax of a long relationship that had become more and more stormy as Juliette had matured and her views had become more decided. If she refused, he would have to deal with her harshly. Not only had he been promising himself and her for years that he would do so in these circumstances but also convention demanded it. If he did nothing he would at best be regarded as weak and ineffectual and at worst his hard-won social prominence would be lost. In the last few days, Juliette had become even more than usually withdrawn and taciturn and he assumed that this was because she too knew that a climax over the engagement was approaching. The incident with Rebecca Phrisio had been forgiven and forgotten, the Luccheses were now pressing him and Antonio visited daily to assure him, if not Juliette, of his devotion. There was nothing for it but to get it over with.

Gasparini asked a servant to see if the Countess was occupied and, if not, to ask her to join him in the salon. The servant returned saying that the Countess was not in her rooms and, upon being asked, that he did not know where she was. The Count then asked for Garzon, who could usually be relied upon to know everything but it appeared that he, Garzon, was also out. Particularly frustrated, having worked himself up to this moment over several hours, Gasparini requested that he should be informed immediately when Maria returned and he retired to the Studiolo.

He did not have long to wait. He joined Maria in the private salon and testily asked where she had been. Unusually for her, she blushed and explained at length that she had been to see friends, then had been shopping and had actually purchased a new hat, which she showed the Count with some pride. The Count was too wrought up to notice or if he noticed to comment on how well Maria was looking; her cheeks were flushed and her eyes bright, her step unusually brisk. The hat was indeed beautiful but, again, the Count did not comment.

"I have decided that we should speak to Juliette about her engagement, this afternoon. In fact, now. I think the time is right that she should begin the next stage of her life and we both know that there is nothing standing in her way..."

Gasparini would have continued but Maria interrupted him to say that she agreed and they sat down on a sofa together and requested that Juliette join them, which, after a long interval, she did. She looked tired. Her eyes were slightly red either from lack of sleep or from crying. She sat down opposite them and waited.

"My dear daughter," said Gasparini with a lightness of tone which he did not feel. "Your mother and I feel the time has come for you to begin the next stage in your life."

"Yes," added Maria, helpfully, "the next stage."

The Count continued without pause. "Now that Cecilia has left us and we are all free to concentrate on your future, your mother and I have been devoting much time in preparations and discussions in regard to it. I do not need to remind you of the duties of your sex now you have come to maturity."

Both Maria and Juliette stiffened in expectation of what was likely to be yet another exercise in the discrimination which they were both already only too familiar with.

"These duties are to marry, bear and raise your children, support your husband in all his activities and do all this with the honor of our name and our family always in mind. Isn't that so, Maria?"

Maria, who was already drifting off, nodded vigorously.

"It has been my happy task, Juliette, my dear," continued the Count, "to have been discussing a suitable match for you with one of the great families in the city and we have now reached agreement with them on all matters. You may be aware of whom we are talking about."

He looked at Juliette for affirmation but she remained mute with her eyes cast towards the floor.

"I am of course talking about the Luccheses and their son Antonio. They are a wealthy and successful family who will provide an invaluable liaison with ourselves and Antonio, as I am sure you know, is one of the most eligible young men in Florence. He has had a great career as a soldier and is now in one of the most important posts in the city government. Also I am told he is extremely good looking. Would you not say so, Maria?"

Maria indicated her acknowledgment with a forced smile.

"And it seems that he has a real affection for you."

Again he waited for some reaction from Juliette but there was neither sound nor movement.

"Well," he said, faltering slightly, "the time has come for us to move forward with the next stage of your life."

At this Maria nudged him in the ribs and he turned to look at her at a loss. He finally uttered the fateful words.

"I propose to announce your betrothal to Antonio Lucchese at a celebration we will arrange jointly with the Luccheses, which will take place here in the palazzo in seven days time."

There was a silence, a long silence. Juliette started to cry silently and her mother leaned over to comfort her. Juliette lifted her head and spoke for the first time since she had entered the room.

"Mama and Papa, I love you both. I know I owe everything to you. You have always been considerate and thoughtful, you have loved me, you have given me a remarkable education and wonderful friends. I know I have not been an easy child and am selfish and irritating to you in many ways. I know what my duty is. I know that this would be what you call a good match both for me and for you. I know that this is what I am expected to do, both by you and by your friends. I know if I don't agree to it, it will be shameful for you and you will not be able to understand me and will hate me for it. But," and here there was a pause and she continued in a firmer voice, "but the future of my life is my life and it should be my decision. And so, I must tell you that, for many reasons, I cannot and will not marry Antonio Lucchese."

At this moment, there was a knock on the door, which was opened in a few moments in spite of the fact that there was no response and a footman announced and ushered in Antonio himself. He bowed and was a little surprised that none of the three members of the family greeted him. There was another silence and finally Gasparini got up and walked over to the visitor.

"I regret Signor Lucchese that this is not an opportune moment for us to receive you," he said. But Juliette also got to her feet and spoke with unaccustomed authority.

"No, Papa, please let him stay."

The Count looked at Juliette and then back at Antonio, bowed and motioned the latter over to a chair. Antonio began to address Juliette but she interrupted him.

"This is a very opportune moment for you to be here, Signor Lucchese," she said. "I was just telling my parents that however much I admire you for your undeniable qualities, your great successes as a soldier, your position in the city and the career that you have ahead of you, your family's name and importance, that despite all of these things and despite the consequences to my own family and myself, I cannot and will not marry you."

Antonio looked at her with an open mouth; not just for what she was saying but the articulate and forthright way she was saying it. There was another silence. No one was sure what should be done next.

Juliette went on, "I am not a fool. I know that this decision will hurt all of you and I regret that very much. But my mind is made up."

Antonio's presence made things even more difficult for Gasparini. He had to appear stern and outraged.

"This is preposterous," he shouted. "You will do what you are told to do. Your mother and I have been discussing this with Antonio's parents for weeks, if not months. Everything is agreed. Everything is prepared. You cannot refuse. I will not allow it. The reputation of the family will be ruined. You will do as you are told. You will never have an offer as good as this. You will never have any other offer at all. Do you realize that? You will never be married if you refuse Signore Lucchese."

"I realize that, Papa," said Juliette, above the noisy sobbing of Maria, who, it seemed, was increasingly likely to have hysterics. "But my mind is made up," she said, repeating herself. "I know the consequences and to make myself less of a burden to you, in fact, no burden at all, I have applied to join the Convent of Santa Caterina in Ferrara. I will leave for there as soon as I have your permission and as soon as arrangements can be made. It would be my greatest wish, dear Papa, that you will forgive me long enough to allow this."

Maria fell back in her chair in a faint. The Count and Juliette got up to attend to her. Antonio, who had not said a word during his brief visit, left without making his farewells. He was disgusted by the whole affair, by the family and suddenly by Juliette. He was white-faced and furious. Once again, he and his family had been made a fool of. It was insupportable. What on earth had prevailed upon him to become involved with these idiotic people? Small-minded parvenus they were and he despised them. In his fury, he suddenly remembered that, in the brief and uncomfortable time he had been with the Gasparinis, he had not had the opportunity to mention the matter which was the reason for his visit. He was now glad that he had not.

CHAPTER 12

Garzon

Following Antonio's request to be informed of all transactions which the Gasparinis had with the Bicci bank, he had just received a report that they had taken out a very large loan secured on all their country estates. He had gone to the Gasparinis that day not only to pay his respects to Juliette but also to check with them, as delicately as he could, whether or not this transaction had been authorized by the Count. In view of what had just happened at the palazzo, he did not feel the slightest inclination to follow through with what was now none of his business. Nevertheless, he was curious about the matter and, on his way back to the Palazzo del Podesta, he stopped at the bank on the Via dei Leone, not far from the Gasparinis, to inquire about the details of the loan.

Antonio met with the director of the bank who gave him the full story. The loan had been negotiated with the steward of the Gasparinis, one Garzon, who had always dealt with their other financial affairs. The latter had explained that as a result of the expenses of the banquet and the wedding, the Gasparinis were in need of temporary financial help and they had decided once again, although this time on a much larger scale, to invest in the wool trade. The bank was fully secured and had confirmed the details of the transaction with the Peruzzis, the wool merchants. Everything seemed to be in order and the bank had not the slightest suspicion of anything untoward.

Antonio, however, had a feeling that there was something odd about the matter. He knew that the Count was not known for his business acumen; it did seem that, at this moment, he was too involved with his family's personal affairs to undertake a transaction of this magnitude and although the expenses of the wedding had been large, they did not seem to have been so large that Gasparini was likely to risk the whole of his estate on a single transaction.

When he returned to his office, he asked an assistant to locate this Garzon and bring him back to the Podesta. He also sent another agent to the Peruzzis to obtain confirmation of the transaction as it had been detailed by the bank. While he waited and still incensed by his treatment at the hands of the Gasparinis, he turned over in his mind a plan that had come to him at the height of his fury.

The first to return to the office was the agent he had sent to the wool merchant, who reported that the story from the bank was accurate. He had also obtained the additional information that the shipment was going to Ferrara and that Garzon had left with it, ostensibly to ensure that when the wool was sold, he would be on hand to receive directly the share due for the Gasparinis' investment, and, furthermore, to ensure that the bank was fully repaid. It was therefore of no surprise to Antonio when the other agent returned to say Garzon was nowhere to be found and no one in the Gasparini household knew where he was. This last fact confirmed Antonio in his suspicions and in his plan.

His last action was to call in two of his most trusted agents, men who had been with him since his days in the Florentine army, men whom he trusted implicitly and for whom he reserved especially difficult but rewarding tasks. He gave them detailed instructions and ordered them to set out at once.

****

I relate now the end of the Garzon affair although details did not come to light until much later, after an investigation which was time-consuming and difficult, since the Ferraran authorities were not cooperative. It appears that the Gasparini wool shipment arrived safely in Ferrara and was sold at the time, place and price expected. The merchant categorically stated that he had handed over the amount of the original investment together with the agreed share of the profit to Garzon in the form of a draft on a Ferraran bank and he had witnesses to this effect. This bank reported that the draft had been presented and that the bearer had been given a large amount of cash. But the office of the Bicci in Ferrara also stated that the Gasparini loan had not been repaid and was still due and owing. No more could be determined. It appeared that none of the intermediaries in the transaction had acted improperly. Two months later, Garzon's body, quite decomposed and almost unrecognizable, was found within Florentine territory. The money had disappeared and the subsequent investigation into the affair by the Bargello yielded no suspects.

Part 2 Constantinople 1439-1453

CHAPTER 13

Eduardo Ferrucci

Ferrucci had lined up at the rail with the other passengers as they approached Constantinople up the Marmora and watched as the vast walls, and the spires, towers and monuments which appeared above them, grew closer and larger. As the ship rounded the point into the Golden Horn, the great church of Santa Sophia which, with its enormous dome, towered over the eastern end of the city, rose into view. They sailed into the Neorion harbor on the western side of the Horn and moored where they were able to find a berth on the busy dock. Eduardo disembarked with the others and on the quay, he paused and looked around. The harbor was full. There were at least twenty ships tied up at the semi-circular dock and dozens of seamen engaged in loading or unloading cargoes. Horses and wagons were stationed alongside the ships or waiting in lines for their turn, hauliers were unloading, officers were shouting orders, the scent of the sea, of fish and of the horses was as thick as the press of people. But for Eduardo it was a relief to be on dry land after his long and uncomfortable voyage at sea.

He walked around the dockyard and, as he had been instructed, found himself a seat on a stone bench, somewhat back from the activity on the quayside. He sat down and waited, the sack of his meager belongings beside him, his legs still weak from the constant movement of the ship which he had endured for the previous two weeks. He felt both apprehensive and excited by the prospects for his future. His greatest and most understandable concern during his journey had been that, in his ignorance of Greek, he would be completely isolated, not only unable to perform the difficult tasks required of him in his new profession which needed subtlety and secrecy but that he would even be unable to pursue a normal daily routine which would allow him to survive in a strange and hostile city without attracting attention. It seemed to him very likely that his inability to communicate would make him an obvious stranger amongst the local inhabitants and would thus stand in the way of his immediate objective, which was to remain hidden and anonymous until he could learn the language, make his plans and carry them out with some certainty of success.

It was therefore a relief for him to hear, as he waited, that many of the sailors and others on the dock were speaking Italian and that his concern on the matter was entirely misplaced. It was a saying in Constantinople that the world contained seventy-two languages and each of them was spoken somewhere in the city. Italian was certainly one of them.

He watched and marveled at the frenzy of activity before him. He had previously not given much thought to the fact that the Greeks and the Turks were not formally at war. The gates and harbors of the city were open to all-comers and the sea lanes were open both from the west and the north where Italian colonies in the Crimea and elsewhere along the shores of the Black Sea provided the supplies necessary to sustain the city and the remains of the once great empire. The harbors of Constantinople were international destinations with ships and sailors from all over the known world.

From where he sat, Eduardo could see through the forest of masts of the ships at the dock and in the harbor and through the gap in the sea walls, over the windblown, grey waters, to the other side of the Golden Horn. Here was another great wall fronting the harbor and more spires above it. This he was soon to discover, was the city of Pera, a small, independent, self-governing, Genoese trading colony, ruled by a Podesta, much like other Italian colonies throughout the Aegean and the Black Sea. The Genoese of Pera viewed themselves as standing apart from the conflicts between Greeks and Turks, and they dominated and jealously guarded the trade between Constantinople, the Latin West and the nations of Asia Minor and the Black Sea.

It was a cold, overcast and blustery day. Eduardo was exhausted from his journey and was very much relieved when a young man who had sat down near him on the bench finally addressed him in Italian.

"The west winds are strong for this time of year, are they not?"

"On the contrary," replied Eduardo, reciting the formula he had been taught, "I have been delayed by strong winds from the east."

"What is your name?"

"I am Nicholas Camerino," said Eduardo.

"And I am .. Andreas," the man replied making it quite clear that this was not his real name. "So you are the traitor." And he turned and looked Eduardo up and down with a scowl.

"I am not a traitor," shouted Eduardo. "I was tricked. I was deceived. I was framed. I did not wish to come to Constantinople but the only other option was to be executed. What would you have done?" This was too much he thought – to be accused and insulted within a few moments of arriving.

"Keep your voice down," said Andreas who nevertheless did not display the slightest sign of alarm and appeared to be enjoying Eduardo's discomfiture. He was dressed as a sailor and might easily have been one, with a lean, bronzed face, dark eyes and hair tied at the back of his head.

"I have no doubt that's what all traitors say. But I know all about you. They have told me everything. You are now under my control and direction. If you disobey my orders in the slightest, if you attempt to leave the city, I will find out and you will be followed and killed. You are still alive for one reason and one reason only which is to discover as much as you can about that Greek, Philip Shamash. I am giving you three months to learn Greek fluently. And then you will get further instructions and be expected to get immediate results. There will be no excuses. No delay. Do you understand?"

As irritated as he was, there was little that Eduardo could do except acquiesce.

Andreas continued, "Lodgings have been arranged for you. The Mascarios will be expecting you. They know nothing about the purpose of your stay in the city. For them you are just another refugee looking for work in the city. You will take a ferry to

Pera which is the other side of the Horn and ask for this address."

He handed Eduardo a piece of paper. "The ferries are those small boats at the side of the harbor, there." He pointed towards the dock.

"If you wish to reach me in the future, you will sit here each morning for half an hour until I contact you. I shall expect you no later than in three months. And one more thing; you should grow a beard to disguise yourself."

Andreas rose and strode off. Eduardo had no option but to follow his instructions. He crossed the dock to the small boats which Andreas had pointed out and made the short crossing to Pera. At least here he felt more at home, since the predominant language was Genoese, which he could understand. The people he passed mostly appeared to be Italian but were dressed in what he assumed was the local style, with long tunics and embroidered cloaks against the cool weather. He knew that they reminded him of something and it was only a few days later that he remembered; they were similar to pictures he had seen in school-books of the garments of ancient Rome.

After making inquiries from passersby, he walked wearily up a steep, narrow, cobbled street, overshadowed by the upper stories of houses which projected out over the roadway until he found the address he had been given. His knock was answered after a short pause by a smiling and buxom middle-aged dark-haired woman who invited him in without waiting for him to speak.

"Yes, yes, you must be Nicholas Camerino, welcome, welcome. I am Angelina Mascario. You look tired. But that is not surprising. We were told to expect you but were not sure when you might arrive. You have had a long journey. But now you are here and we will make sure you do not lack anything. We are about to have our dinner so Clara here will show you to your room and you may come down as soon as you are ready. The dining room is through there. You will meet the rest of my family."

Eduardo who, during the effusive address, had not been able to greet his hostess nor even acknowledge who he was, bowed slightly to the Signora and followed Clara to a room at the far end of the house.

A little later, he came down to the dining room where the evening meal had already begun.

"Ah, Nicholas," said the Signora, "come in, come in. Sit there next to Eudora, my daughter. Let me introduce you to my family. Eudora is betrothed and soon to be married so keep your hands off her."

"Mama, please," interjected Eudora but she was ignored.

"Next to her, is Father Simon who is our guest tonight, then Michaelis, my younger son, the handsome one as you can see, then Roberto who also lodges with us and is my favorite since he adores my cooking. That is Pietro my other son who has just joined the city government so we are all very proud of him. My husband is late, he is always late but then he works very hard and so I forgive him. This, everyone, is Nicholas Camerino, our new guest, who will be staying with us. He has just arrived from Italy."

Eduardo stood up and bowed to the table in general. Before anyone could speak, the Signora began again.

"Now let Nicholas eat. Don't talk to him. Come on, Clara, serve him, hurry, serve him."

Eduardo was indeed famished but his obvious hunger did not stop him being assailed by a barrage of questions, but the Signora held up her hand and the questions ceased. It was only after he had finished two large bowls of soup that the Signora suggested that he might like to relieve them all of their curiosity and tell his story.

He began, "I am afraid my story is very short. I was brought up in Ferrara but all my family died in the plague last year. I fled the city and went to Florence where I worked as a scribe in a book-shop. But the proprietor was old and about to retire and did not need my services for long so I decided to come here to Constantinople and seek my fortune in the East. And that's it. I arrived this afternoon."

"Well," said Signora Angelina "we are sorry to hear of your family. That is a terrible thing, the plague. But at least you survived and now you are here."

"I have always thought that the plague was a punishment from God for some evil-doing," said Eudora, "Wouldn't you say, Father?"

"No, my child," said Father Simon, "the plague strikes the good and the bad, the righteous and the evil-doers equally. The plague, like all other misfortunes and disasters of this world, is a test of our faith. It is sent as a test by God to ensure that we remain strong in our belief, to ensure that despite every setback, every misfortune and all adversity, we accept, even if we do not understand, that it is God's will. We must recognize that his ways are inscrutable but that if we do remain steadfast in our faith in the Lord, we shall, with His grace, always aspire to the beauties of heaven and everlasting….."

"Well, thank you for that, father," said Angelina Mascario, who, fortunately, appeared to have no qualms in interrupting this burgeoning homily as soon as she could.

"And how do you think you are going to make your fortune?" broke in Michaelis changing the subject and with a touch of sarcasm. "Don't think that we are going to give you charity." Although he was the younger of the two brothers, Michaelis was taller, more athletic and, as it turned out, more assertive than his elder brother.

Eduardo reddened a little. He had given much thought as to how he was going to make a living but was still quite uncertain about it.

"I was hoping to get a job in another bookshop and then we shall see," he replied vaguely.

"Ha!" said Michaelis, "Another dreamer. You better talk to my brother. He reads all the time. But you must be out of your mind if you think you can make money out of books."

"If you read a little more," retorted his brother, "in stead of spending every night with your friends in bars, you might have found yourself a good job instead of being taken in by Father."

"Boys, boys, boys," said their mother, "not again please."

Michaelis had indeed recently started working in his father's office. With his aggressive nature, he quickly took offense if he perceived himself slighted but despite his quick tongue, he made friends easily, was naturally gregarious and contrary to the implication of his brother's remarks, he was as likely as anyone to be successful in his father's business which required constant contact and negotiation with traders from all over the East. His father, Alessandro Mascario, was a merchant; he traded principally in wheat, supplying, with other merchants, the constant demand of the granaries of the city. From the earliest days of the empire, the ordinary people of Constantinople had been granted the privilege and security of free daily bread and it was a saying that if the supply of bread ever failed, the city itself would fall. Wheat trading, therefore, under license from the Emperor himself, was a prestigious, lucrative and steady business although, over the years, it had slowly become more and more difficult and even dangerous as Turkish pressure on the imperial territories had grown more intense. As the wheat supplies dropped so did the population and, as a consequence, so did the ability of the empire to defend itself. Michaelis would inherit the management of a business which would require particular skill and determination.

"Don't mind my brother, Eduardo," continued Pietro Mascario, "I will indeed show you the bookshops of the city – it will be a pleasure. But tell us now about Italy. We have had news of the Union of the Churches. No one here thinks that there is any chance of it succeeding. What do the Italians think? Are they going to send an army to help the Greeks?"

"I was in Florence at the time of the Council but I know very little about politics. My feeling is that most people give the matter very little thought. We have heard about the advances of the Turks and that indeed is frightening. But what can we do about it? I really have no idea about that or about the government's plans "

The table fell silent. There was a pause and Eduardo felt that he was obviously a disappointment to his hosts. Characteristically it was Michaelis who expressed the general feeling: "Well you are hopeless. You don't know anything. Why are you really here? No one comes to Constantinople voluntarily any more," said Michaelis, "most people are leaving, if they can."

Eduardo just shrugged his shoulders. He was too tired to argue and he had no wish to respond.

"Anyway," said Roberto, "The Greeks will never ratify this Act of Union. They hate the Latins more than the Turks. And even if they did, no one will send help."

"And what about you, father?" asked Pietro. "What do you feel? Would you join with the Orthodox rite?"

"I shall do whatever my Lord Bishop tells me to do," said Simon, "But as I understand it that is not the purpose of the Union. Each church will retain its own rites. There will be some changes to the Creed so that both churches recite the same wording and the Patriarch will acknowledge the Pope as Supreme Pontiff. Otherwise it will all be much as it was before. But I agree with you, Roberto, the Greeks will never ratify it."

"Well, then we are lost," cried Roberto. "The Greeks cannot hold off the infidel for ever."

"But the Turks will not attack us," said Pietro, with the authority of someone who had inside knowledge. "Even if Constantinople fell, Pera is neutral. The Turks accept us, they need the Genoese for the trade we give them. Take it from me, we are safe. They could have destroyed us, economically or physically, decades ago but they have not. Why? Because the government of Pera takes pains to remain neutral and because we pay taxes on our trade."

The conversation continued but Eduardo did not join in and he soon excused himself from the table. He had heard enough to appreciate that there was, behind their bickering, a real antagonism between the two brothers which went beyond mere sibling rivalry. And although he found Pietro's remarks persuasive and comforting he sensed amongst the whole family a continuous undercurrent of concern, not to say dread, about the future, the future of their lives, of their father's business, of the city itself, at what was now the flashpoint between two great empires and between two, one could even say three, irreconcilable religions, between the Greeks and the Turks, Eastern and Western Christianity and Christianity itself and Islam. In Florence, Ferrucci had not given any thought to politics. He had had no source of information about world or local events and at the time when he had been exiled to Constantinople, he had not had the least appreciation of the reality of the dangers facing the Greeks in the midst of which he now found himself.

CHAPTER 14

The Meeting

And so Pietro Mascarios and Eduardo became friends and, when he was able, Pietro took time to show Eduardo the city and the latter was amazed to find that the Constantinople which he had dreamed of in his imagination was not a city at all in the accepted sense of the word, in the sense that Florence was a city, constructed of row on row of houses on narrow streets tightly enclosed within its protective walls. The city of Constantinople was a collection of villages, fields, woodlands and farms interspersed with churches and monasteries and the monuments and ruins of classical and later times. There were at least eleven separate communities within the walls of the city, some surrounded by their own individual walls or stockades. In the West they would have been small towns in their own right.

On the one hand, he was overwhelmed by the size of the city, by the obvious magnificence of the monuments and of the ancient public buildings, of the churches, of the forums and of the ubiquitous colonnades and the columns with statues of Roman and Greek heroes, gods and famous men. On the other, he felt an overpowering sadness that he would never be able to experience the city as it must have been at the height of its greatness. Everywhere he went, he found the disheartening signs of unmistakable decline and decay which even with his inexperience he knew were irreversible.

On that first day, Pietro asked Eduardo to meet him near his place of work, the new imperial palace of Blachernae, the seat of the Emperor and his administration, in the north-eastern corner of the city, about as far from Pera as it was possible to be. It was an hour's walk from the Neorion harbor to the Palace and the two met early in the evening.

"Let us first go up on the walls, so that you will immediately understand how and why the city has retained its greatness." Pietro spoke with unmistakable pride even though to the eyes of Eduardo, from his very brief acquaintance with the city, the opposite appeared to be the case.

The outer wall of the palace formed the north-eastern corner of the land walls of the city and so they only had a short walk from the palace gates to find steps to the battlements. And when they reached the top, Eduardo immediately understood the pride of his companion. The great wall stretched, as far as he could see, away from the palace down into a low valley and up the other side over a hill. The wall was interspersed with gates and massive towers and between where he was standing, some sixty feet up, and the countryside beyond, there was a second wall only slightly lower and equally as massive and beyond that a third short wall on the inner bank of a wide water-filled ditch. The track where he was standing on top of the wall was wide enough for two wagons to pass easily.

Eduardo turned and looked at his companion, his mouth open in astonishment. Pietro had a self-satisfied smile.

"You see," said Pietro. And there was no need to say more. This was the reason, it was obvious, why Constantinople had survived the sieges and onslaughts of countless invasions, why it had survived intact for more than a thousand years and why it had gained and retained a brilliant reputation as the queen of cities.

That first evening, they walked some way along the wall and then descended and returned through the city back to the harbor and, as they went, Pietro continued to point out the landmarks of the city: the monastery of Chora, the Church of the Holy Apostles, the Forum of Constantine. That evening they did not have time to go as far as Santa Sophia but on subsequent days and evenings, either alone or with Pietro, Eduardo made himself familiar with the other sights of the city, the ruins of the vast Hippodrome, the massive walls of the old Palace, the University, the Acropolis. It was hard work. There were steep inclines all over the city which had been built, as was Rome, on seven hills. Everything he saw made him despondent. Every building, every monument was in a state of disrepair and only Santa Sophia which was maintained by the imperial administration itself, was relatively pristine. It seemed obvious to Eduardo that the reduced population, many of whom were foreigners, could not possibly be large enough to comprise or support even the members of the administration let alone an army or the other elements necessary to sustain and defend a great city and certainly not an empire.

Despite these misgivings, he did not forget the purpose of his visit and now appreciated that he had been sent to live in Pera for good reason. It was at one remove from Constantinople itself and it would enable him to remain inconspicuous in a predominantly Italian quarter where he would be unlikely to encounter Philip Shamash by chance in an unguarded moment.

He set about learning Greek in earnest. This was not too difficult a task; he was an intelligent and determined young man. He worked at it with diligence and the sights and sounds of the language were all around him since the Mascarios and much of the population of Pera were bilingual. By the end of his allotted three months, he could make himself understood and he did not stop his studies until he was a fluent reader and speaker.

With Pietro as his guide, he began to search for employment and again found a position as a part-time scribe in one of the only remaining city booksellers, the Tetrabiblion, in the quarter close to the Philadelphion on the slope leading down to the Marmora from the central ridge of the city on the far side from the Neorion. His knowledge of Latin and now of Greek gave him an advantage. The booksellers in Constantinople, as much as those in Italy, knew where the market lay, books had to be copied and Latin translations of the books that remained in the city, would help sales in the West. The salary Eduardo earned from his job, only a few numismata a day, was hardly enough to live on but it was the best that he could do. There seemed to be few other prospects in the run-down economy of the city and he had the vain hope that he might be able to become a full time employee of the bookshop after a brief apprenticeship. His advance from Antonio Lucchese in Florence was dwindling rapidly.

And so each day, he and Pietro took a ferry across to the city, Pietro set off to the Blachernae along the road inside the wall fronting the Horn and Eduardo continued over to the Philadelphion. One day, after his three month novitiate was over, Eduardo doubled back and took up his position on the bench within the Neorion dock. He had to do this each day for a week before he was joined by the man he knew as Andreas and who, without hesitation and no doubt to test his progress in the language, addressed him in Greek.

"Tomorrow, you will begin to search for Philip Shamash. He lives in the district called Petra off Mese Street and close to the Church of St. John. You must be very careful both here and when you search. It is quite unlikely that he will come often or at all to the harbor district but you should always be on your guard."

"Petra is close to the Blachernae?"

"Yes, that is where Shamash has his office. I remind you that your principal and your most urgent task is to watch him, and do everything you can to discover for whom he is working and to this end to intercept any messages he may be sending."

"If he is working for the Greeks, there is no way I can intercept messages, since presumably he will be meeting his colleagues every day in the normal course of his business," pointed out Eduardo quite reasonably.

"We don't know for certain that he is or was working for the Greeks," replied Andreas. "He may very well be working for others and we have to find out if that is the case."

What Andreas did not tell Eduardo was that Florentine agents under the instructions of Lucchese had followed the courier who had taken the original notes with the secret message and in Constantinople had tracked him to the consignee of these notes. This individual, one Al-Malik, turned out to be of Turkish origin. He had been abducted by Andreas and other Florentine agents and after persuasion had revealed that he always passed on the notes to a further contact outside the city within Turkish territory. He had not revealed the key to the message and it was the opinion of Antonio's agents that he did not know what it was. But progress had been made. Shamash had been revealed to be spying for the Turks and Eduardo had now been given the unenviable task of uncovering his contacts outside the city. Andreas decided not to reveal to Eduardo, at least for the time being, that these contacts were Turkish. He did not wish to limit the scope of Eduardo's investigations and until he had some sense of Eduardo's skill in his new and dangerous trade, he thought it prudent to tell him as little as possible.

Eduardo then brought up the time-honored topic of every new employee, his pay.

"I have a part-time job at the book shop," he said.

"I am aware of that," said Andreas.

"But the pay is not enough to live on. If the job was full-time, which possibly I could arrange, I would have no time for investigating or supervising the activities of Philip Shamash. So I have to be paid for my work for you."

"I am afraid that is out of the question," said Andreas coldly. "You are here in Constantinople for one reason and one reason only. You were guilty of treason and you were given a reprieve on the condition that you work for Florence and that you produce results. How you survive is your own affair. If the information you produce is useful you will be paid for it. If not, you are on your own. Obviously, this gives you an incentive to produce results. And I may also say that if you do not produce results, you will be of no use to us and you will suffer the consequences."

The logic of this argument was obvious but it left Eduardo profoundly nervous. The short novitiate he had been granted during his first few months in the city was now over and he was now being forced to embark on the dangerous activity for which he had been sent. He was almost alone in the city and he really had no idea how to begin. At any moment he might encounter Shamash and be recognized but, at the same time, he had to get close enough to him to find out who he was and what he was doing. That afternoon, after he left work, he walked up the hill to the Forum of Theodosius and then again along Mese Street, which ran along the center of the city, past the Church of Holy Apostles, towards the Charisius Gate in the western land walls of the city which he had seen on his first day with Pietro. In an excess of caution, he walked slowly, kept close to the stores on the side of the road and scanned the passersby well ahead of him. It was at least a two mile walk to Petra and part of the road was through open fields where there were few pedestrians and little traffic on the road. It was clear to him immediately that, if he was to make this journey frequently, he would have to find another route.

Petra, in the north-western corner of the city, was a wealthy community whose inhabitants most likely were attached to the administration or the Emperor's court. Eduardo spent the afternoon surveying the area from the palace to the great monastery of Chora to the Church of St. John. He cautiously walked the narrow streets until he was exhausted. He still had to walk back to the ferry to Pera and get back to his lodgings but he felt he had made a start.

The following day and the day after he repeated his efforts, on this occasion walking right back down to the shore of the Golden Horn and then along to the Blachernae, the center of the administration and the court, taking the same route as did Pietro every day since this route, through the trading communities of the city on the edge of the Horn, was much busier and less exposed. It took him at least an hour just to reach Petra. Day after day he persisted, walking the streets of the quarter in the hope of finding or seeing something that would get him started on his investigation. He did not dare make direct inquiries of the authorities or of people locally, which might alert Shamash to his presence and he did not seem to be making the slightest progress. He was at the point of despairing how to proceed further when, one afternoon, he suddenly saw her. She was on the other side of the street, walking away from him, but he recognized her long brown hair, her figure and height and her confident stride.

He couldn't help himself; "Juliette", he exclaimed.

She stopped, turned round and looked at him. Indeed, it was Juliette. Then he froze as he realized his mistake; it was of course not Juliette but Cecilia.

She came up to him and studied him carefully.

"Yes, I know you in spite of your beard." she said in Italian. "You are the bookseller. What are you doing here?" She smiled and continued: "Whatever it is, I am very pleased to see you. I remember you, of course – you used to come round to Papa's house in Florence and sell us books; I think you were interested in my sister. That was really why you came, was it not? We used to laugh so much that we were buying so many books. We knew we would never be able to read them all but you had to have an excuse to come round. Walk with me a little and tell me what you have been doing and what your purpose is here in the city."

She asked her maid with whom she had been walking to follow behind them and she continued with Eduardo along the street.

"Come," she said. "Our house is quite close. Please take coffee with me. Philip is away and we will have time to gossip about the affairs of Florence."

Eduardo had to think quickly. He could not risk going into Shamash's house even if the latter were away.

"I will walk with you," he said, "but I have business this afternoon. I will not be able to accept your invitation but I would certainly like to meet again very soon. I am in the city to acquire books and will only be here a few days. I have many appointments so perhaps I could ask you to come to the Philadelphion tomorrow. We could meet in Hagia Sophia or the Church of the Holy Apostles and sit and talk about old times."

They had already reached Cecilia's house. Eduardo noted the address and they made an appointment for the following day.

He was on the one hand furious that he had given himself away but childishly pleased that, under the pressure of the moment, he had conceived a coherent explanation of his presence in the city. He was also overwhelmed by memories of Juliette. It was disconcerting to be so close to the double of his loved one, someone who appeared exactly like that person but was not. He felt a tension which, not surprisingly for someone as young as himself, he had never previously experienced. It was like the tension between two former lovers when they meet again much later and feel briefly the old attraction but know it can never again be consummated.

The following afternoon Cecilia and Eduardo met in the loggia of the Church of the Holy Apostles, sat on a stone bench under the portico and talked for an hour. It was early May and a cool and beautiful sunny day. In front of the church there was a small piazza, which separated them from the noise of the street. For the first time since he had arrived in the city Eduardo was relaxed and even happy. He was sitting next to a beautiful woman, he could talk to her at ease in his native language, they were old friends and they had much to discuss. The great marble columns of the portico rose silently above them and this, for a reason he could not understand, added to his feeling of serenity. He looked at Cecilia and smiled happily and she smiled back.

"Yes," he said, "I come to the city every three or four months to buy books. And I have now gone back to live in Ferrara and left Florence so that I do not have any news of Juliette or your mother and father. You must have heard more from them than I have of what goes on in Florence."

"Oh," said Cecilia, "then you do not know. I have so much to tell you. I am so glad to see you – I hardly ever see anyone from the old days, only occasionally someone who comes on a diplomatic mission from Florence to the Emperor but they don't bother much with me in any event."

She gave Eduardo another wide and disarming smile, looked at him straight in the eye and, in spite of himself, he felt his heart beat faster.

"Papa and Mama have lost all their money. They had to sell the palazzo and their estates and retire to their house in the country. They have practically nothing to live on. Garzon, our steward, stole all the money and was then killed. No one knows what happened to the money that he took. And Juliette has entered the Convent of Santa Caterina in Ferrara – she refused to marry Antonio Lucchese and Papa sent her away."

This was not quite true, as we know, but no doubt it was the version put about by Gasparini. Eduardo was elated finally to learn of Juliette's whereabouts but was also surprised to experience a feeling of intense guilt, guilt for the responsibility that it was for love of him that she had been condemned (as he thought) to a life of chastity, isolation and contemplation. What did this mean? Would he ever be able to see her again? Indeed, was there any purpose in trying to see her again? His spirits which had risen over the months since his arrival in the city and particularly in the last twenty-four hours when he appeared finally to have achieved something in his new career, completely dissipated, leaving him suddenly desolate and depressed.

"You are not listening," said Cecilia reaching out and touching him on the arm. He looked up and forced a smile.

"And tell me about Philip," he asked casually. "How is he?" He could not help noticing that she dropped her eyes quickly.

"He is away on business frequently," she said, "I spend most of my time by myself. I have tried to learn Greek but I find it very difficult. To be honest, I am lonely. I used to have so many friends at home. I write frequently to them and Mama and Papa and Juliette but that's only a substitute for the real thing and that's why I am so pleased to see you."

Eduardo thought he saw tears coming to her eyes; he felt sorry for her and he was struck by several thoughts at the same instant. He felt a moment of guilty elation as he realized that here was a beautiful and vulnerable woman who seemed to need him and to whom he was strongly attracted. What was more, a relationship with Cecilia would give him the chance to get close to Shamash and finally and what was most appealing to him, he could begin to get his revenge on his enemy by suborning his wife.

He grasped her hand and held it tightly and she started to sob quietly; she put her head on his shoulder and he did not discourage her. After some moments her tears stopped and he asked her when Shamash was returning home.

"In two days, I believe, although he tells me very little."

"Do you know when he is leaving again and where he goes?"

"No, I don't know how long he will be at home but he goes on diplomatic missions to other Greek cities. He has become quite important, I believe. He even joins in audiences with the Emperor himself."

"I shall be here for a few more days," said Eduardo looking into Cecilia's eyes. "Maybe we can meet again before I go. And I think you should not mention to Philip that I am in the city. That might be a mistake."

She looked back at him, her eyes blank and expressionless, nodded slowly and they continued to talk.

They met every day for the next three days at the same place. They held hands, she leaned her head on his shoulder and they talked. For Eduardo this was not an imposition. Cecilia did not have the intellectual curiosity of Juliette but in every other respect she was the same: in the feel of her arms, in the perfume of her body and in the tone of her voice. She told him that Philip had returned but she had hardly seen him and he was leaving again in two days for Corinth in the Morea. Eduardo told her that he too was leaving, he had already delayed his departure several days, but he would return as soon as he could. In parting, she gave him a shy kiss.

Once again Eduardo repeated the procedure to contact his handler and sure enough, a few days later, early in the morning in the Neorion, Andreas approached him. Eduardo gave him a note.

"I have located Philip Shamash. This is his address. I have made friends with his wife whom I knew in Florence."

"Good," said Andreas.

"Apparently Shamash is employed as an emissary for the Greek administration and he is leaving the city any day now on an embassy to Corinth."

"That is useful information."

"Yes, and I may be able to get further information on his future movements. His wife also tells me that he is privy to the highest counsels of the Greek state and may even have the ear of the Emperor."

"That makes it even more important that you find out what information he is passing on and how."

And with that acid remark, Andreas and Eduardo parted but this first substantive report by Eduardo was in fact of great interest to his superiors although by the time it got back to Antonio in Florence, it was much too late to track Shamash to Corinth, a town which lay on the border between Turkish occupied territory in the north and the Morea, the southern peninsular of European Greece now called the Peloponnese. The question which immediately occupied Antonio was whether or not to share with the Greek authorities the information that he now had about the activities of Shamash. He asked for a meeting with the Bargello and Catania, representing the Committee of Eight, attended again.

"It would seem sensible to pass on to our Christian allies the identity of this traitor who has access to their plans at the highest level," suggested Antonio after outlining the revelations about Philip Shamash.

"There is only one question at issue," responded Catania, "and that is, what is best for the security of the Republic? The question is not what is best for the security of the Greeks. The interests of our two peoples are not identical."

"Well," said Bardini, "the fall of Constantinople would be a grave blow to Florence and to the rest of Christendom. Can we risk contributing to that possibility in any way?"

"The Greeks can look after themselves – if they can," replied Catania. "In spite of all this talk at the Council and in spite of all the things that they have promised, the Greeks have not ratified the Decree of Union. The Emperor cannot control the Patriarch and the Patriarch cannot see the broad political threats to the State. He only has the narrow interest of his church and his clergy in view. He is more afraid of acknowledging the Pope as his spiritual leader than he is afraid of the infidel. As a result he will lose everything. The Greeks are an effete and weak people who cannot defend themselves. They ask for help but do not provide anything in exchange. In any event to send help would be useless in my view."

After this dismal assessment, there was a pause while the three of them contemplated the options.

"With or without Constantinople," continued Catania finally, "the Turks will always press on the borders of Europe. The city has become largely a symbol and will surely not stand forever. To me, what is more important is that the Turks are now just one day's sail away from Italy and we have to devote every resource at our command to discover their plans and we have to do it continuously. If we betray Philip Shamash to the Greeks, they will arrest him and we will lose what might become a valuable source of insight into the Turkish plans."

Antonio could see which way the decision was likely to go and, somewhat against his personal inclination, he suggested, "We have to admit that Ferrucci has had some initial success. I believe that we should give him a little more time to pursue the matter. He may be able to discover the Turkish contacts of Shamash and this might give us opportunities to get an agent inside the Turkish administration."

And so the Florentines decided that they would not reveal the role of Shamash to the Greeks. For the time being they would continue to track him and his activities and not risk the likelihood that he would be immediately arrested and the source of their information cut off. Instructions eventually reached Ferrucci that he was to continue his surveillance and report any information that he obtained even if, to him, it did not appear of great significance.

CHAPTER 15

The Tetrabiblion

The owner of the bookshop was an old man, much older than Patrizzi, with white hair, a white beard and a wild and wandering eye. He went by the ungainly name of Heliogabalus, probably not his real name but one he had acquired long ago in the course of his eccentric career. Eduardo was not sure at first whether Heliogabalus' conversation was exceptionally learned or merely as irrational as his appearance but, in any event, it did not take long him to appreciate that the stock of the Tetrabiblion was quite extraordinary. One reason for this was that, oddly enough, Heliogabalus appeared to have no wish at all to sell books. On the contrary, it seemed that he went out of his way not to sell books and had a variety of tactics to ensure that such a shocking event could not possibly occur. Surprisingly, there was the occasional customer but he always went away dissatisfied. Either the book had just been sold (when Eduardo knew it was on the shelf just round the corner) or it was being copied so that it was not presently available (when he knew that there were already at least two copies) or that it was being rebound (when it was in pristine condition) or that he, Heliogabalus, had just discovered that his copy was the last copy in existence and therefore the price had increased threefold or that it was a holy book and kept under lock and key or (on rare occasions) that it was reserved for the Emperor himself and could not even be touched or that the book did not exist or, most surprisingly, according to Heliogabalus, that the book existed but had not yet been written.

Obviously Eduardo soon began to have questions about the purpose of this bookshop, his own role in the business and that of the two other young men who were employed as copyists and most of all about the state of mind of Heliogabalus. The answers to the first two questions clearly depended on the answer to the last. Maybe there was a purpose to the bookshop or there had been at one time but it was not clear that Heliogabalus now knew what it was. One of the two other scribes had been copying the same book for the last six months; not that it was a long book but he had now made three copies of it, each of which when completed was placed next to the previous one on an empty shelf. What was ominous about this particular exercise was that there was room for at least another thirty copies on the same shelf. When Artaxerxes, the scribe, timidly suggested that he might be given something else to copy, Heliogabalus rolled his eyes, as though in horror, and suggested the Bible. Artaxerxes immediately backed off since no one ever copied the Bible in less than fifteen months. But Heliogabalus still did not vouchsafe why that book had to be copied and recopied. Neither was it clear to Eduardo why scribes were needed at all since neither copies nor originals were ever sold.

After a little time had passed, Eduardo realized that the same customers were returning even though on previous occasions they had always gone away empty-handed and soon he came to understand that Heliogabalus refused to part with his books because of the simple fact that he regarded himself as the guardian of the knowledge contained within every book he possessed. If indeed these were unique copies of some of the most important books of ancient times, and Eduardo began to appreciate that they were, the personal prestige that Heliogabalus bathed in and obviously enjoyed was a reflection of the prestige of his books. To dispose of any book was to diminish his reputation. The balance that was essential for a successful dealer of any kind, not only one of books, was to have great objects for sale and to be able to replace these after they had been sold so that there would always be more stock. The problem for Heliogabalus was that it was almost impossible to acquire new books at reasonable prices; many books had already been sent to the West, those that remained in the imperial or monastic libraries were not for sale and the few remaining in private hands were seen for what they were, easily portable stores of value which could command high prices in the West.

His business and his mind deteriorating, Heliogabalus perversely refused to take or maybe just could not conceive of taking any of the obvious ways out of his dilemma: to hand over the business to a younger man (he had no heirs), to sell all his stock and retire or to emigrate with his stock and set up shop in Italy where he might enjoy great success. Not content even with just retaining his books and allowing customers to view them and perhaps read them on the premises, he had begun to refuse to allow anyone to handle or even look at them. Those customers who returned were generally not serious buyers; such people had long since abandoned hope of tempting him at any price but it was apparent that they knew the value of the books and were concerned for their safety and well-being. But Heliogabalus was intransigent; in the fixations of his old age, he continued the daily round, the copyists copied, his old customers occasionally visited and his reputation as the guardian of the great books remained unchallenged. He just did not make any sales.

After some weeks in his new employment, Eduardo began to understand something of the situation and appreciate that he had been presented with an obligation and an opportunity which were quite unique. His first love had been and still was books and despite the growing pressure of his other duties he realized that he must find the time to devise and execute a plan that could save the treasure trove that was the Tetrabiblion. He did not take into his confidence either of his two colleagues, who also only worked part-time so that in any event he did not even see them every day, and besides which he did not regard them as capable or even likely to be willing to contribute to any plan he might devise.

Heliogabalus spent most of the day at a high desk overlooking the worktable of the scribes. He seemed to spend all his time checking that his books still existed; he would go to the shelves, pull out a volume at random, take it back to his desk, open it and read a little, make a note on a piece of parchment and then after some time take it back to its place on the shelves and apparently at random pick another one. Eduardo took advantage of a break in this monotonous routine to ask whether there was a catalog of the books.

"Ha!" said Heliogabalus. "You want to steal the books, I can tell. I see it in your eyes. I have seen eyes like yours before. You are always looking at my books. Prying eyes. Yes, I have eyes too. I see and my eyes see. I have three eyes (or was it "I"s, Eduardo was not sure). I have an I here (pointing at his head) and that's where my books are."

Eduardo could not help but blush. This accusation, despite the fact that it derived entirely from Heliogabalus' increasing paranoia, was not so far from the truth. He was now certain that Heliogabalus' mind was going but he wanted to continue the exchange and find a dialogue that would engage the two of them. He matched the outburst with one of his own.

"That's not true," he said. "You know that's not possible. You check my bag every day. But I have eyes too. How can I avoid seeing the books since I work here. And I have an I too," he pointed to his head "and my I wishes to learn; I, speaking for my I, wish to learn from your knowledge of the books, I have a winged I, one that flies from book to book, like a bee seeking the nectar in the flowers, wishing to distil this learning in my I."

He paused, pleased with his extempore response and curious how Heliogabalus would react. The latter just sat there regarding Eduardo, the wandering eyes strangely still. There may have been a slight smile about them.

So Eduardo emboldened continued. "Of course, if you had a catalog, it would be easy to check that the books were still in their appointed place."

Heliogabalus ignored this, warming to what was apparently his favorite theme.

"Mente videbo. I see in my mind and the I is in my mind. It is not out there, it is in here, here where I see. Out is an illusion, in is reality. Would the books exist without me? Would the knowledge exist without someone to know? No. No. I guard the knowledge, it is my knowledge, it does not exist out there. You do not have it, no one else has it. Only I, it only exists in my I."

Eduardo began to feel that he was completely out of his depth but nevertheless that there was a kernel of rationality to what Heliogabalus was saying and he had to respond in the same kind.

"But if the I is in your mind, it could be and should be in my mind too. Maybe there is only reality in the I but I have an I too. My I is like your I." He changed his tack. "The only question is whether our Is are the same or different. Is there one universal I or many I's? My I must be different from yours since I know I don't know but I also know that you do know. There must be different Is. Yours and mine for one. Only God is the one I. We know that he is one and that we are many. And my separate I needs to be nourished. It is starved of knowledge and your I can feed it. The bee in me must taste the nectar. Why should my I not also know what is in this book for instance?"[12]

And with that, he pulled out a volume from an upper shelf and handed it to Heliogabalus without taking his eyes off him. Heliogabalus did not look at the book but stroked it gently as he might if he were a blind man.

He sighed and said sadly and slowly, "And I shall know even as also I am known." and a tear began to fall down his wrinkled cheek.

Eduardo realized he had by chance picked out a Bible and he replied, "And I, I know only in part. I look through the glass darkly as in an enigma."

But Heliogabalus ignored him, lifted his head and said to the room at large, "and I stood upon the sand of the sea and saw a beast rise up out of the sea having seven heads and ten horns and upon his horns ten crowns and upon his heads the name of blasphemy."

And, as Eduardo looked at him with an open mouth, he continued, "and I saw a new heaven and a new earth, for the first heaven and the first earth were passed away and there was no more sea."

Eduardo got up, gently removed the Bible from Heliogabalus' grasp, resisting the temptation to put his arm round the old man, and picked another book at random. This time he looked at the title which was *Comedy, Book II of the Poetics*, by Aristotle. Good, he thought, perhaps this will cheer him up. Heliogabalus again felt the book without looking at it and dried his tears with his beard.

Finally he said, still without looking at the book, "So what do you know about comedy?"

"Very little," replied Eduardo, "except that it is to be contrasted with epic and lyric poetry and with tragedy. Tragedy has a sad ending, comedy a happy one."

"On the contrary," said Heliogabalus, his thin voice rising again. "Comedy starts happily and ends badly. Comedy is the progress of mankind from illusion to reality. Don't you see it around us? The city is an illusion. God is playing a game with us. Fate will force reality upon us and we shall soon understand that God has abandoned us. We shall know that our life has just been a comedy played for God."

On this cynical and bitter note, he handed the book back to Eduardo.

Over the next weeks and months, Eduardo had many exchanges with Heliogabalus, some instructive, some histrionic, all inspiring and stimulating. The old man was slowly losing control over the ordered logic of his thoughts and his expositions started to resemble visions or dreams. When the day was over, Eduardo made a secret note for himself of the title of each book and a summary of what Heliogabalus had said about it, although this last became more and more difficult as the weeks passed and the conversation became more whimsical. But it was certainly true, even if Eduardo did not fully realize it, that the stock of the Tetrabiblion was extraordinary. There were the complete works of Aeschylus, fifty of the plays by Sophocles and thirty by Euripedes, the *Fables* of Plato, Aristotle's *Life of Pythagoras*, a collection of the poems of Sappho, the *Dyskolos* of Menander and many others. Time and again, Eduardo wondered to himself what a miracle it was that these works had survived for two thousand years. It also occurred to him that the history of each manuscript, which had been handed down from generation to generation over this long period, must have been at least as fascinating as its content.

Eduardo had written to Patrizzi in Florence. He apologized for the difficulties he had caused his employer and explained without going into details that he had been quite innocently and maybe ingenuously deceived by Shamash. He explained further that he had been exiled to Constantinople, where he was now just barely making a living. He said further that he had found a wonderful source of books which he believed, although he was not sufficiently knowledgeable to be sure, were of great value. He sent a list of those books about which he hitherto made notes as a result of his conversations with Heliogabalus. If Patrizzi would advance him the money to have each book copied one by one, he would be able to send him each copy as it was completed. He realized that this was taking a lot on trust but he believed that the prize was worth it and Patrizzi would only need to risk the outlay for the first copy.

One day, while awaiting Patrizzi's reply and finally succumbing to the temptation to follow up on the manuscript from which he had extracted the secret message in Florence, Eduardo asked Heliogabalus if he had a book by an author named Stobaeus.

"No," said Heliogabalus without hesitation, "and what do you know of this Stobaeus?"

Eduardo explained that he had seen a copy of a work called the Sentences or Eclogues of Stobaeus in Florence and he had been told that there was a companion volume to the one he had seen.

"I have heard of Stobaeus, but I have never seen any of his works."

"Do you know of Michael Psellus and his library?" asked Eduardo taking advantage of Heliogabalus' unaccustomed lucidity and remembering what Shamash had said about the second volume of the Stobaeus in Psellus' library.

"Psellus was the most learned man in Constantinople under the Emperor Constantine Ducas three centuries ago. It is said that that as a boy he knew the whole of Homer by heart. If you wish to know more about him, I have his *Chronographia* in which he relates the history of his own time. But," continued Heliogabalus relapsing into melancholy, "what good did it do him? Time is how God plays with us. God does not need time. He sees all things now and forever in an instant. He gave us time so that we think we have existence but it is an illusion. All life is an illusion."

Eduardo nervously asked Heliogabalus – this was the critical moment – if he could rent the *Chronographia* for a short time to read it. He would pay the rent out of his wages. To his relief, Heliogabalus, whose enthusiasm at the idea of making a little money for the first time overcame his distaste at allowing one of his precious books out of his sight for any time, assented and Eduardo was able to read the relevant parts of the *Chronographia* at his leisure.

He found that Psellus was as enthusiastic to describe his own life as those of the Emperors who were nominally the subject of his book, and he also learned that Psellus, for unknown reasons, had been exiled to, or had himself decided that it was politic to retire for some years to, a monastery on Mount Olympus in Bithynia, where he had spent his time writing. Bithynia was the province now under Turkish rule on the southern shore of the Black Sea across the Bosphorus from Constantinople. The principal town of the region, Bursa, also on the slopes of Mount Olympus, had for a short time, a century before, been the capital of the expanding Turkish Empire. And so, Eduardo supposed, if Psellus had handed on his own books to some institution, there was no reason why it might not have been this one. He determined that, when he had the opportunity, he would seek out the monastery to which Psellus had retired and look for the second volume of the Stobaeus, if in fact it existed.

Not long after, he received a letter from Patrizzi which included a draft on a bank in Constantinople for the equivalent of 100 numismata, enough to pay a scribe to copy the *Chronographia*. He hired an acquaintance, another scribe, to come to his rooms to copy the book - he did not dare let it out of his possession - and demanded that it be finished within one month, an almost impossible task but Heliogabalus was already getting nervous and inquiring about the book's whereabouts, safety and well-being. And so the copying was completed in the allotted time and Eduardo finally had his first book to sell.

CHAPTER 16

The Quest

Eduardo was instructed by Andreas to learn Turkish. To the Florentines, it was obviously essential that someone who was supposed to be conducting surveillance on the Turks should be able to speak the language. For Ferrucci learning another new language was an almost impossible task since he was still in the process of perfecting his Greek. But Andreas insisted and accordingly Eduardo began regular lessons. When therefore he proposed to Andreas that he should venture out of the city into Turkish Bithynia to practice the language and familiarize himself with the condition of the enemy, he was not surprised that Andreas had no hesitation in giving his approval for the journey. And so, a few days later, Eduardo and Michaelis Mascarios crossed the Bosphorus to Turkish occupied Asia.

He would have preferred to take Pietro. The latter was his friend and of the two brothers, the one who was interested in books but Pietro could not take time off from his work with the administration. Eduardo discussed his plan with the Mascarios and Alessandro, after some hesitation, agreed that the journey would be also an opportunity for Michaelis to familiarize himself with the customs of those with whom he was doing business. The fact was that Michaelis was more aggressive and extravert than his brother and a far more accomplished swordsman; for this reason alone Eduardo welcomed his companionship. Although they were not intimate friends, Eduardo and Michaelis occasionally went to exercise together in the gymnasium next to the Hippodrome near the old imperial palace and took time to practice their swordsmanship. Traveling was a dangerous pastime and although Bursa was only fifty miles from Constantinople they would have to make at least one and possibly two overnight stops. However tolerant the locals might be, a traveler alone was vulnerable to theft, injury and possibly worse.

When he heard it was to pursue the purchase of books, Heliogabalus also assented to Eduardo's request for a week off to make the journey although it apparently never crossed his mind to ask the obvious question as to how Eduardo proposed to pay for any books he might find. Eduardo also was not clear about this but assumed that he would be able to arrange to have anything he found copied and paid for later.

They could not afford horses and indeed, under local law, non-Moslems were not permitted to ride horse-back but had to content themselves with mules or donkeys. So Eduardo and Michaelis joined a group of Turks who had come over with them on the ferry and took their places in a large cart pulled by two horses. Since these latter could not be persuaded to proceed faster than a slow walk, it turned out to be a long, tedious three day journey.

When Eduardo had first arrived at the Mascarios, Michaelis had not given him much thought – Eduardo was just another lodger, who was doted on by his mother and befriended by his brother. But after some months he had begun to realize that there were unexplained anomalies in Eduardo's story. Why would any intelligent young man voluntarily leave the security of his homeland and venture into the dangerous environment that was Constantinople in a vague search for his "fortune"? How could he survive on the meager earnings of his part time employment in the bookshop; what was he doing in his long absences in the evenings walking about the city and why had he started to learn Turkish, a difficult and unusual undertaking for anyone in Pera or Constantinople? Furthermore, how was it that Ferrucci, who pretended such an interest in books, was not only such an accomplished swordsman but was also intent on perfecting his mastery of the art? These two aspects of his character did not appear to match. The conversations between them on the journey to Bursa did not assuage Michaelis' curiosity. Eduardo gave no clear answers to any of Michaelis' pointed questions and rather than satisfy him, this tended to aggravate his suspicions.

Bursa was an attractive town on the lower slopes of Mount Olympus with a cool climate and wide views over the open plain below. It was, in a small way, laid out like Constantinople. Each of the main communities, the Turkish administration in the old palace and the Christians and Jews had their own enclaves within the twin city walls. There were wide tree lined streets and imposing buildings, numerous mosques and in the Christian quarter a few remaining churches. As in all the territories that had been taken by the Turks, life for the original inhabitants continued with surprisingly little change from what it had been before.

Eduardo and Michaelis lodged comfortably in a Christian hospice in Bursa and on the morning after their arrival Michaelis visited a business acquaintance of his father's, while Eduardo sought information from the nearest church on the whereabouts of the region's monasteries. He was directed to the only monastery in the city, that of Ayia Giorgios, St. George, which was close by, on a rocky area adjoining the Christian quarter, located in the narrow gap between the twin city walls. To reach it, he had to go through the inner part of the nearest city gate, up over the ramparts and along a deserted and overgrown path between the two sets of walls.

It was a pleasant enough walk but, as he went, he realized that someone else was walking behind him at the same pace on the rampart of the outer wall. Eduardo stopped and turned and the man on the rampart also stopped, turned and began to look out over the battlements. It was immediately evident to Eduardo that he was being followed. He was not in any danger; he was carrying his sword and in any event the wall was too high for anyone to jump down but he was relieved when, after a fifteen minute walk, he reached the gate of the monastery and was admitted.

He was taken to the office of the abbot, a tall gaunt white haired man in his seventies with piercing, intelligent eyes who smiled as he talked. He introduced himself as Father Nicephorus, offered Eduardo as seat and asked him his business.

"I am from Constantinople," Eduardo said in Greek. "I work in a bookshop in the city and I am looking for books which could be available for purchase. In particular, I am looking for one book which we understand is or was in a monastery in Bursa or on Mount Olympus. If that book is in your library and you are willing to sell it, we would like to buy it or, if you are not willing to sell it, I would like to have the facility to copy it."

There was a pause and Nicephorus said "You are indeed an adventurous young man to come so far in a quest for books. There are many in this city who would find it difficult to believe that that was the real reason."

Eduardo stared at Nicephorus with blank eyes. He thought of the man on the ramparts and the implications behind the remark of the Abbot gave him a sudden jolt of disquiet.

"But that is not my business," continued Nicephorus. "Yes, we have books here, I will show you where they are. Yes, we might be willing to sell them or have them copied but I do not believe there will be anything of interest to you. And what is the name of the particular book you seek, why do you want it and why do you think it is here?"

Eduardo told him about the one volume of the Stobaeus and how he was looking for the second volume. He told him about Psellus and the story that he had retired to a monastery on Mount Olympus and how it was possible that he could have left his books at that monastery.

"I have, of course, heard of the learned Psellus, but I was not aware that he came to Mount Olympus nor do I believe that he ever came here. Let me explain. Many centuries ago, before the infidels arrived, there were many monasteries on Mount Olympus. They were, in many cases, sited in remote areas, both for protection and because that is the purpose of a monastery – a place, quiet and inaccessible, where we can contemplate God without the irritating distractions of this world. But over the centuries, partly no doubt because of the incursions of the infidel, many of these houses were abandoned and only a very few remain. This house, St. George, was relocated and rebuilt in its present position for better security many years ago and fortunately, after the Turks took the city they have left us in peace."

"I am curious about that," said Eduardo. "How is that they allow you to survive?"

"It is quite simple," said Nicephorus, allowing himself a smile. "As always, it is a question of money. We and the many other Christians who still live here in Bursa and in other Turkish territories are tolerated because we pay the jisvah or special tribute required by the holy book of Islam. I fear that many of my brothers in Christ would quickly convert to heathenism just to avoid this tax but the Turks do not encourage it. But they are a tolerant people and we live in fragile harmony together."

"I would like very much to look at your books," said Eduardo. "And I would be grateful if you could explain to me how to get to any of the remaining houses on Mount Olympus."

"I can do that," said Nicephorus, "but I must tell you that not only do I believe that these other houses do not possess books of any interest apart from liturgical material but I believe it would be foolhardy of you in the extreme to wander about alone in the countryside in areas which are mountainous and inaccessible. Apart from the physical dangers, inevitably you will arouse the interest of the authorities. You are armed and no doubt able to take of yourself but that in itself is suspect. You are not even Greek, are you? And that makes your journey even more unusual. I have no doubt that it is already known that you have come here."

There was a brief silence while Eduardo considered the matter and again thought of the man who had followed him.

"Very well," he said "I believe you are right. I have a companion but it is most likely too dangerous for us to continue the search outside the city."

"Come then, I will show you the books," said Nicephorus and he led Eduardo out into the cloister. After a short walk through the cool corridors of the monastery, Nicephorus unlocked a small door and motioned Eduardo inside, handing him the lighted candle-holder he was carrying.

"When you have finished, please return to me and tell me what you have found," he said and there may have been a touch of irony in his tone.

There were no windows and even with the door open and with his candle, the light was not sufficient to reach the far corners of the room. Eduardo could barely make out the simple slatted wooden shelves which surrounded the walls and which, in some cases, were broken or had collapsed. On the shelves and on the floor were the books of the monastery, codices bound and unbound, rolls of parchment, single sheets, torn scraps and fragments, all in utter disorder, mostly in piles where they had fallen from the shelves or been thrown by readers who had long abandoned hope of replacing a book in its proper position. It seemed likely to Eduardo that no one had used the room, that no one could have used the room for many years and he immediately realized that his task was hopeless. It would take him weeks just to read the titles of each of the books. He would have loved to spend the time cataloging the books and putting them back in order although he knew he did not have the time. Already they had spent three days of their allotted week just reaching Bursa. On this visit, an extended stay would be impossible.

For an hour he persisted. He developed a routine. He picked up five or six books and took them outside into the light of the cloister where he opened each of them, read the titles and copied these on to an erasable writing tablet he had brought with him. Almost without exception, they were liturgical books, Homilies, Psalters, Hours, individual books of the New Testament, works of the Church fathers, Gregory of Nyssa, Athanasius, John of Damascus. He discovered at the most two or three classical works, of which the most surprising was the Pentabiblios of Musaeus although none of these had any interest for him.

He worked on in solitude interrupted only by the reassuring and deep chime of a bell which rang every fifteen minutes. Otherwise there was complete silence. After two hours or so, a young monk brought him a tray with a jug of water, a few slices of bread, some cheese and soup. Eduardo thanked him in Greek but his benefactor just smiled and said nothing.

Four hours passed and Eduardo was exhausted. He had examined perhaps one hundred books and found nothing of interest. His estimate that there were weeks of work was clearly accurate and at the end of that there still might be nothing of interest. It was obviously hopeless and his initial enthusiasm for cataloging the whole collection had completely dissipated.

He closed the door of the library and returned to the office of Nicephorus.

"Well," said the latter in a more friendly tone than he had used earlier. "How did it go? Did you find anything of interest?"

"I regret not," said Eduardo, "but I am grateful for the opportunity."

"We have little time for such things," said Nicephorus, almost apologetically. "I believe that most of the books are old hymnals, psalters and the like which have become unreadable or unusable since they are so old and we have not wished to dispose of them. But it is not impossible that some rarity is there. Maybe we shall never know."

He did not seem particularly concerned.

"I thank you for your hospitality," said Eduardo. And so they made polite farewells and Nicephorus escorted him to the monastery gate.

His escort on the ramparts had gone and his walk back to the hospice was uneventful. Michaelis had already arrived. His own meeting had gone satisfactorily and he was heartened to hear from Eduardo that there was no purpose in prolonging their stay. The next morning they began their return journey.

It was an indication of Eduardo's naiveté or ingenuousness that although, in his preparations for their journey, he had considered the physical dangers, which is why he had asked Michaelis to accompany him, he had not given any thought to the attitude of the authorities. Such was his enthusiasm to find the Stobaeus, it had just not crossed his mind that the two of them might provoke suspicion. But the Turks, although tolerant of travelers and of the local Christian communities, were certainly not fools. What were they expected to make of two young foreigners, armed, lean and athletic who came to Bursa with almost no baggage and had nothing but the flimsiest of reasons for why they were there and very little money to support the pretext on which they had come? In fact the authorities had been notified immediately after they landed on Turkish soil on the first day and now as the cart in which they intended to travel back to the Bosphorus passed through the gates of Bursa, it was stopped and Eduardo and Michaelis were ordered out by the city guards.

CHAPTER 17

The Court

When Philip Shamash returned to Constantinople in the fall of 1439, Gemistos Plethon did not accompany him. Plethon was eighty-three years old and he decided to retire to his home town, to Mistra, the capital of the Morea in European Greece. This was fortunate for Shamash since, apart from his close friends, Plethon was one of the few people aware that Shamash had not left Florence with the remainder of the delegation of his own accord but had been ordered to leave by the authorities. There had been those in the Greek delegation and in the administration who had always had their doubts about Philip Shamash but he had persuaded Plethon to give him a letter of introduction to the Megadux, the administrative head of the Byzantine court, and this was to prove enough to ensure him a position in the Court. As in all such affairs, personal connections were essential for advancement and to have recommendations from both Plethon and then from Lukas Notaras, the Megadux, was a major step for Shamash, who had no family connections in the city or court. But the administration was to some extent a meritocracy and anyone who could demonstrate faithful service, good looks and intelligence in addition to the diplomatic skills necessary for navigating the intricacies of the court rituals and intrigue, was likely to be well rewarded.

The imperial palace, the Blachernae, had originally been built outside the walls in the north-eastern corner of the city but here it was very vulnerable to attack and at an early stage the city walls had been extended to enclose it. The palace was a collection of at least seven separate buildings which had been constructed over many centuries and they included the Emperor's private apartments, the imperial state rooms, the offices for the administration, which at the height of the Empire employed some hundreds of civil servants, and the homes of many of the most senior officials of the Empire including the Megadux himself. The state rooms were naturally designed so as to impress ambassadors and visitors from other countries with their opulence and grandeur. Some had ceilings of gold, others thrones that could be raised on mechanical devices; there were gardens, courtyards and pools, fountains which flowed with wine, a zoo and an aviary.

Philip Shamash was wealthy, at least for the time being. The money which he had obtained by selling books to Patrizzi and with which he had intended to maintain his household in Florence, he could now use for the same purpose in Constantinople as well as buy himself a position in court. This latter was not by any means an underhanded affair but standard practice in the court and one more way in which the Emperor and his officials gained revenue. A low rate of interest was normally paid on the sum involved but it was tacitly understood that the capital itself would never be returned.

The Emperor retained absolute power in the court and the Empire and all final decisions on the appointment and dismissal of senior advisers, on the question of life or death in judicial matters and on matters of war and peace remained with him. A courtier could be condemned without trial, the execution would be carried out immediately and the victim's head would be displayed to the Emperor in full court to show not only that his orders had been carried out and as a lesson to others but above all as a demonstration of the Emperor's complete and absolute authority.

Such arbitrary authority imposed on a rigid ceremonial spawned a culture of intrigue that was only partly a caricature of Byzantine society. The Emperor had to be continually on alert to enemies within, the spies and assassins of foreign powers, members of his extended family who had ambitions to the throne, courtiers who felt that they had been slighted or overlooked for promotion or reward and victorious generals who knew that real power, despite the vacuous ceremonial of the court, lay with those who commanded the loyalty of the army. Vast numbers of people had access to the palace, foreign representatives or envoys from all over the world, the *koubouklion* or corps of eunuchs, priests, the palace guards, suppliers and slaves. Emperor had a network of informants within and without the court who reported on the rumors and the reality of conspiracy. One false step or ill-considered remark by even his highest confidants could mean immediate execution and yet, despite these dangers, it was almost inevitable that sooner or later a courtier would be forced to choose sides in some palace intrigue or join a faction with dangerous political ambitions.

And so it was with Shamash. At first he flourished in such an atmosphere. His diplomatic experience in the West was particularly desirable in those desperate times for the Empire and, in spite of the reservations of some, there were good reports from the leaders of the delegation to Florence of his judgment, his advice and his activities. Within three months he was appointed to the foreign department headed by Theodore Cydones, the *Logothete tou dromou,* or Minister of Posts and Foreign Affairs.

Cecilia's remark that her husband had the ear of the Emperor was in fact untrue, a natural exaggeration by a proud spouse, particularly one who had no notion of the protocol of the imperial court. However, it was true that, in the performance of his new duties, Shamash became aware the policy of the Greeks toward their western neighbors and allies, such as they were, and these were naturally matters which were of the greatest interest to his real masters.

The small house Philip and Cecilia Shamash had bought was on a narrow street close to the Palace. It had three stories like its neighbors and much like those in Pera, with the upper story, supported on elaborate wooden corbels, extending over the dark and damp street. To provide some protection against intruders, the entrance door was on the second floor, approached by narrow steps running parallel to the street. Next to the entrance door there was a small barred opening through which visitors could be identified. Neither Shamash nor Cecilia were aware that this grille, a feature of all the local houses, had originally been designed, although it had never been used as such, to allow the householder to wield through it a pike or spear to dislodge an attacker from the narrow platform in front of the entrance door.

The entrance floor held three main rooms, one of which Philip Shamash took for his study and another Cecilia used as a parlor. The kitchen was on the floor below where there also rooms for two maids and a door to a walled yard at the rear. On the top floor were three bedrooms. The interior of the house was paneled in plain wood and lit by small windows and wall sconces.

During the first months after their arrival, Cecilia was engaged in setting up their household, although even this was not easy in view of her difficulty with the language. On occasion Shamash visited the marriage bed, although Cecilia soon realized that he had little interest in such conjugal intimacy. Shamash did not dislike her; for the most part he just ignored her but from her point of view, this neglect was worse than dislike or even hatred. However, he was aware of her difficulties with the language and he made arrangements for her to have a teacher and as a result she began to make some acquaintances in the city. But between the two of them there was little friendship and no emotional connection and he for one did not miss either.

Cecilia never went into the Palace. Only the Empress and her attendants, together with the wives of the high officials of the administration, lived there and they were strictly segregated from the remainder of the court. They did not attend court functions and if there was a state banquet to entertain visiting dignitaries, the Empress held a separate banquet for the women visitors. The only officials allowed into her apartments apart from the Emperor himself were the eunuchs who served her. It was impossible for Cecilia to have a social life in the court since such a thing did not exist for women of her station.

Almost the only opportunity the two of them had to participate together in an imperial function was when they joined the Emperor's retinue on one of his rare progresses outside the palace to visit the city granaries. These ceremonies which had originated as no more than a prudent administrative check on what was one of the principal sources of imperial power became formalized, over the centuries, into a ritual procession. At other times, on important saint's days, the Emperor processed again from the Blachernae to the church of Santa Sophia and on these occasions too the whole court was required to take part. It was by this means that the ordinary people of the city, who never entered the gates of the palace, were reminded of the power and the divinity of the imperial person.

The processions were splendid affairs. The streets were strewn with mats, leaves, and branches and many of the inhabitants of the city lined the processional route. First came the priests carrying sacred icons, such as a copy of the Mandylion[13], the most holy of all, a picture of His face supposedly impressed on the cloth by Christ himself. They were followed by members of the court in silks of red, white and green, followed by the personal bodyguards of the Emperor, the Varangian Guard, clad in sky-blue silk and carrying gilded axes. Next there were the eunuchs, pages and patricians, and finally the Emperor himself, accompanied by the *silentarius*, whose job it was to hush the crowd. The Emperor wore his diadem of pearls and gold, his state robes, and the purple cloak and shoes that only he was entitled to wear, and behind him walked his chief minister, who at every two steps reminded him to "think on death", upon which he opened a gold box he was carrying and, with tears in his eyes,[14] kissed the earth it contained,

Shamash had many things on his mind. He was keenly aware of his isolation in the court with neither family from whom he could learn the craft of the courtier nor family to fall back on if his financial position should become impossible. He had to devote his time and energy to his new duties and his salary would only be paid at some indefinite moment in the future if at all.

He still had most of the money from the sale of his books in Florence but this would not last long with his present lifestyle and the big ambitions that he nurtured. It was clear that he had to find additional sources of income as soon as possible. In this, he was in competition with most of the elite of the Byzantine court. The Turkish incursions had curtailed if not eliminated many of the aristocratic estates and, apart from administrative salaries if they had them, selling books had become one of the few acceptable ways for courtiers to make money. After all, even the Emperor himself was known to be decimating the imperial library. So now Shamash had to do the same; he had both to find a source of books and the means to dispose of them. In the past, he had obtained books from Plethon, either from the latter's own library or from introductions which Plethon had given him. But it was one thing to approach a member of an important family with a famous library as the secretary of the great Plethon who had a scholarly reputation second to none and, who was, like all scholars, understandably short of money. It was quite another to be seeking a reputation as a rising star in the court while having to reveal to his peers that he needed money to sustain that reputation.

As disturbing as the state of his finances was his knowledge that some of his former colleagues in the deputation were aware of his precipitate departure from Florence and were understandably curious as to the reason for it. And even more alarming was the possibility that the Florentines might at any moment disclose to the Greeks their suspicions as to his real identity. He could not think of any good reason why they would not. Finally, he had to decide if and how he should once more make contact with his Turkish handlers. Perhaps they might not have further need of his services but it was more than likely that they too would want an explanation of the events in Florence. His previous contact in Constantinople, one Al Maliki to whom his dispatches had been addressed, had disappeared, and uncharacteristically, he was at a loss as to what he should do next.

He had tried to avoid the few friends he had made in Florence and who had returned with him to Constantinople but in the close confines of the court he could not do so for long and he knew it. Sure enough, one evening, soon after he had started in his diplomatic duties and as he was making his way across the outer courtyard of the palace towards the gate on to the city streets, he was accosted by his friend Alkaios who suggested they might have talk about their old times together. Much as Shamash was loath to do this, he knew that there was no point in putting it off. If he made an excuse now, there would always be another time in the near future. So he agreed and they took a seat on the edge of a small pool in the center of the courtyard, where, Shamash noticed, the noise of the fountain made conversation impossible to overhear.

"It's good to see you again," said Alkaios. "I am surprised that we have not had the opportunity before."

"It seems only a few days ago since we were together in Florence," replied Shamash "Yes, as you can imagine, I have been busy at work and busy finding a house. What are you doing?"

"I am now working for General Anemas, as is Phokas."

There was a pause.

"And how is your wife? Is she settling in?"

"As best as she is able. She obviously has difficulty with the language but she is starting to learn it. For anyone in a new country, it takes time."

Shamash was trying to cut short this line of conversation but Alkaios persisted.

"Of course, we were surprised when you decided to return to the Constantinople after your marriage. You seemed to be very well set up there with a good connection to the elite of the city, a beautiful wife and a grand home. What more could a man want?" Alkaios asked and Shamash could not detect any irony.

"If we were not friends," said Shamash, "I would say that this sort of inquiry is none of your business. But I can tell you that Plethon persuaded me that I had a greater chance of advancement back here in the Court than if I were exiled with those effeminate Italians, however great were the other advantages which you mention. I thought then and I still think that he was right."

'Yes, you may indeed be right," replied Alkaios, "but as a friend, I should also tell you that there are rumors about the matter circulating in the Court that may not have come to your ears, rumors which are not all flattering."

Shamash's heart froze but he forced a smile. "What rumors?" he asked, "I have heard no rumors although I have no doubt that you wish to pass them on to me."

"That there was some scandal. That it involved state secrets. That a young man who was a scribe was secretly executed."

"I know of no such rumor nor report. And I work in that department here. I would have heard."

"Nevertheless," continued Alkaios, "that is the rumor. It has certainly reached the General's ears and he has asked me to discuss it with you. He has made inquiries and he finds that there is some truth in the matter. And that you were involved."

"Nonsense," said Shamash, "what would I have to do with Florentine secrets?"

"That's what the General would like to know. Would you like to come and discuss it with the General himself?"

This sounded like an invitation but Shamash knew that it was one that he could not refuse. The two of them looked at each other for a moment.

"I certainly did not expect a friend to treat me in such a way," said Shamash, "but I am happy to meet the General. I have nothing to hide and you know also that I have no choice."

"Indeed, I believe you do not. But I think it will be to your advantage. And this has nothing to do with friendship or otherwise. I am just a messenger and these are my instructions."

With that they parted and three days later, Shamash found himself in an office, also in the Blachernae, where the General awaited him with an aide seated behind him. It was a large room lit by tall windows with thick oriental carpets on the floor and tapestries on the walls. General Anemas, a man in his fifties, tall, dark and heavy-set, was wearing his formal uniform, a body hugging suit of gold chain-mail, with a short leather skirt and a long green cloak fastened at the neck with a brooch. He commanded one of the Tagmata or divisions of the army stationed within the city as a permanent defensive force and he was one of the most senior officers in Constantinople, second only to the Akolythos, the commander of the Varangian guard. He was not one to waste time on preliminaries.

"So you are Shamash. You should know that I have been in contact with my people in Florence. We know that you were involved in the theft of state secrets and were expelled. What do you have to say about it?"

'I have nothing to say about it. I do not know what you are talking about. I deny the suggestion entirely," said Shamash, but he could not keep his voice from wavering.

"Of course, you do," said the General smiling. "But that is not the point. We can either confront you with the evidence or we can force the truth out of you. But there is no need for such measures since I am convinced about the facts of the matter. But you need not be concerned. For the time being, I do not intend to let these 'facts' go beyond the walls of this room. And in return I expect something from you. In due time I shall call on your services and, when that time comes, I shall require an immediate response. I will leave it to you to imagine the consequences if you fail to answer my call or fail to heed my instructions. Do you understand?"

Shamash did not understand but he nodded all the same.

"In return", the General added, "you can be assured that for the time being no one else will get to learn about your activities in Florence or about those on behalf of whom you were acting. Do you have any questions? If not, you may go."

Shamash left by himself but two days later he encountered Alkaios in the palace and angrily confronted him.

"What is going on with your General and what does he mean by services?" he said raising his voice.

"I am not sure what you are talking about, but keep your voice down. If the General has asked or asks you to do something on his behalf, I imagine you should do it or whatever he knows about your stay in Florence will be made public. It seems obvious to me."

"How can I work for the General when I already have a job in the Administration," asked Shamash with irritation.

"You are being ingenuous or pretending to be so," said Alkaios with a smile. "But one day you will understand and then you will have a choice to make."

CHAPTER 18

The Hippodrome

Shamash was unsure whether the protection that the General had promised was to his benefit or not. The more he thought about it, the more he realized that whatever services the General had in mind for him were likely to be equal to the favor that the General was doing for him by saving him from the axe. There seemed to be no doubt that Anemas knew the whole story.

The delicacy, danger and urgency of his situation was brought home to him with even greater force by an incident that had occurred as Shamash was walking the short distance home from the Palace along the crowded streets of Petra. A stranger had tapped him on the shoulder and had handed him a small piece of folded parchment, with the curt remark, "I believe you dropped this."

Shamash looked quickly down to check the loose bag he was carrying with a strap over his shoulder and across his body, in which he did indeed have a number of documents. When he looked up again the stranger was gone. The incident appeared to have gone unnoticed by anyone else in the crowd. Shamash put the parchment in his bag and did not open it until he had reached home and was alone in his study but he did not at first have any idea what to make of the single line written on it:

"St. Praxedes says that books are rivers that water the whole earth; they are the most ancient and holy springs of wisdom."

He thought that it must relate to the purchase and trade of books which he was in the process of organizing but what was the point of it? He looked up St. Praxedes in his almanac and found that this saint's day was just one week away and would be the subject of a festival with a procession that ended at Santa Sophia. He then noticed the words Hagia and Sophia in the text, holy and wisdom, and the message became clear.

The following week he waited in Santa Sophia as the long procession of St. Praxedes entered the church headed by priests carrying icons and relics of the saint. The great church was extremely crowded and when a man gripped his arm and without saying a word motioned for him to follow, Shamash had great difficulty keeping him in sight as they pushed through the crowds of onlookers.

When they reached the outside of the church, it became easier and Shamash kept about twenty paces behind his guide who did not look back. Neither did Shamash who nevertheless suspected that, behind him, there would be other observers to check that he was alone and that they were not being followed. They reached the ruins of the Hippodrome only a short distance away and the guide led him through the maze of arches beneath the ancient stands until they approached another man who, at first sight, appeared to be just one more of those who lived in destitution amongst the ruins. The guide walked on without a word but, as Shamash passed, the second man grabbed him and had addressed him without introduction, rapidly and aggressively.

"Al-Malik was betrayed. We don't know by whom. You have been clumsy and irresponsible. These things are not forgotten. Since you have a new and potentially rewarding position in the Administration, we are continuing to make use of your services. You will give me a full written report here next month. Come to Santa Sophia on the same day, at the same time. If you wish to contact us urgently or if you are being sent away on a mission, you may come on the same day and same time in any week. There will always be someone waiting and watching. Do not make another mistake or your services will be seen as having no value and you will become a liability."

Before Shamash could protest or respond, this man also walked off into the gloom of the arches and passageways and, within twenty seconds, two more men walked up from the direction from which he had come, passed Shamash and followed the first.

Shamash was shocked by the brusqueness of his interrogator, by the news of the disappearance of his contact, Al-Malik, and the fact that he was being blamed for this. If Al-Malik had been arrested it was very likely that his own true allegiance was also known. And yet he was not being offered the option to withdraw from Constantinople but only to continue in his work. And this could mean arrest at any moment. And if he did not continue his work, it was quite plain, as the man had said, that he had, or would, become a liability and this could only have one outcome.

The only small consolation was that since he had not yet, in fact, been arrested and since it was inconceivable that, under torture, Al-Malik had not revealed his own true identity, it must be that the Italians had decided not to pass on to the Greeks his role in the affair. But they might do so at any moment. He turned these things rapidly over in his mind. Such had been the rapidity and confusion of events in Florence after his interrogation and exile that he had not thought of the obvious outcome that the Florentines would trace and arrest the addressee of the package that had been intercepted. If he had thought of it, he would never have returned to Constantinople; it would obviously have been much too dangerous. But now he had returned, he could not leave; his Turkish masters would never permit it. The position he had got himself in the diplomatic service was too valuable for them and they would continue to milk him for information until the end. And then he had another thought. There was only one reason why the Italians would not yet have unmasked him and that was because they were following him in the hope that he would lead them to others.

Suddenly, within the oppressive gloom and dampness of the ruins of the Hippodrome, the realization of his position came to him. His reputation now meant nothing. His fate hung by a slender and twisting thread, which could be cut at any moment. The Italians might abandon him as soon as they perceived he had fulfilled his usefulness, as could the Turks who might reveal his role to the Greeks as the easiest and cleanest method of disposing of him. And this was without the threats of General Amenas who might also turn against him if it suited his purpose. He was entirely at the mercy of people who were quite as ruthless as himself or more so. There appeared no way out. His thoughts suddenly turned to the executioner's passage in the Charisos Gate and the stories of victims' heads being presented to the Emperor in full view of members of the court. As he walked back home to Petra, he began to feel overwhelmingly nauseous.

CHAPTER 19

The Rumor

Philip Shamash had been a small boy when, as an orphan in Bursa, he had been picked out by the Turkish authorities as someone of exceptional intelligence and promise. He had been assigned to a special orphanage, where he was given a handler whom he came to know as his father and, along with other promising candidates, was taught Greek intensively so that, after a short time it became his first language. At the age of eight he was taken to Constantinople and told that he must never reveal anything of his earlier childhood. He was delivered anonymously to a Greek orphanage, which accepted him as a Greek and continued his education. Thereafter his "father" had visited him at intervals and slowly impressed on him the true nature of his vocation, which he had accepted, at first, as some kind of a game and then in earnest. But his activities in Florence had been the first serious exercise of the vocation for which he had been preparing for so long. He had undertaken his secret duties knowing they were dangerous but not fully considering the consequences, involved as he was with the prestige of his liaison with Plethon and his growing personal reputation amongst his Greek colleagues.

Faced with imminent betrayal, the consequence of which almost certainly was summary execution, Shamash immediately set about conceiving plans to neutralize the threats which beset him and to impose his will on the web of fate which entangled him. He would have to find a scapegoat on whom to cast the blame if he were denounced to the Greeks. He would try to come up with a plan that allowed him to pretend that his contact with both Latins and Turks had been at the behest of the administration itself. Then he would build himself a power base in the Court as quickly as possible to assist him in obtaining early warning of any dangers and make him indispensable to his superiors. And he could not forget that he still needed or would soon need a source of income.

To help with these last plans, he needed subordinates to assist him to seek out and approach the owners of the great libraries and through whose skill or connections he could add to his own reputation at Court. He needed a group who would be beholden to him as he rose through the administration and would see the potential of rising with him, a group which would draw attention to his administrative skills but would not excite undue envy or antagonism amongst his superiors. To do this would require more money, but he accepted this as a risk that he would have to take.

Not content with merely familiarizing himself with his own duties in the diplomatic service, he immediately began to consider who might be candidates among the young men of the court to qualify as his assistants. After some months of careful observation, he approached three of them, Demetrius Palamas, Manuel Argyropoulos and a young Italian, Pietro Mascario. All of them, to some extent dazzled by Shamash's reputation and well aware of the advantage of attaching themselves to a rising star in the court, accepted his proposal.

Palamas was an aggressive but well-educated young man, member of an important Byzantine family whom Shamash felt would have an easy and successful entrée to many of the other wealthy households in the city thus enabling him to gain access to their libraries.

Manuel Argyropoulos was the cousin of John Argyropoulos, the scholar, teacher and the natural successor to Plethon in his exposition of the teaching of Plato. Shamash could see that he provided a liaison who not only reflected his own interests but would also gain him connections in both literary and social circles in the city.

Finally, Mascario was one of the few non-Greeks in the administration. He was intelligent and well-educated and he would have the advantage in a diplomatic career of his Italian background and language, which would be obvious and acceptable to Shamash's own superior, the Logothete. Shamash supposed, and this was the real reason for the choice, that not being a Greek, Mascario might be susceptible to a proposal to turn his allegiance towards the Turks whom, it seemed, fate was ineluctably preparing to become the new masters of the Byzantine world.

Shamash insisted that each of them make the usual investment in their new positions. All three could easily afford it, and this naturally made the appointments more palatable to Cydones with whom Shamash shared the proceeds. The speed with which he had organized the appointments and the obvious qualifications of the three candidates added to Shamash's own reputation.

The initial purpose of Shamash's own appointment was to act as liaison with the Greek Despotate at Mistra, capital of the Morea. This, with Thessalonika, was the only Greek territory remaining to the Empire other than Constantinople itself. The Despotate was governed by the Despot Theodore who was the brother of the Emperor and the territory was, nominally at least, still part of the Eastern Empire and kept close relations with the capital. Philip Shamash's job was to read the dispatches sent on an almost daily basis from Mistra, to summarize them and make recommendations to the Logothete on any action that might be necessary. In return he composed the replies, passed on the orders of his own superiors and summarized the relevant news from the capital. The actual letters he dictated to one of his assistants, whose job it was to write them and make copies for the office records. He allowed his assistants to read all the incoming messages. One of his duties, and this suited him perfectly, was to make regular visits to Mistra and other parts of the Morea to confirm the accuracy of the written reports and to make independent recommendations.

Frequently the four of them would meet in Shamash's office in the Blachernae and discuss the political situation at home and in the Morea. It did not take much for Shamash to discover that none of his young protegés was sanguine about the future of the remains of their motherland, the Byzantine Empire, and their hometown, Constantinople. Each of them was diligent in his work, ambitious for his future career and unstinting in his devotion to the Emperor but, as Shamash quickly detected, beneath this youthful enthusiasm they displayed an almost desperate melancholy, a realization that all the panoply of the imperial administration was a façade, that their ambitions would never come to fruition and that their daily work was no more than a hopeless game, a game whose outcome was certain and which they could never win.

It was at one of these meetings that Shamash first broached the subject of books. He gave a short introductory speech, designed, on the surface, to boost the morale of the group and emphasize the continuing importance of their work.

"Our job as diplomats goes far beyond just keeping in touch with the distant parts of the empire or indeed the world outside the empire. It goes beyond making treaties, securing allies, cementing trade relations. One of the most important functions of our job as diplomats is to introduce Byzantine culture to the people we shall be meeting in the outside world. And this is not just because we naturally take pride in our own values and our own way of life. We, as leaders of the empire, have a special responsibility towards the rest of Europe despite the fact that we know that most of the European nations are nothing but barbarians. Why is this? Because Byzantine culture, Greek culture, is the fount, the origin of all European culture. Because that culture has been preserved in this great city in the centuries since its foundation whereas what knowledge they have, or had, of it in the outside world has almost entirely been destroyed. The heritage of literature, of philosophy, of mathematics, of astronomy and the other elements of what we call the *paidea*, our educational curriculum, hardly exists outside the empire."

"Actually," said Palamas, always the first to interrupt or respond, "Greek culture has also influenced the peoples of the north, the Varangian people of Kiev, Moscow and Rus. What about St Cyril and St. Methodius in Serbia and the conversion of Queen Helena of the Rus?"

"And the infidels, the Arabs, and the Ottomans," said Argyropoulos. "They know as much about Aristotle as we do."

"Yes," interjected Mascario, "Was it not the scholars of the House of Wisdom in Baghdad who translated all the Greek works into Arabic?"

"And you sir," said Palamas, directing his question at Shamash. "You were a student of Plethon, were you not? You know as much about the ancient Greeks as anyone. Do you think that what they said and wrote has any relevance, is a living force today?"

"And anyway," interjected Argyropoulos, "why did he call himself Plethon?"

"That's easy," said Palamas. "It's because his favorite philosopher was Plato."

"It was more than that," explained Shamash. "You may not know that his second name is Gemistos and that of course is a synonym for Plethon – both words meaning abundance. But you are right, the coincidence with Plato was too much for him to resist. He was always laughing and chuckling at the coincidence. And yes, I do think that what the ancient Greeks said and wrote has relevance today, both for us and for the rest of the world. We know that Aristotle's works are the foundation of much of our education. And the other Greek philosophers also wrote about justice, how we should live our lives, the meaning of life, of language, of ways to approach God. We know that the work of Plato was used by the original church fathers as the basis of their exposition of Christian theology. We can be proud that our ancestors were the first people to think of these things. And we, generations later, still have a responsibility to ensure that their ideas are passed on, are not lost. They have to be taught anew to every generation, both here and overseas."

"How do we do that in practice?" asked Argyropoulos. "We are not teachers, we have not chosen that career, we shall never know enough to become like Plethon and my cousin who have spent all their lives learning, and it will be years before we get enough experience and seniority to be allowed even to go to any of the Latin countries."

"Yes," replied Shamash, "that is true but there is one thing that we can do and should do. There is one way that we can ensure that the knowledge that is encapsulated in this city and in its ancient scholarly traditions is safeguarded and passed on to other peoples for their benefit. We can try and acquire some of the ancient books that still exist in the private and public libraries of the city, copy them or buy them and send them overseas."

Shamash could not as yet bring himself to say "sell them to the west" but it would soon become obvious that that was his intention.

"I believe," he continued, "that it is our patriotic duty to do this, our duty to our heritage and absolutely an essential part of our role as diplomatic representatives of the culture of the Empire."

It was a resounding and persuasive argument and the young men agreed with it whole-heartedly. After further animated discussion, it was agreed that both Palamas and Argyropoulos would make separate plans to approach their family acquaintances with the proposition that these families should go through their libraries and consider whether they would sell or allow any of their books to be copied. When they got to a discussion of what channels should be used to send books out of the city, Mascario remarked that he had a friend, another Italian, one Nicholas Camerino, who had the means to sell books in Italy and that he would inquire whether this individual would be interested in accepting books from other sources.

Shamash ended the discussion by emphasizing that his name should be not be used in any of the negotiations; if asked, they should say that the project was being promoted by the state itself, whom they represented. This would be quite credible to any owner and potential seller of books who would know only too well the impoverished condition of the imperial administration. He also indicated that he would fund any necessary expense himself and, as an aside, that any profits that were made, which he did not expect to be large, would be shared with the group. He made arrangements to meet with the Logothete to reveal his progress and to confirm that, as was customary, he would share with him the profits of the new enterprise.

He also took advantage of this meeting to reveal to Cydones his plan for the second part of his strategy: to discover who it was that might be passing on information about him to the Italians and to provide cover if his activities were ever betrayed. He proposed to pass a rumor round the Court of some secret action by the Turks against the Italians; if the Italians reacted to this information, he would know that there was indeed a mole in the court and by distributing the information selectively he might discover the individual or individuals who were responsible. To do this would have the double advantage of again boosting his own reputation in the court and he could then say, yes, as they all knew, he had been providing information to the Italians at the request of his own superiors. Hopefully this would be enough to exonerate him from suspicion. He would in fact become a double spy. Also, he would also pass on the same information to his Turkish handlers, again taking care to do this through the medium of a third party and thus safeguard his position from betrayal from this quarter, especially if there was a reaction from the Italians, which would validate the reliability of his information.

"Your honor," said Shamash after explaining his plans for the book business, "To broach a different subject, I have reason to believe that there is an Italian spy operating in the Court."

"That does not surprise me at all. What specifically makes you think this?" replied Cydones without the slightest display of alarm.

"I was talking to a Florentine acquaintance of mine who was visiting the city and he told me that there were rumors circulating in the Florentine administration of details of the recent successes of the Despot in the Morea and Boeotia."

"Such information could have come from Mistra or indeed from Athens," said Cydones.

"That is true, your honor, but I have a plan that will reveal whether the leak is here in the city or is from elsewhere."

"Very well and what is this plan?"

"I propose that we circulate in the Court specific information which, if it is reported to the Italians, will necessarily provoke a response from them. We shall then know that the spy is operating here and not in Mistra. My proposal is we should circulate a rumor, that has come to our attention, that the Turks are proposing to make an assault on Pera to test its state of readiness and its defenses. I believe that this news is sufficiently serious that the Italians would report it back to us if indeed they get to hear of it."

The Logothete stared at Shamash in something close to admiration. "Yes, that is an excellent plan. I personally see no difficulty with it. In fact, it has certain strategic advantages. But before you take it further, I will need to inform the Emperor, which I will do immediately."

And so, in turn, Cydones consulted with the Emperor whose approval was not long in forthcoming; there seemed to be no downside to Shamash's plan since even if the original information was incorrect and there was no Italian mole, nothing would be lost.

Accordingly Shamash began to take into his confidence Pietro Mascario and told him confidentially of the information that had just been received about the Turkish designs on Pera. Pietro was a garrulous young man, who did not seem to have any self-control when it came to sharing gossip both within the court and outside and within days the news was widely known. For the office records, as he put it, Shamash had Mascario write out the plan for the Pera attack and this sheet he handed over to his Turkish contact when he next met him in the Hippodrome. He asked that this should be returned to him when it had been used and so it was. As it turned out passing on this message to his Turkish handlers was a serious error by Shamash. His purpose was to implicate Mascario as the contact with the Turks if he, Shamash, was ever denounced for what he was but Shamash did not think through the wider strategic and political implications of the plan and this proved his downfall.

He also gave some thought to who else could be a possible suspect in the matter and suddenly realized the obvious - that Cecilia was Italian. Now that he knew that prospects for his position, his reputation and indeed his very life, had become precarious, not unnaturally, he had become worried and irascible at home even though he preserved his usual confident façade at Court and in his office. His temper, which at the best of times was often uncontrollable, was frequently vented on her. He realized he did not even like Cecilia, although he now felt an increasing need for both comfort and companionship and in his frustration he reacted by being more aggressive and abusive. During, and in spite of, this downward spiral of domestic discontent, he did pass on to Cecilia more details of his office affairs than he was accustomed to and did slip into these conversations the news of the plan of the Turks to attack Pera. He could not believe that Cecilia could possibly be the source of leaks although he wondered whether she might, in idle moments, be innocently passing on gossip to some of her few friends in the city.

Amidst all this, he was summoned to meet again with General Amenas. He had turned over in his mind whether or not to confess all to the General and seek his protection but he realized that this was what in effect the General has already offered him and to confess would be a sign of weakness that would put him in no stronger a position. All he could do was to obey Amenas' orders and follow him wherever it led.

As it turned out, he did not meet with Amenas himself but with one of his subordinates. This latter without even introducing himself gave Shamash a sealed letter with no address.

"You will deliver this as soon as possible to your Turkish contacts," he said. "And do not be so stupid as to deny you have such contacts. We know what you have been doing in the Hippodrome. You must guard this with your life – if it is lost, the General's protection will be forfeited. Do you understand?"

Shamash once again nodded silently. He knew that he had little alternative. He rose and, after concealing the letter in the inner pocket of his cloak, left as quickly as he had come. He went straight home and into his study, placing the letter on his desk where he studied it intently. It was folded and sealed in two different places and the wax was stamped with a strange device. No doubt this was one which was unknown to anyone except those to whom he had to deliver the letter and this would ensure that the letter could never be traced back to its origin if it was intercepted. He turned the letter over and over, trying to detect if there were any secret marks or other precautions which would indicate if it had been opened. It was likely that there were such marks but he could not detect any and it was a risk that he would have to take. No doubt also the letter was in code so that the undertaking might be fruitless but he decided to try. It was not for nothing that he had been instructed in the techniques of spy-craft.

Cecilia was out but he called one of the maids and told her that under no circumstances was he to be disturbed. He then lit a candle and heated a pin in the flame holding it with a piece of cloth. Using the point of the pin which he continually reheated, he began to soften the wax of one of the seals by touching one side of the seal just above the parchment taking great care not to singe the parchment itself. Very slowly, he was able to lift the wax off the parchment as it softened and then dried again. It took more than an hour to do one side of each seal and lift the fold of the letter without damaging the parchment. Finally, he was able to open the message which turned out as he had feared to be in code, long lines of meaningless letters covering two sheets of parchment. Nevertheless, he decided to copy the message and then he resealed the letter using a similar technique. With a small flat flexible metal tool coated with a small amount of oil, he reheated the whole of the underside of the wax and then pressed it back into the same place on the parchment. It was impossible to tell that it had been tampered with.

He then took up his copy and contemplated it. Without the key to the message it was of course hopeless to try and decode it but there just the possibility that it used a key which he knew. He had been taught and had memorized twenty different keys one of which he used at random each time he had himself sent a coded message. The recipient of the message had to try out each key on the first few letters of the message until he came to the relevant one. It was just possible, thought Shamash, that the same group of keys was used throughout world of Turkish intel-ligence and that one of them would reveal the content of the general's message. Accordingly, he began the painstaking process of using each of the keys that he knew both in Greek and in Turkish and sure enough after several tries he was able to start translating. It was in Turkish and as he read, Shamash felt him-self become colder and colder with fear. The General was offer-ing to betray the city to the Turks in exchange for being con-firmed Emperor. He would open the gates of the city to a limited number of Turkish troops. His own forces would remain intact to act as his personal security guard, the population and the fabric of the city would be respected, the city would pay tribute to the Sultan in the traditional manner and he, the General, as the new Emperor would swear allegiance to the Sultan.

CHAPTER 20

Captives

Eduardo and Michaelis were taken to the palace of the Turkish governor in Bursa. This had much the same function as the Blachernae Palace in Constantinople; it was both the seat of local government and the residence of the governor and many of the local officials. Bursa was the capital city of the whole of the Ottoman province of Anatolia, which was still, formally, a military district so that these officials were officers in the Ottoman army and as such disciplined, efficient and quite accustomed to dealing with suspected espionage.

The two were imprisoned separately and interrogated first in Turkish and then in Greek. On the one hand, they both repeatedly gave the same account of their presence in Bursa, an account which was weak but credible and there was no evidence of wrongdoing against them. On the face of it, they were two innocent travelers whom, as we have seen, the Turks normally tolerated. On the other, it was not surprising that when two young men, foreigners, armed and athletic were seen to be inspecting the site of the headquarters of a military district of a potential enemy on the pretext of looking for a book, the location and details of which neither of them had anything but the vaguest notion, this would arouse considerable suspicion. In due time it was decided that the two of them should not be released but should be taken to the army headquarters, at the court of the Sultan himself in Adrianople, on the far side of the Bosphorus north of Constantinople, where they could be interrogated again and their fate decided.

Three days after the expected date of his return, Michaelis' father, Alessandro Mascario, naturally started to get anxious. He had been nervous enough when Michaelis had told him of the proposed journey but his son was of age, needed the experience

166

with Turkish manners and customs and Alessandro did not want to discourage his iniative. Mascario himself was comfortable in his relations with the Turkish traders; in his long years of doing business in the cities of the Black Sea and Anatolia, many of which were now under Turkish control, he had experienced the ways of these people and had established and maintained contacts amongst them both in their public and private capacities. He decided to dispatch to Bursa one of his most senior employees, Marco Dandi, who spoke fluent Turkish, to investigate the whereabouts of the two young men. It did not take long even after the most cursory inquiry for Dandi to discover what had happened.

When he received the news of their capture and later of their intended transfer to Adrianople, Alessandro realized that there was nothing for it but to mount a rescue operation. He knew that there was no point in alerting the Greek authorities. Quite apart from the obvious fact that the two prisoners were Italian, the Greeks were far too wary of the Turks to risk a major incident or to contemplate antagonizing them over what, to them, would be a petty matter. The same, to a lesser extent, went for the Genoese authorities in Pera. If Alessandro alerted them, he might again risk them ordering him to take no action so as to prevent antagonizing the Turks. He had to organize the rescue operation and carry it out himself and secretly.

Dandi had already told him that it was intended to take the two prisoners to Adrianople. This was good news since it was out of the question for any rescue operation to take place on land in Turkish territory. It would have to be mounted during the brief crossing of the Bosphorus. Not only was it likely that the prisoners would be lightly guarded on a small boat but Alessandro had ships and sailors in his employ. He only needed to hire a dozen mercenaries to perform the actual boarding and rescue and the operation could be swift and might be unnoticed by anyone on the shore. There need be no witnesses.

There were, however, tactical difficulties of which, with his knowledge of the local waters, Alessandro was only too aware. The Bosphorus is not wide; at the narrowest point close to Constantinople, the distance between the two shores is only about

2,000 Greek *pous* (feet). The trip across would be quite quick, which would make it extremely difficult to identify the correct boat in a short time and then, having identified it, to rendezvous with it and board it. These difficulties would be compounded by the very strong current flowing from the Black Sea to the Sea of Marmara which itself was exacerbated by the narrowness of the channel at that point.

Fortunately, he would have a day's notice for the attempt after the prisoners left Bursa and he decided that he would have to have two boats, one stationed on each side of the Bosphorus of which that on the European side would most likely make the interception, going, as it would be, in the opposite direction. But a boat from the Asian side would also be necessary as reinforcement and to indicate which of the many small boats crossing the Bosphorus was the one they were pursuing. It would have to do this by setting sail immediately the prisoners left the Asian shore and following them. Quite apart from the uncertainty of the outcome of a struggle in a confined space which could easily result in the death of the prisoners, there was the possibility of misidentification of the vessel which was transporting them and then the difficulty of the rendezvous in the fast flowing current. The operation could easily turn into a disaster and, unless performed quickly and efficiently, quite apart from the possible loss of his son and his men, might bring down severe penalties on his family and his business.

Nevertheless, Alessandro knew that unless he did something, he might never see his son again and that he had to proceed whatever the risks. And so he did. The mercenaries were hired and lodged in Pera and, as it turned out, they did not have long to wait. Early in the morning, the day after the message was received that the prisoners had left Bursa, the first boat sailed and was anchored close to shore on the Asian side of the Bosphorus, near the point of embarkation for the ferries to Constantinople and the European shore. From this position Alessandro's men were able to monitor all arrivals and departures. Later that afternoon, Eduardo and Michaelis arrived on horseback, shackled to their mounts and accompanied by an escort. They were immediately put on a small sailboat, which apparently was waiting for them. They were still securely shackled but there were only two guards and two sailors. They could normally expect to make the crossing in half an hour.

The first of Mascario's rescue boats immediately weighed anchor and seeing this, the second one started off from the European side. As it happened, the first boat, being larger and faster and sailing in the same direction on the same current, caught up with its quarry when they were both in the middle of the channel. As the larger boat drew alongside, Mascario's men with grappling hooks at the ready, the Turkish guards and sailors saw the inevitable, the overwhelming odds, and the reinforcements closing from the opposite direction. They did the obvious, they immediately pushed the two prisoners, still manacled, overboard and turned downstream. This tactic had the desired effect. Both the pursuers turned up wind and stopped. Sailors from both boats immediately jumped into the water and succeeded in rescuing the two prisoners who were, with much difficulty in view of the strength of the current, dragged on to one of the boats. The whole affair was concluded so quickly that it seemed possible that nothing of the incident had been observed from either shore although the escape of the Turkish boat meant that almost inevitably there would be repercussions.

Eduardo and Michaelis were released from their manacles and given dry clothes. Both the rescue boats sailed on to Pera, where the two of them disembarked and greeted the waiting Alessandro. It was early evening; Michaelis and his father embraced and both wept, Michaelis from exhaustion and Alessandro from relief. After a short time, Mascario turned to the boats and thanked the captain and the crews and walked off with his son up the hill to their home. They ignored Eduardo who, after some hesitation, began to follow them, but found his way barred by one of Alessandro's men.

"You are not wanted," he said. "Consider yourself very fortunate that you also do not find yourself in the water."

Eduardo understood; it was to some degree what he had been expecting. He realized that he had now lost his home, his books and all his other material things although they did not amount to much. His most valuable possession, his sword, had already been confiscated by the Turks. Perhaps it was typical of him that the first thing he thought of was the *Chronographia*, which fortunately he had returned to Heliogabalus just before leaving on the ill-fated journey to Bursa. He had had a foreboding that it would be prudent to tidy up his affairs to some extent so that obligation, at least, was off his conscience and he would still presumably have his job, despite the fact that he had been absent for so long. However the copy that he had had made with Patrizzi's advance and the rest of his money, which he had kept in his room in the Mascarios was now lost to him. He was exhausted mentally and physically. They had not been tortured by the Turks but they had been poorly fed and a week in captivity, with continual interrogation and little sleep, followed by the tiring journey on horse-back from Bursa, had left him weak, dazed and hardly able to think, let alone formulate a coherent plan.

He considered going to Andreas's taverna but at least had sufficient sense to realize that if he did this, it would be the end of his activities for the Florentines and they might, no, they probably would, seeing him as a security risk, kill him there and then. He thought about going to Petra and trying to contact Cecilia but there was no way he could be certain that Shamash was not at home and he could not risk sending her a message. The only other alternative was to go to the Tetrabiblion and hope that Heliogabalus would take him in for the night or at least advance him some money.

It was still early evening although the light was fading. As things stood, Eduardo did not now even have the fare for a ferry over the Golden Horn. The harbor was always full of small boats and, for a fee, many of these took passengers the short ride across to the city. Eduardo had, of course, been making this trip, morning and evening, most days for many months and he knew, at least by sight, most of the ferrymen. He waited until he recognized one of these arriving at the dock and walked over and briefly explained his predicament. The story he told was just not credible but his appearance, disheveled, wet, white-faced, red-eyed, thin and trembling, almost on the verge of collapse, a complete contrast from what he had been just ten days earlier, was enough to persuade one of the boatman to take him on the promise of a later payment of the fare.

Heliogabalus did take him in and give him a meal and after a few days Eduardo had recovered his spirits and his strength. He took new lodgings close to the shop in the area of the Philadelphion in the center of the city and this turned out for the best, since it saved considerable time in his daily commute. Now that he had found where Shamash lived and had grown to know the latter's routine, he was no longer concerned about a chance encounter with him in the center of the city. He began to resume his normal activities; he met with Andreas, he made assignations with Cecilia and he wrestled with Heliogabalus and the problems of the bookshop. The only matter over which he was at a loss was how to recover the book he had promised to Patrizzi and which was now gone. He decided that there was nothing that could be done on that score for the moment and it would have to wait.

When, after a few days, he reported to Andreas, he gave him a description of Bursa with emphasis on the military aspects of that city and on the military headquarters. For the first time, Andreas was impressed with Eduardo's work, although he did not know of the intimate circumstances which had enabled to him to obtain this information since, prudently, Eduardo said nothing about his capture and the subsequent events in the middle of the Bosphorus and in full view of the city. Eduardo did say that he had been stopped and his papers examined and recorded as a result of which he believed he should be given another new identity. You will remember that up to this moment in Constantinople he had been using the alias Nicholas Camerino. Andreas agreed that this was a sensible precaution since it was to be expected that Eduardo would continue traveling in Turkish territory. Accordingly, Andreas said he would take instructions on the matter and attempt to obtain new papers for him. With this agreement, Eduardo believed that he had finally extricated himself from the consequences of his fateful journey and could resume his regular daily routine.

CHAPTER 21

Heliogabalus

As the months passed, Eduardo had increasing difficulty in handling Heliogabalus whose lucid moments were becoming more and more rare. It had become impossible for Heliogabalus to handle his financial affairs and since they were not being paid, Eduardo's two colleagues left the bookshop. Eduardo could have arranged that they be paid but since their output and productivity had become negligible and, in any event, their function purposeless, he did not feel any necessity to do so. He began to look after Heliogabalus, at first obtaining for him his domestic supplies and then later caring for him as he lay, much of the time, in his bed in the room on the second floor. Each day Eduardo brought up a new book from the shop so that, although Heliogabalus could no longer read, he could keep the book in his grasp, holding it, fingering it over and over again, while staring at Eduardo with blank and vacant eyes. Occasionally, he would utter a phrase from the Book of Revelations, which appeared to be his favorite text and which he seemed to know by heart.

During the long period that he was attending the sick man, Eduardo discovered where he kept his money. He knew it had to be somewhere in the building and shortly after Heliogabalus took to his bed, Eduardo noticed in the bedroom a loose board in the wall next to the fireplace. The old man, in his senile state, had become too clumsy to replace it properly and when Eduardo pulled it away and looked inside, his heart almost stopped; in this secret compartment, in addition to several piles of paper each wrapped in a ribbon, there were at least a dozen large cloth bags, each so heavy that he could hardly move it. The bags were full of gold coins and they all appeared to be Venetian gold ducats, which was the preferred currency, the one commonly in use in the city and the one which had retained its value all over the Mediterranean. The old Byzantine solidus, at one time the glory of the empire and the source of its trading wealth, had, over the recent centuries, been gradually devalued as the economic difficulties of the empire had multiplied. By the time of which I am writing, the solidus had become almost valueless and had been supplanted by the Venetian ducat.

After the first shock of his discovery, Eduardo began to use the money for Heliogabalus' every day needs and to pay himself at the rate he had been paid previously. After several months, he had not made even a dent in the first bag and he finally realized why Heliogabalus did not need to sell any books. He made a careful accounting of everything he spent and he repaired and replaced the secret door so that it was no longer visible from the outside.

He also began to befriend some of the regular visitors to the bookshop who came not expecting to buy books but to inquire after or pay their respects to Heliogabalus and check on his condition and that of the stock. Some of them had known the old man for decades and had come to love him in his eccentricity and to appreciate his extraordinary collection. They recognized that Eduardo was now in a position of some authority and indeed was the only person who could communicate with Heliogabalus at all. Eduardo suggested to a number of the most devoted and frequent visitors that they should meet together in the shop and discuss what was to be done now that it was becoming obvious that Heliogabalus would not survive much longer.

"Does a catalog exist?" was one of the first questions.

Eduardo could only answer no, since Heliogabalus appeared to have, or at least he had had, everything in his head. It was agreed that each of them whenever they were able would devote some time to create a catalog.

Was Eduardo legally in a position to dispose of books if that was what was decided?

"No," said Eduardo. "Nothing has changed in that respect."

Then came a more delicate question. Was there a will and did Eduardo know of any heirs?

"I am afraid I don't know. Heliogabalus has never discussed the matter and I have never even considered asking."

"Well," said John Palamas, one of the members of this ad hoc committee, a professor from the university (no relation of Shamash's assistant, Manuel Palamas), "however difficult or distasteful it may be, I think you should ask him or at least see if you can find it. If there is no will, all the property including the books will escheat to the state and it may be years, if ever, before they can be sold."

"Very well," replied Eduardo. "I will see what I can do but I fear it may be impossible to get anything out of the old man. Another thing I can tell you is that when I was living in Italy, in Florence, I was also employed as a scribe at another bookshop, the Libreria Patrizzi. Patrizzi is a very learned man and a well-known book-seller. I am still in touch with him and I am sure that he would give Heliogabalus a fair price if we decide that some of the books should be sold."

A little later when the other visitors had left, Eduardo told Palamas of his interest in the works of Stobaeus and his search for the second volume of the Eclogues.

"Have you been to the library of the Monastery of Khora," asked Palamas. "It is one of the great libraries of the city. It was largely created by the celebrated monk Maximus Planudes a century ago, shortly after the monastery was rebuilt. Planudes was a remarkable man and he created a remarkable library. You should go and see it."

"I will," said Eduardo, displaying his usual enthusiasm when there was a prospect of discovering new books.

"Yes," continued Palamas. "He was one of the first of our scholars to consider Latin as something more than a barbaric language and was one of the first to translate a number of the Greek classics into Latin including Ptolemy's famous *Geography*. He also translated a number of Latin authors into Greek. He was perhaps most famous for his *Life of Aesop*, which you may have heard of."

It was shortly after this meeting and this conversation that Eduardo received, in the Tetrabiblion what was for him a surprise visit from Pietro Mascario. They greeted each other somewhat warily and Eduardo ushered him in to the main room of the Libreria. They took seats at one of the now empty writing tables.

"It is some time since I have seen you," said Eduardo.

"Yes, indeed," replied Pietro. "And it is only with the greatest reluctance that I decided to come. You may not know that our family has been ruined as a result of your escapade in Bursa. They do not know I have come to see you and it must be kept confidential. If my brother ever discovered, he would probably kill both of us."

"I did not know. My God! What happened?"

"The Turks sent a complaint to the Emperor to the effect that one of their ships had been attacked and that if the perpetrators were not punished there would be repercussions. The Greeks, in turn, made inquiries and, as you can imagine, it was not difficult to discover who was responsible. They complained to the authorities in Pera and demanded compensation and the punishment of those who were responsible. Neither of the two governments had any interest in protecting us and risking attacks on Greek or Italian ships or even a complete embargo of the city. So my father lost his license for wheat trading with the Turks which was his principal business."

"I am extremely sorry to hear this," said Eduardo. "I assume there is nothing I can now do to show my regret though it is unfair to blame it all on me. It was certainly my idea but both your brother and your father agreed to it and encouraged it and they knew much more of the risks than I did."

"Be that as it may," Pietro repeated, "my family has been ruined. The house has been sold and my parents have moved to much smaller accommodation. I have moved to a new apartment nearer the Palace and I do not see them very much. Michaelis is still working for my father but their business is a fraction of what it was. And you should be on your guard – Michaelis hates you, not unnaturally since his career has been ruined - and he has a very hot temper."

For the same reason, relationships between Michaelis and Pietro which had never been close, were now as bad as ever. As boys they had fought; this was normal. But Pietro's younger brother had grown up to be the taller, stronger and more athletic of the two and Pietro, in spite of his intelligence, education and now the prospects of an advantageous career, was a little in awe of his younger brother who, as we have seen, was self-absorbed and quick to take offense. Michaelis now, however unreasonably, also saw his brother, because of his former friendship with Eduardo, as somehow responsible for the predicament of his family.

"Well, I thank you for the advice. But in view of what you have told me, I am surprised to see you. What can I do for you?"

"Yes, to come to see you was a difficult decision for me. But I have decided to ignore my family's justified antagonism towards you and to risk my parents' or Michaelis' discovering our relationship because of the importance my superiors attach to what I am going to say to you. Quite frankly there appears to be almost no one else I can approach."

There was a pause.

"I have a proposition for you in connection with the business of the bookshop. I know that you have been selling books to Italy and I am instructed to ask you if you would be willing to act as the agent of the Greek state in similar sales."

Pietro was repeating literally what Shamash had told him to say but the way he put it, no doubt to exaggerate his own importance in the matter, made it sound a much larger affair than it was ever likely to become. Eduardo was certainly taken aback by this unexpected and grandiose proposition but he could immediately see that, if this was real, it was a proposal with huge potential and one which should be explored.

"I should tell you first," he said, "that the proprietor of the Tetrabiblion is very sick and has, for all intents and purposes, ceased doing business. Such business as is done, I do myself. But the contacts in Italy are mine and I see no reason why we should not act in the capacity you suggest. What sort of volume of business is contemplated?"

"At present, I cannot tell but it is likely to start in a small way and then build up considerably."

"In that case," said Eduardo, "you should provide me with details of the books that are available and I will get a price that we are willing to pay and I will arrange for payment. In the first instance, it will take some months to make these arrangements but once the procedure is established we can build a substantial business."

"Good," said Pietro, considerably relieved that he had succeeded in this first simple task that Shamash had given him.

"I would ask you one favor," said Eduardo, "that you retrieve from your parent's house the copy of the *Chronographia* which I had made and which I left there. I imagine it must have been transferred with all the other contents to their new residence."

Pietro was able to do this and after some weeks Eduardo finally retrieved it and sent it on to Florence with a letter to Patrizzi explaining that not only had he found a further source of books, but that it was likely that greater numbers could become available. Thus if he, Patrizzi, wished, he could send Eduardo a further advance so that the business could be expanded.

CHAPTER 22

The Library

Eduardo had the energy and enthusiasm of youth but even so his calendar was now getting more than comfortably full. He had his job in the Tetrabiblion and the increasingly time-consuming business of looking after Heliogabalus. He was establishing his incipient book-exporting business, which was taking up more of his time than he had expected. He also had Cecilia on his hands with whom he lived a double life at once concealing and revealing himself, and he lived constantly with the knowledge that he was being watched by Antonio's agents who expected him to regularly elicit and report information on Shamash's movements and any Turkish activity he could gather. Nevertheless, in spite of all this, he did first what he was most enthusiastic about, his real love: he went to the library in the monastery in Khora, not far from Cecilia's house to look for the Stobaeus.

He had difficulty finding the library – no one seemed to know where it was, a lack of interest matched by the obvious neglect of both the building and its contents. At one time, the structure itself must have been impressive; it was in the long-established tradition of classical libraries, the design of which had addressed, if not solved, the problem that has beset all book repositories, ancient and modern, of how to stabilize temperature and humidity to preserve the fragile nature of the books.

The building was nested in the center of the university protected as much as possible from the elements. It faced towards the east thus being further sheltered from prevailing winds; it had one entrance door with a shaded portico and no windows; light was provided by oil lamps. The rectangular interior had a long table in the midst of the room with wooden book cases in niches around the sides. The niches were high off the floor to protect against flooding and the slatted doors of the cases allowed air circulation. The building itself had double exterior walls with a narrow passage between the two to give added insulation and stabilize the temperature of the interior.

When Eduardo finally found the library, there was no one inside except a guardian sitting near the door and dozing quietly. He remained asleep while Eduardo spent the afternoon searching the bookcases. His task was not helped by the fact that, even though the cases were arranged by subject matter, he did not know in which category the Stobaeus might fall and it was clear that there was no control over or organization in the arrangement of the books. It seemed that there had not been any recent additions to the library. It was more likely that in the absence of real security and with large gaps where there should have been standard references, books were disappearing and probably at a rapid rate. There were now no more than a thousand books remaining and Eduardo saw that it would not take more than a few hours to check them all.

Towards the end of the day, Eduardo found the first volume of the Stobaeus. He could scarcely believe it. There it was, exactly the same size and format as the second volume, which he had first seen what now seemed many years earlier. Carrying the book carefully over to the only table, he opened it and stared for some time at the title page before going through it again, page by page, chapter by chapter, doing what he had done before, copying the first letter of the first word of each chapter. When he had finished he had the following line of text:

Esti tis Arkadies tegen leuro eni kopo euthanemoi pneiousi ipema duo krateres up'anakes.

He returned to his lodgings in high excitement and added the second half of the message, which he knew by heart, on to what he had just found. He was now fluent in Greek and when he read the whole message, he realized that there was something wrong with the first half, just as there had been with the second: the word *ipema*, a word he did not know, appeared to be misplaced and, any event, unnecessary. He looked more carefully and suddenly it came to him; *ipema* was what was missing in the second half. Somehow the chapters, of which these letters were the first in each case, had become transposed from one volume to the other, a not wholly unusual occurrence in the relatively haphazard business of bookmaking at the time. Eduardo placed the missing word in the correct position and the whole phrase read:

"There is a city of Arcadia in a level land where two winds blow by strong compulsion and there is beating and beating back and woe lies on woe. There the life-giving earth holds what you are seeking."

Eduardo did not even know where Arcadia was but it did not take him long to find out; it was a district in the Morea not far from Mistra, the capital. But what about the rest of the phrase? It was obviously what was known as an enigma or riddle but he did not have any idea how to solve it. The only thing he could think of was to take the advice of his new friends from the bookshop, who were, after all, educated and literary and actually the people in the city most likely to be able to help him.

When Palamas next visited the store, Eduardo showed him the riddle and asked him if he had any idea what it meant. Palamas, naturally, asked him in turn where he had obtained it and Eduardo told him the whole story. Palamas was by chance the ideal person to have asked; he was a professor of history at the university and he immediately said that he did know; it was a famous riddle told by Herodotus, the ancient Greek historian, and one which he, Palamas, put to all the students whom he taught. He believed that not one person in the years he had been teaching had solved it but, fortunately, Herodotus himself had provided the answer. The city in Arcadia was Tegea, the wind, the beating back and the woe upon woe referred to a blacksmith: the wind was the bellows, the beating was the hammer and anvil, and the woe referred to the iron which was being worked on since iron was unlucky for the ancient Greeks.

"It probably means nothing," said Palamas. "Authors were and are always playing little tricks like this and remember that the *Stobaeus* was written one thousand years ago and this refers to Herodotus, who wrote a thousand years before that, and he was referring to a pronouncement by the Pythia, the priestess of the oracle of Delphi, made even earlier, probably many centuries earlier! But if you ever get to Tegea, you should try and find a blacksmith's shop or the site of one. Over the years, many people have visited Tegea for exactly that purpose and I don't believe anything has ever been found. And, of course, there is always the possibility that what was there has been found after all and many years ago or perhaps that nothing was ever there. But I am told that the remains of the Temple of Athena Alea at Tegea, which was one of the most important temples in European Greece, can still be seen."

Eduardo had developed an ongoing obsession with his riddle and became unreasonably excited by Palamas' revelation. The riddle had become a lifeline between his former life in Italy and his future life wherever that might lead, a thread, like the thread that Theseus followed in the Minotaur's labyrinth in Crete. He felt that fate had somehow determined that he must hang onto and follow this thread and, indeed, to struggle to do otherwise was pointless and beyond his control. In his ingenuousness, he also became increasingly certain that it was he who had been marked to discover, after more than two thousand years, whatever it was that remained to be discovered. As it turned out the opportunity to visit Tegea came much sooner than he expected.

CHAPTER 23

Cecilia

Several months after their first meeting, Eduardo made a rendezvous with Cecilia and it was not a lie when, pretending that he had just returned from Italy, he said that he had missed her. He also told her that he had arranged with his employer that he should remain in Constantinople for an extended period. This, he had thought, would provide the opportunity for their romance to blossom and allow him more intimate access to the life of Shamash.

As for Cecilia, after Eduardo had left her on that first occasion, she had had time to herself to think about him, about life and about love. She had loved Shamash at the time of her marriage and had entered into their new life with the best intentions. She wholeheartedly had intended to be his support and helpmate. But almost from the beginning he had largely ignored her both in bed and in their daily life and, when he did speak to her, it was usually to indicate his irritation and displeasure. As we know, she had difficulty with Greek and, although with her husband she talked in Italian, he was away much of the time so, as she had confessed, she was lonely to the point of bitterness and depression. Eduardo was more than a potential lover, he was almost her only source of social interaction and perhaps even a lifeline to sanity.

Eduardo's departure and absence, coupled with the knowledge that she would, nevertheless, see him again within a short time, had inflamed Cecilia's imagination. She did not know that Eduardo had been Juliette's lover but she did know that he had been her sister's first love and, for this reason, the thought that she, Cecilia, might also become his lover provoked greater than ordinary feelings of guilt and hesitation. But he was gentle and kind to her, he was good looking, he was intelligent, he understood her loneliness, he seemed to love her and he was very persistent. They never discussed Juliette, she had no idea whether he ever thought about her and Cecilia's concerns on this score evaporated quickly before the mounting pressure of her needs and his demands. And so, she did not need much persuasion to come with him to his new lodgings in the Philadelphion and this first visit quickly became a regular rendezvous. She loved him in her imagination and she loved him in reality. On every such visit, her greatest anxiety was that it would be the last, that some accident or other change in his fortunes would take him from her and this concern gave added urgency to her growing love and her love-making.

He would bring something for them to eat at lunch time: a loaf of bread with vegetables, cereals, eggs or a salad and sometimes fish or a chicken which he bought from his landlord who kept a coop in the backyard. If they cooked they would take turns. And after lunch and several glasses of wine they would make love, sometimes resting or sleeping all afternoon in the heavy summer heat. He told her and he meant it how much he loved her and how much he depended on her. As the months went by he became more and more obsessed by her, by the soft silky smoothness and the subtle scent of her skin as he held her in his arms, the peculiar timbre of her voice, the particular lilt of her walk, her sudden smile which showed for him and for her, both, that everything was right between them and with the world.

She did most of the talking on these encounters. Deprived of friends and most other outlets for feminine intercourse, she poured out her heart to Eduardo without reservation and he did not discourage this although, after a short time, it became apparent to him that the only real information she possessed was limited to nothing more than Shamash's travel plans. He kept this insight from Andreas so as not to diminish his own role and importance but he knew he would have to come up with something more concrete if he were to remain of use to his Florentine superiors.

Partly at the urging of Andreas and partly since he was beginning to hate the days when she was not with him, he began to urge her that he should visit her at home when Shamash was away. To his surprise, she readily agreed; her frequent afternoon absences from home were arousing attention among the neighbors and the servants and she wanted him as much as he did her. And so, at the first opportunity, late in the evening, long after the city had become dark, he quietly climbed the front steps of the house in Petra and tapped on the door. Cecilia was waiting inside. She had not wanted to risk waking the maids who slept on the floor below.

They embraced in the gloom of the hallway lit only by a single candle on a fixture on the opposite wall and then she led him by the hand up the staircase to her bedroom.

"Are you sure that it is safe?" asked Eduardo warily. "How long is Philip away for?"

"He left yesterday. He said he would be away for a week. And he is always accurate. And it is never less than four days."

"Where has he gone?"

"I don't know," replied Cecilia, "I don't know and I don't care. Come on darling. Stop talking and kiss me."

And so they kissed, standing fully clothed in the midst of the room, in the dark and then they undressed each other. Cecilia guided him to the bed, they covered themselves with the coverlets and held each other tightly almost as though they feared that this would be the last time they would ever be together.

An hour later, they were both asleep and when Eduardo woke up it was still dark. He waited until he was sure that Cecilia was still asleep and then got up, found his clothes and got dressed. The candle in the hall had gone out but he had brought with him a small beeswax candle which would make no odor and a flint and steel to light it. He went slowly down the staircase keeping close to the wall to avoid the creaking boards and inspected all three rooms leading off the hallway. He looked carefully around the room that was obviously Shamash's study. It had shelves covered with papers and books, two or three comfortable chairs, and a desk with three drawers which he tried to open but they were locked with large iron locks. He glanced quickly at some of the papers on the shelves but decided not to risk further delay; detailed examination would have to wait for another time. He returned to the bedroom and kissing Cecilia softly, made his way out of the house.

A pattern was established. They would meet in his lodgings once a week and also at least once at her house on each occasion that Shamash was away, usually on the first night after he left. Eduardo examined the papers in Shamash's study at regular intervals and made quick notes of what he found which he reported to Andreas. There did not appear to be much of significance but Eduardo had now become the best source of information which the Italians had in Constantinople. In addition, Cecilia was still confiding in him and she told him quite casually of the planned attack on Pera by the Turks which her husband had let slip on one of the few occasions when he shared with her anything substantive about his work. She saw no reason not to tell Eduardo. Even if it had been a secret, which she did not, for a moment, think it was, since her husband had given her the information, she still saw herself as Italian and if she could help her country, why should she not? Eduardo reported this news to Andreas who at once passed it on to his superiors although as usual even the most urgent communication would take several weeks to reach Florence. Eduardo also suggested that he should learn how to pick locks and it took only a few weeks of practice before he was proficient.

It was not difficult to open the drawers in Shamash's desk. They looked much more impressive than they were; the design of the interior of lock mechanisms had not changed since Roman times and the large metal plates on the exterior were merely decorative. After just a few moments feeling through the key hole into the lock mechanism with a piece of thin angled iron he had brought with him, Eduardo was able to open all three drawers and extract the contents. Most of these were personal items but one of the drawers held a pile of parchments of which the top one particularly caught his eye since it was in Turkish. He sat down at the desk to read it, but before he had finished more than a couple of lines, he was startled by the sound of steps on the stairway. He knew in a moment that he would have no time to lock the drawers which he had to do before he left but in any event it was too late, he knew she would see the faint light beneath the door. When she came in there was nothing he could but stand there with the papers in his hand. She looked at him silently with her hand to her mouth and finally he went over to her and put his arm round her shoulder: "I can explain", he said "Let us go back upstairs."

They sat close together on the bed. Cecilia had started to cry.

"Let me explain," he said again. "I have never told you the full story. I was exiled from Florence for ten years. The authorities believed I was a spy for the Greeks but I was not. It was Philip who put the blame on me to throw suspicion off himself. But he was asked to leave also. He betrayed me although I was completely innocent. Just now I was trying to find evidence that would clear me."

She stared at him. This was a lot to absorb in one moment. "So that was why we had to leave Florence so quickly?" she said. "I never really understood but Philip always said that he had changed his mind about staying, that he was advised that he would be able to advance his career here in Constantinople rather better than if he was left in Florence."

Eduardo turned over in his mind quickly whether to tell her any more of the story but decided that for her sake he should not. If she learned the whole truth, her future life with her husband would understandably become intolerable.

"I know nothing about the real reasons why he decided to leave but that's what I was told."

"And did you find anything downstairs?"

"No, I did not. It may be that it was too long ago and there will be nothing." said Eduardo, "but I should tidy up there before I go."

Cecilia was still crying. "So this was why you wanted to make love to me," she sobbed gently. "You never loved me at all. It was just to get close to him. To get into this house. You must go now. I cannot believe it."

Eduardo put his arm round her and covered her with kisses. "You must not believe it," he said. "You must not. Do you really think that that is what I have been thinking about over the whole of the last two years? You know I love you. If it had not been for Philip, we would never have got together."

Slowly she responded to his caresses and they got back into bed and made love again. Cecilia fell asleep but Eduardo could not and soon he got up and woke her again to say goodbye. Still half asleep, she murmured,

"You must promise never to go in there again. It is too dangerous. If he ever discovered anything moved or disturbed, he would blame me. I will look in there when he is away and see if there is anything about Florence or you. I know how he keeps his papers."

"Thank you," said Eduardo "Goodbye, darling," and, as he left, he went again into the study, tidied the desk and relocked the drawers. He decided to take the Turkish parchment with him; he needed time to read it, he might want to copy it and he had a feeling that it might be something which could be a hold over Shamash in the future. He decided he would have to risk the consequences for Cecilia. But when he got home and read it, he grew cold as he realized the enormity of what he had by chance discovered and for which he now had the responsibility. He turned over the alternatives in his mind. If he revealed it to his superiors, it would certainly be the end of Shamash though that would suit his purpose. But what would happen to Cecilia? She would be left penniless or even worse she might suffer the same fate as her husband. He spent a sleepless night going over and over the possibilities and finally decided that he would have to reveal the discovery. This after all was what he had been seeking all these years – revenge on Shamash - and he rationalized that it was his duty in any event. If the plot succeeded and Constantinople fell it would be on his conscience.

He copied the parchment and gave the original to Andreas as soon as he had the opportunity. He learnt for the first time that, surprisingly, the latter did not read Turkish and Eduardo had to read it to him.

"The main weakness with this document is that it is not signed and not addressed to anyone," pointed out Andreas. "Nevertheless, that would be expected if it was genuine and I assume it would not be difficult to establish which of the commanders of the several Tagmata is involved. We know that Sha-mash is in contact with the Turks, so presumably this was given to him to pass on to them. What we do not know is whether this was the copy that he was supposed to deliver or whether he co-pied it for his own purposes. Bring me an Italian translation to-morrow and I will send them both back to Florence. Then we will see what they want to do."

When they received Andreas' two reports some six weeks later, the Florentines were in the same dilemma as they had been earlier. The Florentines were rivals of the Genoese, a powerful trading nation, as powerful or more so than the Venetians in the Greek and Black Sea trade. It was likely that Genoese power and influence would be weakened by the fall of Pera and would pro-vide an opportunity for the Florentines to take the place of the Genoese traders.

It was of course this rivalry between the European nations and city states and also the rivalry between the Latins and Greeks that the Turks took advantage of in the expansion of their own power. The Turks regarded these rivalries as weak-ness, evidence of the decadence of the Christian nations and one more sign of the coming victory that they saw as inevitably theirs. And there was another indication of this weakness, of both the greed and the lack of discipline of the European na-tions, which the Turks rightly saw as contributing to their even-tual downfall. Much of the war materiel used by the Muslim ar-mies was bought from western merchants with the sanction of their governments. Even the Papacy was well aware of what was going on and, in effect, took shares in the business of arms ex-porting by selling licenses to the arms' merchants to carry out this trade.

The revelation of an imminent plot to surrender Constan-tinople to the enemy could not however be ignored and the Flo-rentines decided that both pieces of information should be turned over to both the Greeks and the Genoese. They also decided, however, that for the same reasons as before, they would not reveal the source of their information.

Eduardo continued to see Cecilia but from that time on their relationship began to deteriorate. She was becoming noticeably restless and less affectionate. At first he thought it must be his revelations about her husband for which, for some reason, she blamed him or that she still believed her first reaction that he had just been using her in his search for information about his exile. He also wondered quite simply whether she was just growing tired of him or perhaps, on the contrary, she was thinking of leaving Shamash and Constantinople and returning to Italy. Maybe the trauma of this prospect was making her understandably tense and irritable. He tried to talk about it with her but she denied that her feelings had changed and refused to discuss it. It therefore came as a surprise not to say shock when finally she revealed that, over the last months, her husband had become much more attentive to her, that he appeared to be much more needy of her affection and that she was beginning to have doubts about her relationship with Eduardo. He was surprised to find that this revelation upset him deeply, particularly since Cecilia further revealed that it was not even that Shamash was being loving towards her but, on the contrary, had become increasingly vicious, bullying and even abusive, and that he appeared to be going through some kind of crisis which she, despite herself, felt the necessity of helping him through and, as a result, felt more and more drawn to him.

Much of the time, they argued over trivial things although both of them knew that these were not the real grounds for their disagreements. Finally, Cecilia said that she wanted to end their affair at least until the difficulties with her husband had resolved themselves. Eduardo tried to dissuade her. He loved her, he would miss her, he would be lonely without her but these protestations did not dissuade her. She said she would contact him again when she was ready and that, in the meantime, he should find himself another woman with whom he might find happiness and a permanent relationship. This last suggestion was particularly galling for Eduardo since it seemed a genuine expression of her lack of feeling for him although it was more likely an indication of her kindness and good nature.

During their final meeting, as though it were a symbol of their parting and with a slightly quizzical smile, she handed him a letter.

"This is for you. I received it from Juliette some weeks ago and I have not wanted to give it to you until now."

Eduardo looked at it, his proper name, Eduardo Ferrucci, was on the outside of the folded parchment and it was in Juliette's handwriting. As he turned it over, broke the seal and unfolded it, Cecilia left the room.

CHAPTER 24

The Letter

To Eduardo my only earthly love – greetings.

It is only now, after the passing of several years, that I have taken up my pen to write to you. I had from my sister a letter in which, amongst many other things, she told me that she had met you and that you were now living in Constantinople. Of course, I knew that you had gone there but how was I to know your address? I have received no letters from you but I imagine that in the same way you did not know my address, so your encounter with Cecilia was very fortunate. The silence from you over the years has often made me wonder whether it was just desire rather than affection which drew you to me during that happy time together in Florence. I came to this convent shortly after you left the city and you left me. I am sure that my sister has told you that they asked me to marry Antonio Lucchese but I refused, preferring to become a bride of Christ than to marry someone I could not love. It was you I loved and will always love. And sometimes I miss you greatly. Life is very quiet here but mostly we are happy. There is a large garden, cloisters and a library where, of course, I spend much of my time. I read books and I copy books and I write books. Sometimes, I copy the books that I have already written and we send them out to other convents, together with the other books we have copied, so that, at least, as Horace says, my books, like swans, are flying slowly over this Earth. In return we get other books back. Cecilia tells me that you are again working in a bookshop so perhaps you can send me some books. We have many books by the Church Fathers but little of the classical authors. We cannot afford to pay for them; we are very poor and have very little money. You know, of course, that my father and mother lost all their money; it was stolen from them by their steward Garzon who then was killed. No one knows what happened to the money but they had to sell the palazzo in town and most of their estate in the country. They now live very poorly in their country house and I don't think that either of them is happy. I too am poor but I have my thoughts, my love of God and my books, which sustain me. I also have quite a number of visitors whom I am happy to see. Strangely enough, Antonio Lucchese comes to Ferrara frequently and when he does, he visits me. I do not know why he comes, he does not tell me. He does not come just to see me, but for some other reason, but despite that we have become friendly and he tells me all the news from home. He is no longer interested in me as a lover, he married Rebecca Phrisio. Perhaps you remember her? She was in love with him from the beginning. They have two children already and he tells me he is very happy with her. He has become very successful, rich and important. They say that he will be the next chief of police even though he is still young. But I still think of you even though I have forgotten what you look like; since I have imagined your face so often, the image has faded away like the impression in a wax tablet fades away. But I remember our meetings, our love and the last night we spent together. Should I not have these feelings which were the most vivid of my whole life? I sometimes feel guilty about our time together and about my thoughts about you, which will perhaps always continue. I wonder whether God understands me and whether he forgives me or whether I need to be forgiven. What we did and what we were is the most beautiful thing on this earth and the most natural. That is something I think about. How can something that is so natural be at the same time so beautiful and bring forth such beautiful consequences? We live very simply here and all the walls are plain and white and there is no decoration, which we are told is sinful. But I have always struggled with understanding that, understanding how the beauty of this world, which, after all, is created by God, can be sinful. Sometimes I want to cry out and sing of the beauty, the poetry, of God's creation, which should be enjoyed rather than suppressed. This is how I feel that we can best express the nature of God, as something beautiful, something that is reflected in the beauty of our nature, His nature. Nature is God's book and we turn the leaves of the book and find Him. And we express our appreciation for, our respect for, our love for God as revealed in his book, by writing, as it were, the scholia and marginalia in his book, by enjoying his creation. I have been writing poetry to reflect God's poetry. Often I wonder whether it was God's will that I came to live in this convent or whether I had any choice in the matter. I struggle with these things. If it is God's will, how do we have choice in the matter, how do we have our own will, how do we choose between right and wrong. And if we have no will to choose, how does God choose us at the Day of Judgment? How does he know if we are among the righteous or elect? If there is nothing to do but to submit to His will, to submit to fate, we become like the mechanical clock they installed in Santa Maria del Fiore. And this is what I write about, about God's will for us, how we can understand his will and his nature, and about beauty, about love. How love of this world, love of beauty, even my love for you is just a prelude for, a preliminary to, a taste of the love of God, the love that God has in store for us. How love is an attraction to beauty and as much as you were attracted to me for my beauty, and you fell in love with me, how much more is the beauty of God and how much more is the love of God, for God. The beauty of God is expressed imperfectly in the nature of this Earth, which he made for us, and can only be expressed perfectly through the symbols of his own nature. We cannot perceive the essence of God directly since, as it says in the Book of Genesis, we cannot look upon His face which is too glorious to behold and we must content ourselves just with viewing the symbols of His nature, sometimes monstrous symbols, that have come down to us through the ages. And so I write in symbols, each one of which depicts some view of God or some moral injunction, a study of which will help us to approach God and His kingdom. Each of my symbols has a picture and a poem and a motto and each part of the symbol represents the whole in some way. It is only by studying each part and then the whole, meditating and contemplating at length, that the meaning of each symbol becomes clear. You perhaps remember the first simple examples that I created and gave to you before you were sent away and you said when I visited you, for I remember everything from that time, that you were surprised I knew Greek since the mottos were in Greek. But at that time I didn't know Greek. I just copied the mottos from the walls of father's study, which he called his studiolo. I believe now that they are not phrases or mottos at all but possibly the titles of Plato's dialogs even though there are many more titles in the studiolo than there are dialogs. Maybe there are more to be discovered. But I too have been learning Greek just as I imagine you have been. I have taught myself during the long hours we have to ourselves. We have services in the chapel, we tend to the garden, we eat well and pass time in conversation with the others but yet we have many hours to ourselves, which I spend writing or reading or thinking about God. But sometimes I get lonely and I think about you and I wish I were with you and that we could share our lives and the beautiful things we have created. I long to hold you and to be held by you and to talk to you about intimate things and about the things that I love. But everyone in the world has their sad moments and we are fortunate to be safe and well and, most of the time, we are happy here. And it would make me happy to have a letter from you, to tell me that you also are safe and well and that sometimes you think of me. As God wills.

Farewell Eduardo; your earthly bride, Juliette.

CHAPTER 25

Deception

Eduardo did not immediately reply to this eloquent letter. His thoughts and emotions were almost wholly taken up with Cecilia and their recent parting and these emotions were much more immediate and intense than any memories he still had of Juliette. He was uncertain whether or not the memory of her was a reality or merely the memory of a memory. In his mind, the two women had become one and his only distinct thought for Juliette was, as it had been ever since he had first had news of her, one of guilt, guilt which, after all the time that had passed, he hesitated to acknowledge, guilt that because of him she had been relegated to a life of contemplation and retirement from what even she described as the beautiful life outside the convent. He put her letter aside, promising himself that he would, as soon as he could, give thought how best to respond, how best to advise her. He wanted to tell her to leave the convent, go out into the world, live and enjoy life which she of all women had the capacity to do. But how? Without money, without a husband, it was almost impossible for her. He tried to salve his conscience and promised himself that, if ever he had any money, he would first give of it what he could to Juliette to enable her to be free.

Finally, he forced himself to write to back to her. He was as kind and comforting as he could be while making it clear that the love he had felt those many years before had dissipated. He explained that he felt responsible for her present unhappy circumstances of which she had hinted so eloquently in her letter and that he had arranged to deposit a little money in a bank in Ferrara for her use and that there would be more to come. He ended by hoping that she would continue to send him news of herself and that she remained happy and healthy.

Eduardo spent most of his time in the Tetrabiblion. The members of his committee came at intervals and pursued the task of making a catalog of the books. Eduardo himself continued to tend to Heliogabalus, who became weaker and weaker; he slept most of the time and ate and spoke little. Eduardo also began to search for the will, looking in all Heliogabalus' favorite books, in all the shelves of the bookstore and then finally in the secret compartment in the bedroom. Eduardo pulled out the several bundles of papers he had found there and examined them one by one as Heliogabalus slept. Most of these appeared to be financial papers, relating to the purchase of books, and dating back over many years.

After looking through and putting aside hundreds of documents written in the flowery script that Eduardo assumed was that of Heliogabalus (Eduardo had never actually witnessed Heliogabalus write anything), there remained three pieces of parchment, folded and sealed and on the outside of which was written *diatheke* or testament. Eduardo could tell from the script on each of these, which ranged from strong to almost illegible, that the latter was probably the most recent. It was therefore with some confidence that he told what he thought of as the book committee that he had found what he believed to be Heliogabalus' last will, news that was greeted by everyone in the room with relief.

He also continued to see Pietro Mascario who, on the first occasion that he returned, brought a bag of papers.

"The first books that I have available are the Moralia by Plutarch and Marcus Tullius' De Re Publica. I have here a summary of each of them which you can send to Italy. What are you willing to pay for them?"

"I fear I personally cannot tell you that. I have never heard of these books but I will ask my contact in Florence and will let you know as soon as I can. I will have to get authority each time you bring a book so I suggest that you bring more suggestions as quickly as possible so that we can start a continuous correspondence with Italy. As you know, it will take two or three months to get a first reply but if you agree we will soon have a constant revolving correspondence going."

Mascario agreed and Eduardo sent on the details to Patrizzi. It was not surprising that he had not heard of the two books – they were completely unknown in the West and therefore Patrizzi was able to make a high offer which Mascario, on behalf of Shamash's group, was delighted to accept. Eduardo had already received notification of a further deposit from Patrizzi in the branch of the Bicci Bank in Pera so he had the funds for an initial purchase but had no idea of the value of the books and so thought it prudent to wait for further instructions from Patrizzi. With each courier, the latter instructed Eduardo of the amount he was prepared to pay and at the same time this figure was credited to Eduardo's account in the bank. He was then able to add a small amount to the price for himself.

Never one to care much about money, Eduardo had recently, to his surprise, been accumulating it without much effort. The book exporting business was expanding both with the material provided by Pietro Mascario and the books from the Tetrabiblion which, under the instruction and guidance of his committee, he had tentatively begun to dispose of. He had already opened three accounts in the Bicci Bank in Pera: one for Patrizzi, one for himself and one for Heliogabalus. Patrizzi deposited money in the bank in Florence and after a month or two, after the regular bank courier had reached Constantinople, this amount was credited to Patrizzi's account in Pera and Eduardo could draw on it to pay for the books. Depending on the book in question, he either gave the money in cash to Pietro, or put it in Heliogabalus' account, in each case transferring his own share to his own account.

On the occasions when Pietro came to visit Eduardo, he was quite happy to gossip about the affairs of his office and the imperial court and he thus provided for Eduardo a substitute for Cecilia as a source of information. In fact he provided much more information and much better quality information than Cecilia had ever been able to do and so gave Eduardo's career in espionage and, ironically, that of Shamash a longer lease on life, since, again, there was no incentive for the Florentines to eliminate either of these two links in the chain of information.

In the meantime, in spite of this absorbing news, we must not forget Michaelis Mascario. Even before the ill-fated journey to Bursa, he had already remarked on Eduardo's unusual and unexplained activities and his dubious background. There were gaps in Eduardo's story and oddities in his behavior and his daily routine, especially after he had first arrived in the city. After their narrow escape from the Turks, Michaelis had developed a hatred for Eduardo, which was fuelled by the knowledge that it was only by a miracle, the devotion of his father and the enormous risk that had been taken on his behalf that he had escaped an almost certain death.

The suspicions that he had had, and continued to have, on the score of Eduardo, developed into an unreasoning obsession to resolve his doubts and exact his revenge. He started to follow Eduardo whenever he could and to inquire about him from his neighbors. But this turned out to be a fruitless exercise. Eduardo no longer spent any time walking about the city since he had long since discovered Shamash's address and almost all his activities were centered on the Tetrabiblion. None of the neighbors whom Michaelis approached had much to say about him except that he was a quiet young man who led a regular and unexceptional life.

It was only months later when Michaelis had almost entirely abandoned his efforts and, out of habit, happened to be walking in the quarter of the Philadelphion in the center of the city when he suddenly saw his brother leaving the Tetrabiblion.

Without hesitation, Michaelis went up to and accosted Pietro.

"What are you doing here?" he asked.

"It's none of your business," replied Pietro, who was nevertheless taken aback to see his brother. "And I mean that. I am here on affairs of state."

"Nonsense. I don't believe it," said Michaelis, raising his voice. "You are here to see Nicholas Camerino. How could you do that? You know he is an enemy of our family. How could you betray us?"

Pietro turned away and started walking up the hill. Michaelis put his hand on Pietro's shoulder and pulled him round to face him again.

Said Pietro, "I told you. I have come to the bookshop for reasons to do with my employment at the palace. I cannot tell you and will not tell you what it is. What are you doing here anyway? You should be at work and not following me around like a pet dog. Now let me go. And find something better to do."

And again, leaving Michaelis flushed and shaking with anger, he turned and walked away. But Michaelis was not satisfied. Reasonably or unreasonably, he became convinced that Eduardo and his brother were involved in some clandestine activity and he was determined to pursue the matter to the end.

After this incident, the relationship between the two brothers continued to deteriorate. They did not discuss the matter again at home but then they did not talk to each other at all and it was clear that sooner or later the latent and longstanding antagonism between them would come to the surface, leading to blows or worse. Only because Pietro left shortly afterwards with the delegation to Mistra was there no further immediate opportunity for them to quarrel.

CHAPTER 26

The Morea

After several months had passed, Theodore Cydones, the Logothete, was asked to receive a newly-arrived delegation from Florence. The meeting, arranged at short notice, was said to be urgent and confidential and the Florentines immediately presented Cydones with a copy of the message to the Turks discovered by Ferrucci as well as the further information about the anticipated Turkish attack on Pera. The Florentines drew attention to the fact that the message was unsigned but was believed genuine since it came from a reliable source and they suggested that the Pera attack could be an early stage in the plan revealed in the message. They, the Florentines, could not anticipate who might be the author of the message but no doubt the Greeks would have no difficulty in discovering this if they believed it was genuine. When asked, the Florentine delegation refused to divulge the source of either piece of information even though it was pointed out to them that knowledge of this would assist the Greeks in their investigation.

A few days later, a similar delegation arrived from the Genoese in Pera, again with the news of the rumored attack and with a request for reinforcements. The Genoese pointed out, not unreasonably that if Pera was attacked, it could only be a prelude to an attack on the city itself and, if Pera fell, it would be a serious and perhaps fatal blow to the Greek defenses. The Greeks replied that they would consider the request and they suggested that all parties should redouble their efforts to monitor the enemy so as to prevent any chance of a surprise attack. This last was, in fact, unlikely because it would take weeks, if not more, for the Turks to build up forces to besiege even the lightly defended walls of Pera and it would soon become obvious what was intended.

Since Cydones knew that rumor of the attack was just that, a rumor, he could ignore it but the Turkish message was a different matter. Although there were constant threats to the Emperor both from within and without the palace and each one of these had to be investigated, this last appeared to be credible and had to be given immediate priority since it was now nearly three months since the message had been discovered. He informed the Emperor who in turn gave the task of the investigation to his most trusted lieutenant, the Akolythos, the commander of the Varangian guard.

A few days later, Shamash was called into Cydones' office.

"I congratulate you on the success of your scheme to unmask the Italian spy. It appears to have borne fruit and we now know for certain that there is a traitor in the Court. We have received information from both the Florentines and the Genoese repeating the rumor that you put about. I suggest that we should now take the matter to the next stage. What would you propose we do next to unmask this traitor?"

"Maybe, Excellency," replied Shamash. "we should repeat the exercise but on a more restricted scale. We should document further information and give it very limited circulation, which would narrow down the source of the leak. I will reflect on this and recommend to you what information would be the most credible."

"Very well but you should consider that the leak may come through your own office and therefore you should prepare the documentation personally."

"Certainly, Excellency, I will do that as soon as I can."

The irony was that Shamash had no intention of going to the next stage in the search. His efforts would now be concentrated on ensuring that the source of the leak was not discovered since if this individual were found and denounced then it was certain that in turn the Italians would denounce Shamash himself.

"Whoever it is," said Cydones, "the leak appears to have had the unintended effect that the Genoese may now be sending reinforcements to Pera and perhaps to the city itself which, of course, is excellent news."

Shamash bowed in response.

"And now we can turn to another matter," said Cydones. "I propose to arrange for a delegation to travel to Mistra and in view of your recent successes, I want you to organize and lead this delegation. You are to present yourself to the Despot and discuss the increasing military pressure by the Turks on European Greece and, so that you can report firsthand to us, you should ask him to give you personally the results of his recent campaign in Boeotia."

"Certainly, Excellency, I would be honored and happy to do this. I believe we could leave within the week."

"Very well," said Cydones and the meeting was over.

Shamash was delighted with the success of his tactic, the smokescreen to hide his real activity. He had gained a greater reputation, he had been brought to the attention of the Emperor himself and he had probably neutralized any subsequent attempt by the Italians to turn him over to the Greek authorities. What's more, he had unwittingly put in the hands of the Greek government a tool to wring more help out of the countries of the Latin West which were much more likely to send assistance to reinforce the Genoese than they were to help the Greeks themselves. It was this aspect of Shamash's plan, which was as obvious to the Turkish authorities as to the Greeks, that proved to be his downfall. How could the Turks be expected to tolerate one of their own who had not only interfered in matters of state way above his station, but, in so doing, had made a strategic error which might, and in fact did, have major implications for their policy?

He had no response to the message he had delivered on behalf of Anemas to the Turks nor did he even notice that his own copy was missing. Although on two occasions, he had been approached by members of the General's staff to inquire whether there had been a reply, it appeared now that the Turks did not wish to pursue the suggestion and that the matter was closed. This was a great relief to him although he still harbored some hope that his reputation with his Turkish masters would be enhanced by recognition of his role in acting as go-between with such a high ranking official.

The delegation to the Morea led by Shamash left the city by ship and after a three day voyage landed at a small village, Lechaion, on the east coast of the Isthmus of Corinth at the northern point of the Morea. There they found horses awaiting them. As part of his task of inspecting all the main cities of the region, Shamash had decided to visit the city of Corinth on his way to Mistra and at the same time examine the state of what was called the Hexamilion Wall. The Wall had been built a thousand years earlier across the Isthmus of Corinth which connects northern Greece with the Morea and which is only four miles wide at its narrowest point. It was the only land route into the Morea and the Despot foreseeing a Turkish attack, had ordered that the Wall be repaired.

The Despot Constantine, who had succeeded his uncle Theodore, was the most able of the five sons of the Emperor, John Palaeologus. Constantine had recovered all of the Morea for the Greeks and recently he had gone over the Isthmus and reconquered Boeotia, the province immediately to the north of the Morea, which had been under Turkish control. He had even recovered most of the city of Athens itself, apart from the Acropolis which remained in the hands of the Florentine family who ruled the city. But being a prudent strategist, Constantine foresaw that it might be necessary for him to retreat back to his homeland and he had given instructions for the Hexamilion to be fully restored.

Out of all the places he had to visit, the Wall, and its state of repair, was actually Shamash's main interest in the Morea and when the party reached it the day after they had landed and travelled along it, he found that although work was not complete and appeared to be progressing slowly, it was thorough and there appeared to be no reason why it should not be finished long before any counter-attack by the Turks. He made careful notes and was amused to think that he would be submitting identical reports to both his masters. His conclusion was that, when the repairs were completed, the wall would be a formidable obstacle to an invader and would be difficult to breach without the use of siege engines or cannons. As it turned out, this advice was a substantial contribution to the success of the Turkish invasion of the Morea, which came much sooner than he might have expected.

The party spent the night in the city of Corinth and slowly journeyed on to Mistra, the capital city of the Morea, where they were to meet the Despot and receive a firsthand report on his successes in Boeotia. He had asked Pietro Mascario to accompany him to Mistra and during the journey, Shamash took every opportunity of engaging in conversation with him, mainly on the topic that was at the forefront of everyone's thoughts, the progress of the Turkish armies into and around Europe and Greece. Just a year earlier the Turks under the Sultan Murad had routed the Christian forces at Varna on the Black Sea and established Turkish influence over Bulgaria, Albania and Serbia. The city of Thessalonika had also been lost. All that remained now to the Greeks was Constantinople itself, the Morea and the newly-won province of Boeotia over which Constantine held a tenuous grip.

"What is your opinion of the progress of the struggle with the Moslems?" Shamash, with feigned innocence, asked of Mascario on one occasion.

Mascario had replied with what was no doubt the official line, one encouraged by the administration to enhance the morale of the remaining inhabitants of the Constantinople.

"I would think that if both Greeks and Latins continue to oppose the infidels with vigor, with God's help their strength will be weakened, they will be repulsed and finally destroyed. In any event, we know that the Sultan is a man of peace."

"Yes, that appears to be true, but the Sultan wishes to retire in favor of his son Mehmet and they say that Mehmet hates the Greeks with a great passion."

"Well, the city has stood for more than one thousand years, it has withstood many sieges and its walls are impregnable and God will continue to protect us."

"You seem very confident," said Shamash, "but I notice that when you talk about it with your friends, you are not so confident, you actually seem quite melancholic about the future. Please be aware that I think confidence is admirable, we certainly cannot overcome the Turk unless we are determined to do so, but I have to tell you that I share your doubts."

"I am surprised to hear that, "replied Mascario. "You have always appeared very confident of the strength of the city and the Empire."

"Unfortunately," continued Shamash, "walls alone are not enough to protect us, we need also defenders for those walls, we need money and resources to pay for those defenders and we need a future we believe in to fight for. I am beginning to feel that my fellow citizens do not see the future very clearly and beyond that are blinded by unreasonable prejudice."

"You mean in their refusal to embrace the Latins and ratify the Decree of Union."

"Yes. Our countrymen refuse to endorse the union which would certainly have brought us help from the West, they seem unwilling to stand up for their own defense and they will not pay for mercenaries to effect that defense."

"But what else can we do to contribute," asked Mascario with some desperation.

"Well, history shows us that there come times when we have to recognize that there is nothing we can do, that the responsible thing is   to recognize the inevitable, and submit to our fate. Indeed to do otherwise is not only pointless but is no doubt going against the design that God may have for us. It may be hard for us to accept even though we know that God's ways are mysterious and that we must accept His will."

Mascario was silent and did not respond and from this silence Shamash understood that his reasoning had resonated with the doubts that Mascario and his friends and presumably many others in the city entertained. Not only did they perceive the inevitable flow of history but they also knew that, if the city did not resist, both under Islamic law and the Turkish practice of that law, the city would be spared, no lives would be taken and no property damaged. The Christian community would not only survive but be tolerated and cohabit in harmony with both Muslims and Jews and with the greater vigor of the Muslim economy and culture, the decline of the city might very well be reversed.

Shamash and Mascario had several more such discussions during their journey to Mistra and it was clear that Mascario was struggling to determine where his loyalties should lie. On the one hand, he was someone whose opinions were easily swayed and was thus a good choice for what Shamash had in mind but even Mascario recognized that what they were discussing was close to treason.

"Even if we did approach the Turks, what could we, the two of us alone, achieve by ourselves?" was his reasonable question during one of these conversations.

"Very little," replied Shamash "all we could do would be to open a channel of communication, explore the possibilities, see if our suggestions receive any encouragement. At that stage we could sound out other members of the Court and we would have something positive to discuss. This is the normal way of diplomacy. If our approaches are rejected nothing is lost. If we succeed, it could be the saving of the city. Someone has to take the first step especially if this is something we believe in and which is of such historic importance. For our own sakes and for the sake of the city at large, I think it should be us."

By the time they had reached Mistra, Shamash believed that he had persuaded Pietro Mascario that it would be prudent for them at least to find a way to discuss these things with the Turks and obtain at least some preliminary indication of how their enemies would view peaceful overtures. Shamash made it clear that this was not the official line but, if it appeared that the Turks were open to such ideas, he would present such proposals to his own superiors.

CHAPTER 27

Tegea

Before he left for the Morea, Pietro Mascario had a last meeting with Eduardo Ferrucci in the bookshop.

"I will not be able to meet with you for some weeks," said Mascario, "I have been asked to join a delegation from the administration which is going to Mistra in the Morea."

"Very well," replied Eduardo, "And congratulations. I will continue to pursue sales as we have done before and if and when I get further information from Italy, I will keep it all together for your return. And what are you going to do in Mistra? I hear that it is a very beautiful city."

"I am not sure exactly but I am told by my superior, Philip Shamash, that we are going to see the Despot. I imagine we shall have some personal communications to him from the Emperor and that we will hear the latest situation on his campaigns against the Turk."

"I wish you well," said Eduardo, "and we will meet again on your return."

Eduardo could hardly believe his good fortune; if he could persuade Andreas that he should follow the delegation to Mistra and report on its activities, it would give him an opportunity to make a detour to Tegea and continue to search for the answer to his riddle and the remains of the blacksmith's shop.

"Mascario tells me that Shamash and he are leaving shortly for Mistra in the Morea. I think I should follow them there and make some attempt to discover what is going on between the Despot and the Turks," said Eduardo at his next meeting with Andreas.

"I see no harm in that," replied Andreas. "You will have nothing to do here if Shamash is away. However, do not expect us to pay for the journey. You are still earning a reprieve from your offences in Florence."

Eduardo did not even bother to protest. He knew it was hopeless and did not care anymore. He had the money himself and was excited by the prospect of making further progress on his obsession with the riddle. He decided however that he would have to have a partner to handle things in the bookshop while he was away and he asked John Palamas if he would be willing to undertake this. Now that the procedure had been established, the correspondence with Patrizzi was not time-consuming and indeed they could have sent many more books at any one time; the bottleneck now was Patrizzi's ability to sell them. As it was, they sent him details of several books each month and received back a list of the prices he was prepared to pay. If these were acceptable to the committee, Eduardo arranged the delivery and the payment. This is all that Palamas would have to do in Eduardo's absence. He no longer had to resort to the cash in the hidden closet since Heliogabalus had sufficient in his account to pay for his daily needs, which in any event were now becoming fewer and fewer. Eduardo hired a local woman to take over the task of nursing Heliogabalus while he was away although this required little work and no one believed that her services would be needed for very long.

It was impossible for Ferrucci to follow Shamash's party closely. He certainly could not take the same ship that Shamash and his delegation had traveled on and he was not able to find any other ship that could be persuaded to take him to Lechaion where Shamash had disembarked. When he finally reached the Morea, at the port of Navplion further to the south, he had no idea where Shamash was and, even if he had known, it would have been almost impossible to catch up with him. But he reconciled himself to ending his journey at Mistra, which he knew was Shamash's final destination and in the meantime he would pursue his investigations in Tegea, which was some two days ride away.

As he approached the modern village, Tikli, which had been built on and around the ancient ruins he became increasingly excited at the possibility of finding the answer to his riddle, despite the fact that apparently no one over the last two thousand years had succeeded in doing this. But when he actually reached the ruins of Tegea, he quickly realized how hopeless his task was. He had to find evidence of a blacksmith's shop that had possibly existed in pre-classical times although all that remained of buildings from that era was a rectangular stone platform, the foundation for the great Temple of Athena Alea. Numerous pieces of fluted Doric columns and capitals and other lumps of weathered stone, also lay in the field around the foundation, where they had fallen when the temple collapsed. No doubt much of the original stone had been used for other purposes in the centuries since its destruction. He inquired but no one in the village had any further information about the site of the temple other than what could be seen in this one field and there appeared to be no other visible ancient ruins in or around the village.

After wandering several times round the site, looking at the stone work and seeking inspiration, Eduardo sat and rested on the side of the stone platform which had been the base of the temple. He remembered the words of Palamas, that many people had sought what he was looking for but no one had found anything at all. As he sat, his gaze alighted on some of the larger stone blocks which had the outlines of figures carved in relief but which, as a result of centuries of weathering, had become almost completely eroded. One of these, he noticed, seemed to consist of two figures seated one behind the other. The figure at the back appeared to be holding a spear and wore a helmet; this was obviously Athena and the figure at the front also held something upright but it was much shorter. It could have been a scepter or an axe. He idled through his small knowledge of the myths and then suddenly had an epiphany. His heart stopped. Of course. Of course. This was Hephaestus, the blacksmith god. The figure was holding an axe. The myth told that Hephaestus, in a moment of anger, had struck Zeus on the skull with his axe and Athena had been born fully formed out of the head of Zeus. This was the blacksmith. He had found it.

He could tell from their irregular shape that the large stone blocks had fallen from the front pediment of the building, the triangular space forming the front of the roof of the temple and supported by the Doric columns. He could tell from the size of each of the stones where in the pediment it had been placed. According to the riddle, he had to look in the earth under the original position of the depiction of Athena and Hephaestus. He immediately ran back to the village and bought a spade. No one in the village bothered to inquire what a stranger was proposing to do with such a thing and when he returned, he started to dig against the foundation stones at the front of the temple. After he had completed a trench about two feet deep by six feet long, he started to uncover an inscription carved into the stonework of the foundation. His excitement mounting, he cleaned off the letters and was able to read:

En Attike estin alsos esuokon timon ena os meta duoin oi eisin eis protos esosen ena ton trion proton enthade anapausauton. Ekei sun te Athenes filia e ge e zoefooros ekei o zeteis[15]

There is a peaceful grove in Attica which honors one who with two that are one first saved one of three who first rested here. There with the love of Athena the life-giving earth holds what you are seeking.

Eduardo knew that since this new riddle was in the same form as the first one he must have found what he was looking for. In his excitement, he almost decided to return immediately to Constantinople and consult Palamas as to its meaning about which he had no idea. But he soon realized that he had no alternative but to continue to Mistra and at least pretend that he had been shadowing Shamash.

CHAPTER 28

Mistra

He arrived in Mistra three days later and found accommodation in a small hospice. The city, the capital of the Morea, with a population of some fifty thousand people, was built on the foothills of the Taygettos Mountains and was dominated by a castle constructed some two hundred years earlier by the French count Villehardouin and now used by the Despot as his palace. The city was prosperous, its churches were filled with ancient and famous mosaics and its markets overflowed with merchants and produce from the valley beneath. From the city walls there were views over the ancient town of Sparta itself.

Before Eduardo even had had time to settle in his room, there was a knock on the door and he was told that he had a visitor. He hurried down the one flight of stairs to find Andreas waiting in the lobby. He could hardly believe it.

"What are you doing here?" he blurted out. "And how did you know where I was? I have only this moment arrived."

"Never mind that," said Andreas, "what matters is what you have been doing and what you have found out. You seem to have taken your time getting here. As you see, I was able to get here well before you and I began my journey after you."

"I couldn't find a ship to take me to Lechaion where Shamash and his party had gone. I had to go to Navplion and by that time it was too late to get up there and follow them. But I got here as soon as I could and I was going to start making inquiries about Shamash tomorrow."

"So in reality all you have done is nothing and you have taken two weeks to do it. You will certainly have to think of something better than that. Tomorrow morning we are to see some old friends of yours from Florence and you will have some explaining to do. I am depending on you to show that my recommendations have been worthwhile."

"What visitors and what recommendations?" asked Eduardo.

"You will see in due time," said Andreas, "but remember that I have been commending your work to my superiors these years past and if it had not been for these commendations, I have no doubt that you and your services would have been found wanting."

Andreas's presence in the city made Eduardo suddenly very nervous though he had no option but to agree and the following morning the two of them made their way up the steep, narrow and winding streets of the lower town and entered a house close to the castle walls. A guard in Italian dress, waiting inside the door, relieved Eduardo of his sword and a poignard, which he had also taken to carrying, and the two of them made their way up to the second floor and entered what appeared to be the main room of the house. As Eduardo entered, his heart sank. Behind a table and flanked by two more guards sat Antonio Lucchese.

"Good morning, Ferrucci," said Antonio amiably but in the same low, dark tone that Eduardo remembered.

"Good morning, Signore," he replied, hardly believing the accommodating voice he heard himself using.

"Sit down," ordered Antonio.

And Eduardo did so, his legs numb with fear. He looked at Antonio who, in the years since they had last met, had grown heavier in face and figure and seemed even more menacing than he remembered.

The intervening years had been good to Lucchese and he had enjoyed rapid success in his position as chief of security for the Republic of Florence. After the conclusion of the Shamash affair and his success in dealing with the Gasparinis, it seemed that he had grasped quickly and comprehensively a policy of utter ruthlessness, and he applied it to whatever was the task in hand. He was wealthy, he came from an influential family, he had the protection of the Bargello and the Duke, and he did his job well, which was all that these latter cared about. He had no hesitation in using his position to obtain power over his peers.

After every social occasion he attended, which in one form or another he did every day he was in the city, he made it a habit to sit in his study and record every piece of gossip and information that he had picked up and cross-reference this in the dossiers of the individuals concerned.

It was not long before the élite of Florence realized that any failure to invite him and Rebecca to even the smallest celebration risked an insult that they could not afford and the couple soon had far more invitations than they could make use of. Rebecca loved it and Antonio compiled his dossiers and strengthened his influence. With the rationale that it was necessary for state security and using the example of the peculations of Garzon, he required all the banks in the city to report to him any unusual financial transactions. He did not hesitate to make use of all the information which he gained and as a result many of the families of the city had found it convenient over the years to pay "fines" to the head of security rather than risk having salacious or disgraceful information made public. Thus his reputation and influence increased and, with them, his draconian methods and his ambition.

He had not come to Mistra solely with the purpose of interviewing Eduardo. He had been sent as leader of a delegation of Florentines to pay respects to the Despot Constantine and to exchange views on the status of military campaign against the Ottomans. It was coincidental that he had arrived at the same time as Shamash but in fact the purpose of their two embassies was identical. Shamash was as shocked as Eduardo to find Antonio in Mistra, particularly since he had no advance notice of the encounter with Antonio. The Despot had found it convenient to brief both delegations at the same time and the two first met in the austere audience chamber of the palace in the presence of the Despot.

"I introduce you to the Lord Antonio Lucchese," said the Despot who was seated on an ornate chair on a low dais accompanied by half a dozen officials who stood round him. "Lucchese leads an embassy from Florence, our valuable friend and ally."

Turning to Antonio, he repeated the introduction. "This is the Honorable Philip Shamash, who has recently arrived from Constantinople. He represents the Emperor himself. Since our interests in this struggle against the Turk are identical, I will be informing you both of the present status of my campaign."

Antonio had been forewarned of Shamash's presence and showed no surprise when they were introduced. He greeted Shamash with an amused smile and a deep bow and flourish in the Italian style.

"A pleasure to see you again, Messer Shamash. It is many years since we last met in Florence. And that long interval seems to have treated you well. I see that you are now a diplomat and Head of Delegation. Your decision to return to Constantinople must have been the correct one."

Shamash's reaction was noticeably different and not at all diplomatic. He paled, stiffened and only after a considerable interval did he return the bow without, however, returning Antonio's greeting, a reaction the Despot did not fail to notice and which clearly irritated him.

"I see you know each other. That is something I applaud, especially if we are to improve relations between our two countries. It is however customary to give our guests a proper welcome," said the Despot curtly.

Shamash bowed to the Despot and again to Antonio. "Welcome to Greece," he said and then in the same lifeless tone and without enthusiasm, "I trust your stay will be a pleasant one."

After the Despot's briefing, Antonio exchanged a few more words with Shamash, mainly devoted to the health and welfare of Cecilia, but he made it clear, with his fixed and cynical smile, that he held Shamash's career and his life in his hands. But he had already decided that the time was still not ripe to turn Shamash over to the Greek authorities; he would wait at least until he talked to Ferrucci.

But as far as Despot Constantine was concerned, the damage for Shamash was already done. He decided to make further inquiries about the man and at the earliest opportunity he asked Gemistos Plethon, who you will remember, had retired to Mistra, to come to the palace, at his leisure, to discuss a matter of importance. Plethon was now approaching ninety years old but he was still able to recall his visit to Florence and the circumstances of Shamash's departure. After this conversation, which took place some weeks later, the Despot, somewhat uneasy, sent a special courier direct to the Emperor in Constantinople suggesting that he discreetly investigate the background of his emissary Shamash about whom he, the Despot, had obtained disturbing information.

The interview between Eduardo and Antonio was brief; Antonio had already decided on Eduardo's fate.

"So I understand that you have been following that Turkish spy from Constantinople. What information did you discover?"

Eduardo did not wish to lie but he evaded the truth.

"Very little, I'm afraid. I have been unable to get very close to him without giving myself away. I know he landed in the northern Morea, probably went to Corinth and then came straight here."

"You have been following this man for several years now. Would you summarize what you have discovered and what you have achieved."

Eduardo recited how he had been able to report the timing of each of Shamash journeys outside Constantinople. He also summarized the result of his visit to Bursa, the reports he had provided on the possible assault on Pera and the discovery of the conspiracy to betray the city to the Turks. As he proceeded through this impressive list, he felt confident that he had been successful and would be recognized as such. But Lucchese would have none of it.

"You were also asked to become part of the social and court life of the city so that you might supply us with information provided by the members of the court. Have you made any progress there?"

"Unfortunately not," said Eduardo, "the court and the aristocratic circle are now much too small and enclosed. I would immediately have become known to Philip Shamash if I had tried to become part of the court."

Antonio looked at Eduardo. He remembered the old antipathy between them and he saw again what he had originally believed, that the State of Florence had little use for Eduardo Ferrucci. He now had the authority and saw no purpose in further delay. He had no hesitation in abandoning him.

"Very well," he said, "return to Constantinople immediately and await further instructions. You may go."

Eduardo left the room, picked up his weapons at the door and was happy to do what he had been ordered. He left for Constantinople at once. As for Antonio, he decided that, rather than put himself or his subordinates to any trouble, he would amuse himself by arranging for his two enemies to destroy each other. He wrote a letter in which he enclosed a copy of the report from Ferrucci on the activities of Shamash. He instructed Andreas to deliver this to Shamash soon as he returned to Constantinople. The letter stated simply: "Cecilia has betrayed you."

CHAPTER 29

The Will

Eduardo had only been away for three weeks but, when he stepped back through the door of the Tetrabiblion, he immediately noticed that something was different. The books were still there, apparently in place, but there was a ghostly silence throughout the house. He ran up the stairs and into the bedroom and, sure enough, the bed was empty. He sat down, his head in his hands, and a cold sadness filled his heart. He had not been able to say goodbye to the old man whom he had grown to love despite or perhaps because of his eccentricities. He had lost one of the few friends he had in the world.

After a short time, he set out for the university to find Palamas and inquire what had happened.

"He died a week ago," said Palamas, "and we buried him on Tuesday at the Church of the Holy Apostles. We can visit the grave together when I am finished here. There were over a hundred people at the ceremony; he had many friends, he had a long and a good life and you should not grieve. You were a good friend to him and I believe he loved you too."

Later they went together to visit the graveside and Palamas suggested that he should arrange that they all meet the following week, read the will and depending on its terms, they could then decide what to do with the remaining books.

The following week, the committee met in the bookshop, and Eduardo gave the will to Palamas who passed it round the table so that all those present could acknowledge the script of Heliogabalus. Then he unsealed and unfolded it and started to read:

"Let it be known that John Mystike, called Heliogabalus, of his own free will and of his own purpose and intention, knowing that death is certain and the hour of death is not, and after commending his soul to God, makes, for the spiritual health of his soul, the testament of his last wishes concerning the goods which God has given him, in the manner which follows."

The will appointed an executor, a lawyer in the city whom the others knew, and then continued with many single gifts, mostly of books none of which, Eduardo was pleased to note, had already been sold, gifts both to individuals, including members of the committee and to the churches in the city. After thirty or more of these, and as Palamas continued his recitation, Eduardo was beginning to feel drowsy but realized thankfully that they were approaching the end as Palamas read,

"And all the remainder of my goods, including my house, my books and any other chattels therein, after payment of all just debts and in the absence of progeny or descendants of my flesh, I leave to my friend ......"

At this point Palamas slowed down to a halt and looked openmouthed at Eduardo who was slouching in his chair almost asleep.

"I leave to my friend, assistant and caretaker, Nicholas Camerino."

Eduardo sat bolt upright and in the silence that followed and, with the eyes of the committee upon him, blushed profusely as though he had just been caught in the commission of a crime, which was indeed somewhat how he felt. He opened his mouth to say something but nothing came out. He shook his head in disbelief and the silence continued until Palamas smiled gently at him and said,

"Well, it seems that you have become a fortunate young man in every sense of the word. You are now in charge of the shop legally as well as practically. What are your instructions?"

"I don't know," gasped Eduardo. "I mean, is this true? There is no mistake? What should I do next?"

"The will has to be deposited with and accepted by the court. I will go with you to the executor's office and explain the circumstances and he will deal with the rest. In the meantime, I suggest we go to the nearest taverna and celebrate – at your expense!"

The others agreed and crowded round with their congratulations and during the celebration later, Eduardo told them of his exploits at the Temple of Athena at Tegea and recited the new riddle.

"Well, what an extraordinary thing!" said Palamas, "you have found something which was hidden for 2,000 years, presumably since the Temple was built. Another reason for congratulations. You are indeed a clever young man."

"No, no," said Eduardo with genuine modesty, "it was complete luck. I was just sitting there without any idea what to do and the myth of Athena and Hephaestus just flashed into my mind. It could have happened to anyone."

"No, only to you," said Palamas with a laugh, "let us drink again to the scholar amongst us." At which Eduardo once again ordered a further round for his friends.

"But we can't give up now," shouted Eduardo, who despite the increasing hilarity of the party, persisted with his obsession. "What does it mean? Concentrate! What does the riddle mean?" But none of them had ever heard the riddle before and no one, in their present state, could solve it there and then.

"Well," said Palamas, "I will do some research and discuss it with my colleagues and see if we can throw any light on it and come back to you when I can."

"Thank you," said Eduardo, "and a further question, if I can change the subject. Am I legally able to dispose of the books immediately?"

"In theory," said Palamas, "I think not but in practice there is little doubt that your claim will be confirmed and no one will know anyway, so you should just proceed as you wish."

"Well what I wish is that each of you should take whatever books you want from the Libreria. That would be the least I can do for you all, for all the help you have given and all the kindness you have shown our old friend."

And so it was. They all finally agreed that they would each choose one book, their favorite, and they duly thanked Eduardo for that.

CHAPTER 30

Discovered

During Shamash' absence, the city of Constantinople was a scene of extraordinary activity. One evening the inhabitants of the populated areas of the city were informed by the town heralds that, effective immediately, a curfew was imposed and that, on pain of arrest, no one was to leave their dwellings until further notice. At the same time, large numbers of the Skythikoi, the Scythian mercenaries who were the city police, were deployed and reinforced by elements of the Tagmata. This curfew lasted for forty-eight hours at the end of which it was lifted during the day-time, normal life slowly resumed and the Skythikoi were withdrawn. Naturally enough, rumors of the cause of this deployment abounded and eventually it came to light that one of the generals of the army had been arrested for treason together with his senior officers. His regiments had been confined in their barracks under guard.

A few days after these events, very early in the morning, there was a succession of thunderous bangs on the front door of Cecilia's house and she awoke to demands to open the door which otherwise, she was told, would be broken in. Peering through the grille next to the door, Cecilia saw armed Skythikoi outside and more of them on the street. When she opened the door, they burst into the house and, ignoring her protests, scattered all over the house and began to ransack the contents.

"What are you doing," she screamed. "Stop it! Stop."

"Keep quiet, lady," said the officer in charge, "and you will not get hurt."

And that was all she was told. The searchers at once located Shamash's study, broke open his desk and removed all the papers which were in it and on the shelves. All other texts or parchments anywhere in the house were also removed and placed in a cart which had been brought for the purpose. The search lasted for more than an hour after which the Skythikoi departed. The whole episode was conducted in silence while the women sat in the hall weeping and watching their home destroyed. No one even asked where Shamash was; it was likely that they knew he was away and when he would return.

When he did return, much earlier than expected, the house had been cleaned up but the news of the arrest of Anemas and his aides was devastating. On learning of the raid on the house, Shamash immediately remembered the copy of Anemas' message that had been in his desk. As a result of the incident in Mistra, his clash with Antonio and the remarks of the Despot, he had already lost the confidence, the hubris, that he had regained before he had left, but now he knew that the end had come.

When therefore, shortly after his return, he received Antonio's anonymous note, he was in no state to consider it other than at face value even though initially he mistook the import of it and initially assumed it referred to the recent raid on his house. Only when he read the enclosed report did he realize the full implications of the letter.

Shamash was by nature a coward and a bully and Cecilia was not only the one person to whom, without consequence, he could risk displaying his real character and concerns, she was also someone from whom he need not expect any emotional or physical retaliation.

He called Cecilia into his study in their home and handed her the note, which naturally did not take long to read. She lifted up her eyes to his, which were blazing with anger and frustration.

"Well," he shouted, "what does this mean?"

She, to her misfortune, was not able conceal her feelings and immediately blushed a deep red, a reaction which Shamash perceived and interpreted for what it was, an admission of guilt. He immediately struck her hard on the face. She went reeling to the floor, where she curled up and started to sob quietly holding her face in her hands. But she could not protect herself from her husband's anger. He bent down and pulled her to her feet. Holding her by the arm he slapped her again so hard that he cut her cheek with the inside of a ring on one of his fingers. Her face was now bruised on both sides and blood flowed down her cheek onto her dress. She screamed and he hit her again.

"Why did you do this?" he shouted again, "I shall continue until you tell me why."

Unable to stand, she sagged onto the floor and, not strong enough to hold her with one hand, he let her drop and kicked her as she continued to scream.

Finally, she whispered, "It was Eduardo Ferrucci, it was Eduardo."

Shamash sat down heavily into a chair and for a moment was speechless.

And then, "Ferrucci, Ferrucci. What does Ferrucci have to do with it? Ferrucci is dead. He was executed in Florence."

Cecilia was silent and lay still, with blood dripping from the deep cut in her face through her hands onto the floor. Shamash ignored her, recovering his composure as he slowly began to understand what had occurred.

"So they deceived me. He is here. He has been here all these years. He betrayed me and you were the source of the information. How clever."

He sat back and the blood drained from his face as further realization sunk in.

"How do you know Ferrucci? What have you been doing with Ferrucci?"

It was not that Shamash felt any lingering jealousy. He was beyond that. He was furious with himself and with Cecilia. He knew that he could be arrested at any moment and execution would follow immediately.

"Through the weakness of a woman. I should have known."

And he gave her another kick and she whimpered.

"So where is he?"

Another vicious kick. She whimpered again and whispered Eduardo's address which he calmly wrote down.

"Now," he said, "get out, I never want to see you again. Get out of this house at once."

Cecilia could hardly move but she forced herself to her feet and limped out of the room.

Later, Cecilia's maid knocked on the study door and asked if she could call a doctor, saying that her mistress was in bed and had a fever.

"No," said Shamash. "No doctor. Your mistress and you must leave the house by tomorrow night."

Timidly the maid started to explain that unless Cecilia was attended to, she would be scarred for life but Shamash cut her short and shouted at her to get out.

There was nothing more he could do that evening but he stayed awake most of the night struggling with his predicament. He could not understand why he had not been arrested as he entered the city and before he had even reached home. That would have been what he would have expected in the circumstances. There was therefore just a chance that the copy of Anemas' message had not been discovered but if not where was it? And who had sent the anonymous letter? On reflection, he realized it could not have been in reference to the seizure of his papers. Who would care about Cecilia in the context of the treason of Anemas? It could have been sent by the Italians but why would they want to discredit their own agent, Ferrucci? He remembered the meeting with Antonio and finally understood that the only explanation was that this latter had now decided, on behalf of the Florentines, to eliminate both their agent Ferrucci and himself, Shamash, in one stroke.

There was no alternative, he thought, but for him to leave Constantinople and return to his homeland. But where could he go? The full force of the obvious came to him with an empty coldness; he had no home, no family and nothing other than what he possessed in the city, his house, its contents and a little money, which would, in any event, be useless in territories controlled by the Turks. But he had to do something. He could not remain. He would have to throw himself on the mercy of his Turkish masters whom he had served so long.

Early in the morning, he sent for one of the officers of the palace guard and ordered the arrest of Eduardo Ferrucci who was to be held pending further instructions. He did not dare go to his office but he sent a message requesting that Pietro Mascario should come to his home immediately and when he arrived, he dictated to him a report on the journey to the Morea with particular emphasis on the state of repair of the Hexamilion Wall and his views on its efficacy in withstanding an invading force. He asked Pietro to make three copies of the report. The first, he emphasized, was for the office files, the second was for the Logothete and the third, he said, was for his own records. In reality, he intended to pass this copy on to his Turkish handlers in exchange for a promise to conduct him secretly out of the city.

Immediately after Mascario had finished the report and its copies, Shamash asked him to bring them and accompany him to a meeting. Although Shamash refused to indicate what the meeting might be about, Mascario had no choice but to agree and the two of them set out on the long walk to the Hippodrome at once.

CHAPTER 31

The Hippodrome

It was the first day back for Mascario as it was for Shamash. And Michaelis Mascario who, during the latter's absence overseas, had been nursing his obsession with the dark activities of his brother, was still determined to discover the true nature of Pietro's secrets. As Shamash and Pietro walked the several miles from the Blachernae Palace to the Hippodrome at the opposite end of the city, Michaelis followed them. When they reached the Hippodrome, they had to wait at least half an hour in the appointed place beneath the ruins, no doubt to allow Shamash's Turkish contact to be located and fetched. When the Turks finally approached them in the gloom, Shamash saw that the man was accompanied by several armed companions.

"Give me one copy of the report," said Shamash. "These are the Turks with whom I have been able to make contact. With this report, I can establish our credentials."

"I don't like this," said Mascario.

"Give it to me," shouted Shamash, "this report contains nothing that they don't know already. Wait here until I ask you to join us."

Shamash went forward to greet them but as he approached, the group of Turks at a silent signal drew their swords, surrounded him, disarmed him, bound his hands and started to take him away. Mascario, not a coward, drew his own sword and started towards the departing band, which was disappearing into the darkness of the ruins. As he approached, the bodyguards turned and Mascario could see that all the courage in the world would not prevail against odds of five to one; he turned and fled.

As he came running out of the tunnels beneath the Hippodrome, with his drawn sword, he almost knocked down his brother, Michaelis, who was waiting at the entrance. It was a moment which shows the unyielding power of Fate. Michaelis, fearing that Pietro had ambushed him, hoping to end once and for all the enmity between them, drew his own sword and engaged his brother. Michaelis was by far the more accomplished swordsman and Pietro surprised by an attack from a different direction than he had been expecting, put up a fragile defense. Before they had had a moment to utter a word of explanation to each other, Michaelis ran Pietro through with a thrust to the chest. Pietro collapsed to the ground, blood pouring from his wound. In shock, Michaelis threw away his sword, knelt over his brother and cradled his head. He shouted for help from the crowd which had already gathered. But nothing could be done, Pietro's face rapidly paled, became white, his eyes glazed, perhaps he did not even recognize who had been his assailant, and he died within two minutes. Michaelis sobbed uncontrollably, clasping his brother in his arms, rocking to and fro, his clothes covered with his brother's blood.

Within a short time the Skythikoi arrived. The onlookers gave contradictory accounts of what had occurred but they all agreed on one thing: Michaelis had attacked Pietro without provocation; without doubt it was murder. Michaelis was arrested, Pietro's body was taken away and since there was not the slightest indication of who he was, since Michaelis had picked up the bag which contained all his papers, Pietro was buried in the common grave and his parents never knew what had happened to him. Michaelis was taken to the barracks of the Skythikoi, put in a cell and his papers and other belongings including the contents of Pietro's bag were taken from him. When the paper which Pietro had been taking to the Turkish contact was found and read, the importance of it was quickly realized and Michaelis was transferred to the jail in the Blachernae palace.

At almost the same moment, during the afternoon of 11th April 1447, Eduardo was sitting in the upstairs bedroom of the Tetrabiblion, doing what anyone else would have been doing in the circumstances, he was counting his money, the money in the bags in Heliogabalus' secret closet. It began to dawn on him that he had inherited an enormous fortune. There were eleven bags full of gold coins, Venetian ducats, the common trading currency of the world, each coin more than 99% pure gold and weighing 3.5 grams. Eduardo had received just one of these each month for his wages and it had been enough to live on. He guessed that there were more than five hundred coins in each bag, perhaps seven thousand in all. For a few moments he allowed his imagination to wander. What was he going to do with this great fortune? And more immediately, how he could deposit it all in the Pera banks?

At that moment his reverie was interrupted by a violent knocking at the door of the shop. Hastily he put the money into its bag, pushed the bag back into the closet and carefully closed the concealed compartment.

He went downstairs and opened the door. Outside there were six armed Skythikoi.

"Are you Eduardo Ferrucci?"

Eduardo was so taken aback at being addressed by his real name and not by either of his two aliases that he nodded despite himself.

"You are under arrest in the name of the Emperor," said the officer. The soldiers seized Eduardo, tied his hands, threw him across a horse and, in this ignominious and agonizing position, they took him through the city to the Blachernae, where he was processed and deposited in a cell.

The two prisoners never knew of the other's presence in the same prison even though they were held not far from each other. Eduardo's fate was in some ways the worse because he had been arrested on the orders of Shamash to be held at his pleasure, no one else knew he was in jail and Shamash as it turned out, subsequently disappeared. The warders were going to do what they had been told to do and would hold him until they were ordered otherwise. In the meantime, even if they had wanted to, they were unable to tell Eduardo when or if a date for his release might ever come.

As for Michaelis, the paper with the secret information was damning. He was interrogated in the presence of the Logothete himself to whom he told the true story that the paper was in the bag of his brother, which he had picked up after his brother had died. He had no idea where his brother had got it or what he was doing with it except that Pietro had been walking with another man when he went into the Hippodrome and that man was easily identifiable as Philip Shamash. He had not read the paper and did not know what it contained. Even under torture, Michaelis did not reveal anything else and eventually it was reluctantly acknowledged that he probably was an innocent pawn in the affair. Nevertheless, he was accused of murder and fratricide and after a brief trial, since he could put up no credible defense, was sentenced to fifteen years in prison. His mother and father were never informed what had happened to him and for them, sadly, their two sons had disappeared without trace and no inquiry they made yielded any further information.

Shamash also disappeared. He got his wish since his Turkish captors secretly transported him out of the city and he was taken to Adrianople where he was interrogated by the Sultan's officials. His worst fears were then realized although his end came not from his enemies the Greeks or the Italians, whom he had so feared, but from his own countrymen whom he was relying upon to save him. As a result of the foolish scheme to save his skin, the Genoese had begun sending reinforcements to Pera to aid in its defense against possible Turkish attack and, to the discomfiture of the Turks, these reinforcements played a crucial role in the subsequent siege of Constantinople itself. Shamash had succeeded in betraying everyone with whom he came into contact and shortly after he reached Adrianople, he was executed for treason.

As for Cecilia, her face was disfigured for life with a scar across her cheek, her husband had disappeared, no one knew where he was or whether or not he was still alive and she had no idea where Shamash kept his money. When she went to look for Eduardo to seek his help, he also had disappeared. As a Florentine, she was not someone who was going to be assisted either by the Greek authorities or the Genoese of Pera and she had no one else to turn to in the city itself. Shamash had few friends outside the Court and most of those that knew him distantly did not like him. She had no alternative but to sell the house which they had bought together and move to a small apartment where for the time being she was able to live on the proceeds. After the trial of Michaelis Mascario when the details of the work of Philip Shamash for the Turks were revealed, the authorities ordered that all his possessions should be confiscated but by then it was too late to expropriate the house itself. Cecilia was left to correspond with her family and to decide whether or not she should return to Italy.

CHAPTER 32

Prison

Conditions for Eduardo were by no means as harsh as they could have been. Since he had not been accused of anything and had just been ordered held at the pleasure of an official of the court, the warders did not see reason to mistreat him. They were accustomed to political prisoners and it was customary, that if the fortunes of such prisoners turned and they were released and brought back into favor, they would remember and repay the kindnesses of their jailors. After a few months therefore, Eduardo, on the promise of the appropriate recompense, was able to persuade the warders to forward a letter to Palamas explaining what had happened and where he was, asking, at the same time, for money, books and writing materials. Shortly afterwards, Palamas came to visit him, bringing what he asked and relating the news of the outside world.

"Needless to say, we came to believe after some time had passed, that you were dead. Otherwise, we could not imagine that you would abandon the bookshop so soon after Heliogabalus' death. But the executor has done nothing since, if you were dead, the state would have taken everything in the absence of heirs. I shall now tell him to proceed and complete the formalities in your name. But why are you here? What have you done?"

"I don't know," said Eduardo. "The warders don't tell me anything. I believe the fact is that they don't know either. The worst of it is that they say there is no date set for my release or for a trial. I am here at the pleasure of a member of the court."

"I will try and discover who it is that has ordered this," said Palamas. "Possibly one of the great families who sold you books through that Pietro Mascario you were telling me about. Maybe they were disgruntled about the price of the books that they received although that doesn't sound very likely. But such people have absolute power here. You can never be certain. Mascario has never been back to the bookshop since you disappeared so maybe that does have something to do with it."

"I can give you both his address and that of his parents. He worked for the administration so you may be right that it is something to do with the book sales by the state. If you inquire of his parents, you must be careful because they hate me. He also has a brother, Michaelis, who dislikes both me and his brother. It is not a happy family."

"Very well," said Palamas, "I will try and find Pietro first."

"And did you ever manage to decipher the riddle?" asked Eduardo who, even in the midst of his present painful predicament, was of all things most interested in pursuing his obsession.

"I am afraid not, but one of the books I have brought you is a copy of the *Library* by Apollodorus, which is a compilation of the ancient myths from classical times. It is in Greek so it will take you some time to read but you may find something relevant. In the meantime, I am continuing to send books from the bookshop to your friend Patrizzi in Florence and he is continuing to pay for them, so you should have no worries there. I will come and see you again shortly and bring more books and money and hopefully some news."

With the money he received at regular intervals, Eduardo was able to pay the warders who, thereupon, were happy to ensure that he had a comfortable existence and that he was provided with every amenity he asked for except his freedom. He took regular exercise, he read and he wrote, so after the first uncertain months, he slowly became reconciled to his lot and even content, if not happy, with life. These were, after all, the occupations which, of all others, he most enjoyed and it was no more and no less an existence than that enjoyed by the many thousands of Christian monks who lived in similar conditions, throughout the city and the regions beyond the city, both under Greek and Turkish rule.

Palamas visited him at intervals and brought more books and more news.

"I have not been able to discover anything from the authorities about the purpose of your confinement, who ordered it or when it might end. To be frank I could not get much interest in your case. The political situation is deteriorating and I cannot get anyone to focus on the plight of a single prisoner out of the hundreds in the city jails. And what's more, both the two brothers, Mascario, have disappeared. I went round to the address of Pietro and they were occupied by someone else. No one even remembered him. So then I went to his parent's house. I did not mention your name but asked after Pietro and they confirmed that both brothers left without a trace. The parents did not seem to know anything. I was only there for a few minutes but obviously they were desperate for some information themselves."

Eduardo considered this for a few minutes.

"Pietro worked in the Foreign Service for a man called Philip Shamash," he said. "I believe it was his idea to sell books owned by the State. You might be able to find out if he or his office knows where Pietro is. But be very careful, Shamash is a well-connected and dangerous man. Do not under any circumstances mention my name."

Palamas looked at Eduardo quizzically, surprised at the authoritative tone of his voice. "Very well," he said. "I will try and do that. And there is some good news. The will has been approved and you are now officially the old man's heir. I also have here copies of the latest accounts of the book sales. They are continuing at a brisk pace and we are both getting richer!"

On the occasion of another visit, they discussed the riddle. Eduardo had found nothing in Apollodorus or in any other of the mythologies that Palamas had given him.

"Focus on the clues that are given," suggested Palamas. "We know that there were three people who rested at Tegea. We know that one was subsequently rescued and was, presumably, a captive at the time he was at Tegea. We are told that this was the first time they were rescued so look for someone who was taken captive at least twice. We are told that three people did the rescuing of which two were one. What does that mean? And we are told that the grove honors only one of the three and that Athena also has a connection. Those are a lot of clues. Here is another book that might help: Pausanias' *Description of Greece*. He was a contemporary writer and his book contains large amounts of information about classical Greece which he witnessed personally. Read it carefully. You have time on your hands." He ended with a wry smile in an attempt to lighten the atmosphere.

"And what else is going on in the world?" asked Eduardo glancing at the book and then putting it aside

"You haven't heard?" said Palamas. "We have a new Emperor - Constantine. John died some months ago. His brothers are now joint Despots. The Turks invaded Morea and destroyed the wall that Constantine had just rebuilt and he was forced while he was still Despot to pay the Sultan an annual tribute. We also hear that the Ottomans defeated the Hungarians last year at Kosovo and have occupied Hungary. The infidels advance and the Latins do nothing to help us or cannot help us and neither do our countrymen do anything to help themselves. They still refuse to honor the decree of union of the Council of Florence and I really believe that they would prefer to submit to the Turks rather than to the Latin Church. I am very worried about our future."

On yet another visit, Palamas revealed that he had made progress on discovering the reason for Eduardo's incarceration.

"It appears that you were jailed at the pleasure of that official you mentioned, Philip Shamash. He was the one who initiated the book sales. But he also has since left Constantinople, maybe for good. There seems to be some kind of scandal attached to him and to his departure and no one will take it on themselves to override his order for your imprisonment. They have to get the authority of the Emperor and no one regards it as important to discuss it with him especially in the current circumstances. Did you know this Shamash?"

"Yes, I did," said Eduardo who had gone white and had sat down. "Listen," he said after a moment, "Try and get a message to Cecilia Shamash, his wife. I used to know them both in Florence when he was with the delegation to the Council. She may know where he is." He gave Palamas the address.

On his next visit, Palamas had to report that he could not find Cecilia. She had moved shortly after Eduardo had been jailed and no one now knew where she now was. Eduardo thereupon wrote to Juliette, which up to now he had been reluctant to do, although he had continued to send her money as it came

233

in from the continuing sale of books. He was somewhat ashamed that he now found himself in the same forced confinement that she had endured but the pessimistic outlook for his future overcame his reluctance and after some months a letter came back. Palamas was able to locate Cecilia who immediately also came to visit Eduardo in prison.

Her visit was very brief. Female visitors were not generally permitted and only Eduardo's special status and particular generosity with the guards enabled this one exception. The two of them were reserved and distant. Cecilia felt some guilt that it was she who was responsible for Eduardo's predicament although she did not tell him the truth of how she had betrayed him.

"My God! What happened to your face." Eduardo could not help himself. Her disfigurement could not be concealed even by the veil she was wearing or the makeup she always applied.

"It was Philip, when he found out about us." And she handed him the letter which she had discovered in her husband few remaining papers. With it was the report implicating Eduardo.

"So you lied to me all that time," she continued. "You never loved me. You just used me to get at Philip. I shall never forgive you."

She started to cry. She did still love him and she cried both for his predicament as well as his betrayal and her own prospects.

Eduardo could not help himself. He could not meet her gaze. She was right and there was nothing he could now do. It went through his mind that unwittingly he had been responsible for the ruin of both sisters who now were both condemned to a life of loneliness and penury.

"You are wrong," he murmured. "I can understand if you do not believe me but I did and I do love you."

"I have decided not to return to Italy," she said. "I have sold the house and now have a little money. And I have been able to make a living as a seamstress. I actually enjoy the work and now I have moved away from the palace circle, I have been able to make some friends, particularly amongst the Italians. It feels good doing something for myself and supporting myself.

Besides if I go back, I will never be accepted by our old friends in Florence since we have lost all our money. And I won't have anywhere to live better than I have here. I don't believe Philip will ever come back though it would be nice to know where he and is that he is safe."

There was little else to be said. There was nothing she could do to make his confinement any easier or to press for his release since she had no influence of any kind with the Greek administration. They embraced and sadly parted. He asked her to give him the letter and the report which she did. She said she would come and visit him again if he could get permission but both of them knew that this was very unlikely.

CHAPTER 33

The Great Book

Eduardo's confinement continued, seemingly without the prospect of an end. He corresponded with Juliette on what was a quite formal level since she, by now, had apparently accepted that his feelings for her had largely dissipated. They mostly exchanged views on the books they were reading and on her philosophical and mystical beliefs, which she was trying to express in her writing. Eduardo at first had little interest in these matters and exchanged views with her because it seemed that they were the only subjects she wished to write about. But he had time on his hands, he was intelligent, thoughtful and increasingly well-read in both Latin and Greek and he recognized that if he was going to achieve anything in his present state it was obviously only going to be by virtue of his pen and not by any more war-like instrument. It was then that he decided that he would turn his own energies and thoughts to writing.

His book would be called *Mystical Consolations*[16] and, apart from following up and enlarging on the correspondence with Juliette, would be dedicated to Heliogabalus, whose insightful outbursts and comforting simplicity Eduardo greatly missed. He was becoming increasingly despondent about his future. He wondered why it seemed to be that, each time he was on the point of reaching some meaningful goal in his young life, he was dealt a cruel blow by fate: the death of his parents, the loss of Juliette, his first love, and now the loss of the great fortune that he had been left by Heliogabalus and the deprivation of his liberty. How could God be doing this to him? Why would God be doing this to him? Juliette seemed optimistic and fulfilled and, she said, happy with the lot that God had chosen for her. But Eduardo could not be happy and the book was to an extent a catharsis for his frustrations, an attempt to work out, by reason or by contemplation, an answer that would give him also comfort and perhaps fulfillment.

The book began with Eduardo falling asleep in his darkened prison cell and dreaming. He dreamed that he was writing in a book of gold in the company of a beautiful young woman with long golden hair who was dressed in a flowing white robe and holding the book for him to write. As the writing proceeds, the Angel, Mystiké, and Eduardo, discuss what he is writing and she guides him and corrects him as they contemplate the nature of God. The idea for the book he takes from Heliogabalus and the Book of Revelations, the great book of the Apocalypse, the revelation of the mystery of God. Inspired by Juliette's compositions of poetry and pictures, Eduardo fills his book with both words and pictures. He asks the Angel for help in understanding why human reason is not enough to comprehend the nature of God.

"I am a man and my nature is defined by my ability to reason. Why would God give me reason and single me out from all the animals and creatures of the earth as one who is closest to God and yet not permit me to approach him as a man, the rational man?"

"Reason is given to you as a man, yes, but to live as a man on this earth and to use as a man when you approach other men but not when you approach God," says the Angel. "When you approach God, you must abandon your reason, you must release yourself from your senses, you must eschew language and as you reach the presence of God, you must cast out words and thoughts altogether."

Eduardo obeys the Angel and as he turns the pages of the great book, he continues to draw pictures but words become fewer and fewer and now only a continuous succession of monstrous images fill his book, symbols, reflections, images, icons, representations of God, an aesthetic of the invisible and the unknowable. As his story proceeds, he realizes that he can never see God face to face but only in reflection as in a mirror. He begins to grasp the paradox that God cannot be understood, that the ways and purposes of God cannot be understood, that understanding is not an appropriate attribute of God or for those seeking Him. Eduardo throughout the book pursues his love and his lover, Beauty, and when, at the end, his love achieves consummation, he sees that this is only because he has abandoned earthly and bestial beauty and finally achieved spiritual union with the beauty of God and given up his will to the will of God. When the book is finally closed by the Angel, Mystike, Eduardo has achieved peace.

In the midst of these flights of inspiration and intuition which characterized his book, Eduardo pursued the mundane matters of his everyday life. He learned that, due to some temporary construction work in their own wing of the prison, a group of prisoners had been transferred to cells close to his own. One day he thought he recognized the voice of one of these newcomers and, yes, it must be, it was, that of Michaelis Mascario with his distinctive Genoese accent. He could not believe it. He asked the warder if he could speak to the prisoner and, when this request was granted, he went to visit him in his cell. When he first saw Eduardo, Michaelis did not realize that Eduardo was also a prisoner and he had a twinge of the old antagonism but he was so glad to have a visitor, to see someone he knew, that this was immediately forgotten. The two embraced and Michaelis wept.

Michaelis, who had been convicted of fratricide and suspected espionage, had been kept under a much more stringent regime than Eduardo. Michaelis was thin, sickly and white-faced. He obviously had no strength; both emotionally and physically he was close to the end. Five years imprisonment had left him without hope and he was wasting away. With the help of further largesse, Eduardo persuaded the warders that Michaelis should remain in a cell close to him and receive the same treatment that he did. As a result Michaelis' vigor and health improved and, after a few months, his old robustness had returned. They even resumed their old practice of sparring together during the daily exercise breaks using short staves which on one occasion Palamas brought them for the purpose.

This visit of Palamas was to be his last. He bought Eduardo further books including a copy of Plutarch's *Lives* which he had found in the Tetrabiblion. He explained that he was leaving on a trip to Italy, to Florence, with the purpose of visiting Patrizzi who had not responded to their recent letters. He was afraid that

Patrizzi might have died or gone out of business. When Eduardo asked him when he might be back, for an instant a shadow passed over Palamas' face, and Eduardo realized that he did not intend to come back, and thus it happened. As though in confirmation of this, Palamas gave him the news that the old Sultan, Murad, had died and been succeeded by his son Mehmet. At first this news had been greeted by the Greeks, and indeed the Latins, with relief, since Mehmet was young and, it was assumed, would be ineffectual, but it soon became clear that, on the contrary, he was vigorous, determined and much more aggressive than his father. He was already issuing threats against the city and had started to assemble an army, although for what specific purpose was not yet known.

Then Palamas said, 'I have submitted a petition to the Emperor for your release. It was signed by all your old friends on the book committee as well as many of my friends from the university. We explained as best we could the circumstances of your imprisonment, how you have never been accused of any crime, how your accuser has disappeared and how it is against the natural law for someone to be imprisoned without indictment let alone without trial. If I can get the Emperor just to see and accept the petition, there may be some hope."

"I cannot say how grateful, I am to you," said Eduardo. "Needless to say some hope is preferable to no hope."

"I will be taking to Italy as many books from the shop as I can and I will credit your account in the bank in Florence when they have been sold. Here are the details of your account in Pera. As you can see this is now a considerable sum. I fervently hope you will soon have the opportunity to spend it."

"I do too," said Eduardo, smiling grimly.

"And here is more money. There are many books remaining in the Tetrabiblion but I believe that the most valuable have already been sent to Italy. I will leave keys at the University in case you are able to use them during my absence."

In return, Eduardo gave him the manuscript of his own book and urged Palamas to take it with him to Italy, get it copied and attempt to sell it and this, of course, Palamas agreed to. With tears in his eyes, Eduardo thanked Palamas for all his advice, assistance and his devotion; they embraced and Palamas departed.

As soon as he had recovered his composure and to take his mind off what he knew to be the loss of yet another friend, in effect his only lifeline to the outside world, Eduardo, with a heavy heart, started to read the Plutarch. Within a few minutes it came to him that, finally, after all this time, he had found the answer to the riddle. The first of Plutarch's *Lives* is that of Theseus, the great hero, most famous as the slayer of the Minotaur. It appears that when Theseus was in middle age, he traveled to Sparta with his friend Pirithous, where they were received by the king of that country. This king had a beautiful daughter whose name was Helen – yes, *the* Helen. Even at the age of ten, she was so beautiful that the two visitors decided to steal her and that one of them would marry her. And so they did, but naturally they were pursued by all the king's men and it wasn't until they reached Tegea that Theseus and Pirithous lost their pursuers. At Tegea they rested (the three with one) and drew lots to decide which of them should take Helen to wife. Theseus won. Since Helen was too young to marry, they took her secretly to Aphidnae, where she was cared for by Theseus' mother. The two then set out again to seek a wife for Pirithous but on this occasion the expedition turned sour. This time, the father of the princess they had their eye on realized what they were up to and turned his dogs on them. Pirithous was eaten alive by the dogs and Theseus barely escaped. Later Helen's two brothers, the twins Castor and Pollux, (the two who are one) led an army against Athens to rescue Helen although the Athenians had no idea where she was. Fortunately for Athens, a member of the Spartan army, Hekademos, discovered that she was in Aphidnae, so Athens was spared and Helen was rescued (the first rescue). In honor of Hekademos, who had saved the city, the Athenians set aside a grove in his name outside the city walls and later a sanctuary to Athena was built there.

Not unnaturally, Eduardo was overjoyed by his new discovery, although his utter inability to do anything about it made the conclusion of his research an anticlimax which, on reflection, more than outweighed the pleasure of having solved the riddle.

He once again lapsed into depression. He had finished writing his book, he had solved the riddle, he had lost his principal friend and contact with the outside world, he had no new books and the future stretched on indefinitely with little hope and little to occupy his mind.

As it turned out, in this his darkest hour, fate came to his rescue. Early one morning there was an unaccustomed commotion in the far reaches of the prison. A warder appeared to be going to each of the cells and reciting something to each of the prisoners. As the warder came closer to Eduardo's cell, he could hear that, after this reading, there were loud cheers and shouts of joy.

"I, Constantine XI, Palaeologus Dragases, Emperor of the Greeks, hereby grants an amnesty to all prisoners confined within the city. They will be released and put under the authority of Lucas Notaras, Megadux, and formed into a regiment to aid in defending the city. Any prisoners refusing to serve or attempting to escape will be executed without trial. At the conclusion of their service, and on my authority, all prisoners will be freed.

Sealed with the Imperial Seal: Constantine.

February 14th in the year of our Savior 1453."

CHAPTER 34

The Siege

It was obvious to those on the outside that events were rapidly coming to a crisis point upon which the future of the city and that of the Greek empire would depend for many years. The determination of the young Sultan was demonstrated when, in defiance of an earlier treaty, he began the construction of a fortress on the Asian shore of the Bosphorus upstream from the city. Three thousand workers completed the work in only four months. Within the fortress, the Sultan placed cannons which commanded the waterway and in effect closed the Bosphorus. When a Venetian galley tried to run the blockade, it was sunk with a single shot and the few survivors immediately executed. Nothing could have better demonstrated the Sultan's intentions. Constantinople was now cut off from the Black Sea and its trade and particularly the supplies of grain that fed the city. In case anyone had missed the point that he was making, shortly after his new fortress was completed, Mehmet, with his army, marched up to the renowned land walls of the city and inspected them at his leisure.

The Emperor and the inhabitants of Constantinople had no doubt what was about to happen. The Emperor, for his part, did everything that he humanly could. The proposal for the union of the eastern and western churches was again raised amongst the Emperor's advisers and the Pope sent a small mercenary force to aid in the defense of the city as an earnest of his intentions if the Orthodox faithful could be persuaded to submit to his authority. And so, in December of the previous year, at a solemn ceremony in Santa Sophia in the presence of the Emperor, the Decree of Union agreed at the Council of Florence was finally ratified by the Patriarch and some of the Orthodox clergy. Most of the congregations of the Eastern Church, however, ignored the ceremony and the Orthodox rites were practiced as they had always been. Again it was put about by some of the Emperor's advisers and no doubt it was true that many in the Eastern Church, if they were to be forced to submit to a foreigner, would prefer the Sultan's turban to the Cardinal's hat. As it turned out, even this gesture by the Emperor was useless – no more help was sent by the Pope and by this time many of the inhabitants who could afford it, including, as we have seen, John Palamas, started to abandon the city.

The Sultan continued his preparations although even he had misgivings and many of his advisers were against any attempt at besieging the city. Constantinople had withstood many sieges over the centuries, some of the Turks thought that the strategic importance of the city had diminished and was not worth the enormous effort that would be required. In spite of the over-whelming numbers in favor of the attackers, the outcome was by no means certain. How were they going to overcome those massive walls?

The Sultan had a secret weapon. He had taken into his employ a Hungarian engineer named Urban, who professed to be able to build a cannon that would be large enough to destroy the ancient walls. To be fair to Urban, he had first offered his services to the Emperor but the latter could not afford the salary that Urban asked for and, more importantly, the Emperor did not have the materials with which to make a cannon. And when the Sultan offered Urban four times this salary, who can blame him for taking up the offer? Urban's prototype cannon was the one that sank the Venetian ship in the Bosphorus and on the success of this, he was ordered to proceed with his full-size model which, on completion, had a barrel twenty-eight feet long, a projectile weighing over half a ton and a team of seven hundred men to service it.

In addition, the Sultan had assembled a large naval force consisting of some thirty triremes and biremes and perhaps one hundred smaller vessels. None of these was as large as the ships of the Venetians, the Genoese or the Greeks themselves but there were many more of them and when they sailed past the city in a show of force and to demonstrate that the Turks now had control of the seas, the Greeks were understandably shocked; they had had no idea that the Sultan had anything approaching such numbers of ships. The orders of the Turkish fleet were to prevent any reinforcements or supplies from reaching the city by sea and this they were able effectively to do during the first weeks of the siege.

Upon their release from their cells, Eduardo, Michaelis and their fellow inmates were taken out of the prison and escorted by a small contingent of the Skythikoi to their barracks on Mese Street. There the prisoners were housed in quarters not much better than those they had come from and guarded much as they had been before but they were equipped and armed and they exercised and trained every day. They were not able to leave the barracks but, as well as anyone in the city, they heard the news and they knew what was expected of them. The swordsmanship of both Eduardo and Michaelis was so much superior to any of the others that they were given command of the two battalions, each of about eighty men, that comprised their regiment.

The numbers of the regiment were included in the census that, on the orders of the Emperor, was taken of the fighting men in the city. The Emperor was horrified to learn that he had less than seven thousand men at his disposal including a contingent of some seven hundred Genoese under a professional soldier, Giovanni Giustiniani, who, in view of his experience, was put in general charge of all the defenses of the city. In spite of the presumed neutrality of the Genoese and Pera, the Genoese colony, the authorities in Pera were as concerned about the outcome of the siege as was the Emperor. They had no doubt that if Constantinople fell, Pera would be next.

The Turkish army under the command of the Sultan himself started to arrive in front of the walls of Constantinople at the beginning of April 1453. It was impossible for the defenders to know the size of the force that opposed them, perhaps it was as well that they did not, but it was obvious that they were far outnumbered. The Emperor had already ordered the gates of the city closed and all bridges destroyed. He had also ordered that a boom was to be constructed across the mouth of the Golden Horn. This was attached to the walls of the two cities on each shore and supported on boats and this effectively prevented any attack on the harbor from the sea.

A preliminary bombardment on the land walls was started by the Turks immediately after they had encamped, after which the Sultan ordered a pause of a few days while he assessed the situation and repositioned his cannons including Urban's monster. This latter could only fire about seven shots a day but its effects were disastrous; after a week part of the outer wall was completely destroyed and the outer ditch was filled with rubble from the collapsed wall. But all was not yet lost. The defenders, mostly women from the city, repaired the walls each night with barrels of earth and wooden stockades and also had some success in clearing the ditch of the debris that had filled it the day before. At the same time, an attack by the Turks on the boom across the Golden Horn was repulsed by the defending ships stationed inside the harbor. These stood too far out of the water for the smaller Turkish craft to make any impression on.

The battalions of Eduardo and Michaelis were ordered to join the force of Genoese under Giustiniani, which was placed at the weakest part of the great triple wall where it joined the wall of the Blachernae palace at the north-western corner of the city. The soldiers were armed with swords and javelins and were accompanied by some archers. The defense had little or no cannon; the guns they had could not be hauled up onto the walls and, in any event, they had almost no gunpowder. But the defending soldiers did have good body armor, better than the Turks, many of whom had no armor at all. After the initial bombardment, the Turks made an assault on that point of the walls, which had been most damaged but this was repulsed with no loss of life for the defenders and this again greatly boosted their morale.

And then there was another diversion for both armies and a pause in the fighting. A flotilla of four large Italian ships, filled with provisions and weapons, sailed to within sight of the city before it was observed by either side. It was then immediately attacked by the Turkish fleet but the small, low Turkish ships could make little impression on the Italian galleons, which poured down fire on the Turks and the very number of attackers

245

did not give them any advantage in the confined space around just four ships. Sailing with a strong wind behind them, the Italians were within reach of the Golden Horn when the wind suddenly fell and, caught in the strong current coming out of the Bosphorus, the four ships started drifting backwards towards that very spot on the shore where the Sultan was waiting in fury at the impotence of his sailors. On occasion, in his excitement, he would ride into the water so as to get closer to the action and shout orders to his admiral. Fighting on land ceased entirely as the soldiers of both sides crowded onto the shore, or onto the sea walls of the city, to watch the action on the water. The Italian ships, in their desperation, managed to lash themselves together in a square in order to concentrate their forces and they were able to make use of quantities of Greek fire[17] to ward off their attackers. And then, at the final moment, when they had almost succumbed, a strong wind rose again and the four ships were able to make way, crushing the opposition and entering the harbor.

This episode was another boost in morale for the defenders, quite apart from the provisions and material that the ships had brought, and it was another setback for the Sultan who took his revenge on his admiral by torturing and cashiering him. But it also energized him into undertaking a desperate scheme that almost changed the course of the siege. He knew he had to get control of the Golden Horn and he determined that he would bypass the boom that was protecting the harbor by pulling his ships overland from the shore of the Bosphorus behind Pera into the back of the harbor. He had been preparing a road along this route for some time and overnight a number of ships were hauled along the road and into the top end of the harbor. When the defenders awoke in the morning, they were horrified to find they had lost control of the Golden Horn. Skirmishes, which were inconclusive, took place between the ships of the opposing navies within the harbor but the Turks were now in position, on the least protected side of the city, and they could not be dislodged.

Despite this success, the occupation of the harbor did little to assist the progress of the Turks, except by harassing the

Greek fleet, and the action now returned to the land walls. All the guns were concentrated on one place on the wall where it was thought to be weakest, the Mesoteichion, the lowest place on the whole western side of the city, where the River Lycus ran into the city and then to the Marmara. Further Turkish assaults on this position followed but they were all heroically repulsed. Each time the walls were damaged, they were repaired with wooden stockades and earth. The besiegers also attempted on frequent occasions to breach the walls by mining them but, in every case, the mines were discovered and destroyed so that this tactic had to be abandoned. The Turks also erected siege towers to protect those who were filling in the ditch with the purpose of enabling an easier traverse for the soldiers trying to assault the walls. Again, the towers were destroyed by the defenders. After six weeks of continuous attacks and no real progress to be shown for them, it seemed as if stalemate had been reached and, on 25th May, the Sultan not only held a council at which some of his advisors recommended that the siege be abandoned, he even sent an emissary to the Emperor offering surrender terms. These terms were rejected and both leaders determined to fight on.

But in spite of, or perhaps because of, the extraordinary resistance put up by the defenders, they were in fact at the end of their endurance. The fighting had lasted for more than six weeks and, during this time, they had not left their positions on the walls where they got little sleep, since cannon fire often continued throughout the night, as did the Turkish assaults. The city was running out of food and other provisions, there was no sign of the reinforcements promised by the Venetians and many parts of the wall had collapsed beyond repair. On Sunday 27th May, the Turks managed to fill in some of the ditch and actually stockpiled arms on the inner side. The Sultan instructed his commanders that, on the 29th, the whole army was to attack at once, along the entire length of the wall, and his navy was to attempt to attack the seaward and harbor walls if only to provide a diversion and to engage as many of the defenders as possible. He promised gold beyond his dreams for the man who first reached the top of the wall and he then ordered a day of rest for

247

the following day. For the first time for many weeks, the guns were silent. The defenders knew that the moment of crisis had come.

During this day of rest, church bells rang throughout the city, processions formed outside the churches and the holiest relics were brought out for the faithful to view, perhaps for the last time, and were carried round the walls of the city. The Emperor headed the procession and then addressed his soldiers and the multitude.

"Gentlemen, illustrious captains of the army, and our most Christian comrades in arms: we now see the hour of battle approaching. I have therefore elected to assemble you here to make it clear that you must stand together with firmer resolution than ever. You have always fought with glory against the enemies of Christ. Now the defense of your fatherland and of the city known the world over, which the infidel and evil Turks have been besieging for two and fifty days, is committed to your lofty spirits.

Be not afraid because its walls have been worn down by the enemy's battering. For your strength lies in the protection of God and you must show it with your arms quivering and your swords brandished against the enemy. I know that this undisciplined mob will, as is their custom, rush upon you with loud cries and ceaseless volleys of arrows. These will do you no bodily harm, for I see that you are well covered in armor. They will strike the walls, our breastplates and our shields. So do not imitate the Romans who, when the Carthaginians went into battle against them, allowed their cavalry to be terrified by the fearsome sight and sound of elephants.

In this battle you must stand firm and have no fear, no thought of flight, but be inspired to resist with ever more herculean strength. Animals may run away from animals. But you are men, men of stout heart, and you will hold at bay these dumb brutes, thrusting your spears and swords into them, so that they will know that they are fighting not against their own kind but against the masters of animals.

Now he threatens to capture the city of Constantine the Great, your fatherland, the place of ready refuge for all Christians, the guardian of all Greeks, and to profane its holy shrines of God by turning them into stables for his horses. Oh my lords, my brothers, my sons, the everlasting honor of Christians is in your hands.

You, my comrades in arms, obey the commands of your leaders in the knowledge that this is the day of your glory -- a day on which, if you shed but a drop of blood, you will win for yourselves crowns of martyrdom and eternal fame."[18]

Eduardo and Michaelis had left their men in position in the charge of their principal subordinates and they had joined the other commanders to listen to this stirring exhortation. At its conclusion, they joined the throngs of citizens who were making their way to Santa Sophia. For the first and only time since the proclamation of union between the Eastern and Western Churches had been ratified five months earlier, the Liturgy was performed beneath the great dome of the cathedral and all parties, both those who opposed union and those who supported it, participated and embraced their fellow Christians. By chance, in the crowd, Eduardo encountered Cecilia. They hugged each other, Cecilia hung close to him and sobbed quietly.

"It is you," she said through her tears. "Here, after all this time." And she said the only thing that could be said, "I love you."

"I love you too," he replied and when she had calmed a little, "and what are you going to do?"

"I shall be fine," she said. "I have a friend. He has a place to hide me in the sewers beneath his house. I shall wait there until the worst is over. I shall have food and water and some other friends will join me. Hopefully, the Muslims will not find us."

"Yes, you will be safe and knowledge of that will give me some relief. I shall be thinking of you. God willing, you will one day return to your family and tell of the great deeds that you have witnessed."

"I will, I will and God keep you and spare you and save you," she said her tears starting again.

All around them, people were embracing and crying, clinging to each other in the knowledge that this would most likely be their last human contact for all time.

Finally, the two of them parted and Eduardo and Michaelis returned to their posts on the wall, where they exhorted their own men and had something to eat. For a few minutes, Eduardo stood on the wall, looking out over the enemy camp. On the far side of the now almost completely filled-in ditch, there was a wooden stockade, which the Turks had constructed early on in the siege to withstand any unexpected counterattack by the defenders. Beyond and inside the stockade were the white tents of the enemy illuminated by the flicker of their fires. In the unaccustomed quiet of this last night he could, at times, hear occasional murmurs of conversation and music interspersed with the larger sounds of the final preparations for the assault. Around him, on the wall, were great piles of stones and javelins as well as pails of water for refreshment, which had been brought up to the ramparts during the day. There was nothing more he could do and Eduardo, leaving the sentries to continue the watch, lay down for a few hours sleep.

And so, early in the morning of the 29th May 1453, the attack began. The number of the Sultan's forces was variously estimated at between fifty thousand and two hundred and fifty thousand and they were pitted against only five to seven thousand defenders stationed along fourteen miles of walls. The first wave of attackers rushed over the ditch and laid their ladders up against the walls. Eduardo and Michaelis and their men, who with the Genoese under the command of Giustiniani, were positioned near the Blachernae Palace, the walls of which, perceived to be the weakest, received the brunt of the attack. But the first wave had been chosen by the Sultan merely to exhaust the defenders. They were the camp-followers, mercenaries and other adventurers excited by the promise of booty and riches. They were easily repulsed, their ladders thrown down and thousands crushed by the stones thrown from the battlements. They could not retreat since the Sultan had stationed seasoned troops behind them who cut them down when they attempted to recross the ditch. After two hours, the Sultan gave up and the survivors were permitted to retire but they had done their work; the defenders were already exhausted even though they were sustained by the women of the city, who had joined them on the ramparts with fresh buckets of water and more stones and to aid in the continuous task of repairing the walls.

The second wave of the attack, consisting of more disciplined troops from the Anatolian heartland, failed equally, despite the fact that a whole section of the wall was once more demolished by cannon fire. Eduardo and Michaelis fought with their men throwing rocks and javelins, firing arrows and using the few small-arms that they possessed. They were joined by Giustiniani and encouraged by the Emperor himself, who rode along the wall giving continual exhortation and orders to his men. Not one of the enemy reached the top of the wall.

But now the Sultan committed his finest troops, the famed Janissaries, his personal bodyguard, young men who had spent their lives as soldiers and who were disciplined and fearless. The noise of the cannon was drowned by their drums, trumpets and shouts as they approached. Several of these mighty soldiers carrying scimitars and shields managed to climb the ladders and reach the top of the wall but even they were thrown off.

It seemed as if this final assault had also failed when disaster struck. Giustiniani, the leader of the Genoese and the rock upon which the defense had stood, was wounded and, despite the entreaties of the Emperor that he should remain in position, was carried off into the city. His men, seeing this and assuming that he had been killed, panicked and started to retreat from the Parateichion, the gap between the inner and outer wall, where they had been stationed, and this sudden collapse of the defense gave the Turks their chance. They poured over the outer wall into the area where the Genoese had been stationed.

At the same moment, the Turks noticed that a small postern gate, the Kerkoporta, at the very corner where the triple walls joined the single wall of the Blachernae Palace, had been left open. They crept into the area before the defenders noticed and by then it was too late. The Emperor himself with his companion, his cousin Don Francisco of Toledo, galloped to the palace to rally a counterattack. As he passed the positions of Eduardo and Michaelis, he called on them and any of their men who were still standing to join him, which they did. The Emperor threw off his cloak, the imperial purple, and his other regalia signifying his divinity, and, with his three companions, personally led a charge against the infiltrating enemy. It was hopeless; the Emperor was killed almost immediately by a javelin shot, as was his cousin, and Eduardo and Michaelis and their party, fighting valiantly, were surrounded and disarmed.

The Turkish forces now poured into the city and the defense, disorganized and disheartened, broke up. At once the destruction, the slaughter and the looting began. Under the rules of war, at least those of the Turks in accordance with the Koran, and perfectly well known to the Greeks, those who resisted the faithful could expect three days of rapine and pillage; this indeed was the principal motivation of every individual in the besieging forces. The fighters could earn a fortune in one hour from the goods they seized, more, much more than they earned in a lifetime of soldiering.

When the church bells started to ring again signaling that the walls had fallen, many of the remaining population of the city crowded into Santa Sophia and barred the great doors in a vain attempt to seek sanctuary. It took the Turks, unfamiliar with the layout of the city, some time to traverse the several miles between the Blachernae and Santa Sophia and, by the time they reached the cathedral, their bloodlust had somewhat abated. It did not take much to break down the door but, by then, the prospect of making money by selling their captives as slaves rather than just slaughtering them, spared most of those who were sheltering inside.

At the same time, the sailors of the Turkish navy, seeing and hearing the success of their compatriots in breaching the walls, and themselves not wishing to lose the opportunity for plunder, poured into the city from the Golden Horn. This left the harbor and the Bosphorus unguarded and many of the defenders, especially the Italians, were able to escape and they sailed away to spread the news to a shocked and horrified world that, after more than two thousand years of glorious history, the Roman Empire had finally ceased to be.

The destruction and the looting might have been much greater if it had not been for two factors. The first was that the city within its majestic outer walls was, in truth, as we have seen, a collection of small rural communities many of which had their own defensive palisades or walls. When the inhabitants of these enclaves surrendered without a fight, the Turks were prepared to apply their own rules of war – the inhabitants and their property were spared. The second was the decision of the Sultan himself. When, later in the day, he entered the city attended by a great procession of his notables and taken aback, as he himself admitted, by the grandeur of the city and its buildings, palaces, churches and monuments, he ordered that the looting and destruction should stop and the regiments he had kept in reserve for this very purpose enforced his order.

One of the first acts of the Sultan was to send for the body of the Emperor to confirm, as he had been informed, that the Emperor was in fact dead. Eduardo and Michaelis were still with the body, and with that of Don Toledo, and they too, manacled and disheveled, were brought into the presence of the Sultan as, on his white horse, he progressed down Mese Street in the center of the city. Since he had rid himself of his imperial cloak, the Emperor's body had been identified only by the eagles embroidered on his shoes, but the Sultan recognized the features of Constantine and accepted the identification.

"Who are these men?" he asked of their guards referring to Eduardo and Michaelis, who were kneeling on the side of the road with their eyes lowered and their hands tied behind their back.

"They were fighting with the Emperor and appear to be among his personal bodyguards," said one of the guards.

The Sultan looked briefly at the two men and was about to turn away when Eduardo, without looking up, said in Turkish.

"Great Lord. I submit to your mercy. My name is Eduardo Ferrucci and I am from Florence. My companion is Michaelis Mascario. He is from Pera."

Eduardo knew that the Sultan had an admiration for the city of Florence, for the Medicis and for the culture of that city.

"Florence, indeed," said the Sultan. "You must be a friend of his Grace, Duke Cosimo."

"I am, Great Lord," lied Eduardo, sensing a last opportunity for salvation.

The Sultan spoke briefly to one of his companions, who in turn quietly gave orders to one of the guards. This latter came up to Michaelis, took out his scimitar and with one stroke cut off Michaelis' head, which rolled in front of the horrified Eduardo. The same guard then cut off the head of the Emperor and that of Don Toledo and thereupon the Sultan rode on. The Emperor's body and his head were buried separately and were never again discovered. Eduardo, in shock, his shirt soaked with the blood of his friend, was led away.[19]

Part 3 The Return 1453

CHAPTER 35

The Sultan

A short time after the siege had ended, the Sultan returned to his capital and to his palace in Adrianople. From this, it seemed as if he intended to abandon Constantinople to its decay and destruction. But he had other, grander plans. He ordered the rebuilding of many of the destroyed monuments, palaces and churches, some of which were turned into mosques, and he began the construction of a great palace for himself, the new Roman Emperor, at the eastern end of the city. Constantinople was to be his future capital. He forcibly repopulated the city with Turkish families and with Greeks who had originally fled. Then, after it became obvious that the city had not only survived but was flourishing, peoples of many nations and of all classes returned of their own accord and with enthusiasm. As in the other parts of his dominions, the Sultan tolerated and indeed encouraged the local religions. He arranged to have his own nominee, George Scholarius, known as Gennadius, appointed as Patriarch of the Orthodox Church and he confirmed all the privileges of the Church as they had previously existed. In this way, he showed that not only the church in Constantinople but also the whole Christian hierarchy and community throughout his empire were fully in his gift and under his authority.

Eduardo found himself back in the prison of the Blachernae. The palace had been looted and largely destroyed but the jail was intact – there had been little or nothing in that part of the great building to attract the looters. Again, he was not treated harshly but was received with courtesy and afforded some comfort since he was apparently being held under the particular orders of the Sultan. He was able to converse with his new captors in their own language unlike many of the other prisoners who, having escaped the initial slaughter, were rounded up almost at random by the Sultan's police regiments and imprisoned, as much for their own protection as for any misdeeds they might have committed. Many of these prisoners suffered harsh privations and did not survive. Others were eventually sold into slavery. But, as before, Eduardo had a relatively easy existence though his future remained as uncertain as it had been during his previous imprisonment. It was clear that the Sultan had spared him for what seemed good reason at the time but, as Eduardo questioned time and time again: would he, the Sultan, amidst all the other pressing affairs of state that he must have, remember and give any further thought to Eduardo's existence? It seemed to him, in the dark hours of his confinement, that this was very unlikely. He had no books or any other type of recreation, he was not able to pay the warders for them, and he had no visitors.

As it turned out, after two months confinement just as he was beginning to succumb to desperation, he was summoned without warning to an audience with the Sultan. He was taken in his prison attire to one of the areas of the Blachernae that had escaped destruction where the Sultan had made his temporary administrative quarters. He was given a bath, clothed in Turkish dress, combed and perfumed until he looked, as he thought, when he was given a looking glass, a perfectly accoutered Turkish courtier. Dressed richly for perhaps the first time in his life, he made an imposing figure. His height, his coloring and his youth provided a notable contrast to the other courtiers around him. He began to feel more confident. After these preparations, he was led through several state rooms until he reached an antechamber crowded with many others who were seated and also waiting for an audience with the Sultan. Eduardo was introduced by his guards to an official who from the splendor of his dress was clearly of the highest rank and who, he learnt later, was Zaganos Pasha, one of the Sultan's most intimate advisers.

"If you wish to keep your head, you will follow these instructions precisely," said Zaganos.

"Very well," said Eduardo.

"When you enter, you will follow behind me with your eyes cast down. You will kneel on the floor when I say so and not rise until you are bidden. You will never look the Sultan in the eye.

You will not speak unless spoken to. You will address his Highness as 'Great Caesar'. And when you are dismissed, you will back out of the room. Is that clear?"

"Yes, Excellency," said Eduardo.

"His Highness will be asking you questions about Duke Cosimo and Florence, about the culture of Italy, about the differences between the court of the Duke and this court and how an embassy from his Highness should best approach the Duke. Do you feel that you can answer these questions adequately?"

"I believe I can, Excellency," said Eduardo although, in truth, suddenly realizing what he had let himself in for, he did not feel confident at all, and his legs had suddenly become so lifeless that he almost collapsed. But it was now too late; he had no option but to proceed.

After this conversation, his escort took Eduardo into an adjoining chamber where, in the presence of another guard, he was told to remove all his clothes and he and his clothing were thoroughly inspected for weapons. After this examination, he was led back into the antechamber where, with the others, he waited his turn.

After some little time, the door opposite him, guarded by two janissaries, opened and Zaganos Pasha beckoned him to enter. He walked in slowly, with his head bowed, following behind Zaganos and across some thirty feet of floor until Zaganos stopped and stepped aside. Eduardo fell to his knees and continued to look down; he could see nothing before him, even out of the corner of his eyes, except the steps of a dais. As instructed he waited and said nothing.

"You are the friend of Cosimo," said a voice above him, a surprisingly young voice and one which he recognized from his previous brief encounter with the Sultan in that terrible moment in Mese Street.

"Yes, Great Caesar," said Eduardo, speaking to the floor.

"Describe the Duke to me and describe Florence."

Eduardo had never seen Cosimo but he knew he must not falter so he invented an elegant description largely based on his memory of Antonio Lucchese. He described how the Duke was a patron of the arts, how he used his wealth to encourage sculpture, painting and architecture. He described how the Duke collected books from ancient Roman and Greek times. He hurried on to what was easier for him, a description of the city of Florence, its narrow streets, its great churches and its new cathedral, its walls, the river running through the city, the bridge over the river, the wealth of the citizens, the shops and the banks.

"I understand that there is in Italy a great revival of the art and literature of the Romans."

"That is true, Great Caesar."

"I understand that the city of Florence is governed by its citizens. Tell me about that," said the Sultan.

"That used to be the case, Great Caesar, but that time has passed. Now Duke Cosimo is the acknowledged governor of the city."

"And what is the basis of the wealth of the city? The Florentines do not appear to be merchants. We do not see them in great numbers in our dominions."

"No, Great Caesar, the wealth of the city is based on the wool trade and on the banking business of some of the great families of the city including the Duke."

"Tell me about these banks. I know there are some of these so-called banks in Pera. How do they add to the prosperity of the city?"

Eduardo was getting out of his depth here but he struggled on and described what he understood to be the workings of a bank: how they funded trade in wool and other commodities, including the trade of those Italian cities, Venice and Genoa, which did or had done business with Constantinople; how citizens could deposit money in a bank, which the bank could then use to lend out itself.

"And do you think any benefit would be derived from my making contact with the Duke?"

"Indeed, yes, Great Caesar, there is always benefit in learning about other civilizations and teaching others about your own. It leads to greater understanding and more peaceful relationships." Eduardo sensed that an opportunity might be opening here and he forced himself to expand on his point. "There would be benefit in opening trade agreements, and in sharing the knowledge of new cultural developments and the traditions of the classical age which you, as the new Emperor of Rome, have inherited."

Eduardo suddenly feared that here he had gone too far and that, in any event, his enthusiasm sounded a little hollow. There was a short silence and then the Sultan said:

"Look up and look at me."

Eduardo did so and looked at the Sultan, face to face, for the first time. He saw a young face, with a long aquiline nose, clear skin, piercing, unsmiling eyes, a large bushy black beard and his head topped by a large turban. In turn, the Sultan studied Eduardo for a few seconds.

"You may go."

As Eduardo backed out, Zaganos whispered to him to wait in the anteroom, which he did and, after a few minutes, Zaganos joined him.

"You have made a good impression on his Highness. In due course, he will be asking you to go with a delegation to Florence and present his compliments to Duke Cosimo. In the meantime, you are free. You may not leave the city. You will be given no travel documents until we decide that the time is right for the delegation to go. Until you go, you will be paid three Venetian ducats a month. You may go now to my office and they will prepare the papers."

He motioned to a guard, gave him instructions to accompany Eduardo and within an hour Eduardo found himself outside the palace in the street with three ducats in his pocket and a pass to give him safe passage throughout the city signed by Zaganos himself. It was still early afternoon and Eduardo walked slowly down Mese Street overwhelmed by the sights of destruction and desolation of the neighborhoods and buildings that he knew so well and that had become his home. His splendid court dress, which he had been given to keep and his bearing and new-found confidence, contrasted with the appearance of most of the passersby who were either Turkish soldiers or other Turkish inhabitants dressed like Eduardo but more modestly or Greeks who, even two months after the siege had ended, were in rags, barefoot, grim-faced, dirty and ill-nourished. His first concern was for Cecilia but he had not the slightest idea where to start to look for her even if she were still alive.

Slowly he walked amidst the ruins, towards the Tetrabiblion. It took him more than an hour to get there to find his worst fears realized. The door had been broken in and the windows smashed. He saw immediately that there were no books left at all; the whole of the ground floor was a ruin, water had gotten in through the broken windows and vandals had finished the destruction begun by the Turkish soldiers. There was, in the center of the room, the remains of a fire where obviously a great number of books had been burned – all that remained was a large pile of cinders and the occasional charred scrap of parchment on the edges of the patch of singed floor. Sick to his stomach, he walked slowly up the stairs. The upper room seemed to be relatively untouched. The single window was broken and glass lay on the floor but the bed was still standing. Most important of all, there was no sign that the secret door had been found. He carefully removed the panel and his heart began to pound; yes, all the money-bags were still there.

Eduardo was exhausted. Apart from the emotional stress of his imprisonment and release, his interview with the Sultan, the sight of the suffering in the streets of those he had come to know as his fellow countrymen and the destruction of what was in effect his home, he had to deal with the fact that he had become, or would become, an enormously wealthy man if and only if he could somehow smuggle all this money out of the city without the source of it becoming known. He lay down on the bed without any covering, since there was none, and went straight to sleep.

He woke later in the evening and went out to get something to eat. Over the next few days, he began to get his bearings and resume his composure. He bought some more clothes, still in the Turkish style but things that were altogether more modest than his court dress and he was able to find someone who could help him replace the door and the windows of the Tetrabiblion, not a difficult task compared to the reconstruction of the ruins of much of the remainder of the city. He visited those few of his acquaintances who had survived the onslaught and had returned to their homes but there were very few. He had of course been away for more than five years and almost no one other than the elderly had survived the final attack; most of his neighbors had either been killed or sold into slavery. The families who were to be resettled into the city had not yet arrived and some neighborhoods were completely deserted. He went to what he thought was Cecilia's last address but it also was deserted.

After a few days, he crossed over to Pera to check whether the Mascarios were still there and to see if any banks were still operating. Contrary to what the leaders and the people of Pera had been expecting as reprisals for aiding the Greeks, the Sultan had not exacted revenge on the Genoese. On the contrary, almost his first official act after entering Constantinople was to grant the people of Pera protection and freedom from interference in their customs and worship. In return, Pera had to accept the sovereignty of the Sultan and pay the tax required of all non-Muslims. Weapons were to be confiscated, the city walls were to be demolished but property rights would be observed unless those who had fled the city did not return in which case their property would revert to the Sultan. In the event, many of those who had fled did return to their homes to start a new life under Muslim rule.

The contrast between the two cities that Eduardo found when he made this first visit was astonishing. Pera had been untouched by the besieging forces, it was completely undamaged and to all appearances remained a typical, bustling, small Italian city. But the mood of the citizens was still somber and downcast; they could not yet be certain that the Sultan with his well-known volatility would not change his mind or that some diplomatic misstep by their own leaders or by the Genoese on the Italian mainland or indeed by any of the other Italian cities, would not provoke a reaction from the Turks. But, for the time being, life in Pera went on much as usual.

The Mascario house was boarded up and from the brief inquiries that Eduardo made it appeared that the Mascarios had left many months previously. In a way, Eduardo was relieved. This spared him the difficult decision as to whether to call on the family and relate to them the fate of Michaelis. On the one

hand, he felt he had a duty to do this but he also knew that however irrational this might be, they would blame him to some degree for their son's fate.

He next visited the bank where he had his account and was
relieved to see it was open for business and that, as Palamas had
promised, he now had a very considerable balance owed to him.
That day, he opened an account in each of the four other Italian
banks operating in Pera and, on the following day and every day
for several weeks, he took as many of the coins out of the hoard
in the Tetrabiblion as he could carry discreetly, hid them within
his cloak and deposited them by turn in each of the banks, until,
finally, the cache in the secret closet was exhausted.

He also arranged to send more money to Juliette in Ferrara.
He had not heard anything from her since their correspondence
when he was first imprisoned and now since he had time on his
hands and apart from his wish to hear news of Juliette and her
family, he felt an overwhelming need to record the extraordinary
events in which he had taken part during the last months. He
wrote Juliette a long letter describing the siege, his interview with
the Sultan and the likelihood that he would be sent to Florence
as the emissary of the Sultan. If that were to be the case, he
would be able to visit Juliette on the way. He asked Juliette if she
had heard anything from Cecilia and if so to let him know as
soon as possible and also to tell him that she, Juliette, was safe
and in good health. He was not certain that this letter would
even reach Juliette although communications from Pera to the
Italian mainland still appeared to be running normally. He did
not expect to get a reply before he himself left for Florence but
Juliette was now the only real friend he had left either in Constantinople or in Italy and in the desolation of the city, the future
of which, at that moment, still appeared quite uncertain, he felt
strongly the need for companionship. He had still not the slightest idea how to discover the fate of Cecilia. He did not know
the whereabouts of the friend she had referred to who had been
able to hide her. The few inhabitants of the city who remained
all had their own grief to deal with and were not the least inclined to help when he inquired.

Each week, Eduardo had to report to the office of Zaganos Pasha in order to revalidate his safe conduct and to hear whether or when they had decided to schedule the departure of the delegation. On one of these occasions, he asked the secretary with whom he had been dealing for help in locating Cecilia.

"Your honor", he said, "I would like to request your assistance. I had a friend here before the Sultan's liberation of the city. I have not been able to find her and if she is still alive, it is possible that the authorities might be able to do so."

"Very well," said the clerk. "I will take it up with my superiors. But I do not hold out hope that either they will have any interest in doing so or that they will be successful. Give me the details."

"Her name is Cecilia Shamash. She is from Florence but she was married to an important official of Emperor Constantine's court, one Philip Shamash, a diplomat. Philip Shamash disappeared from the city some five years ago but he had contacts with the court of the Great Caesar. Cecilia Shamash has lived in the city since that time. It may be that you would have knowledge of her whereabouts or her death or her enslavement. It would be a very great comfort to me to know of her fate."

Eduardo seemed to be asking the impossible; that the authorities would be able to find a single individual in a city which had been ransacked and largely destroyed and the inhabitants of which had either been killed or enslaved. But it has to be said for the organization and determination of the Turkish authorities that they were making serious attempts to record the whereabouts of all survivors. They had started a census of the property in the city and of those who had survived and claimed ownership and they also required details from the buyers of all persons who had been sold into slavery even if they had been taken out of the city. When these inventories and censuses were complete, there were large gaps; many, many people had been killed on the final day of the assault and buried without any attempt or any possibility of recording who they were but, nevertheless, there was a chance that Cecilia would be on the list and the secretary, aware that Eduardo was held in favor by the Sultan himself, said he would make inquiries.

Another month passed and Eduardo was beginning to wonder how he should spend his time. The Tetrabiblion was repaired and habitable and his money safely banked. He had instructed the bankers to send the majority of his fortune to Italy, where he assumed it would be safer. He did not wish to flaunt his wealth, in fact, he had little idea what he was going to do with it, but he was impatient to get on with life and was looking forward to returning to Italy. He did have time to give further thought to the riddle of Tegea which he was still intent on pursuing. But without his friends from the university or anyone else who could help him and without books to pursue some research, he was helpless to make further progress. It was obvious that he would have to be able to get to Attica and search locally.

As it turned out, on his next visit to the office in the Blachernae he was told to wait and that Zaganos would see him personally.

"Ah," said Zaganos, when Eduardo finally entered the inner office. "Ferrucci. You will be glad to hear that his Highness' plans for the visit to Florence have finally matured. However, before I give you the details, we have something for you."

So saying, he motioned to a guard at an inner door, which was opened and Cecilia came into the room. At first, as she looked about her, she seemed nervous and fearful but when she saw Eduardo standing there, she couldn't help herself, she broke into a great smile, ran over to him and threw herself in his arms. She was dressed in the Turkish style, she also had been groomed and perfumed and to Eduardo she looked and felt extraordinarily beautiful in spite of the scar on her cheek. They held each other for a few moments and then Zaganos said,

"That will do. Mrs. Shamash, please leave. When our business is concluded, you may rejoin Ferrucci."

As Cecilia left, Eduardo started to express his thanks but Zaganos waved these aside.

"You will leave for Venice by the end of the week. You will head up the delegation, which will consist of twenty of my men and a contingent of janissaries to act as an escort. You will present gifts and letters from his Highness to the Duke. These letters will indicate that his Highness holds the Duke in very great esteem, that he has long heard of the great contributions made by the Duke to the governance and culture of his city, that he, the Sultan, wishes to establish good relations with the city of Florence, that he wishes to learn about the ancient traditions that are being revived within the city and that he wishes to establish improved trading contacts with the merchants of the city so as to benefit both Florence and the dominions of his Highness. You, Ferrucci, will have the responsibility of achieving these aims and we will give you ample time to do so. We shall expect you back here within six months. Do you think you can achieve this?"

"I believe I can, Excellency," said Eduardo, "and I have one request."

"And what is that?"

"That on the journey over to Italy, we be permitted to stop in Athens. I would much like to see the city that was the cradle and origin of the civilization of the Greeks while I have the opportunity and it would not take us out of our way."

Zaganos looked at him for a moment and said, "I believe that would not be a problem. We can give you further letters to take to the governor of Athens."

Eduardo nodded his head and Zaganos continued:

"And now let us talk about Mrs. Shamash. She is very beautiful, is she not?" Eduardo blushed despite himself and Zaganos continued, "She, herself, will tell you the story of how we found her. It was not very difficult. We have confirmed that her husband died five years ago and she has told us about her relationship with you during her marriage."

Despite himself, at this remark, Eduardo again blushed like a child and Zaganos could not repress a slight smile. He continued:

"I may say that the Great Caesar himself has looked favorably on Mrs. Shamash."

When Eduardo heard this last remark, his heart went cold.

"But," continued Zaganos, quite well aware of the inference of his statement, "she will be permitted to live here safely in Constantinople under the protection of his Highness until you return. Is that quite understood?"

266

Eduardo nodded slowly.

"Good," continued Zaganos. "I have here papers which confirm your appointment, give you safe conduct through his Highness' territories and give you full instructions on the mission as well as the names of all your companions. The letters to the Duke and the gifts will be brought, under guard, by my people when you leave. Mrs. Shamash will be permitted to go with you now. Do you have somewhere for her to stay and the means to support her while you are away? If so, give me the address."

Eduardo confirmed that he did, thanked Zaganos and gave him the address of the Tetrabiblion. He and Cecilia walked out of the office and the palace together hardly daring to breath.

"How did they find you?" asked Eduardo.

"We waited for two weeks in our hiding place beneath the house until we ran out of water and food. They ransacked the house above us. We could hear them. And then my friend went out and found that the whole neighborhood was in ruins and deserted except for Muslim soldiers. He found some more food and also discovered that some areas of the city were almost untouched where we could possibly find accommodation. After another week, we all came out and went to the district of Phanar down by the sea, where we have friends who have let us live with them. And after a month, they started to take a census of everyone who was still living there. It did not take long because so many had died. And then after another week, the Sultan's soldiers suddenly came for me. It was a complete surprise and my friends assumed that it was the end for me, as I did, but I have since been treated very well. I don't understand it. What did you do and what is now going to happen?"

As they walked along Mese Street one more time, Eduardo related his story from the time they had parted in Santa Sophia on the eve of the final assault. He explained how he had been picked to lead the delegation to Florence and that, for better or worse, she was going to be held hostage in Constantinople to ensure that he would carry out the task he had been given and that he would return to the city when his mission had been completed. He comforted her by telling her she would be safe, she would be well looked after, that he had every intention of returning and that when he did they would finally be together. This was little comfort to her; she was sickened by the realization that, after all this time apart, they would only have a few days together before he left again. Hand in hand and immersed silently in these somber thoughts, they reached the Tetrabiblion.

CHAPTER 36

Athens

In less than two weeks, Eduardo left Constantinople and arrived a few days later at the Piraeus, the port of Athens. He had under his command a party of twenty officials and another twenty janissaries as well as the captain of the ship, one Ekrem Zeki, and his sailors. They had brought with them, safely enclosed in a wheeled iron chest with four locks, the gifts for Duke Cosimo and a considerable sum of money to pay for the whole expedition. Eduardo's deputy, a Turk named Manuel Bryseis, an older man and a professional diplomat, long in the service of the Sultan and the Sultan's father, had advised him after they had arrived at the Piraeus that he, Bryseis, should go in advance of the main party, with a small escort, and inform the ruler of Athens of their arrival and the purpose of their visit. Accordingly, Eduardo waited on board their galley for twenty-four hours and then he disembarked with the remainder of his party, leaving some janissaries to guard the ship, and proceeded the few miles to Athens on horses they had hired for the purpose.

They found themselves in a city that was even more desolate than Constantinople had been before the siege. The Athens of the Hellenistic Age had been about six hundred acres in extent, surrounded by powerful walls erected by Themistocles in the 5th century BCE. It was now reduced to a small fraction of its former extent, a town less than five hundred yards square with just thousand homes protected by later Roman walls that hugged the citadel of the Acropolis, the impregnable rock that served as the seat of the ruling Florentine family, the Acciajuoli. This family had inherited the governorship of the city from the Frankish crusaders who had overrun the province of Attica at the time of the crusade two hundred and fifty years earlier. The walls of Themistocles had now completely collapsed; in most places no trace of them could be seen and the outer city was nothing but a patchwork of pastures interspersed with earlier Byzantine churches and numerous classical ruins in various stages of decay, although what remained still gave some indication of the former beauty of the earlier city.

When Constantine, as Despot of the Morea, had invaded Boeotia a decade earlier, he occupied Athens but had been unable to dislodge the Italians from the Acropolis. After only a short time the Turks had counterattacked, reoccupying Boeotia, including Athens, destroying the Hexamilion Wall across the Isthmus of Corinth and advancing far into the Morea. On this occasion, the Acciajuoli felt it prudent to submit to the invaders and the present Duke, Bartolemeo Contarini, survived by acknowledging the overlordship of the Turks and paying them tribute. He was therefore in no position to object to the visit of the Turkish delegation even if he had wished to.

During the short voyage to Athens, Bryseis handed Eduardo two sets of keys to the chest.

"Your honor," he said, "these two keys are for you. They open two of the locks. I shall keep the other two so that we can both open the chest at the same time and there need never be any misunderstanding. I am told that the letters both for Duke Cosimo and for Contarini are in the chest so I suggest we read these now to prepare ourselves."

"I know what they contain," said Eduardo. "I translated them myself at the request of Zaganos Pasha."

The letters to Contarini were much more brusque in tone than the similar letters to Duke Cosimo. And, as befitting a visit to someone who was his vassal, the Sultan did not send any gifts. The Sultan informed Contarini (in case he had not heard) that he, the Sultan, was now the new Emperor of Rome, that the tribute that was the due of an Emperor was double what had been paid hitherto, that he, Contarini, should remain firm in his loyalty and that if he did so his titles and authority would be confirmed. He was also enjoined to give every hospitality and assistance to his emissary, Eduardo Ferrucci, and the remainder of the delegation.

When Eduardo finally reached the top of the Acropolis, he first walked past the Parthenon, which had long since become the principal place of Christian worship in Athens, the Church of St. Mary, and then was received by the Duke himself in the great hall of his palace, the ancient Propylaea. Eduardo, in the splendid attire of the ambassador, with his youthful good looks, his athleticism and his hard edge of leanness and authority, not to say aggression, derived from his many years incarceration, was an impressive figure.

"Your Grace, allow me to introduce my advisors," said Eduardo in Italian, bowing to the Duke, a tall but overweight and florid figure, whom Eduardo immediately supposed regarded the territories of Attica as his personal fief to be milked for his own benefit rather than that of his subjects. He motioned forward Bryseis and the other senior officials in his party. The Duke did the same.

"We can converse in Italian or Greek," continued Eduardo, "and I will translated for the benefit of the rest of my party."

Eduardo was the only person in either his own delegation or in the Duke's court who could speak all three languages: Italian, which was spoken in the court, Greek, which was the official language of Athens and Turkish, which was the language of the delegation. Eduardo made it clear from the beginning that he understood what was being said by everyone in the room and that therefore there was no question of deceptive translations or secret agreements.

"The Great Caesar presents his compliments to the Lord of Athens. He has asked me to give you these letters which outline the terms on which he, the Great Caesar, will confirm the authority and privileges which you enjoy at present over the territories of Attica and as result of which he will give you his beneficent protection."

There was complete silence in the audience chamber while the Duke unfolded and read the letters. All the Duke's advisers knew that whatever the Sultan was offering, it was not likely to be less than what they had enjoyed from his predecessor. The Duke's countenance became more and more inflamed as he continued to read and finally he threw the letters on to the floor in a rage.

"This is impossible," he exclaimed. "How can we pay more than we pay at present? My subjects are completely impoverished. Their land has been ravaged by the recent war. My treasury is empty. This is out of the question."

Eduardo translated for the benefit of Bryseis and his companions and then replied calmly. "This aspect of the matter is not for negotiation. If you are unwilling to meet the generous terms of the Great Caesar then he will have no difficulty in finding someone who will. I shall remain for week at the end of which I shall expect your answer. And as an earnest of your loyalty to the Great Caesar, he will require a payment on account of five thousand gold ducats which you will provide us on our departure. In the meantime, while we wait for your response, I shall wish to visit the town and the surrounding country."

The Duke, flouting diplomatic convention in his fury, had already turned to leave but he paused on hearing this last, taking it to mean, as Eduardo intended, that he would be inspecting the city's defenses. Although he had not had specific instructions to do this, it seemed to Eduardo at the time that this would be a good cover for his search for the Grove of Hekademos, which was the real reason for his visit.

"What can you tell me of the Grove of Hekademos, for instance?" he asked the Duke in a casual tone.

The Duke was surprised by the question; he could not immediately think of any possible tactical importance for the Grove. Eduardo was equally surprised by the immediacy of the answer.

"The Grove of Hekademos is about one mile from the outer walls of the city towards the northwest."

Eduardo could hardly conceal his excitement.

"I would like a guide to take a small party of us there tomorrow," he said.

"Very well," said the Duke forcing himself to be accommodating. "That can be easily arranged. And now you will want to see your quarters and to rest."

At that, the two bowed to each other and each left the room.

The next day, Eduardo instructed most of the delegation to go out over the old city and spend the day examining the state of its defenses. He himself, accompanied by four of his bodyguards and two others from the delegation and with a Greek guide rode out to the Grove of Hekademos. They went across the mostly deserted fields of the ancient outer city with the guide enthusiastically pointing out the name, origin and history of every ruined building that they passed.

"Here is where the ancient walls stood," said the guide, although all that could be seen was a low mound which stretched away in both directions through the fields.

"And this was the celebrated Dipylon Gate," he said as they made their way round an arch which had long since collapsed. Beyond the arch there was a long straight track on each side of which appeared to be a cemetery with the remains of monuments and mausoleums.

"Yes, indeed," explained the guide in answer to a question from Eduardo, "this was the People's Grave where, despite its name, many of the most famous persons in the history of Greece were buried. There for instance is the grave of Pericles himself, and, there, those of Zeno and Chrysippus."

On another occasion perhaps, Eduardo might have shown some interest in these revelations but he rode on in silence and impatience. Finally after a short time, not more than a mile as the Duke had said, they reached what the guide said was the Grove, a lightly wooded area with a stream running through it and evidence of several ancient structures lying on the ground in their decay.

The party dismounted and Eduardo asked the guide, "Please explain in detail the history of this area."

"It was one of the three gymnasia of the ancient city, an area where citizens would come and exercise or just rest and relax by the stream or walk around amongst the trees. It was said to be founded by one Hekademos who saved the city in the time of Theseus by telling the invading Spartans the whereabouts of Helen whom Theseus had abducted from her home in Sparta."

"Theseus, you say?" asked Eduardo.

"Yes," replied the guide. "Theseus, the founder of the city. In return, the Spartans spared the city. At one time as well as the gymnasium, there was a temple to honor Athena, a shrine to Castor and Pollux, the brothers of Helen, and other shrines or altars to Hermes, Heracles and Hephaestus. It is said that this is where Plato held what became known as his Academy. He apparently owned land nearby and he would come here with his students and sit among the trees and teach them."

Eduardo told the rest of his party to rest by the stream and wait for him. He left with the guide and walked back and forth across the grove through and among the traces of ruined structures.

"Tell me more," he said.

"Races were run from here to the city, some of them at night. They started from the Promemeikos altar, which was dedicated to Prometheus, here in the center of the grove. There were other altars and shrines here also."

They walked around what he was told were the remains of the temple of Athena but there were even fewer stones remaining than there had been in Tegea and none of which he could discern the slightest indication of carving or inscriptions. And yet he was certain that somewhere here, somewhere beneath the ground was what he was seeking.

"And what else?" he asked. "Where was the Promemeikos?"

"Over here."

They walked over to an undistinguished slab of gray and weathered stone largely covered by lichen and grass. Eduardo examined it closely but could not find a single mark or sign that might have helped him.

"Are there any other remaining structures of any kind from that era?"

"It is believed," said the guide, "that there was an altar to Eros near the entrance to the grove by the roadway. Let me show you."

They walked back to the road and found another smaller slab of stone also covered by the grass and undergrowth. There was nothing to indicate that it was dedicated to love or anything else.

"This may have been the altar," said the guide. "What are you looking for?"

Eduardo truthfully said that he did not know but nevertheless, although he was downcast, he had reason to be pleased with himself. He had successfully solved the riddle, found the Grove and found resonances both with Eros and with Athena. He also had the resources of the Sultan and a large body of men at his disposal and he had been granted time to make use of them. He did not believe he even needed the permission of Duke Contarini to deploy them in the Grove, since the latter's authority only ran as far as the walls of the city itself. He decided that, however bizarre it might seem, he would request the assistance of local hired men, slaves or otherwise and he would, over the following week, dig up the whole area. He would dig around the two altars that had been identified, around the whole base of the temple of Athena and if necessary elsewhere in the Grove.

The Duke, irascible by nature, was furious at the new demands of the Sultan and by the unexpected burden on his meager resources and the potential threat of forty well-armed foreigners within his home or close by. He was also not a little nervous from his ignorance of the true reason for the visit of this large and obviously high-level delegation, and at first he refused to accommodate Eduardo in his request for able-bodied workmen or slaves but Eduardo stood his ground and the Duke had no choice. By noon on the following day, the party was ready. Eduardo had dismissed all his companions except ten of the janissaries, whom he took with him to guard the twenty-five or so workmen he had enlisted. He did not permit any representative of the Duke to accompany him or any of his own staff to whom he explained that he was engaged in a task for which he had direct orders from the Sultan.

When they arrived at the Grove, he divided the workmen among the different ruins on the site and they started to dig. By the end of the afternoon, they had dug trenches along one side of the temple foundation, almost completely around the Promemeithion and around what was thought to be the altar of

Eros and had found nothing. The following day, despite Eduardo's growing misgivings, which he kept to himself, they continued. As dusk was falling on this second day, there was a call from the party at the altar of Eros; at a depth of four feet at the back of the altar, they had struck metal and as they continued down they unearthed what was revealed as a large box measuring four by two by two feet. It was now getting dark and Eduardo decided that there was nothing further he could do that night; they were in any event quite unable to move the box, let alone lift it. He left four of the janissaries on guard and told them that he would send others to relieve them throughout the night, which he did.

The following day he set out again with the workmen and their guards and this time with a strong tripod, block, tackle and rope. They slowly dug under the box and inserted the ropes and with the help of several of the horses on which they had ridden to the Grove, they were able to lift and finally extract it. A second similar operation was required to place the box on the heavy four-wheeled cart they had brought for the purpose. After this operation was completed, they returned immediately towards Athens but bypassed the inner city and the Acropolis, proceeding directly on to the Piraeus and the ship that had brought them. Eduardo supervised the loading of the box, which required the requisitioning of heavy planks and the construction of a wide gangway so that the cart could be led onto the boat which was then secured to the deck.

Although there was another three days before the deadline in the Sultan's ultimatum for the acceptance of his terms would expire, Eduardo on his return to the palace requested a further audience with the Duke. The latter who was happy enough to get rid of the burden of his guests as soon as he could, informed Eduardo that he accepted the Sultan's terms and that the additional tribute that was required of him would be handed over the following day. Eduardo insisted, to avoid the possibility that his party would be attacked on the short journey between Athens and the Piraeus, that this should take place on board his ship. Accordingly, the next morning in a brief ceremony, in exchange for the agreed tribute, Eduardo presented the Duke with the letters under the Sultan's seal confirming the Accaijiulo as the overlords of Attica. Immediately thereafter Eduardo gave orders to weigh anchor and depart.

Eduardo and Bryseis placed the bags of gold coins into the money chest and then between them they locked it again. They looked at each other and each broke out into a broad grin. Their first diplomatic mission had been a success.

"Now," said Bryseis, "you must tell me about the other chest. I received no instructions about that. What is in it?"

Eduardo continued to stare at Bryseis.

"I don't know what is in it," he answered. "I received permission from Zaganos to stop in Athens and I asked for permission because I have known of the possible existence of this box for many years. I wanted the opportunity to search for it. I believe it may contain objects or documents important to Greek history and which may throw light on subsequent Italian history. What is important now is that we find a way to open the box without damaging what may be inside. Let us now examine it and see what is to be done."

The box was still resting in the cart which had been lashed to the deck. It was extremely heavy and apparently very robust, probably as they had guessed if not entirely of lead at least with a lead lining. There appeared to be no lid or other natural opening and while it was still encrusted with dirt, there was no question that it was intact. Captain Zeki who had joined them summoned two of his crew who scraped away the dirt from the exterior, and they could then see on the top of the box the single word, *Aristokles*.

"This must be the name of the owner," said Eduardo for the benefit of the others. "As far as I know it has no other meaning."

"You see," pointed out Zeki, "there is a raised line round the center." And he ran his finger along an almost invisible line which ran round all four sides of the box. "The top has been sealed with hot lead. It will be very difficult to remove."

"I believe the contents may be fragile," said Eduardo. "So we have to exercise the utmost care. Do you have any suggestions?"

"It is possible that a blacksmith could apply a hot instrument which would slowly melt the lead but it would be a long and difficult job if the contents are to be absolutely safe. And what if I may ask do you expect to find when you do open it."

Again Eduardo had to explain that he did not know but he believed that it contained ancient documents or relics – probably of little material value but of historical importance.

"I have to tell you," said Zeki , "that my men have already formed the opinion that the box contains a treasure which they, as participants in the discovery, are entitled to share in. You will not be surprised at that in view of the trouble you have taken to find and safeguard it. I think it important that we get open as soon as possible so that their expectations are not raised to a level that they become uncontrollable."

"Very well," said Eduardo, "we will not wait until we get to Venice. You may put into the first port we get to where you think we could find a blacksmith. And in the meantime you should put about to the crew the strong likelihood that the box contains only documents and nothing of value. In any event, I will ensure that your men and everyone else are properly rewarded for their trouble."

This suggestion suited Eduardo since he did not wish to open the box in Venice, where even his status as the emissary of the Sultan would not protect him if the Doge should decide that the box was rightfully his. However outrageous such an action might be and whatever might be the diplomatic consequences, the Doge had the temperament and certainly the power easily to confiscate from visitors to the city anything that might add to his own prestige and wealth. Eduardo and Zeki therefore decided that they would put into the ancient Roman town of Split on the Adriatic coast.

There, on the advice of the harbor-master and encouraged by an advance from Eduardo's own pocket, the best smith in the city was persuaded to examine the box, which was still on board, secured and guarded on its cart. This latter proclaimed himself able to cut through the seal but this procedure would have to be done in his shop since only his furnace was hot enough to heat an iron knife to a temperature that would melt the lead. And so, after a further delay while the box was transported to his shop, the smith, by applying the red-hot iron knife gently to the seal and thus softening the lead, did indeed manage to cut a groove slowly round the box. He repeated the application three times to ensure that he did not pierce the box and damage the contents and each time he was able to cut the groove deeper and deeper. Finally, after the fourth round he had cut right through the seal and the top of the box could be removed, although even this was still too heavy to do by hand. In any event Eduardo, now consumed by excitement, decided that he would perform this next operation on board the ship and away from curious eyes.

And so, again using block and tackle and levering the ends of the lid up sufficiently so as to insert grappling irons, they lifted up the lid. Eduardo had dismissed the whole of his party except Bryseis, whom he wanted present as a witness, and the two of them watched as the lid was lifted and they peered in to find another box, this time of iron, which fitted neatly into the first. This one also had the word *Aristokles* on the top and, in this case, the lid was secured by hinges and bolts. This inner box was much lighter and Eduardo was able to have it removed to his cabin where the hinges of the lid were knocked out and, when the two of them were alone, he opened the inner box. Inside were ten small cylindrical packages sewn up in protective sheepskin. Carefully, he lifted one up and it was very light; his immediate thought was that it was a manuscript or possibly even one more in his trail of riddles although, on reflection, he realized it was much more likely the former; it just did not seem credible that anyone would go to such trouble to hide a simple riddle. As the two of them, somewhat disappointed, gazed at the rolls, nestling in the iron box, Eduardo was uncertain what his next step should be. He knew enough about manuscripts to understand that, if they were on parchment or papyrus, they were durable but might not survive a sudden exposure to the air after what might have been a thousand years or more in their airtight covering.

Exercising the most extraordinary restraint, which perhaps no one other than a true lover of books could have done, he decided to contain himself and not cut open any of the rolls until he was able to take the advice of some expert in the handling of ancient manuscripts and this he knew would have to wait at least until they got to Florence when he would have time to do this at his leisure and where there might be someone he could consult. If he attempted to do this in Venice or another city on his journey to Florence, the Doge or any other ruler would be sure to get wind of the discovery and might confiscate the packages.

For now his immediate thought was to assuage the curiosity of all the remainder of his party who, over the last week, had become certain that the box contained treasure which they, as participants in the discovery, would be entitled to a share of and Eduardo knew that, if they were not immediately persuaded that this was not the case, they would believe that he was cheating them and would very quickly make an end of him. And so, within a few minutes of the time he had taken the box into his cabin, he and Bryseis carried it out again, placed it on the deck and invited everyone on board, including the janissaries, to inspect it and the rolls inside. He made a short speech to the assembled company and crew reflecting his disappointment and that of everyone else. He told them he assumed that these rolls were letters or manuscripts that had little or no value and that, in any event, in view of their great age, he did not dare open them until they reached Florence and could get expert advice. If there were value to them, he would still share this in the time-honored manner and in the meantime, he would make a distribution on account out of his own pocket, to every man his due, in recognition of the extra work they had put in and the disappointment they had suffered. And now, as he said, they must make haste and continue their journey. The sighs of the company were audible, the disappointment was palpable but mostly they believed Eduardo, they trusted him and in any event, they knew that he had had no time to change the contents of the box even if he wished to. When later he distributed his small bonuses, they grunted their thanks and this reflected a genuine appreciation of his generosity. They then consigned the cart and its leaden burden to the Adriatic and continued on their way to Venice. The whole matter of possible treasure was forgotten within a week, which was as Eduardo had hoped.

CHAPTER 37

Venice

The Lagoon, the port of Venice, was the biggest and the busiest harbor in the world. As they sailed in from the Adriatic, Eduardo, Bryseis and the captain, Zeki, for the last two of whom it was their first visit, were standing together on deck with their eyes fixed on the distant view of the city. Slowly, as they gazed around, they began to take in the full extent of the Lagoon. The three men looked at each other in frank amazement. Even Eduardo, who had sailed out of Venice nearly fifteen years earlier, had forgotten or perhaps had never fully appreciated the extraordinary scene. It was said that the merchants of Venice could muster more than three thousand vessels and, at first glance, it seemed that most of these were there at anchor or slowly moving about the Lagoon. The actual number was far fewer but, nevertheless, probably reached several hundred, a figure augmented by the dozens of smaller craft loading or offloading passengers and freight. There were double deck transport ships, galleys of all sizes, some with sails, and older cogs and hulks for carrying heavy goods. Not surprisingly, many of the vessels were the distinctive Venetian galleys themselves, manned by freemen rather than slaves, and these were particularly renowned for their speed and maneuverability. When necessary the Venetian galleys could also be requisitioned for service in war and thus they all carried a permanent stock of armor and munitions for emergency use.

Threading their way slowly through the maze of vessels, Zeki found a suitable place to anchor and, as soon as they could, Eduardo and Bryseis, with a small escort, made their way to land and to the office of the harbor-master, the *direttore di porto*. This, as one might imagine, was overwhelmed by a mass of sailors and officials all seeking to promote their own affairs and Eduardo's imposing appearance in the dress of an ambassador and his escort availed him not at all; he had to wait his turn. When this came, Eduardo presented his credentials and explained his business to the impatient official: that he was the emissary of the Sultan himself, that he sought safe conduct through Venice and Venetian territory for himself and his party on the way to their final destination, which was Florence, and that the ship on which they had come would depart immediately after they had disembarked. He was asked to wait while the official consulted with his superiors and finally was told to return the same time the following day when he would be given an answer. Eduardo asked if his crew and other members of the party could, in the meantime, disembark and see the city. After further consultations, he was told, and given letters to the effect, that eight of his party including himself could disembark at any one time but all of them must remain on board at night.

They sent the boat on which they had come back to the ship with instructions to Zeki to allow six more men to land and be back at the ship by nightfall. Eduardo and Bryseis, in the meantime, set off for the Turkish agent in the city to introduce themselves, to obtain any recent instructions that he might have received from the Sultan and to get as much information on Venice and their onward journey as he could give. They crossed St. Marks Square, marveling at the ancient cathedral upon which had been placed the great bronze horses that had brought from Constantinople as booty after the crusaders had sacked the city during the infamous crusade and made their way towards the Rialto across the canals and over the bridges. The Turkish agent had no further instructions but he did have a mass of letters for Eduardo, the crew and the remainder of the party, which had arrived in the last few days by a ship that had overtaken them while they were in Athens. Eduardo and Bryseis pulled out those that were their own and said they would send for the rest on the following day. They also asked the Agent to arrange to hire horses for the whole party on the mainland for later that week, by which time they assumed that they would be permitted to leave.

As they were crossing St. Marks Square again and walking towards the quayside where their boat was waiting, Eduardo noticed three women walking towards them. One of them must have been a maid; she was alone and slightly behind the other two, who were talking animatedly to each other. Both of them were dressed extravagantly, one was dark and the other much fairer with golden brown hair and a long white gown with gold embroidered trim. Eduardo was so taken by the beauty of the latter that he stopped and stared as the two passed him by and was rewarded with a turn of the head and, what he fancied, was an acknowledgment, as their eyes locked for just a second. He could not help himself, he turned and watched them as they strolled slowly away over the square in the direction from which he had just come. Bryseis had also stopped a few yards further on and was watching Eduardo with an amused smile.

"Ah," he said. "I can see you are glad to be back amongst your countrymen."

Eduardo grinned, "Yes," he said. "There are some things which the Italians are particularly good at. And there, you can see, are a few of them."

Back in the ship, in the quiet of his cabin, he took out his few letters, of which the only one that he was interested in was the one from Cecilia, which turned out to enclose another, which he recognized, from the distinctive yet fragile handwriting, as being from Juliette. Both letters contained similar sentiments, hovering between passion and restraint as though they both knew what the other sister was saying (although Juliette's letter was still sealed) and wanted to respect the other's right to the man they both loved. Eduardo's reaction was again guilt and confusion; he once more found it difficult to distinguish between the two women whom he possibly loved as one. But the letter from Juliette was the more immediate and disturbing:

"We have thought you were dead and it is the greatest of good news to hear otherwise. We heard nothing from my sister but your letter and your description of the battle with the infidels and your part in it and how you were saved and how now you are the ambassador of the Sultan is the most remarkable thing I have ever read. I have shown it to everyone. They all wonder at the miracle of your deliverance and how God has saved you for what must be further great deeds and we await your arrival in the most urgent expectation. It is so long since we have seen each other and I have thought of you continuously over the years. You, I am sure, have not thought of me but that is the lot of women. But now I am tired and sad and have been sick but I place my faith and soul in the hands of God who will, I know, allow me to see you again. This letter will be short since I have difficulty in writing and I must dispatch it quickly so that it arrives before you leave. In any event, I have a beautiful surprise for you so please hurry."

Eduardo read and reread the letter several times attempting to extract from it the hidden significance of some of Juliette's remarks. How sick was she? The fact that she had difficulty writing suggested that she was very sick. Why was there a continual reference to "we"? What was the surprise? After a time, he took up his pen and wrote a reply, which he determined to send to her in the morning and which would probably reach Ferrara before he did. He told her that he had arrived in Venice and was awaiting permission to continue his journey, that he was very concerned about her and her health, that he wished her a speedy recovery and that he hoped to see her very shortly. But when he reread it, he recognized a certain hollowness; the fact was that if it had not been for his fresh memory of Cecilia, he would not have been able to visualize Juliette at all, let alone feel the emotions which, out of a certain sense of obligation, he was expressing and when he slept he dreamed not of Cecilia nor of Juliette but of a certain young woman with golden brown hair, fine features and a white gown.

He was wakened the next morning earlier than he was accustomed to by a violent knocking on the door of his cabin and a voice which cried:

"Captain says, please would you come on deck immediately!"

He seized a robe and ran up to the deck where Zeki and Bryseis were already standing. They were watching a large Venetian galley, which in the early morning light had sailed up to their anchorage and, at that moment, was itself dropping anchor about one hundred and fifty feet away on their starboard side. There was a shout from the lookout, the three men turned and another similar galley was coming to the same position on the port side.

"Sound the alarm," ordered Eduardo. "If they had wanted to attack us they would already have done so and would not be dropping anchor, but we should be prepared."

Zeki gave the order, a bell was struck and within a remarkably short time the janissaries and crew, fully armed, had taken their defensive stations. But it was obvious that, if it came to it, although the natural advantage always lay with the defenders, they would be far outnumbered; both the Venetian ships were patently bristling with soldiers. But nothing happened immediately and, after a time, a boat put out from one of the Venetian ships carrying what looked like senior officers and when they arrived at Zeki's ship, they requested permission to board. Eduardo saw no choice but to agree, even though he and his colleagues were in some embarrassment since they had not had time to dress.

"Captain Edmundo Silvestri at your service," said the leading Venetian when his whole party had boarded.

Eduardo bowed, "And I am Eduardo Ferrucci, emissary of the Great Caesar, Sultan Mehmet II. You have us at a disadvantage with so early a visit. What is the nature of your business?"

"I am sent by the government of Venice to inquire as to your purpose in the city," said Silvestri briefly and to the point.

No doubt that was the excuse but from the glances that Silvestri and his companions were making around the ship and at the janissaries who were lined up on the deck, it was obvious that the real reason for their visit was to assess the strength of the ship's complement and the nature of its defenses. Eduardo smiled to himself. It was a simple trick and one which, in the circumstances, he supposed was fair.

"As I explained yesterday in the office of the *direttore*, our purpose is simply and solely to obtain safe conduct through the territory of the Veneto on our journey to Florence, which is our destination. Do we have that permission?"

"You will have to obtain the papers for any safe conduct from that office, as you were informed yesterday. My government, however, takes seriously the presence of foreign soldiers in the city and we shall ask you to disarm your escort if you are to remain here or travel through Venice or its territories."

"We do not intend to remain in the city. We do not intend to go through the city. As soon as permission is granted, we shall ferry our party to the shore and leave. We are already arranging for horses. Obviously, an escort cannot fulfill its purpose without the means to defend itself. We are on a diplomatic mission and expect to be recognized as such. If you wish to provide a further escort while we remain in the Veneto, we will have no objection. We have agreed to the request that, while we wait for the safe conduct, no more than eight of us will visit the city at any one time. Hopefully if we get permission today, we shall leave today and that will be the last you will see of us, at least until we return," he concluded with a smile.

Silvestri bowed in his turn. "I shall take your answer back to my superiors. And you should present yourself today, as arranged, at the office of the *direttore*. In the meantime my ships will remain in their present position and you will kindly obtain my permission before your ship is moved."

Eduardo bowed also and Silvestri turned, climbed down into the boat in which he had come and he and his party crossed the short distance to their own ship.

Eduardo translated the exchanges to Bryseis and Zeki and the three of them agreed that the visit and the requests of Silvestri were not only reasonable but normal in the circumstances, although the presence of the two military galleys could not be ignored. They would have to mount a continuous guard, which would put an extra burden on the soldiers and crew who had been expecting some time for rest and relaxation in the city. After the arrangements had been made and they had finally dressed and breakfasted, Eduardo and Bryseis, with six other members of the party who were given shore leave, set off again for the office of the *direttore*. On this occasion, they were received immediately but were told that their safe-conduct had not yet been granted and that an appointment had been made for them to discuss their request with officials in the government. They should present themselves, in two days time, at the palace of the Doge in St. Marks Square and ask for Messer Francesco Dome-nichino, who would be their contact and guide. In the meantime, the restrictions regarding the number of their people who were allowed ashore still applied and it was pointed out, as they knew perfectly well, that these restrictions would and could be enforced by sanctions, including the seizure of their vessel, if they were not adhered to.

Eduardo and Bryseis were furious at the delay but had no alternative but to comply. Eduardo was granted permission to arrange for provisions for the ship but apart from that they had little to do but wait. Bryseis decided to return to the ship but Eduardo remained on shore with the excuse that he wished to take the opportunity to look at the city. Of course, the first thing he did was to go to St. Marks Square in the unlikely and romantic hope of seeing the woman in the white dress. He waited until the same hour as on the previous day and, sure enough, she and the maid appeared on cue, walking slowly in the same direction as they had the day before. Eduardo got up from where he had been waiting and walked towards her. As she approached, she again looked him straight in the eye and gave him a wide and inviting smile. He stopped, took off his hat, bowed low.

"Signorina," he said, "my name is Eduardo Ferrucci. Please excuse me. I am a stranger to Venice. I am not familiar with the customs and habits of the city. I have come here only two days ago from Constantinople but I have already been fortunate enough to experience that passion that only the beauty of the women of Venice could excite so quickly – the passion of love. Since I saw you yesterday, I have been thinking of nothing but when I should see you again and I thank God that he has taken pity on me and allowed my prayers to be fulfilled so quickly. Will you permit me to walk with you a short distance?"

She nodded her head and then said, in a soft and sensuous voice, which he judged to have the intonation of a Neapolitan,

"I am Vittoria Orsini. I am a widow. Please walk with me and tell me your story. You must have escaped that frightful battle with the infidel that everyone in Venice has heard about. But you don't look like someone who has fled from defeat. You seem much too grandly dressed for a refugee. Tell me about it."

Eduardo turned to her and bowed again at the compliment. He looked again into the brown eyes with long lashes and at the delicate nose, the slightly freckled forehead framed with golden brown hair and admiring the immediacy and unexpected frankness of her speech, he fell deeply in love.

"Let me first say, Signora, that you seem much too young to have already suffered the pain of widowhood and that this sad state cannot, in the least, have marred your beauty, which overwhelms me to the point of suffocation."

She laughed good-naturedly, "Messer Ferrucci, I can see that you have not lost the Italian manner during your stay in the Orient. But go on, tell me about yourself. How is it that you find yourself in Venice?"

"No, madam, I am not a refugee. Do not be alarmed but I am, in point of fact, the ambassador of the Sultan of the Turks himself. I and my retinue are awaiting permission and safe conduct through Venice for our embassy to Florence."

Like everyone who is in love, Eduardo wanted to put himself to his beloved in his best light although not only was what he had said the simple truth it was, actually, in the context of their meeting, quite unnecessary. Vittoria already found him very attractive, particularly his eyes, which were gentle and, she thought, displayed traces of intense suffering, a suffering that endeared him to her. The revelation that he was the Sultan's ambassador did, however, stop her in her tracks and she also turned, facing him.

"Indeed sir," she said, "you too seem much too young to be an ambassador. If what you say is true, you must have exceptional qualities. Pray proceed. I still have to hear your story."

They walked slowly round the square and then walked round again and Eduardo told Vittoria his story or part of it; how, as a young man, he had been forced to go to Constantinople and spy on the Greeks, how eventually he had been discovered and sent to prison, how he had fought in the siege and then been saved because he spoke Turkish and how because of his acquaintance with Florence, the Sultan, who had an admiration for the Medicis and their works, had chosen him to lead an embassy to that city. He did not tell her of his relationships with Juliette or Cecilia – he thought that would be boorish.

She, for her part, told him that she had been married when she was seventeen to Giannantonio Orsini of Taranto, a man who was forty years older than her, a great statesman, a soldier and ally of the King of Naples but a man whom she had never met before her marriage and whom she had never loved. They had had no children and he had no other heirs and thus, when he had died only a few months before, all his property had reverted to the King of Naples and she had decided to come home to Venice, where she now lived with her parents. She did not feel it necessary to observe the normal rituals of mourning since no one in the city knew of her husband or cared. She had only been back in the city for three months and for the time being, with her newfound freedom, was enjoying herself immensely.

They agreed to meet at the same time the following day and Eduardo, his heart and mind in turmoil, returned to the quayside to find the boat, which was waiting for him. On the following day, he returned, at the same time and to the same place, and she was there waiting and they walked and talked for two hours and admired each other. He told her about his book-exporting business, about how and why he had been forced to learn Greek and Turkish and how this had resulted in his life being saved. He told her about his relations with Juliette and Cecilia which, surprisingly to him, fazed her not at all. After all how would such an attractive man not have had several mistresses during his youth and why should he not? He did not tell her of the vast fortune he had inherited; he was in love but he had retained sufficient good sense to realize that there were limits to such disclosures at such a time.

She told him of her life as the chatelaine of Taranto, which had been mostly unutterably dull since being so much younger than her husband, she had hardly ever been taken into his confidence and all his advisers regarded her with disdain. But from her experience as the leading lady in her husband's court, she had acquired an ease and confidence in conversation and an experience in worldly matters, which, for him, added to her attraction. She did not have an intense interest in books but was widely read, was highly intelligent as well as practical and Eduardo admired her for that. She did not tell him that although her husband had lost his property, he had left her a fortune in jewels and cash which she had brought home with her to Venice. Despite the fact that she did not perceive Eduardo as being excessively wealthy, she thought that he was just the sort of man for her, a man of the world, good-looking, intelligent, well-traveled, an international diplomat and, most important of all, not a native of Venice, her home town, the great families of which despite their acceptance of her widowed state but because of it, would not entertain the possibility of entering into a marital alliance with her.

Both of them were already beginning to think of the future. After a couple of hours Vittoria said, for no particular reason except that she thought it might appear unseemly for her to stay longer, that she had to go, but she invited Eduardo to see her home and meet her parents on the following day. He agreed, in fact said he would be delighted to do so, but that he had his meeting at the palace of the Doge and he would only be able to come when that was over.

The following day, Eduardo and Bryseis in their full formal dress, presented themselves at the palace and were met by Messer Francesco Domenichino as arranged. He took them through the corridors of the palace where they caught glimpses of the great state rooms in which the organs of the Venetian democracy functioned, including the vast Sala del Maggior Consiglio, the meeting place for the city legislature. Domenichino finally led them into another chamber where they were asked to wait. This he told them was the Chamber of the Council of Ten, the body to which was delegated the executive power to run the city, and which had practical control over all matters pertaining to both peace and war. After a few minutes, four men, very grandly dressed, entered the room together with some assistants and secretaries and sat opposite the two visitors, who had risen out of respect.

"My lords Bembo, Giustinian, Morosini and Foscari," announced an usher, pausing after each name to allow that individual to bow his head to which the visitors bowed in return. These individuals were in point of fact the most powerful men in Venice although Eduardo was not to know this.

"I am Eduardo Ferrucci," said Eduardo. "I am the emissary of the Great Caesar, Emperor of the Romans, Sultan Mehmet II of Constantinople and the Turkish dominions. This is my colleague Manuel Bryseis. With your lordships' permission, for his benefit and as we proceed, I will translate everything that is said. We seek permission and safe conduct to travel through the Veneto to Florence, which is our destination. We have an escort but we have no objection to a further escort also being provided, during our journey through Venetian territory, if your lordships should think it appropriate."

Bembo spoke first. He seemed to be the principal spokesman for the group.

"We welcome the embassy of his lordship, the Sultan, to Venice."

Eduardo bowed in acknowledgement and quietly translated to Bryseis.

"We trust your stay has hitherto been pleasant and you have not been inconvenienced by the small precautions we have taken to ensure the safety of the city."

Eduardo bowed again.

"Of course we are aware of the great events that have occurred in Constantinople and the triumph of his lordship, the Sultan, over the Greeks. As you would expect, we view these events with great seriousness and it is our hope that we can, today, and perhaps over the next few days, discuss with you what you know of his lordship's future intentions."

In reply, Eduardo said, "Your lordships will understand, as I have just explained, that my embassy is to Florence and not to Venice. I have no instructions and indeed no knowledge in regard to his lordship's 'intentions'," here he emphasized the word which Bembo had already used. "I can tell you however that our embassy to Florence is of a purely cultural nature and I have no authority to discuss political matters. There is very little for me to add to that. I cannot, of course, reveal what I have been instructed to say the government of Florence and I do not think anything will be served by protracted discussions with your lord-ships."

It was then Justinian's turn. "Can we ask how you, who are, we imagine, a Florentine, came to be appointed ambassador for his lordship, the Sultan?"

"Your lordships will excuse me. It is a very long story. Suf-fice it to say, I have lived in Constantinople for nearly fifteen years. I speak Greek and Turkish. I fought through the whole siege together with the great Giustiniani of Genoa, who was the bulwark of the defense and when the city fell, I came to the at-tention of the Sultan in view of the fact that, to the last, I had been fighting alongside the Emperor himself, in the final despe-rate effort that he personally made to repel the enemy."

"You saw the Emperor killed," said one of the others.

"I did. I was by his side," said Eduardo.

The diplomatic reserve fell apart as the four great lords of Venice fired questions at Eduardo in their curiosity, and indeed excitement, to hear the details of the siege in which the most impregnable city in the world had fallen to the Turkish on-slaught.

Towards the end of this barrage of questions, one of the se-cretaries approached Bembo and whispered at length into his ear.

"Tell me, Ambassador Ferrucci," asked Bembo. "Are you related in any way to the Ferruccis of Ferrara?"

"Yes, indeed, my lord. My father was Sylvestro Ferrucci of that family. He, my mother and the remainder of my immediate family died in the great plague of 1438. I left the city and jour-neyed to Florence and avoided infection."

There was some whispered discussion amongst the four lords which Eduardo could not hear.

"You should know, Ferrucci, that there is a possibility that you may be the last surviving member of the Ferrucci family. The last Count, who may have been your uncle, died a few months ago. His children also died in the same outbreak of pla-gue as your parents. You should stop in Ferrara on your way to Florence and get further information. You may have inherited the title of Count and the fortune of your uncle."

Eduardo had the presence of mind to bow again in acknowledgement of this suggestion.

"And now I ask you again," said Bembo, "you are an Italian, I cannot imagine that your loyalties do not ultimately belong to your countrymen in Ferrara and the other nations of Italy. You fought against the Sultan. We have not asked you why you have changed sides. We imagine that the Sultan has coerced you in some way. So is there nothing you can tell us of the ambitions of his Lordship, the Sultan, towards the West, towards Europe, towards Italy?"

"My lords," said Eduardo, "I am not a fool. I know as well as anyone the dangers represented by the actions and ambitions of his lordship, the Sultan. But I have no knowledge of his intentions. I believe I was chosen to lead this delegation because I am from Florence and know the city well, because I speak the three languages and, indeed, because the Sultan has a hold over me by which he can ensure that I fulfill my mission. He holds hostages who are dear to me. It may very well be that he will in the immediate future send a further mission, political or cultural, to Venice itself but I have no knowledge of this. But I will tell you that you should not underestimate the Sultan. He is young, vigorous, ambitious, determined and capable. I would think it very likely that he will make further moves against the West. That is all I can tell you. As for myself, I request again for permission for my party to make an immediate departure from Venice to Florence."

The four lords of the Council of Ten looked at each other and, by some unspoken sign, acquiesced in Eduardo's request.

"You have our permission," said Bembo. "You have spoken frankly and I thank you. If you wait here, the safe-conduct will be given to you immediately. We wish you well and Godspeed with your journey."

They rose and left the Chamber and Eduardo and Bryseis, after they had obtained their safe-conduct, left the palace in the company of Domenichino. Outside, Bryseis turned towards the quayside where their boat was waiting. Eduardo, however, stopped him and told him that he did not intend to return to the ship at once but would do so later the same evening. Bryseis was astonished:

"But sir, our safe-conduct gives us permission to leave at once. We can be on our way this afternoon and stay the first night on shore."

"I know that," said Eduardo, "but I have other business that I must attend to. In fact, we may not be able to leave until the day after tomorrow."

"Surely that is out of the question. We have already been here four days, our arrival in Florence, which is expected, will be seriously delayed, Zeki and the ship are also waiting to leave and the escort is becoming restless confined on board. We should leave at once."

"That is out of the question," blustered Eduardo. "We will leave when I say we should leave. Return to the ship and do as I instruct."

So saying, he walked off across the Piazza in the direction of the Rialto towards Vittoria's house. Bryseis in the meantime returned to the ship, deeply disturbed, and had a long talk with Captain Zeki.

The main entrance to the Querini Palace was, as Vittoria had said, on the Calle Cavalli on the southern side of the Canal Grande onto which the palace fronted. Eduardo, even with his ambassadorial status, his newfound confidence and his imposing attire felt some trepidation as he contemplated the vast, silent and from the narrow alley from which he approached, the dark and forbidding aspect of the palace. The ground floor walls of the palace on the alley had no windows, only a large iron double door, at least twelve feet high, with a lion's head knocker. This, he could hardly lift and when he did and let it fall, it resounded with the ponderous echo of a deep and heavy bell. After some little time, a grille in the door was opened, he announced himself and he was let into the palace courtyard through a wicket gate in the great door. This courtyard seemed just as quiet and lifeless as the exterior of the building and until Vittoria ran out of a side door and greeted him with an amused curtsey and her wide smile, he was starting to imagine himself back in the Blachernae dungeons.

The Querini Palace was indeed just that, beyond anything Eduardo had previously experienced. He was overwhelmed by the grandeur of the interior although as they walked together, Vittoria with her arm in his, up the main staircase and through the state rooms, he tried not to show it. Vittoria, of course, was naturally oblivious to it; she was just at home.

Eduardo had never mixed in the highest levels of Italian society. His own family house in Ferrara was quite modest, as were those of his other relatives and the palaces he had visited in Florence in his capacity as a bookseller, including that of the Gasparinis, were decorated in a severely medieval style. In any event, he had never entered the salons of Florence since, after all, he was only a tradesman, a mere purveyor of books. The houses in Constantinople, almost without exception, had been run down to the point of decay and he had never seen the state rooms of the Blachernae.

But the tall rooms of the Querini were filled with glass chandeliers, rich carpets and curtains, gilded furniture, immense vases. Some of the rooms had whitewashed walls with tapestries and extraordinary beamed and inlaid ceilings, others had textiled walls and decorated ceilings. The fact that all this decoration appeared somewhat worn and faded and the lack of the slightest indication that any of these rooms were actually used, added to the overall effect of antique opulence.

Finally, they reached what was apparently the grand salon where Vittoria's mother and father, the Marchese and Marchesa Querini, (as Vittoria informed Eduardo when they walked in) were seated quietly in one corner, apparently waiting for them. The room was like the others: quiet, faded and opulent. So quiet that if Vittoria had not gone up to her mother and father to introduce Eduardo, he might not even have noticed them. Just a little life and light was admitted to this room through the great windows on one side of the salon, which led in turn to an arcaded loggia overlooking the Grand Canal.

The luncheon that he had come for was a disaster. It was served at a small table at the other end of the salon and they were joined by Vittoria's brother, Nicholas and his wife Alaria, who had brought their two small children. None of the family had any interest in Eduardo at all and apparently not even in each other. The Marchese, a tall, thin, bearded, still handsome man in his seventies, said nothing to Eduardo during the whole time he was there. He did not appear to notice him, or if he did, it seemed that he did not wish to know why he was there and did not feel the necessity of inquiring. If he spoke at all, it was briefly and monotonously to his wife, who ignored him. He sat there stiff and upright at the head of the table, noisily ate whatever was placed before him without looking at it and when the meal was over, got up and left without a word. The Marchesa, also thin and gaunt, at least acknowledged Eduardo and tried a little conversation, responding to his own attempts to engage her, but, again, she did not show the slightest curiosity about why he was there, what was his relationship with Vittoria, what was his background or what were his plans. He was uncertain whether she hated him on sight, was bored with him, possibly as just one more of Vittoria's many suitors, or just plain stupid. Finally, charitably, he decided that this was the aristocratic style, certainly in Venice, probably elsewhere. By definition, small talk was just that; it was important not to say anything that mattered or that showed you cared about anything. That would be beneath the aristocratic dignity.

Alaria, Vittoria's sister-in-law also ignored everyone, not speaking to any member of the family including her husband and certainly not Eduardo, despite his efforts, from the time she arrived until she left. Only her husband, Nicholas, who was apparently in charge of the family finances evinced some interest in Eduardo, not for his personal story, but just as in his interview earlier that day, in an attempt to obtain from Eduardo an indication of the ambitions and immediate plans of the Turks, of the situation of the Genoese who remained in Pera, who were, of course, the principal rivals of the Venetians, and whether and when it was likely that the Sultan would open the Bosphorus. Eduardo told him what he could, which was not very much, but at least the conversation helped to pass the time.

When the lunch was finally over, Vittoria excused herself and taking Eduardo by the arm, she took him out onto the loggia. She was mortified by the whole affair.

"I did want you to see my home while you are in Venice and understand my background," she said in embarrassment.

But Eduardo waved away her protestations and they stood quietly at the front of the loggia watching the scene on the Canal, which was crowded with gondolas and other river traffic and was yet another indication of the extraordinary prosperity of the city. Eduardo told her that they had received permission to leave Florence and that he was planning on going the day after tomorrow so that they could have one more day together. He could not put it off any longer. He told her that more than anything he wanted to see her again, that tomorrow they would make arrangements as to how and when they could meet again, that she was the most beautiful woman he had ever seen and that he loved her. She turned and pressed herself to him and in the magical, cool, clear air of the fall afternoon overlooking the Grand Canal, they embraced.

When they went back into the salon, it was cold and empty. Perhaps it had always been empty and he had dreamed the whole affair. They made plans for a rendezvous the following day and Vittoria led him out through the courtyard and the great iron door and he made his way back to the quayside and his ship. When he boarded he found Bryseis pacing up and down in some impatience; he immediately asked Eduardo for the safe-conduct. Eduardo showed it to him but said he would keep it himself at which Bryseis allowed himself a frown. Without further words between them, Eduardo retired to his cabin to collect and calm his thoughts. There was no doubt about the seriousness of his feelings for Vittoria and the fact, which she had assured him, that they were reciprocated. On the one hand, he was prepared to do anything to ensure he did not lose her but, on the other, he had serious duties to perform in the next few months and lives depended on his success in doing so. He would discuss it with her on the following day; he already had such confidence in her experience and practicality that he believed that she would think of a way they could soon see each other.

He was awoken the next morning by an unaccustomed motion of the ship and after some moments collecting himself, realized that the ship was underway. He rapidly dressed and tried to open the door of his cabin to go on deck but found immediately that he could not, the door was locked. He pounded on the door but to no avail. He considered shouting but knew it was pointless and he settled back on his bunk seething with fury. After a short time, it could not have been more than three quarters of an hour, the ship slowed and he could hear the anchor being dropped. The door to his cabin was opened and he was invited outside by Bryseis who was accompanied by Captain Zeki and two of the janissaries who were fully armed. They went up on deck and Eduardo saw that they were now anchored close to the mainland and one of the two military galleys, which had accompanied them, was also dropping anchor next to them

"I regret that we have had to do this," said Bryseis "but, as you know, our orders from his Highness were to proceed as quickly as possible. I believe that you will agree that what we have done was preferable to further delay, the cause of which I would have had to report to his Highness and the consequences of which could not have been desirable for anyone. I shall regard the episode of the last few days as a temporary mania that you have been able to overcome. I ask you now to hand over the safe-conduct or we shall be forced to take it from you."

Eduardo knew it was pointless to resist and he also knew that Bryseis was right. He was too embarrassed even to expostulate at his treatment. He realized how it must have seemed to the others. At the first test of his leadership, he had fallen prey to the wiles of a beautiful woman and had, in effect, deserted his post. He said nothing but merely bowed to Bryseis and handed over the safe-conduct and thereafter nothing further was said of the matter. He and Bryseis waited while Zeki supervised the disembarkation and unloading of the ship and then they too went ashore. Eduardo proceeded to assemble his party while Zeki weighed anchor and sailed away.

CHAPTER 38

Ferrara

Eduardo had told no one about the possibility that he might inherit the title of Count and he had omitted this from the translation he had passed on to Bryseis during their interview in the
Doge's palace in Venice. He did not want to be disappointed or
disappoint others but nevertheless he obviously wished to investigate the possibility of the report being true and this, in addition
to his rising excitement about the prospect of finally meeting
Juliette again, completely absorbed him as they approached Ferrara. He decided to take Bryseis into his confidence since he
needed to give him an explanation as to why they would have to
stay several days in the city despite their obligation to press on to
Florence as quickly as possible. He found that Bryseis was ame-
nable to the idea that they should all take some time to rest. It
had been an exhausting journey; it was difficult arranging accommodations for such a large party in the small towns along
their route and, on every occasion they crossed into new territory, they had to obtain permission and safe-conducts from the
authorities, which was always a long-winded process. After
weeks at sea, the whole party was tired from the unaccustomed
exertion of long days on horseback and it was time to give them
all some opportunity for rest and relaxation. Ferrara was a large
enough city to be able to provide this.

And so the morning after they arrived and after all members
of the party had been settled into various inns about the city, he
set off alone, on horseback, to the Convent of Santa Caterina,
which lay within its own enclosure about two miles beyond the
city walls. He pulled the bell-pull on the main gate of the convent and heard the bell chime within. A few minutes later, the
grille in the door was opened and a woman asked him who he
was and what was his business. He told her that he wished to see

Juliette Gasparini, that he was a very old friend who had not seen her for fifteen years and that she had been expecting him. When he mentioned Juliette's name, the Sister's face immediately relapsed into a grave expression. She let him in and started to talk.

"My name is Sister Joanna. You presumably know that Juliette is very ill."

"She wrote to me and said that she was sick but did not say how sick or what was wrong with her," replied Eduardo.

"She has lung sickness, she has been very ill for some months and is deteriorating."

A cold grip seized Eduardo's heart. He stopped in his tracks. He knew immediately the likely outcome.

"Oh God," he said. "Is there nothing that can be done? How long has she got?"

"The doctor comes most days. It is a matter of weeks, not more. We have been doing everything we can for her. I do not believe there is anything more that can be done. Maria is with her now."

"Maria – her mother," said Eduardo in surprise.

"No, no, her daughter."

"Her daughter!"

"Yes, her daughter. Did you not know? She has two daughters. Maria and Francesca."

Eduardo was struck dumb. At once, a dozen questions ran through his head.

"How old are her daughters?" he asked.

"You can ask them yourself," said Sister Joanna. "Wait here until I let you in."

So saying, she stopped outside a door on which she knocked softly, opened and entered. There was a brief pause while Eduardo tried to collect his thoughts. He could hear a few murmurs of conversation and then the door opened again and Sister Joanna beckoned him in.

The room was large and light with a big window on the opposite wall through which Eduardo could see a garden. There was a bed in one corner, a long desk with books on it, there were bookshelves and chairs, pictures and a crucifix. The room had a comfortable feel to it. In the bed was a figure lying on one side, her face turned to the wall and apparently asleep. Even from where he stood, Eduardo could see that the figure was frighteningly thin. Waiting at the foot of the bed, looking at him, was a young woman. His heart stopped. She was just as Eduardo remembered Juliette at the moment they had parted. She looked at him for a moment with large open eyes and then looked down without smiling. He could see now that she seemed younger than Juliette had been and that there was something different about her. Yes, yes, he was certain, he was positive, he could see himself in her as well as Juliette.

He walked over and held her in his arms. She burst out in uncontrollable sobs. He held her tightly and waited until the outburst was over and then held her away from him looking at her closely. My God, she is so beautiful, he thought, flawless white skin, clear, deep brown eyes with long lashes, a full mouth with the corners turned up like her mother's and long curly brown hair. The cheek bones were a little higher than Juliette's. That was where he saw himself.

"I never knew," he said. "I never knew. She never told me."

After a pause, Maria answered through her sobs "Yes, we decided not to tell you. We knew you could not get away. We knew there was nothing that you could do and then later we thought you were dead."

"And where is Francesca?"

"She is out. She will be back soon."

"And how is your mother?"

"She is very bad. She has been sick for three months and has been getting worse all the time. Everything that could be done is being done. One of us or one of the sisters stays with her all the time."

There was a knock on the door.

"I will get it," said Maria and went to the door. She opened it, said something to the person outside and Francesca came in.

"This is Francesca," said Maria to Eduardo although this introduction was unnecessary since the two sisters were identical apart from the dresses they were wearing. Eduardo took her also in his arms and held her.

"I did not know," he repeated. "I did not know."

At length, the three of them drew up chairs at the side of the bed and began talking in low voices.

"So tell us how you are, Papa," said Francesca, blushing as she said the word. "You cannot believe how I have longed to be able to say that to you. You look so handsome in all these fine clothes. We understand you are an ambassador now. Tell us all about it. Tell us about the siege. Tell us everything," she continued with girlish enthusiasm.

So Eduardo began his story, which, of course, is a very long one and he had not got far when there was a moan from the bed and Juliette stirred and started to turn over.

"You should leave the room, Papa. She will wake up now. And we will call you in when she is ready for you."

Eduardo left the room to a paroxysm of coughing and the soothing murmurs of Maria and Francesca. After a while, he was called back in again and Juliette was sitting up in her bed wearing fresh night clothes, her eyes open and a thin smile on her lips. Eduardo tried to force a smile himself and hide the shock he felt at seeing her haggard face, which he hardly recognized. He leant over her, clasped the thin frail body in his arms and gave her a gentle hug.

"And so, my darling, you are finally back," she whispered, "and you have to see me in this condition. I wanted to be beautiful for you but now I cannot. You will have to see me in our daughters. What do you think of them?"

Eduardo could not help himself. Tears came to his eyes.

"Our daughters are beautiful," he whispered. "They are just like you. And you will get better to be like them again."

"No," she said, "I will not. You will have to look after them now. And you can remember me through them."

She started coughing again and blood spattered onto her clothes. Eduardo turned away. He could no longer bear it. Maria put her arm around him.

"You should go now," she said. "This has been a lot for all of us. Come again tomorrow morning and we will talk again."

Eduardo nodded, tears streaming down his face and walked out. He met Sister Joanna outside in the cloister. His tears had stopped but his eyes were red.

"I am their father and I didn't know," he said to her and the tears started again and Joanna held him until they stopped.

"I will come back tomorrow morning and see how they are," he said and Joanna let him out of the convent where his horse was waiting for him.

The ride back was long enough to allow him to recover a little from his shock and the emotional turmoil of learning of the existence of his daughters and of seeing Juliette, after all these years, on what he knew was her deathbed. He knew he had to go on, it was the only way and that, in any event, he could not afford to relax, he had much to do before he would again have to continue his journey. Besides, he would now have to take responsibility for his daughters and this would happen whether Juliette was to live or die. They were new factors in his plans, which would obviously have to take priority. He stopped at his lodgings to get some refreshment and then went straight on to the seat of the city government, the Castello Estense, where he sought an audience with the senior official in the department in which wills were deposited. He explained his situation: that he had been told that he was the heir to the last of the Counts Ferrucci and, accordingly, he believed that this title and the property of the Ferrucci family now belonged to him.

This gentleman, one Giovanni Borromeo, did indeed know the whole story in view of the fact that the Ferruccis were one of the most prominent families in the city and that the death of the old Count without heirs had, at the time, been the talk of the town. Borromeo confirmed that if he, Eduardo Ferrucci, could prove that he was who he said he was, id est, the only surviving child of the second son of Vitaliano Ferrucci, his grandfather, the eldest son, the count, having died, his own children having predeceased him and his, Eduardo's, elder brother and his children also having all died in the time of plague in 1438, he, Eduardo Ferrucci would indeed inherit the title and the considerable estates of the family. Eduardo endured this long recital of the legal position with increasing expectations. He was told that he should seek the help of a lawyer who would advise him as to the next steps in the recovery of his estate. And if he did not know a lawyer, these were the gentlemen whom he would recommend and, accordingly, Borromeo handed Eduardo a list on which there were about half a dozen names and addresses. Finally, as befitted the completion of a long speech to someone who seemed to be on the verge of becoming one of the wealthiest and therefore most powerful men in the city, Borromeo, with a bow and a scrape, wished his Lordship a very good afternoon.

Eduardo did not know whether to laugh or cry and decided in his confusion he had done enough for that day; he would return to his lodgings and on the following day seek out a lawyer. He got back to find Bryseis resting in his rooms and they sat down together to talk. Over the weeks that they had been together, Eduardo and Bryseis had become friends. We saw that Manuel Bryseis was a diplomat who had seen many years in the service of the Sultan. He was perhaps twenty years older than Eduardo and he had no animosity towards this young Italian who, in spite of his lack of experience, had conducted himself well during the whole journey apart from the one incident of the woman of Venice, an incident which he, Bryseis, regarded only with amusement rather than concern.

As for Eduardo, in spite of the fact that Bryseis was one of the enemy, of a different faith and with different agenda, he was beginning to see him, for the time being at least, as someone whom he could trust and confide in. He told Bryseis of his extraordinary day. How here, in his own city, he had found that he had two grown children who he did not even know existed, how the mother of these children whom he had not seen for fifteen years and whom he had loved, was now dying and how it also appeared that he had inherited a title and a large fortune. Bryseis, by nature goodhearted and sympathetic, did not need much sensitivity to realize that for anyone, friend or foe, this was a lot to absorb in a single day; he therefore counseled a good meal, a large drink and a long rest. Accordingly, the two of them ended the day in a nearby taverna and Eduardo bathed his feverish thoughts in at least one bottle of wine, maybe more. Bryseis matched him glass for glass and each time he refilled his glass, he put his little finger into the wine and shook a drop onto the floor.

"That," he said, "is the drop that Allah tells me not to drink!"

On the following day, in the morning, Eduardo returned to the convent. Juliette's condition was unchanged and she slept during most of his visit. He met the doctor who gave him the same story; that the condition was far advanced, that there was little that he or anyone else could do except make things as comfortable as possible and that the end would most likely come within a few weeks. The two girls were also waiting for him. They talked for hours and he told them more of his story.

"And so I have to leave for Florence in a few days but I will return as soon as I can. I am in charge of a party of forty people and we have an international mission that I just cannot abandon. But I will write immediately and you can write to me. And I have today received some good news. My family, as I am sure your mother has told you, originally came from this city and it seems that I am the last in the line of the Ferruccis. It appears that since all the other heirs died of the plague many years ago, I will inherit the family title and fortune."

"What does that mean, Papa?" asked Francesca.

"It means that I will be a Count, that I have inherited a large palazzo from my uncle in the city and the money to keep it up."

"My goodness," said Maria, "that sounds wonderful."

"Yes," said Eduardo, "you need have no fear for your future. You can grow up and live either in Ferrara or in Florence, as you wish. My family has or had many friends in the city here and I have friends in Florence. You will be able to meet more young people."

His two daughters could not restrain themselves and eagerly related the story of their life in the convent.

"You know," said Maria, "we have been very happy here. The sisters have adopted us and cared for us. With the money that you have sent in the past, we have been able to buy books and Mama paid Monsignor Grave, the Convent Visitor, to be our tutor."

"But," added Francesca, "it would have been nice if there had been more children our own age. Sometimes it has been lonely and Mama too has been sad. We often found her crying when she thought she was alone."

"Your mother said that she was happy because she had written many books and these had been circulated to other convents and she had become quite famous."

"Yes," said Francesca, "she has had many letters and visitors who came to talk to her and, apparently, she has become quite famous with her new style of writing."

"And," added Maria, "recently we had a big surprise. Someone sent a copy of your book to the convent, *The Mystical Consolations*. We did not even know you had written a book. So you are famous too."

Eduardo was as surprised as they were and, despite himself, experienced a thrill of pleasure at this news.

"Yes," said Francesca, "and we would like to be writers too and go to the university if it were possible."

"Well," said their father, "one thing at a time. We will see."

And so it went on. They talked and talked. They told him that one of their visitors was Antonio Lucchese who came quite often, every three or four months, but only stayed briefly and did not talk about books but only gave them news of events and people in Florence. They had discussed these visits among themselves and none of them could understand his real purpose. None of them liked Lucchese and, in return, he only seemed to have a superficial interest in them. Their mother had explained that, at one stage, Lucchese had wished to marry her but she had refused him and this they would have expected to mean that he would never have wished to see her again but quite the opposite seemed to have happened. He appeared to want to give the impression of years of attentive and devoted friendship. They had finally come to the conclusion that Juliette's presence in Ferrara was just fortuitous for Lucchese and that he was making use of it as a cover for other business that he had in the city, which he wished to remain secret.

As Eduardo left Juliette's room, he had a long talk with Sister Joanna. He said that, if it were possible, he would like to mar-

306

ry Juliette, even in her present state, even if she were dying. Joanna looked at him and nodded. Yes, she thought that would be a wonderful thing. She would talk to the Mother Superior and no doubt the latter would have to talk to the Bishop. Eduardo explained his position: that he was an ambassador on an important mission and he could not stay more than a few days and he might not be able to get back until it was too late. Joanna said she understood and she would try and get an answer for him tomorrow.

Eduardo returned to the city and decided to spend the rest of the afternoon visiting old friends of his family. He began with his parents' best friends, the Fieschis, who had lived in the same street as his own home, in the Via Del Turco. He would not have been surprised, if the fate of his own family was anything to go by, to find that none of the family remained alive. He could not remember or perhaps never knew whether the Fieschis had survived the epidemic. But the old man and his wife, Angelo and Katerina Fieschi, had survived and were at home, no doubt because at their age, in their seventies, they had no business and possibly no social life to attend to.

They were, needless to say, surprised that it was Eduardo Ferrucci who was calling on them and then overjoyed. They had not heard from him for more than fifteen years and not unnaturally assumed that he, like the other members of his family, had died. They gave him refreshment and some of the most recent news. Yes indeed, the old Count Ferrucci had had no heirs and, as far as they could tell, Eduardo would indeed inherit. If he wished, they could ask their own lawyer, Gianfranco Medello, to act for him. Medello had been their family lawyer for as long as they could remember and he was on the Council of Advisers and very influential in the government of the city. Eduardo would probably have to make an appearance in the city court to prove his identity but that could be done on his return. They told him that his parent's house had been sold long before but that the old Count had a magnificent if rundown palazzo, which they assumed would be part of his inheritance.

He told them briefly of some of his adventures in Constantinople, of the purpose of his mission, of the plight of Juliette, of

307

his intention of marrying her, if possible, and of the existence of his two daughters. The two old people listened with open mouths and great interest and excitement and said they would only be too happy to help in any way they could. They could look after the two girls, while Eduardo's plans matured, and indeed they would do more, they would be happy to introduce them into Ferraran society. Two of their own sons had survived the epidemic and now had their own children who were not as old as Maria and Francesca but that did not matter. They would be one happy family together. From the light that had gathered in the eyes of Katerina and Angelo Fieschi, as they talked together of their plans, Eduardo knew that he was doing them as much a favor as they were him. A new and bright episode had opened in their life. Eduardo asked if he could bring the two girls to be introduced to them the following afternoon and he also asked if it would be possible for him to meet the attorney at the same time. Angelo said he would try and arrange it.

Eduardo returned to his lodgings satisfied with the day's achievements and the next morning he returned to the convent. Joanna took him to meet the Mother Superior to whom he repeated his wish to marry Juliette, if possible on the following day. He explained the position: he was on an important international embassy upon which lives depended and he had a party of forty people, all of whom were waiting for him to proceed to Florence. He just could not wait longer.

While he was speaking they were joined by the Convent Visitor, Monsignor Alberto Grave. Mother Superior explained that the Monsignor had the authority to conduct a marriage both under civil and church law and he also had the authority, in emergency, to waive the notices required under church law. She also said that she was convinced, having now met Eduardo and knowing the girls all these many years as they had grown up in the convent, that he was indeed the father. Eduardo told his story again to the Monsignor and then admitted a little sheepishly that he had not yet told either Juliette or the girls of his plan, which he would now do if the Monsignor would give his blessing to it. The Monsignor agreed and the ceremony was set for the following morning. All that was left was for Eduardo to ask Juliette.

He went down to Juliette's cell with Joanna and as before she was asleep. The two girls were waiting at her bedside; they were subdued but unable to restrain their happiness at seeing and being with their father. He told them of his plan and, after the initial surprise, they were overjoyed at the idea. While they waited, they talked and Eduardo told them that he would like to take them this afternoon to meet some friends of his in the city who could take care of them while he was away. He realized that they could remain in the convent and that they would, of course, have money for their upkeep but a change of scene and an introduction to people their own age would, he was sure, do them good. It would be his first act as their parent to help them go out into the world. It would hopefully only be for a short time while he was away in Florence and they could always go back and forth to the convent whenever they wished. The girls of course agreed; they would never have admitted it openly but they were longing to get out and meet people outside the convent.

When Juliette awoke and when they had made her comfortable, the two girls left the room and Eduardo settled down at her bedside.

"How are you feeling?" he asked.

"I am feeling fine," she said. "I am better after sleeping but I sleep so much and I am always tired."

He told her about the events since he had left her the day before. How it appeared quite certain that he was going to become the Count Ferrucci and inherit property in Ferrara and how he had arranged with some close friends of his family to take an interest in the girls and how they could go and stay with these friends occasionally in the city. And then plucking up courage he said to her.

"I have something important that I want to ask you"

"What is it, darling?" she said.

He took out a ring that the Mother Superior had lent him. He had quite forgotten, during his trip in the city the day before, that he would need one.

"Will you marry me?"

She opened her eyes in surprise, started to breathe heavily and then started coughing. When the girls outside heard this, they rushed in but waited and watched at the foot of the bed. After the fit had ceased, Juliette smiled, nodded her head and Eduardo slipped the ring on her finger. It was too big but this did not matter.

He stayed for another hour, they had lunch, which the girls brought in, and Juliette went back to sleep. Eduardo went to talk to the Mother Superior about the arrangements for the following day and then all three of them left for the city in a carriage he had ordered. They arrived at the Via del Turco and Eduardo first showed his daughters the house where he had grown up. At the Fieschis, they went up to the salon where Angelo and Katerina were waiting for them. He introduced the two girls, they talked for a short time, and Katerina asked them whether they would like to look round the house, which indeed they did, and they left the room. Angelo then introduced Eduardo to Gianfranco Medello, who had been waiting patiently while the girls talked. He was a man in his sixties, tall, lean with a dark but graying beard and piercing, intelligent eyes.

"Ambassador," he said to Eduardo bowing as he spoke.

Eduardo bowed back.

"I have just heard your story or, at least, what I imagine is a small part of it. If the rest of it is anything like what you have experienced in the last few days, it must be very well worth telling."

"You are right," said Eduardo and he could not resist a smile. "You have just given me an idea. I should certainly write a book about my experiences. If only I could find the time." And they both laughed.

"Obtaining your right and title to the estate of your uncle will not be difficult. I will start the process immediately and in due course you will have to appear in court to prove the will and your identity and to sign the papers. That will not be for another few months. When you are settled in Florence, you can contact me and inform me when it will be convenient for you to make the journey."

"Thank you, Messer Medello, I am grateful to you. I should tell you that I have just five more months for my mission to Florence, at the end of which I have to return to Constantinople."

"That should give us ample time," said Medello.

"And," said Eduardo, "there is something else I would like your help with."

So saying, he turned and walked up the salon. Medello followed him. When they were out of earshot of Angelo Fieschi, Eduardo spoke:

"This will be a more difficult task and you may wish to give it some consideration before you agree to carry it out. There is a man whom I wish to get information about. He is a very dangerous, powerful and ambitious man. His name is Antonio Lucchese. He is a Florentine but he has business in Ferrara, which he conducts in secret. He comes to Ferrara frequently, at least four times a year. He is or was the head of security for the Republic of Florence, he may now have a higher rank. I wish to find out what the business is which he conducts in Ferrara."

Eduardo took out from his jacket a bag of coins.

"Here are 5,000 Venetian ducats, which will enable you to make a start on this undertaking, if you agree to take it on."

"That is not necessary," said Medello, "I shall be paid in due course out of the funds in the Ferrucci estate."

"I know it is not necessary," said Eduardo, "but it is an earnest of my urgent need to find out what Lucchese is doing. I need to know the whole story going right back to when it started, which may be many years ago."

"Very well," said Medello as he took the money, "and this may be a matter of state security for the city itself. It would be very unusual, and may be illegal, for a high ranking officer from a foreign state to do business in the city without obtaining permission. I will give it thought and will make preliminary inquiries. It may be possible to make use of state resources."

"Above all," said Eduardo, "the inquiries must be discreet. Lucchese must not be given the slightest indication that he is being investigated. That might make things very difficult for me in Florence. I know for a fact that he has spies in every city."

"I understand," said Medello. "Very well. I shall proceed accordingly."

They walked back across the salon to Angelo and the ladies, who had returned from their tour of the house. After some further discussion, it was agreed that the girls would come and visit on a regular basis and on these occasions Katerina would arrange for them to meet other young people of their own age. Maria and Francesca were overjoyed by the prospect. Eduardo also told the Fieschis about his proposed marriage on the following day and invited them to attend, which they agreed to do. Eduardo put the girls back into the carriage and they returned to the convent while he made his own way back to his lodgings.

When he told Bryseis that evening that he was getting married the following day, Bryseis burst out laughing.

"You certainly have a weakness for the ladies, my boy," he said. "Are you sure you are doing the right thing?"

After Eduardo had explained at length the full circumstances, Bryseis' expression changed to one of frank admiration.

"You are doing the right thing," he said. "I congratulate you."

Eduardo asked him if he would like to attend the ceremony and Bryseis readily agreed.

The following morning all four of them, Eduardo, Bryseis and the Fieschis traveled in the same carriage to the convent and when they arrived, the preparations for the ceremony were under way. At the appointed time, Juliette, who had been dressed in a scarlet gown, was brought into the chapel on a litter and with the help of some carefully applied makeup looked palely beautiful, if not radiant. Maria and Francesca were wearing similar green and gold gowns, which they had made themselves, and they stood next to their mother. Eduardo was dressed in his most formal court dress and, by all accounts, looked extraordinarily handsome. Bryseis stood next to him. All the sisters and the Mother Superior attended. They sang and said prayers together and Monsignor Grave officiated with the appropriate words. It was not long before Juliette and Eduardo were formally married. All the ladies including Juliette cried but Juliette, when Eduardo tried to kiss her, shook her head violently and adamantly refused.

"No, my darling," she said "One sick person in the family is already enough."

She was soon exhausted, the fits of coughing had begun again and so they took her back to her room where she quickly fell asleep. The Sisters had prepared food to celebrate and they all ate their fill. Eduardo said he would stay with Juliette until nightfall and the others returned to the city where Bryseis was to make preparations for the departure of their party the following morning. Eduardo sat with Juliette and with the girls the whole afternoon. Juliette woke occasionally, talked, then drifted back to sleep and during these long interludes, Eduardo, Maria and Francesca talked and laughed and became closer. He told them more of his story and they told him their thoughts, feelings and ambitions, which, despite their secluded upbringing, were much the same as all young women of sixteen who are about to enter the world. Eduardo finally had to leave, promising them all that it would not be long before he returned. He took Juliette into his arms and said goodbye.

"I trust myself unto God," she said. "Our lives and our love have just been feathers on His breath."

She started to cry but nothing could be done. Fate was once again taking him away from her and her from him.

CHAPTER 39

Florence

Count Eduardo Ferrucci sat in the peace and beauty of the Studiolo in the Palazzo Gasparini and contemplated the progress of his embassy in Florence during the three months since he had returned to the city. Those who had already seen the new decoration of the palazzo assumed that the funds for the renovation were part of the expenses of the embassy to Florence and had been provided by the Sultan. In fact, Eduardo had purchased the house and the furnishings in his own name and with his own money but he went to great trouble to conceal this and to foster the illusion that the opulence of his establishment was in furtherance of his mission on behalf of the Turks. Bryseis had also taken up residence in the palazzo with a number of the other senior members of the Turkish party and he was the only other person who was aware of the actual source of the funds.

One of Eduardo's first actions after he moved into the palazzo was to make inquiries about the whereabouts and the welfare of the old Count, Federigo Gasparini and his wife, Maria. His intention was that they should be invited to stay in, or at least visit, their old home. As it turned out, this was not possible. Federigo had died years earlier and Maria, his wife, had become increasingly deranged and now lived alone with a nurse in the small house close to their old country estate, which was all that the family had retained after the bankruptcy.

Before Eduardo had even moved into the Palazzo Gasparini he had written a long letter to Vittoria Orsini in Venice. He explained why he had failed to appear at the agreed rendezvous; he did not expect that she would believe him but it was true nevertheless and he hoped that she would forgive him. He gave her a detailed account of the events that had unfolded in Ferrara and told her that, despite his marriage, he still loved her and hoped that they would be able to meet again soon.

Very quickly he received a reply in which she said, yes, she had been very upset when he had disappeared but was overjoyed to receive his letter. She was very happy that he still loved her and she loved him in return. She thought that everything he had done in Ferrara including his marriage had been the right thing to do and she looked forward to meeting his daughters. What's more, since she knew that it was impossible for him to return to Venice in the immediate future, she would be very happy to come to Florence and visit him if he would have her.

Eduardo was surprised and delighted. Surprised because it was unusual enough for a respectable young woman to stay in the home of a single man and unheard of that she should invite herself. He did not hesitate to accept her suggestion and no more than a few weeks passed before Vittoria arrived in Florence with an escort which Eduardo had arranged to accompany her. As Eduardo would discover, Vittoria was an unusual woman. She did not have the slightest concern with what other people might think of her or her actions, although in fact her presence in the palazzo and her background seemed no more and no less bizarre to the outside world than did the remainder of the household, with the attendants in Turkish dress and the janissaries who were always on guard at the door of the Palazzo in full regalia with scimitars and turbans. Her extraordinary beauty raised much excited comment amongst the gossips of Florentine society, particularly since it was assumed that this must have been cultivated in the delicate and rarified atmosphere of a Turkish seraglio.

Vittoria was single-minded and authoritative. Fortunately for Eduardo, as he told himself, she seemed determined that he was the man for her. After she arrived, she immediately started exercising authority over the domestic affairs of the palazzo. This was what she had done as mistress of the court of Taranto and she going to relieve him of the burden of these duties. After some initial adjustment, Eduardo accepted and welcomed her involvement. Even Bryseis, after a week or two under this new management, had to admit that she was marvelous.

315

That day would be the first time that Eduardo would entertain in his official capacity in his official residence. As the representative of the Sultan and as part of his mission to demonstrate both the desire of the Sultan to establish friendly relations with the Florentines and to show something of the wealth and power of the empire of the Turks, he would be host to the Duke, his advisers and many of the aristocracy of the city at a great **banquet.**

He had presented his credentials to Duke Cosimo shortly after they had arrived in the city at a ceremony in the did not seem able or willing to get out of the habit. She always consulted Eduardo, she recognized his ultimate authority, she deferred to him and was sensitive to his feelings, but she made it clear to everyone else that she was in control and that she was Medici Palace. The construction of the Palace in the Via Larga, with its imposing exterior and its light and airy inner courtyard, had begun only a few years earlier and was not yet completed but it was to become, as befitted the ruler of the city, the largest palace in Florence. Eduardo was quite nervous about this ceremony. Not only was this the moment for which he and his retinue had journeyed so far and for so long and one in which he had to exhibit an uncharacteristic gravitas but also he had no doubt that Antonio Lucchese would be on hand as one of the Duke's principal advisers. In his mind, he had been preparing for an encounter with Antonio for years. Even so he was not looking forward to it.

Of course, Lucchese knew of their arrival in the city. No doubt he had been informed at the moment they had applied for safe-conduct on the Florentine frontier and it was probable that he knew of their intentions from his more distant spies even earlier. He had not attempted to contact Eduardo but Eduardo had learned from the inquiries he had made since he had arrived, that Antonio had inherited his father's title of Count, that he had indeed been promoted to the position of Bargello, chief of police, and that he was now the most powerful and feared man in the city excepting only Duke Cosimo himself. Eduardo had to be very careful; he could not travel around the city without a guard, he had to watch what he ate and drank for fear of poisoning and he did not keep any of his money in Florentine banks except for nominal sums. Guards accompanied all the members of his household, including and especially Vittoria, whenever they left the palazzo.

On the day of the presentation of his credentials, the whole entourage from Constantinople, except a half dozen janissaries who remained behind to guard the palace, prepared themselves in formal court dress. Bryseis and his colleagues wore Turkish clothes including turbans. Eduardo wore Italian court dress, which he had purchased since his arrival. The arrangements for the procession to the Medici Palace had been made and approved in advance and there were many onlookers in the streets as they passed on horseback. When they arrived in the Via Larga a formal honor guard was waiting for them. The horses and soldiers, except for those who were carrying the boxes of gifts, remained in the courtyard of the palace and the rest of the party climbed the stairs to the Grand Salon where Duke Cosimo and his advisers were waiting.

The room was not as imposing as Eduardo had imagined it might be. The room was not particularly large, the building was still under construction and much of the decoration was not yet complete. The dress of Cosimo and his courtiers and the furnishing were a sumptuous contrast to the simplicity of the decor. Eduardo walked slowly across the hall to the Duke, seated at the back, amongst his advisers, and bowed deeply.

"Your Grace, your Lordships, I am Count Eduardo Ferrucci. I come to Florence on behalf of his Highness Sultan Mehmet II, Great Caesar, Emperor of the Romans, Lord of Constantinople and of all the Turkish dominions. I present my credentials."

So saying, he handed over to Cosimo a scroll containing his letter of authority in Italian and Turkish to which the seal of the Sultan was attached. Cosimo took it and, without taking his eyes off Eduardo, handed it to a secretary who was standing next to him. The secretary proceeded to read the letter aloud and when he finished, Cosimo replied:

"Ambassador Ferrucci, your credentials are in order, you are welcome to Florence. We are honored to receive you on behalf of his Highness, the Sultan, Emperor of the Romans, of whose great prowess, abilities and deeds we are, of course, aware. We are impatient to learn of the purpose of your embassy. We are also curious to know how or why you, who we understand, were a former resident of Florence, came to occupy your present position."

"Your Grace," said Eduardo, "I have no doubt that Count Lucchese has already informed you of my personal history and, with your permission, I do believe that the details need not concern us at this time."

As he said that, he slowly turned his head scanning the faces of the men standing next to the Duke until he came to Antonio whose heavy features, darker and more sinister with age, were unmistakable. He stopped sufficiently long to indicate to whom he was referring but did not blink or incline his head in the least. It gave him a brief opportunity to confront his old adversary.

"Your Grace," continued Eduardo, "I have with me letters from his Highness, the Sultan, which set out the reasons for my embassy to Florence but first his Highness has asked me to present to you some indications of his esteem and admiration for your Grace."

At that Eduardo stepped aside and beckoned forward the janissaries who were carrying the boxes of gifts from the Sultan. The boxes were laid on the floor before the Duke who motioned to a secretary to open them. The first was a casket about two feet long by eighteen by eighteen inches. It was not locked and as it was opened, the Florentines, despite themselves, could not hold back a gasp of surprise and admiration. It was full to the top with loose precious stones: rubies, emeralds, diamonds of a size, brilliance and color, more spectacular, than most of the on-lookers had ever seen. The second box was much larger: about the size of a traveler's trunk. This contained a set of embroidered cloths of gold. The third box, which was of an intermediate size but so heavy that it required four of the janissaries to carry, contained a engraved cross of solid gold, each arm of which was about eighteen inches long and an inch in diameter.

There was a moment's pause and then the Duke said:

"Please convey to his Highness the appreciation and the thanks of the people of the Republic of Florence for these extraordinary gifts, which reveal the munificence of his Highness and no doubt reflect his wish for a sincere friendship with our country."

If there was any irony in this statement, it was very carefully concealed.

"I will convey your appreciation to his Highness," said Eduardo with a slight bow. "They are indeed tokens of his understanding and appreciation of the contributions that you, personally, have made to the culture and governance of the city and a confirmation of his sincerity in wishing to establish good relations with you and the city of Florence. He views the city under your guidance as the foremost in all Italy in reviving the ancient traditions of which he is now the representative and thus it is natural that, of all cities, he should choose Florence to bestow the favor of his friendship. At the same time, he wishes to learn more about the civilization and culture of Florence, past and present, and to encourage the economic links between the two countries. To this end, he desires to establish trading contacts between Florence and Constantinople. The details are recorded in these letters from his Highness and we would wish to discuss these further when your Grace has had an opportunity to consider them."

Eduardo was aware that some of what he was saying was outrageously brazen and even he could hardly keep a straight face during parts of his speech. He handed over the Sultan's letters and requested that in due course his Grace would contact him to arrange further discussions. At that, the ceremony came to an end, Eduardo and his party left the hall and progressed back to the Palazzo Gasparini in the same way that they had come.

In fact since this first meeting, he had not received any invitation from the Duke or his advisers to participate in further discussions and his hope of advancing the negotiations was the rationale behind the proposed banquet. He was becoming concerned about what he should do if the Florentines continued to ignore him.

The Duke had convened his advisers after the meeting with Eduardo and they came to the consensus was that his embassy was nothing more than an initial and transparent attempt to drive a diplomatic wedge between the nations of Italy. Although the offer of trading privileges was attractive since it would place Florence on a par with Genoa and Venice in the Turkish territories, the benefits of this had to be weighed against the danger of opening up Italy to Turkish influence, which could only be the prelude to more direct intervention.

His diplomatic duties in limbo as he waited for contact from Duke Cosimo, Eduardo continued to be extremely busy. Only three weeks after his arrival in Florence, he received a letter from Angelo Fieschi with the news that Juliette had died quietly the previous night. The funeral was to be the following Monday, but this day had already passed by the time Eduardo received the letter. Angelo wrote that he had asked the girls to come and live with them after the funeral and they had agreed.

Although he had known the inevitable outcome of Juliette's condition, on receiving the letter Eduardo was devastated by sadness and remorse. It was his fault, he had not been able to do more to help her, he had not been at her bedside during the final hours. He left immediately for Ferrara, handing the affairs of the palazzo temporarily over to Bryseis. When he reached Ferrara, he first visited Juliette's grave in the convent in the company of the Fieschis and his daughters. He added his own flowers to those scattered over the grave in the convent cloister and the three of them stood in silence, hand in hand, for some minutes.

"It was peaceful, Papa," said Maria. "One morning, she was very, very weak and the doctor said we should call the Monsignor. He came and gave the last rites. We were all at the bedside, Sister Joanna and the Mother Superior and ourselves. We sat there while her breathing became slower and slower and eventually stopped. It was the most terrible thing I have ever known."

The two girls started to cry again and Eduardo took them in his arms and held them until the tears had passed. Mother Superior tried to comfort them.

"Life has to be lived in the shadow of dying, my children," she said. "To love means both pain and joy, and death cannot destroy these. Juliette now lives with God and she lives always in our memories."

They remained there for a few more minutes and then Eduardo thanked the Mother Superior, the other sisters and especially Sister Joanna for their kindness. They in turn invited Eduardo and his daughters to visit the convent and grave whenever they wished. The three of them then returned to the city and in the carriage Eduardo discussed with the girls where they should live.

"I would like to take you back with me to Florence, but I shall only be there for a few more weeks. Besides it is not very safe there for you. As you know, I represent the Turkish Sultan and he is still the enemy of all Italy. I have people who guard me but one can never be certain. I think it would be better for you to remain here."

"But," said Francesca, "we shall miss you, Papa. When shall we see you again?"

"I shall stop here again when I go back to Constantinople. And after that we shall have to see."

"There is no need for anyone to worry," said Fieschi. "We will look after them. We are very happy to do so. They will have a wonderful time in Ferrara."

"Yes, Papa," repeated Maria. "Don't worry. We will be happy here. We will look after Mama's grave. There is no need to be sad. Mama had a good life. She did the thing that she wanted to do which was to write. She became famous through her books and her name will be remembered. We will see you soon and then you can tell us more of your extraordinary adventures. Besides, I want to see more of the city here. I want to see your new palazzo. We both want to meet new people. We will write to you and you can write to us."

Eduardo smiled, despite himself, at the brave attempts of his daughters to give him comfort and it was agreed that the two girls had had enough change and disruption in their lives for the time being. They would stay with the Fieschis, enjoy their freedom and their new status as the Ferrucci heirs.

Eduardo next went to visit Medello in his office. He signed the papers relating to his inheritance and Medello informed him that he would not after all have to attend the court. Medello had taken care of the formalities and although these were not complete, for all intents and purposes Eduardo could now regard himself as Count Ferrucci. Medello was making an inventory of the estate and he would be pleased to manage it on his behalf if Eduardo so agreed, which he was happy to do. Medello then reported on his investigations into the activities of Lucchese.

"I used my authority with the city government to request of all the banks any knowledge they had of accounts opened in the name of Lucchese. They were, of course, reluctant to do so but since they are licensed by the city to do business, they had no option but to comply. We did this at the highest level in each bank, so I believe there is no possibility that Lucchese would discover that he is being investigated. It appears that his interest in Ferrara began about fifteen years ago when one very large deposit was made in one bank in his name. Shortly thereafter, this money was distributed amongst the other banks in Ferrara in different names, which we assume were pseudonyms for Lucchese. Over the years, these amounts have gradually been reduced and we assume that, little by little, he has been repatriating the money in cash to Florence and this is the reason for his frequent visits."

"How much was the original deposit," asked Eduardo.

"About 300,000 florins," said Medello.

"That is a very large sum," said Eduardo. "Where would he have gotten such a sum and why would he bring it into Ferrara in the first place?"

"We have investigated that and we believe, although it will be extremely difficult, perhaps impossible, to prove after such a long interval, that this was the money that was stolen from the Gasparini family of Florence. The only thing we can really show towards any proof is that the amounts were the same."

"The Gasparinis," interjected Eduardo. "Did you realize that my daughters' mother was a Gasparini? I don't know anything about this – explain it to me."

Medello then recited the story of how fifteen years earlier, the elder Gasparini, Count Federigo, had invested in a consignment of wool from Florence that had been sold in Ferrara but the loan from the bank to effect the transaction, handled by his steward Garzon, had never been repaid. Garzon was later found dead and the money had disappeared.

"Yes," said Eduardo, "that explains it. Gasparini went bankrupt and died some years later. His widow is still alive but has become senile."

"Lucchese must have discovered about the investment and used his position to set up the robbery and the murder of Garzon. The only mistake he made was to put the original deposit in his own name, which I suppose he did to prevent the people he had hired to do the robbery from subsequently taking the money themselves. And he would never have been discovered if it had not been for your inquiry."

"Can he be arrested next time he comes to the city?" asked Eduardo.

"We could certainly detain him. We could certainly question him. I don't think there is sufficient proof to tie him to the robbery. Using false names for his bank accounts is certainly illegal but we would never be able to convict him in view of his diplomatic immunity. It would cause enough disruption in our relations with Florence just to detain him. My advice is that I should recommend to the Council of Advisers that the balance of the deposits be frozen and confiscated. Since the deposits are in false names, there will be no one to complain and, if Lucchese himself makes a formal complaint, we can then take action against him."

"That is a clever idea," said Eduardo. "I certainly approve. And how much of the money is left?"

"Approximately a total of one hundred thousand florins in the various accounts. What's more, if you provide for me full details of the Gasparini family, the circumstances of the bankruptcy and anything else you can find out in Florence about the robbery and murder, I will submit them to the Council and recommend that the money be turned over to the Gasparini heirs. The only remaining question is when should we do this? Lucchese will inevitably suspect your involvement; the coincidence of timing is so great. This would put you in some danger."

Eduardo told Medello of the precautions he was already taking and they agreed that Medello should proceed immediately since Lucchese would not even discover the loss of the money until he next came to Ferrara, which might not be for some months.

Eduardo returned to the Fieschis to bid them and his daughters and returned to Florence. On his way he gave further thought to Antonio Lucchese. Not only had Antonio exiled him to Constantinople, Eduardo also suspected that it was Antonio who had written the letter to Philip Shamash betraying Cecilia and thus had brought about his imprisonment. Now it also appeared that it was Antonio who had ruined the Gasparinis and committed murder along the way. Eduardo had spent many hours thinking about Lucchese before and during his imprisonment in Constantinople and contemplating ways of obtaining his revenge but the latest revelations sharpened his anger and resentment as well as his determination to bring about an early and ignominious downfall of Lucchese.

On his return, he took comfort in the company of Vittoria. He had told her at the beginning of his relationships with Cecilia and Juliette and then, when she arrived in Florence, had given her the further revelation about his two daughters who would henceforth be part of their lives. She fully supported him during these difficult moments and their love and dependence on each other continued to mature.

During the next few weeks, Eduardo and Vittoria received and accepted many invitations from the elite of Florentine society all of whom were anxious to entertain the exotic ambassador of the fabulously wealthy and aggressive Sultan of the Turks. The whole city had by now heard Eduardo's story, which was not surprising since he himself had discreetly circulated it in advance. It seemed that everyone knew that he had been sent to Constantinople as a spy on behalf of the city of Florence, that he had been betrayed by someone inside the Florentine administration, that he had spent many years in the horrific dungeons of the Blachernae, that he had fought alongside the Emperor in the last desperate stand of the defenders of Constantinople, that he had been pardoned by the Sultan himself and finally, because of his fluency in languages and knowledge of the city, he had been sent as ambassador to Florence to set up cultural and trading contacts between the two cities.

It did not take much of this propaganda and much of his continual social interaction for his reputation to continue to grow over the time of his stay in the city until it reached nearly mythical proportions. Everywhere he went in the city, easily recognizable with his escort of janissaries, people stopped, bowed and even clapped as he passed. At the aristocratic salons, conversation stopped completely when he entered and all eyes focused on the young, handsome, noble hero of the Republic. There was talk that a special medal should be struck to commemorate his exploits but this idea seemed to meet opposition from the administration, which used the reasonable excuse that it would not be right to honor the representative of the archenemy of all Christendom.

During these social gatherings, Eduardo met many of the political and social leaders of the city and he discovered that there was widespread resentment and even hatred of Antonio Lucchese as a result of his activities during his rise to power. Lucchese had not hesitated to use the information he had gathered on most of the prominent individuals in the city to obtain their support for his own interests, to block any activity he did not approve of or for outright blackmail. As a result of this resentment, many of the people that Eduardo talked to were only too happy to voice their grievances especially to an outsider and it was not difficult for Eduardo to accumulate detailed information about Lucchese's family, his career and his business interests.

As we have seen, during this time Eduardo and Vittoria discussed between themselves different ways of entrapping and destroying Antonio Lucchese and finally decided to put into effect the plan which she herself suggested. They would initiate it at the banquet at the Palazzo which Antonio would attend.

From the diplomatic point of view, the banquet at the Palazzo Gasparini was a disaster despite all the efforts of Eduardo and Bryseis. It was certainly a glittering affair. The Duke and Duchess attended, as did their advisers and all the aristocracy of the city but Eduardo did not get the slightest indication from the Duke that he was interested in pursuing negotiations on the matters that had been outlined at their first meeting. They were still considering them, said the Duke. These were very weighty matters. They needed to be given due care and attention. It would take some time before the reply of the city of Florence to the Sultan's proposal could be formulated. When Eduardo asked when such a reply might be forthcoming, the Duke was vague. He could not say. At present it was in the hands of his advisers. They deliberated carefully. It could be some months.

It was immediately obvious to Eduardo, even with his inexperience in affairs of state, that they were not going to get a reply. It was the diplomatic way of saying that the Medicis and Florence were not interested in any form of association with the Sultan and this rejection was reinforced by the nature of the gifts that the Duke presented in his turn to Eduardo as representative of the Sultan. By comparison with what Eduardo had brought to Florence, they were meager if not insulting: a copy of the works of Cicero in a jewel-encrusted binding, a small painting of the Madonna by a Florentine artist, Filippo Lippi, a silver goblet inlaid with emblems of gold. The very fact that the gifts were presented at the banquet at all indicated that, for the Florentines, the embassy of the Turks was at an end and they should depart.

At the banquet, Vittoria was seated next to Antonio Lucchese. They got on well. They found they had a lot in common. He knew her former husband, the Lord of Taranto, with whom he had corresponded many times. He asked her what her relationship was with Eduardo and she was happy to tell him. She had met him in Venice and he had asked her to visit him in Florence to which she had agreed. She found him attractive but rather young and quite naïve, particularly in matters of state. She was used to older men. She liked powerful men. In any event Ferrucci would be returning soon to Constantinople and she would be left alone, a young widow with no one to turn to.

While Antonio was absorbing Vittoria's extraordinary beauty which he found irresistible and while he was considering the implication of her pointed and sensuous remarks, a note was delivered to him by a footman. He opened it. It said:

"I have the letter by which you delivered me into the hands of the enemy, by which you betrayed your office and your country. I have the evidence of how you stole the patrimony of the Gasparinis and committed murder to do it. Your money in Ferrara is gone. Unless you resign and leave Florence within seven days, the letter and this evidence will be made public and you will suffer the fate of all traitors.

Signed: Ferrucci."

Antonio went white, his hands started to tremble, he pushed his chair back and got up.

"I have to leave," he said to Vittoria. "Please excuse me."

"Not bad news, I hope," she said sweetly. "In any event, please let us meet again. I have enjoyed our talk. Send for me. I shall be waiting."

As he left, she gave him her widest and most inviting smile.

CHAPTER 40

The Iron Box

Eduardo had not forgotten his iron box in which were deposited ten rolls of sheepskin. The box had traveled with him, close to him, throughout his journey to Florence and was now sitting next to his desk in the Studiolo. He had found the time to start making inquiries about experts in the city who could advise him on how he could safely examine the contents of the rolls. One morning he walked the still familiar route from the Palazzo to the Libreria Patrizzi, only to find it closed. He made inquiries and discovered that Patrizzi had died five months earlier. It seemed that his widow had, at first, tried to keep the business going but had been unable to and the books were now being dispersed. He returned to the Studiolo to give further thought as to how he should proceed when he had an unexpected visitor. John Palamas was shown in.

"My dear friend," said Eduardo, "what a wonderful surprise."

They embraced.

"How did you know I was here?" continued Eduardo.

"Now don't be ingenuous," laughed Palamas, "the whole city knows you are here. I just had to follow the gossip. Although, I confess that I was not absolutely certain since when we last met you had a different name, did you not? I have no doubt there were good reasons for that!"

"Indeed," said Eduardo, "but it is very good to see you. What have you been doing? It seems incredible that it is less than a year since we last met."

"I have a post in the Studio of Florence, teaching Greek and Greek History," said Palamas. "Everyone wants to learn Greek! When I first came to the city, I visited Patrizzi but he was very old and could only work with difficulty. He died only recently and I have tried to help his widow but I do not have the time nor the ability nor the contacts that he did, so the business is being wound up. I am helping her sell the remaining stock and, when that is done, she will certainly have enough to live on. But I have no need to ask you what you have been doing. I know the story by heart as everyone else does! And I have good news about the book that you wrote and gave to me. I had it copied and gave it to each of the booksellers in Florence. Apparently it is selling well."

"So that's how it happened." said Eduardo, "I had almost completely forgotten about it but I have heard since arriving in the city that it has been quite well received. It is naturally very gratifying to hear that and once again I am very grateful for your efforts."

"Yes, needless to say, the booksellers are now capitalizing on your notoriety as a statesman to compare you with Boethius."

"Yes I have heard this. Let us hope that I don't meet a similar fate. And since you are here, if you wish, you can help me again on another matter or at least advise me about how I should proceed."

Eduardo related the story of how he had found the answer to the second riddle in the copy of Plutarch's *Lives* which Palamas had left with him in the Blachernae and how he had discovered the iron box in the Grove of Hekademos outside Athens. And in the box was … At this point, Eduardo gestured with a flourish to the box next to his desk and slowly and carefully opened the lid disclosing the rolls seated within it. But Palamas was not looking at the rolls, he was looking at the name on the lid – *Aristokles*.

"Do you know what that name is?" asked Palamas. His face had gone white.

"No," said Eduardo.

There was a pause.

"It is the family name of Plato himself."

The two men looked at each other with open mouths. Eduardo felt his stomach sink away and his heart stop.

He sat down and motioned to Palamas to do the same and there was another long pause.

"What shall we do?" he asked.

"We must take some advice. We have many manuscripts that come into the Studio and there is a specialist who handles them all and who is an expert in conserving them. I am friendly with him. We could ask him here and show him one of the rolls without disclosing where it came from. If it turns out to be something important, it will be difficult to keep it secret if that is what you want. And it may take a long time to deal with so many, perhaps even years."

"Very well," said Eduardo. "Ask him here as soon as possible."

The next day, Palamas presented himself at the Palazzo with his friend, Gianni Gabriele, a man of about fifty with a tidy grey beard, untidy wild grey hair and kind, intelligent eyes. He was awed to be in the presence of the famous ambassador known over all Florence as well as by the magnificence of the palazzo and beauty of the Studiolo. He bowed to Eduardo, who helped him to a seat at a table upon which one of the scrolls was waiting.

"This has recently come into my possession," said Eduardo. "I believe, from where it was found, that it may be as much as two thousand years old. We want your advice as to how we should deal with it."

Gabriele picked up the roll and inspected it. It was very tightly sewn up.

"It appears to be airtight and the contents may be intact. If it is a scroll, it will be brittle and difficult to unroll without breaking. Each layer will have to be very carefully wiped with a damp cloth until it becomes soft and then that part can be slowly unrolled and then the next part will be softened. It may take weeks to do. It is very difficult and can be done only by someone with much experience. If you ask me to do it, I would have to take it to my own rooms, where I have the equipment."

"How much do you charge?" asked Eduardo.

"Since we do not know what condition it is in, I would have to charge by the day. And I have my other work at the Studio to do so I cannot guarantee how long it would take. My fee is five florins a day."

"This is my proposal," said Eduardo. "I am not prepared to allow the scroll out of my possession. If you will come here to the palazzo and bring your equipment, I will set aside a room here for you to work in. You must work fulltime and I will pay you four times the fee that you have just mentioned. There are more similar scrolls so I can promise you work for a considerable time. There is one condition. Absolute secrecy must be maintained. If I hear from any outside source the slightest rumor of the nature of your work or the nature of the contents of the scrolls, your employment will be terminated and we shall consider what other sanctions to employ. In addition, half of your salary will be kept in abeyance until the whole job is complete and if secrecy has been maintained, this balance will be released. Please take your time to consider whether you will accept."

It did not take Gabriele long to agree and it was decided he would begin the next day. He brought with him and set up his equipment: a shallow dish to hold water in which to dampen the scroll, large amounts of muslin on which to place any pieces of the scroll that needed to dry, fine instruments for picking up pieces of the manuscript or for prying it apart, rollers on which to reroll a scroll, lenses for reading indistinct writing, brushes for applying water or glue, a concave board to hold the scroll while it was worked on and much else.

With Eduardo and Palamas watching, he took up the first roll and, with a fine knife, began to cut the threads with which the package was sewn together. As he cut away the cover, they could see that inside there was a tightly rolled scroll of papyrus, which had turned brown with age. It seemed that the scroll was intact. When the final piece of packing had been removed, Gabriele, with gloved hands, placed the scroll on his working board. They could see the fine edges of the scroll, which appeared to be hard and brittle.

"Now the work will start," said Gabriele. "I shall apply a very small amount of water with this fine brush along the edge and continue to do this slowly until it begins to soften. This will take hours and the whole scroll will take days to do, so I would prefer to work alone. This evening you can see whether there is any progress."

When the two of them returned that evening about six inches of the scroll had been unrolled and a sufficient amount was showing that they could see that the text on the scroll was in Greek. Gabriele said that he would leave the unrolled part between two pieces of slightly damp muslin overnight. When this unrolled part became sufficiently long, he would wrap it round a roller again, separating each layer with muslin and each morning he would unwind the roller to check on the flexibility of the restored scroll. He advised that they should transcribe the scroll as he proceeded in case the process of softening the papyrus affected the ink. It was always possible that some or all of the script would fade or become washed out.

Eduardo and Palamas discussed the matter. Neither of them had the time to do the transcription themselves. Eduardo had his diplomatic duties and Palamas had his job at the university and besides he did not consider that his Latin was yet good enough for the long task of transcribing and then translating all the scrolls. He thought for a moment. Yes, he knew of someone else who might be prepared to help. His name was Ficino, Marsiglio Ficino, a young man about twenty years old, who was a brilliant scholar and knew both Latin and Greek. Palamas would ask him if he was interested and, if so, would bring him to meet Eduardo.

They returned to Gabriele's worktable and they could already see the first few lines of the first scroll and its title, *Kalliope*.

"I know that name from somewhere," said Eduardo.

"Kalliope was the goddess of poetry," said Palamas.

"No, it's something else. I have a vague memory of a specific incident in my life. Yes, I have got it. I remember. The first piece that Juliette ever showed me that she had written, was entitled Kalliope. I remember. She said she thought it came from Plato. Come with me."

He ran upstairs into the Studiolo with Palamas following him and began looking round the walls at the inlaid pictures of the symbols of the arts and sciences, each of which had inlaid Greek titles or mottos above them.

"Look there," he said. 'Kalliope'. I remember she said that she had got the inspiration from her father's studiolo, although she didn't know at the time what it meant."

They walked round the Studiolo and Palamas started to copy down all the Greek titles.

"Maybe these are all titles of works by Plato," he said.

"But how would anyone else know of such works if they are contained in my box and have been buried for two thousand years."

"Well," said Palamas, "other writers must have known of their existence, even if the content was unknown. It will be the task of another day for us to trace the origin of all these titles. For now we have more than enough to do."

A few days later, Palamas brought Marsiglio Ficino to see Eduardo and the two of them struck a deal similar to the arrangements Eduardo had made with Gabriele. Ficino would transcribe and translate the scrolls as they were recovered and would remain in Eduardo's employ until all ten scrolls were completed. Eduardo also asked Palamas if, for the sake of their long friendship, he would like to come to live with him in the Palazzo. He could continue to work in the university and, at the same time, supervise progress on the scrolls. Looking ahead, when Eduardo had to leave, Palamas could remain in the Palazzo and have a magnificent residence of his own until they were able to return. Palamas readily agreed.

Ficino also agreed to begin at once and the first dialog took about a month to complete. It turned out to be a conversation between Socrates and Kalliope as they were seated on the banks of a river near Athens. Neither Palamas nor Eduardo had ever heard of this dialog but, clearly, as evidenced by the pictures of the Studiolo, someone else had.[20]

By the time of Eduardo's banquet, three of the scrolls had been translated and the work was proceeding at the rate of about one a month. It also seemed that secrecy was being maintained; Eduardo had not even told Vittoria although she was curious about what was going on behind the locked door of the room on the second floor of the Palazzo. He told her truthfully that he was employing someone from the university to translate some manuscripts he had found and this seemed to satisfy her. She was not particularly interested in such things and besides which she now had her hands full with Antonio.

CHAPTER 41

Death

Vittoria had sent Antonio a message after the banquet asking him where they could meet. It was several days before she got a reply and he apologized for this lack of attentiveness, which, he said, she should not take as an indication of how he felt for her but he had had to make a journey outside the city and had only just returned. He was going to the salon of the Strozzis that evening and they could meet there.

They met at the Strozzis and, on the following evening, the Tuornabuonis and then the Gherardis and so on every night, for five or six nights. Each evening, Vittoria dressed exquisitely in a different gown and looked overwhelmingly beautiful. She spent every evening in the company of Antonio so much so that, by the end of the week, it was assumed by society they had already become lovers and would and should be invited as a couple. The speed of this attachment was unusual even for the circles in which Antonio moved, but his reputation was such that no one dared pass an untoward comment on the relationship. He had been estranged from his wife Rebecca for many years and so a liaison with a beautiful young woman was not to be wondered at. He was besotted with Vittoria, who had succeeded in allowing him to forget his increasing problems, at least part of the time, to the extent that he was now even more obsessed with that greater problem of how and where they might consummate their love.

"Darling," she said one evening. "You don't look well. In fact I think you have been looking less well every night this week. What is the matter?"

It was true. He had become more and more haggard as the week had worn on.

"I have severe problems of state that are weighing upon me," he replied.

"Well," she said laying her head on his shoulder so that he could not help but sense every element of her perfume. "Tell me about them. It is not good to keep them to yourself. May be I can help. That is what I am for; to help you, make you relax, to discuss things with. Maybe the woman's point of view could help."

Antonio Lucchese was no fool. In spite of his admiration for Vittoria, he did not wholly trust her. But he could see no downside to the proposal that he was about to make. If she was discovered, it would not be he who would suffer. In any event, he only had a few days left before Ferrucci's ultimatum would expire and she was his only connection to the Ferrucci household. He had to risk it. His visit to Ferrara had been a disaster. He had been briefly detained at the city gates and informed that he was now persona non grata in Ferrara and that he would be arrested if he ever returned. It appeared that Ferrucci was a formidable opponent; what he had said in his letter had turned out to be true and he, Antonio, had likely lost the remainder of his fortune in Ferrara.

"Yes, perhaps you can help," he said. "It is a complicated matter but the city has a problem with the Turkish embassy led by your friend Ferrucci. I am in charge of the police and the security in the city and so I have to solve this difficulty."

"First of all, let us be clear, he is not my friend. Well, tell me, what is it?

"You understand that this is highly secret and I have to rely on you not to divulge it to anyone. Can I do that?"

"Of course, my darling," said Vittoria, caressing him with her most intimate smile.

"The Turks have obtained from us some papers, which they are using to force concessions out of the city. Naturally if we could get these papers back, their position would be undermined."

"How exciting," exclaimed Vittoria in her most melodramatic tone. "And I could help by taking the papers back. I am sure I could do that. I think it would be easy. I know where Ferrucci keeps his papers. But how would I recognize them?"

"Well," said Antonio, "let's start with one at a time. The first one is a letter to a man in Constantinople called Philip Shamash. It suggests that his wife is betraying him. And indeed she was passing on secrets to her lover who was one of our agents. By recovering this letter we may be able to save her and the agent involved."

"How exciting!" Vittoria repeated. "Of course, if the letter is there, I can find it easily. You know these young men. They are so naïve. He tells me everything. And you said there was a second paper?"

"Yes," said Antonio, "this may be more difficult to find. It is evidence of a large sum of money that was used to fund the assassination fifteen years ago of a traitor and spy. This money was subsequently deposited in a bank or banks in Ferrara."

"I will look tonight," said Vittoria in high excitement. "I am so pleased to help. It will be my contribution to saving Italy from the Turk. If I succeed tonight, I will send you a message to your office and we can meet and I will give you the documents."

"Very well, darling," said Antonio, "but be careful. I hope to hear from you tomorrow."

Sure enough, on the following day at about noon, the following message was delivered to Antonio's office:

> "I have what your heart desires. If you wish to obtain this gift, tell me where we should meet."

Antonio admired the tone of the message. Vittoria was entering into the spirit of the game of espionage. If the message was intercepted, it would be assumed that she was making a rendezvous and, since everyone already knew that they were lovers, this was perfectly natural. Besides which, Antonio considered, it might be that she really did intend that they should be lovers and that prospect made Antonio's heart leap. But, above all, he was hopeful that Vittoria's intervention would enable him to escape the terrible dilemma that beset him. He sent the following message back to her with instructions that the messenger was to deliver it to Vittoria's hands only or, if he could not, he should return with it to the office.

"Five in the afternoon at 31 Viale dei Fiori."

31 Viale dei Fiori was a small house owned by the city and used for the accommodation of diplomatic visitors to the city. It was fully furnished but, at that moment, unoccupied.

Antonio arrived at the house some thirty minutes before the appointed hour and he took with him the four bodyguards who always accompanied him when he walked the streets of Florence. As he started to unlock the main door, it was opened precipitously inwards and Eduardo stepped out, his sword in his hand. Before Antonio could react, the point of Eduardo's sword was in his neck. At least six of Eduardo's men ran after him into the street.

"Tell your men to drop their weapons," said Eduardo.

Antonio motioned accordingly, his bodyguards were restrained and their swords removed.

"Now draw your sword and fight – for your life," said Eduardo stepping back, on guard.

Even in his prime, Antonio would most likely have been no match for Eduardo and now he was middle-aged, dissolute, out of condition and out of practice. He had not conceived for years that he might actually have to use the sword that he carried and certainly not against a battle-hardened master such as Eduardo. The outcome was not in doubt. They cut and thrust for twenty or so strokes and then Eduardo nicked Antonio on his left arm. It was nothing. A more experienced fighter would have scarcely felt it but it was enough of a shock to Antonio that he perceptibly paused and Eduardo took his opportunity. He struck Antonio on the head and split his skull.

Antonio fell back, landing heavily on the cobbles of the little alley, and blood gushed from his wound. Eduardo knelt beside him. Antonio opened his eyes, looked at Eduardo, reached up and with one finger touched Eduardo's hand, his final human contact. Then his eyes rolled and he was gone.

"Bring their swords," Eduardo said to his men. And to Antonio's bodyguards, "Take him away." He and his party walked off towards the palazzo.

The next morning, an envoy from the Duke arrived at the Palazzo Gasparini demanding that Eduardo Ferrucci surrender himself and face charges of murder. The envoy was accompanied by a troop of Florentine guards who took up positions in the street in front of the palazzo. Eduardo sent the envoy back with the following reply which he also had made public:

> "Your Grace, I have received your request to appear before you and my peers on the charge of the murder of Antonio Lucchese. I reject this request and this charge for the following reasons.
>
> Item 1: I am an accredited ambassador of a foreign power and as such cannot be subjected to the laws of the Republic of Florence.
>
> Item 2: Antonio Lucchese died in a duel in which he engaged freely and of his own accord.
>
> Item 3: Antonio Lucchese was a traitor to the Republic of Florence in that in the course of his duties and on foreign soil he betrayed his own agents to the enemy. I have proof to that effect.
>
> Item 4: Antonio Lucchese was a thief and a murderer. He stole the patrimony of the Gasparini family of Florence and murdered their steward to do this. I have proof to that effect.
>
> With respectful salutations
> Ambassador Count Eduardo Ferrucci."

The proof for Items 3 and 4 was, as we have seen, a little weak but, in any event, according to a further letter that arrived shortly after, Duke Cosimo did not accept any of Eduardo's arguments.

> "The customs governing the special treatment of foreign ambassadors and envoys do not extend to allowing them to slaughter high ranking officials of the state in the streets of the city in broad daylight. As for evidence of wrongdoing by Lucchese, this can be presented before the court in the proper time and place. We repeat that you should surrender yourself and let justice take its course.
> Cosimo de Medici"

While this exchange was continuing, more Florentine soldiers were arriving in front of the palazzo. The interest and the excitement in the city over the incident and the prospect of an assault on the palazzo were naturally intense. Huge crowds gathered in the vicinity although they were prevented by the authorities from getting too close. Eduardo arranged to have distributed further copies of the correspondence and of the evidence of Antonio's treachery, making it appear that this was only a part of the documentation he possessed. We know that Antonio had been very unpopular and by contrast Eduardo was the hero of the moment, one who had risked his life for the Republic, who had fought to the last in the great siege, who was the complete courtier, the now-famous author and mystic, equally adept with pen as with sword.

For a short time there was a standoff in the negotiations but the sympathy of the people of Florence was on the side of Eduardo and his men, besieged for performing what was now seen to be an act of justice. Cosimo could not afford to ignore the mood of public opinion. The citizens of Florence prided themselves that their city was a democracy despite the fact that, at present, Cosimo was the unchallenged leader. He did not need to be reminded that his political fortunes could change rapidly and indeed had done so once before; only ten years earlier he had been imprisoned on political grounds and had only just escaped with his life.

Eduardo decided that it would be politic to try and resolve the stalemate with a generous offer to Cosimo, which he believed that the latter could not refuse. He wrote a private letter to the Duke revealing that he had in his possession three recently discovered dialogs of Plato. He would be prepared to donate these to the Republic of Florence (meaning, of course, Cosimo himself), on three conditions: that he and his party were allowed safe-conduct out of the city, that all charges against him were dropped and that he personally, and his family, would be permitted to travel within Florentine territory or live there whenever he wished. He would release one of the dialogs when the agreement was signed, one when their party left the city and the final one as they crossed the frontier of Florentine territory.

And so it turned out. As Eduardo had expected, Cosimo de Medici, with his thirst for knowledge and his love of the Greek philosophers, particularly Plato whom he had first learned of from the speech of Plethon fifteen years earlier during the Council of Florence, could not resist the offer. The agreement was signed, the first dialog, the *Kalliope*, was presented to Cosimo and the Turks made preparations for departure. On the appointed day, the whole party headed by Bryseis, Vittoria Orsini and Eduardo Ferrucci left Florence on their way to Venice and Constantinople.

Postscript

The Sultan required Eduardo to remain in Constantinople for more than two years until it was clear that his diplomatic overtures to the Italian states had completely failed and he had no further use for him. Eduardo Ferrucci was then released from the Sultan's service and allowed to return to Italy. Vittoria and he were married and they had four children and many grandchildren, passing their time between their palaces in Florence and Ferrara. Eduardo spent the rest of his long life reading the works of the great authors of antiquity and writing about his experiences. He also amassed a book collection that vied with the greatest in Italy, with Bessarion's in Venice, with Parentocelli's (later Pope Nicholas V) in Rome and Montefeltro's in Urbino. Cecilia Shamash, neé Gasparini, decided to remain in Constantinople. It is not known whether she remarried and thereafter she passes out of history. Maria and Francesca lived nearly all their lives in Ferrara where they also married, had children and kept in close and happy contact with their father. Marsiglio Ficino completed the translation of Eduardo Ferrucci's Platonic Dialogs and it was as a result of the experience and enthusiasm that he gained from this work that, a little later, Duke Cosimo asked him to head up the newly founded Platonic Academy in Florence, the activities of which had a decisive influence on the cultural and literary history of the European Renaissance. The Greek inscriptions decorating the Studiolo in the Palazzo Gasparini were found to contain the titles of all the known Dialogs of Plato as well additional unknown ones presumed to be lost. It is my sincere hope that the story of the discovery of these remaining dialogs will one day also be told.

NOTES

1 After the events related in this book, Gasparini's studiolo suffered many vicissitudes but it survived as a whole and is now displayed in the Metropolitan Museum of Art in New York City.

2 Ferrucci has obtained accurate versions of extracts from these speeches which can now be read in full in the citations given in this and the following two notes. The first is translated by Joseph Gill and excerpted from his *Council of Florence* Cambridge: University Press, 1959.

3 The whole of the speech of Albergati can be read at http://www.beavervalleysoftware.com/historysources/historycontent where it is translated anonymously.

4 The speech of Plethon is translated by C .M. Woodhouse and is excerpted from his *George Gemistos Plethon: the last of the Hellenes* Oxford: Clarendon Press, 1986.

5 This poem is taken from the *Epistre D'Hector* by Christine de Pisane in the translation by Steven Scrope.

6 The description of Cecilia's carriage is excerpted from the description of the Triumphs viewed by Poliphilo in the *Hypnerotomachia Poliphili* first published by Aldus in 1499 and translated by Joscelyne Godwin in the edition of Thames and Hudson: New York, 1999.

7 See Barbara Santich *The Original Mediterranean Cusine* Prospect Books, 1995 for full enjoyment of this wedding feast.

8 Excerpted from *Ad Conjugatos* by Alanus de Insulis and translated by D'Avray and Tausche. This and the following three extracts are excerpted from Anthony F. D'Elia *Wedding Orations of Fifteenth Century Italy* in *Renaissance Quarterly* LV 2002, 2.

9 Lorenzo Valla *On Pleasure*.

10 Ludovico Carbone *Dictus in nuptiis*.

11 Pietro Parleo *Epithalamium in nuptiis Julii Ceasariis Varani*.

12 For those who are interested in Heliogabalus' concept of the eye of God further discussion can be found in Meister Eckhart's *Predigt 12* excerpted conveniently in *Meister Eckhart: Die deutschen und lateinischen Werke* Stuttgart-Berlin: Kohlhammer, 1936 1:201.5-8.

13 The original of the Mandylion disappeared from Constantinople during the sack of the city in 1204 by the Crusaders and is thought by some to be the origin of the Turin shroud.

14 Excerpted from a description by Nicolas of Bracton quoted at www.florilegium.org.

15 Adapted from a translation by Eleanor Dickey, Associate Professor of Classics, Columbia University in New York City.

[16] The original title is *De Consolatione Mystike*, a mixture of Latin and Greek, a not uncommon practice amongst pretentious authors of the time. Some insensitive translators of the work no doubt aiming at a wider readership render the title as *The Consolations of Miss Tickle* which nevertheless does give something of the flavor of the personified heroine.

[17] Greek fire was a weapon of which the secret belonged to the Greeks of Constantinople. It was a flammable chemical which burned on water and which they used with great effect in many battles over hundreds of years. Its precise composition is still unknown.

[18] From the contemporary account of Leonard of Chios translated and excerpted from Donal M. Nichols, *The Immortal Emperor*, Cambridge University Press, 1992.

[19] There are numerous good accounts of the siege including those of two eyewitnesses, Nicholas Barbaro printed as *Giornale dell'assedio di Constantinopoli* Vienna: 1856 and George Phrantzes *Chronicon* edited by E. Bekker *Corpus Scriptorum Historiae Byzantinae* Bonn: 1828-1897. Gibbon's *Decline and Fall* has a florid description and a good summary is provided by S. Runciman *The Fall of Constantinople 1453* Cambridge: 1965 which has a full bibliography.

[20] An English translation of the *Kalliope* is contained in the Appendix to the present work.

APPENDIX

The Kalliope[1]

[The first dialog found by Eduardo Ferrucci in Athens in 1453, translated from the Greek into Latin with commentary by Marsiglio Ficino and further translated by Robin Raybould from the first edition of the Plato's *Opera* (Venice: de Alopa, 1484-5).The lines are not numbered and the references to other dialogs do not give line numbers. The conventional line numbering for Plato's works was not used until the Stephanus edition of 1574.]

(Translator's Note: It is remarkable that the first dialog translated by Ficino appears to have been the last or almost the last written by Plato and, as Ficino suggests, in this work Plato appears to reach definitive and final conclusions on many of the elements of his life's work. One of these, which Ficino perhaps fails sufficiently to emphasize (although see Note 11), perhaps because he was too close to events to appreciate the full significance of the developments which he witnessed, is the ontological thread of Order as the ultimate Good in an uncertain world, Beauty as a synonym for Order and Harmony, Love as the attraction that draws man towards Beauty, and in this struggle for union with Beauty, Virtue as the moral force that enables man in an heroic effort to overcome the vicissitudes of Fate and Fortune. The emergence of this last element, Virtue as the conqueror of Fate, *domitrice della Fortuna* as Giordano Bruno puts it, or Man with his new self-confidence, and with a will independent of God's will, was the catalyst and essence of the Renaissance itself. Plato, in his genius, we now know, had already foreseen that this notion of reason and of the independent will of man was an essential element in the logical structure of his philosophical system.)

Commentary: The choice of *Kalliope* as the name of this dialog tells us two things. The first is that at the end of his life, Plato had reconsidered the status of women in Greek

---

[1] Kalliope is the name of the Muse of epic poetry.

345

society. Remember that in the *Symposium* Plato takes the view conventional for his time that romantic love occurs by choice between men and youths and that in so far as it occurs between men and women it is solely for the function of procreation. In the *Republic* he goes so far as to suggest that women should be common property. But, by the time of the *Laws,* he was suggesting that pederasty should be banned and, in the *Kalliope,* romantic love between men and women is accepted openly and without reservation. He emphasizes this by repeating the story of Alcibiades from the *Symposium,* of how Socrates had resisted his sexual advances but this time he puts it in the mouth of Kalliope.

The second signal illustrates what Plato must have regarded as one of the major themes of his entire corpus: the status of poetry as the principal vehicle for the perpetuation of culture and as such its relationship with philosophy. It is well known that in the *Republic,* Plato bans poets from his ideal state on the grounds that the enthusiasm of poetry might infect citizens and incite unrest. This is taken to be a corollary of his theory of Forms. At the time of the composition of the Republic, the natural world was for Plato an unreal world, a reflection or symbol of the only true Reality, which was that of the Forms. Poetry (and other kinds of art) which was a symbolic representation of the natural world was thus doubly removed from Reality and was thus doubly unacceptable to right thinking people, that is to the citizens of his Republic. But by his final works, Plato had shifted his stance on the nature of the material world and accepted that this latter also represented a reality of some kind.

Something even more fundamental in his thinking however is hinted at by Plato's reference in the *Republic* to the 'ancient' dichotomy of poetry and philosophy in the context of his banishment of the poets. The fact that it is ancient indicates that this reference has nothing to do with Plato's own notions of the Forms. Poetry had been the principal vehicle for the perpetuation of primitive Greek culture. Before the invention of writing, the only way that culture could be preserved was by word of mouth and poetry, often in the form of song and probably through constant repetition in early mystical rites as an aid to memorization, was the chosen medium. Poetry was the preeminent art form (and see note 17 below) and in the earliest poems we have, the Iliad and the Odyssey, we see some of these different techniques for memorization, for example, consistent adjectival qualifiers -'the wine-dark sea'. For these early peoples, poetry was knowledge, was philosophy. But Plato and some of his predecessors were champions of a new and revolutionary idea that reasoning from first principles, logic or dialectic, was the proper mechanism for discovering the truth. This was the ancient dichotomy. What the Kalliope tells us is that by the end of his life Plato had come to recognize that poetry as well as reason, art as well as logic, could make a contribution to an understanding of truth and the choice of Kalliope, the Muse of poetry, as his last protagonist is an indication of his final acceptance of this compromise.

M. Ficino 10th January 1454

Kalliope

Kalliope: Socrates. What are you doing here?

Socrates: Kalliope! Come, sit down for a moment and we can talk. I was feeling warm and very drowsy in the sun; you just caught me as I was dozing off.[2]

Kalliope: Well, how have you been? It's been an age since I've seen you. What have you been doing?

Socrates: I do what I always do. I write and I think. Sometimes, as the poet said, I sit and think, sometimes I just sit.[3] Today I am just sitting admiring the river.[4] And you? You are looking very slim and fit; all this exercise does you good.

---

[2] Plato is telling us of the likelihood that the dialog is a dream of Socrates. The reference is to the *Timaeus* where Socrates says "we look at [the Forms] in a kind of dream". We thus understand that in the *Kalliope* Plato is proposing to make a final and definitive statement on the nature of his Forms and emphasizing what he must have believed was his greatest contribution to philosophy.

[3] The poet is Simonides who was a lyric poet from the island of Ceos although he spent most of his life in Athens. He was probably the first to write victory odes for winners at the Olympic games a genre in which Pindar excelled. He is by legend the originator of the Art of Memory. Socrates has already referred to a poem of Simonides in an earlier dialog (*Protagoras*) and he (Simonides) is also made to define justice at the beginning of the *Republic*.

[4] The scene is thus similar to that of the *Phaedrus* where Socrates and Phaedrus sit on the bank of the Illissus. In the *Kalliope* the river is not named but it could again be the Ilissus which ran through Athens or the Eridanos, a tributary of the Ilissus or the Kephisos which also ran close to Athens.

Kalliope: That's nice of you. It's true the river is particularly beautiful today; for once it is not so humid and the exercise has cleared my head. I <u>am</u> pleased to see you; we can have a stimulating talk while I take a rest.

Socrates: That's fine with me. Take my cloak and keep yourself warm.[5] What would you like to talk about?

Kalliope: Let's talk about the river. Why is it so beautiful today? Is it the light? Is it the water? Or is it just me, because I feel so good today?

Socrates: Yes. That certainly sounds like it would give us scope for a discussion. I hope you are not in a hurry.

Kalliope: No, no, no. I am ready for a long debate. You know I love your company and I am now rested. Let's look at the old question. What is beauty? How is it that some days the beauty is there and some days it is not?

Socrates: Well, we could try it in both the ways you have suggested: either subjectively, as an expression of your good mood or objectively as an absolute standard which we have to identify and analyze. I think we should start at the beginning and define what you just meant when you used the word good. Do you agree?

Kalliope: Yes, let's start there especially since that is an easy one. Here goes. Good is something which contributes to the well-being of society.

Socrates: You thought of that one quickly. But it doesn't sound related to what you just said, that you feel good, that

---

[5] It is well-known that Greek athletes exercised in the nude and thus covering Kalliope was more than just a matter of keeping her warm. It also gives added point to Socrates' later remark where he uncharacteristically lets his guard down.

you feel as though you were contributing towards the well-being of society and that is why the river is beautiful.

Kalliope: You are right, it doesn't seem to have anything to do with what I was feeling.

Socrates: You see, good is not primarily an ethical term at all. At bottom it just means effective, effective for the purpose you have in mind.[6] For example, what do you say if you have just eaten and enjoyed an especially succulent slice of cake. You say that it was good cake and what you mean is that served its purpose as cake. It was very effective as cakes go.

Kalliope: You're teasing me. You know I never eat cake so I wouldn't have said anything of the kind!

Socrates: So let's take another example. You do go to the theater don't you. You probably come away from the theater thinking 'that performance was good.' And you mean that it was well written, well acted and directed, it left a lasting impression, it had deeper meaning; it fulfilled all the goals that you set for achieving the purpose of theater-going. Or take a look at your shoes.[7] They are comfortable, hardwearing and attractive. No doubt you think they are good shoes. They are effective for the purpose for which you bought them. There is certainly nothing about society or about beauty in this use of good is there?

Kalliope: No, of course not.

---

[6] Here Plato echoes what he had previously indicated in the *Hippias Major*. "Virtue and Beauty and Rightness of every manufactured article, living creature, and action is assessed only in relation to the purpose for which it was made or naturally produced."

[7] Greek athletes are usually depicted without shoes but it is not surprising that they were necessary when pounding the rough streets of Athens.

Socrates: But apart from this you are right that there is also the ethical use of good and good in such a context has the same inference as the one we were just describing; effectiveness towards a purpose. In this case the purpose is the orderly progress of society as a whole. Ethics concerns itself with the behavior of individuals within society and thus a good man is deemed to be he who contributes to the goals of society at large. He is usually seen as someone who is trustworthy, unselfish, devotes time to public affairs; someone who contributes to public life. The uses of the adjective good have the same meaning in both these contexts, describing the effectiveness of a thing for its purpose and for the effectiveness of a person or activity in pursuing the goals of society. We could say in the latter case that it is effectiveness in pursuing the common good. Would you agree?

Kalliope: Yes, now it is obvious.

Socrates: I have played a little trick on you. Can you see what it is?

Kalliope: No, I can't, but you always succeed in turning the tables on me.[8]

Socrates: In the phrase common good I just used, good is a noun and not an adjective so without your noticing we shifted our position on good. We were first dealing with good as an adjective, a good shoe, an effective shoe or a good man, a man who contributes to civil affairs but now suddenly we find good as a noun, the common good. In the shoe context good tells us nothing about purpose; as it happens the function of your shoes is to be comfortable, hardwearing and attractive but good did not tell us that. You knew the pur-

---

[8] As is typical in his dialogs, Plato starts with an *elenchos*, the figure where Socrates' companion and protagonist starts the dialog with a statement which Socrates proves to be wrong and upon which he then builds his own argument.

pose before you tried the shoes on in the store. And then you found that the shoes were effective for their purpose, they were good shoes. But in the context of the common good the word has shifted from a simple meaning – effective in the pursuit of an aim – to something much more complex - an aim itself. In fact we could use the words aim or purpose in place of good in this context and it would mean the same. We could say that the customs of society work towards the common purpose and this would actually lead to a lot less confusion in ethical discussions. And there is another shade of meaning for good which could be used in the same context; we could use the word benefit, the customs of society work towards the common benefit, the common good. Do you agree?

Kalliope: Yes I do but now we have four meanings for the word good and we still don't seem to have got any closer to our analysis of beauty.

Socrates: You always were impatient but wait, you will see, we are making progress. All the meanings of good we have outlined are related in the following way. What has happened is a three stage process: first, good as effectiveness in society, the good man, has become subtly transferred to mean a helpful, beneficent, kind, tolerant man, secondly, good as effectiveness towards an aim has been transferred to mean an aim or purpose itself and thirdly the kind beneficence of the good individual has been transferred to the aim itself, the common good, the common benefit of all.[9] However, this does not tell us what the common benefit is or should be. The definition is circular; the aim or purpose as beneficial is defined in terms of those pursuing the aim, the beneficent and vice-versa. We are no further forward.

---

[9] The forgoing sentences in this paragraph are corrupt in the original and what is stated here is my own interpretation of the meaning.

Kalliope: I would say that since society does not have an existence apart from its members, the goals of society must be those of its members.

Socrates: You are right and one of the advantages of living in society is that it enforces the pursuit of logical dialog. If you are to persuade your fellow citizens of the correctness of your point of view, of the superiority of your personal goals, then you have to make him accept the logic of your argument by discussion. The politician must debate with his opponents, the leader must persuade his subordinates. Of course there are occasions when dialog and diplomacy are finally exhausted and the remaining option is seen to be only violence or war. But even war is not random but is undertaken for a purpose. We can say therefore that a responsible citizen has the following duties: to determine his goal in life, to learn and perfect the means of persuading his fellow citizens without violence of the virtue of this goal and after the debate is over to pursue the agreed and common goal with enthusiasm and without rancor.

Kalliope: This sounds an ideal state of affairs but even you must admit is only half the story. Very little of human activity or behavior is intelligent, rational or aimed at a goal. We have appetites, we have desires, we have emotions. We can and mostly do pursue activities which have nothing to do with logic or purpose. In most of our actions we are motivated by what we feel rather than what we believe. Most of the time, we are pushed by our feelings and only occasionally pulled by any logic towards this ultimate good that you have described. Not only that but so far we have not even been able to identify this common good.

Socrates: Let me ask you then; you are intelligent and rational, I know that you have a fine mind and you must have thought about these things. Is your life entirely purposeless? Do you have no desires? Do you live without a thought for the future?

Kalliope: Well that's easy, in fact I know you know what I think since we have talked about it before. My desire is love and as much of it as possible!

Socrates: Of course you are teasing although looking at you it is no weakness to say that indeed you were made for love and you may be right that the common good is love. Let us discuss that but first we should be clear that we haven't missed anything. We should eliminate other options. Do you think society's goal is truth?

Kalliope: No.[10]

Socrates. Justice?

Kalliope: No.

Socrates. Virtue?

Kalliope: Definitely not.

Socrates: I can see you are know what you want and are determined to pursue it. But that was not the implication of virtue that I was referring to. Virtue is synonymous with good in its ethical sense. The virtuous man is the one who pursues the Good. Virtue does not describe the goal itself, only the capacity to pursue it.[11] What about Knowledge?[12]

---

[10] In the *Philebus* Plato has already indicated that truth was less than knowledge and knowledge was not the Good.

[11] Virtue is the ethical equivalent of valor which it is easy to see was, in ancient times, the most admired of human characteristics. Indeed Virtue is related to Valor etymologically, that is vir – tus, the strength of virility, the strength of the will, the only power that can tame Fortune or Fate through reason, the supreme and representative characteristic of the individual human of our time.

[12] In the *Philebus* Plato has already indicated that pleasure and knowledge alone cannot form the Good.

Kalliope: No

Socrates: Pleasure?

Kalliope: Pleasure accompanies love but it doesn't seem right as the ultimate objective of society.

Socrates: I agree that that sort of behavior would not likely be shared by anyone other than the younger members of society and is not compatible with the concepts we are discussing and the life-style we profess. Do you have any other ideas?

Kalliope: Well, what about happiness?

Socrates: Happiness just begs the question. It just requires us to ask what makes us happy and we are back to the beginning.

Kalliope: Since we are trying to define beauty, what if we substitute beauty for good.[13]

Socrates: Does that help? If beauty is an exact synonym of good we are no further forward in the analysis. For the substitution to be of any help beauty has to have different characteristics from good and since we are trying to define beauty we are not yet in a position to make that substitution. But you may be on to something. Let us try and define beauty. I know you have been trying to do this from the beginning.

---

[13] These words echo those of Diotima in the *Symposium*. In that case, they form the basis of the argument for and the description of the Ladder of Love which is the kernel of the *Symposium*, of Western mysticism and of the philosophy of the love of the divine which I call Platonic love. However, at this point in the *Kalliope*, Plato firmly rejects this arbitrary substitution of beauty for good but returns to it later by through another line of argument.

Kalliope: Finally!

Socrates: Let's start with beauty as something you are attracted to. You said earlier that the river was beautiful because you felt good. I think you were using good in an unusual way; you really meant that you were in a fresh, open state of mind in which your feelings could have free rein and you were attracted to the sight, the sound, maybe even the smell of the river. Am I right?

Kalliope: Yes I suppose you are – but that's not all of it, is it?

Socrates: No, of course not, we are just getting to the start of the story. We must analyze what this attraction is. It may be that beauty does not exist objectively at all but is merely a terminus for this attraction. Possibly, anything which excites this attraction is called beautiful. Perhaps beauty is just an attribute of this attraction and itself is entirely an illusion. So the next step is to examine the nature of the attraction. I am sure you know what we call it.

Kalliope: Let me guess. I would say that the attraction is called love. Ah, I thought we would never get there.

Socrates: You are right but love is a big word.[14] It accommodates all manner of activities and feelings. There is a long, long spectrum of desire at many levels of intensity and for an infinite variety of objects. We have to be a little selective.

---

[14] Socrates uses the word *eros* here. Greek had several words for love, *eros, filia, storge, agape* just as there are in many languages e.g. like, adore. *Eros* was generally recognized as indicating desire and usually sexual desire rather than affection whereas *filia* is more akin to like. See the *Laws* where a distinction is made between the two and the story of Alcestis in the *Symposium* whose *eros* for her husband surpassed his parent's *filia* since she was prepared to die for him. *Storge* was further down the spectrum reserved for love of family and *agape* was a later word which became exclusively used in Christian theology for God's love for humanity.

Kalliope: How so?

Socrates: I can say that I am in love with you, I can say I love to go to the theater, I can say I love my children. Like good, love is an ancient word and has many shades of meaning. We can talk about love as a disease,[15] love as the force which moves the universe,[16] love between man and woman or love of the Good.[17] We could certainly dwell all night on this subject so let's remember that we are actually trying to investigate the nature of beauty.

Kalliope: Yes and I remember when we last talked on the delicate matter of love, you did stay all night! Do you remember? I remember every moment. Whatever I did to entice you, you eluded me. You just wanted to talk and I just wanted to make love. Even when I spread my blanket[18] over

---

[15] The Greeks recognized the symptoms of unrequited love as a disease *hereos*.

[16] Both Hesiod and Empedocles use *filia* rather than *eros* in their description of the creation of the universe as the product of a union of prior elements.

[17] Surprisingly, perhaps, Plato in the *Symposium* uses *eros* to describe spiritual love indicating the intense nature of such desire and its affinity to physical love.

[18] The blanket had an ancient and powerful symbolism for the Greeks. Spinning and weaving (together with pottery) were the earliest of all manufacturing techniques for primitive peoples, the Greeks not excepted. The importance of spinning and weaving are reflected in the etymology of the Greek words and in the continuing usage of elements and symbols derived from these techniques. We can point to Plato's use of the spindle as the center and turning point of the universe in the *Republic* and his extensive discussion of weaving in the *Politicus*. The Greek word to weave is *hyphainein* or to throw light on from below and is exactly analogous to *epiphainein* (from which the Christian epiphany is derived) to throw light on from above. The weaving patterns were not imagined by the weaver but were revealed by the gods and reflected the *kosmos*, the order of the universe, just as poetry itself was inspired by the gods. Said

you and cuddled up to you, you remained aloof and unresponsive so that eventually I just fell asleep.[19] This very aloofness of course made you even more desirable and attractive. So I am happy to talk about love and your talk here makes me love you even more.

Socrates: Yes, well, I don't believe it is helpful to dwell on our personal feelings and our physical desires which are necessarily vulgar and bestial. We should focus on whether the attraction between a man and a woman is as you say the product of a force which we call love, over which we have no rational control and where the object of this force is by convention called beauty or whether this attraction is the result of a conscious and rational decision to reach for an ideal which we can identify and by virtue of being an ideal, a good, is a candidate for the common good to which we can all aspire and which can lead us to fulfillment in this life and thereafter.

Kalliope: That was a pretty speech but I cannot agree that our earthly love is vulgar. I don't believe it is in the least. I think love is beautiful and natural. And what I feel for you is beautiful and natural.

Socrates referring to poets and poetry, "for not by art do they utter these things, but by divine influence" (*Ion*). A weaving, a blanket, was a sacred thing. The presentation of a new *peplos* or sacred skirt to the statue of the goddess Athenae in the Parthenon was the highlight of the annual Panathenaien festival in Athens. The sacred *peplos* took nine months to weave and was depicted as the centerpiece of the frieze on the front of the Parthenon. To cover someone with a blanket was thus a moment of epiphany, of supreme ecstasy, an extraordinary compliment whereby a person was willing to share his most sacred object.

[19] These remarks echo those of Alcibiades in the *Symposium* where he relates how he spent the night with Socrates but Socrates ignored his advances.

Socrates: You flatter me but you can hardly say that your so-called love for me is the love of the beautiful since I am just an ordinary ugly old man.

Kalliope: Nonsense. I love the sound of your voice, the sound of your voice is beautiful, I love what you think and say, your wit, that is beautiful. I love your eloquence and that is beautiful. Actually, I believe my love is not of the beautiful, it is of you. I have no reason to love you but I do. Beauty is nothing; it is an illusion, it is just a convenient short-hand for the object of the word love. Everything we love is called beautiful because we have to have something to describe the indescribable, to describe the reason for the passion and bittersweet of love. There is nothing of reason in love, it is a sickness and like any other sickness it catches us unawares, at inconvenient times, it leaves us breathless and gasping. And why do we catch this sickness, this hereos? For the prosaic reason that it is nature's way of ensuring that the human race perpetuates itself. It is to ensure that we engage wholeheartedly in the messy business of procreation. Take me.[20] I long to have your babies. We can do our duty for the species and just think, with your brains and my beauty what paragons our offspring would be.

Socrates: Yes but I am not sure I would want to take the chance of that outcome. And in spite of the sickness of love, as you describe it, I believe we can identify an objective beauty. Not only can we identify it, we can also show that it is the common good and that to pursue it will lead to fulfillment.

Kalliope: That sounds like a difficult task even for you.

Socrates. The greatest challenge facing the frail human mind has always been uncertainty and change. Change is uncomfortable and unsettling at best and at worst life-threatening.

---

[20] A suggestive double-entendre which is expressed even in the original Greek.

From the beginning mankind has sought the means to understand the causes of changes in the world, changes of climate, of the seasons, of growth and development, of disease and death. To understand and explain these phenomena is a step in allowing us a measure of control over the natural forces that surround us, dominate our activities and control our fate.

Kalliope: That is true. Certainly, we have always been at the mercy of an unexpected change in our fortunes.

Socrates: Yes, and that is why our greatest desire is for stability, for order, that is why we see order and harmony in art and in life as beauty. Beauty is order. Beauty is the proper relationship of parts to a whole, of form and subject, of action and objective.[21]

Kalliope: That sounds like a reasonable definition of beauty but I am still not wholly convinced.

Socrates: Well, there is another reason why change is a challenge to human thought. If an object, a man or an animal, the skies or the sea, all nature is continuously in a state of change how can they retain identity and meaning.[22] How

---

[21] So this, in the words of Diotima (*Symposium*), seems final and appears to be Plato's final and considered word on the subject. Beauty is order and beauty as order is the supreme Good. It is not surprising that it should be so when Plato's principal contribution towards metaphysics and ethics was the notion of the Forms and the Good and the driving force behind these concepts was the imperative to impose order on a changing and dangerous world. This is also confirmed by Plotinus in his treatise on Love (*Enneads* III, 5, 1). 'Nature produces by looking towards the Good, for it looks towards Order'

[22] Socrates says the same in the *Cratylus* 'Nor can we reasonably say, Cratylus, that there is knowledge at all, if everything is in a state of transition and there is nothing abiding; for knowledge too cannot continue to be knowledge unless continuing always to abide and exist.'

360

can we define the meaning of something which is continually changing and therefore has no identity? How can we profitably use in communication a word which has no meaning?

Kalliope: I agree that to be useful a word has to have meaning and conversely we have to be able to identify an object in order to describe it and give it a name but how then are we to describe something which is constantly changing?

Socrates: First, we must enumerate the attributes of the object, and identify the essential ones, the ones which are common at all times to objects of that sort. We can then state that the object itself is defined as consisting, at the least, in its lowest common denominator, of those attributes. This will give us what we can call an Idea of the object, a universal definition of the object, which although it does not exist in the material world nevertheless has real existence as an object of thought. And we can go further. We can do the same with the attributes of the object. Each abstract attribute of an object, such as flatness or roundness or dare I say it beauty, will also exist as an Idea which itself is an object of thought independent of the instances of it which exist in nature.

Kalliope: Yes I understand that.

Socrates: And the Idea of beauty, that of order and stability and harmony, that which we most yearn after is the ultimate, the common good. So you were right; we can substitute beauty for good.

Kalliope: Well I'm glad I was right about something.

Socrates: Then you must also see that when we reach towards beauty, towards the common good, we reach beyond the bestial and the vulgar levels of love, which are only in the service of what you call the perpetuation of the human species, we reach to the level of the spiritual, to that view of beauty which gives humanity its purpose for existence. The contemplation of Beauty is the Good, the proper objective of the human spirit.

Kalliope: Look, the lights are dancing on the water but you tell me that the river is never the same and cannot be beautiful.[23] What I see is only an idle paradox, beauty and not beauty.[24] You tell me I should not love you but should only contemplate the Idea of beauty. Too bad, this is not enough for me. I should go.

Socrates: When you came, it was warm and sunny and I was dozing. Now it is dark and I am wide awake and ready for the sounds and lights of the city. Yes, let us go, I will walk you home and we will see what the evening brings.

---

[23] Here in his final words Plato hints at the famous dictum of Heraclitus which he has already referred to in the *Cratylus* "We step and do not step twice into the same river, we are and we are not." (Heraclitus Homericus *Homeric Questions* 24).

[24] Even at the end, Plato is reluctant to draw a final conclusion on the matter. This uncertainty is the figure of *aporia* and is typical of the ending of many of the Platonic dialogs.

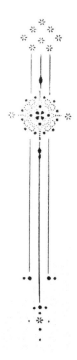

9297431R0

Made in the USA
Lexington, KY
14 April 2011